'The Mary Russell series is the m[...] in mystery fiction today, and this is the best instalment yet'
Lee Child

'These . . . are bestselling books because Laurie R. King captures the voice and character of Holmes as well as any of the thousand and more pastiches that have been written in imitation of Conan Doyle. But this is more than a mere copy. The narrative . . . is completely absorbing and motivates the reader to want to read the rest of the series'
Historical Novels Review

'Excellent . . . King never forgets the true spirit of Conan Doyle'
Chicago Tribune

'Outstanding examples of the Sherlock Holmes pastiche . . . the depiction of Holmes and the addition of his partner, Mary, is superbly done'
Mystery Women

'All [Laurie R. King books] without exception, leave me with a feeling of immense satisfaction at the quality of the story and the writing'
It's a Crime Blog

LAURIE R. KING lives in northern California. Her background includes such diverse interests as Old Testament theology and construction work, and she has been writing crime fiction since 1987. The winner of the Edgar, the Nero, the Macavity and the John Creasey awards, she is the author of highly praised stand-alone suspense novels and a contemporary mystery series, as well as the Mary Russell/Sherlock Holmes series.

By Laurie R. King

The Beekeeper's Apprentice

A Monstrous Regiment of Women

A Letter of Mary

The Moor

O Jerusalem

Justice Hall

The Game

Locked Rooms

The Language of Bees

The God of the Hive

Pirate King

Beekeeping for Beginners

(a novella)

Garment of Shadows

Touchstone

The Bones of Paris

JUSTICE HALL

LAURIE R. KING

Allison & Busby Limited
12 Fitzroy Mews
London W1T 6DW
www.allisonandbusby.com

First published in 2002.
This paperback edition published by Allison & Busby in 2014.

Published by arrangement with Bantam Books,
an imprint of The Random House Publishing Group,
a division of Random House, Inc., New York, NY, USA.
All rights reserved.

A CIP catalogue record for this book is available from
the British Library.

10 9 8 7 6 5 4 3 2

ISBN 978-0-7490-1525-1

Typeset in 10.5/15.5 pt Adobe Garamond Pro by
Allison & Busby Ltd.

The paper used for this Allison & Busby publication
has been produced from trees that have been legally sourced
from well-managed and credibly certified forests.

Printed and bound by
CPI Group (UK) Ltd, Croydon, CR0 4YY

For my family
(YOU KNOW WHO YOU ARE)
Familia fortitudo mea est

EDITOR'S PREFACE

THIS VOLUME IS THE sixth chapter in the chronicles of Mary Russell and her partner, the near mythic (even, it would seem, in the 1920s) Sherlock Holmes. It comes chronologically after their 1923 adventure described in *The Moor*, but is linked with the characters from *O Jerusalem*, which took place in 1919.

I, Miss Russell's literary agent and editor, had a certain amount of assistance in the preparation of this book, people who assisted in the task of ensuring that Miss Russell's narrative did not stray too far from the path of historical truth. Ms Anabel Scott helped this poor Colonial to sort out the rules, regs, and terminology regarding the British aristocracy. Ms Tara Lengsfelder uncovered the paper written by Miss Russell on the boat to New York, running it to earth in an obscure American university journal from the spring of 1924. Mr Stuart Bennett, antiquarian bookseller extraordinaire, confirmed the titles of the books in the Justice Hall library.

Thanks to them all, and to nameless others, not the least of whom was the kind and anonymous soul who sent me Miss Russell's manuscripts in the first place, for the benefit, and the puzzlement, of all.

LAURIE R. KING

Let justice roll down like the waters,
and righteousness like an
everflowing stream.
– *Amos* 5:24

CHAPTER ONE

Home, my soul sighed. I stood on the worn flagstones and breathed in the many and varied fragrances of the old flint-walled cottage: Fresh beeswax and lavender told me that Mrs Hudson had indulged in an orgy of housecleaning in the freedom of our prolonged absence; the smoke from the wood fire seemed cleaner than the heavy peat-tinged air I'd been inhaling in recent weeks; the month-old pipe tobacco was a ghost of its usual self; and beneath it all the faint, dangerous, seductive tang of chemicals from the laboratory overhead.

And scones.

Holmes grumbled his way past, jostling me from my reverie. I stepped back out into the crisp, sea-scented afternoon to thank my farm manager, Patrick, for meeting us at the station, but he was already away down the drive, so I closed the heavy door, slid its two-hundred-year-old bolt, and leant my back against the wood with all the mingled relief and determination of a feudal lord shutting out an unruly mob.

Domus, my mind offered. *Familia*, my heart replied. Home.

'Mrs Hudson!' Holmes shouted from the main room. 'We're home.' His unnecessary declaration (she knew we were coming; else why the fresh baking?) was accompanied by the characteristic thumps and cracks of possessions being shed onto any convenient surface, freshly polished or not. At the sound of her voice answering from the kitchen, I had to smile. How many times had I returned here, to that ritual exchange? Dozens: following an absence of two days in London when the only things shed were furled umbrella and silk hat, or after three months in Europe when two burly men had helped to haul inside our equipage, consisting of a trunk filled with mud-caked climbing equipment, three crates of costumes, many arcane and ancient volumes of worldly wisdom, and two-thirds of a motorcycle.

The only time I had come to this house with less than joy was the day when Holmes and my nineteen-year-old self had been acting out a play of alienation, and I could see in his haggard features the toll it was taking on him. Other than that time, to enter the house was to feel the touch of comforting hands. Home.

I caught up my discarded rucksack and followed Holmes through to the fire; to tea, and buttered scones, and welcome.

Hot tea and scalding baths, conversations with Mrs Hudson, and the accumulated post carried us to dinner: urgent enquiries from my solicitor regarding a property sale in California; a cheerful letter from Holmes' old comrade-at-arms, Dr Watson, currently on holiday in Egypt; a demand from Scotland Yard for pieces of evidence in regard to a case over the summer. Over the dinner table, however, the momentum of normality came to its peak over Mrs Hudson's fiery curry, faltered with the apple tart, and then receded, leaving us washed up in our chairs before the fire, listening to the silence.

I sighed to myself. Each time I managed to forget this phase – or not forget, exactly, just to hope the interim would be longer, the transition less of a jolt. Instead, the drear aftermath of a case came down with all the gentleness of a collapsing wall.

One would think that, following several taut, urgent weeks of considerable physical discomfort on Dartmoor, a person would sink into the undemanding Downland quiet with a bone-deep pleasure, wrapping indolence around her like a fur coat, welcoming a period of blank inertia, the gears of the mind allowed to move slowly, if at all. One would think.

Instead of which, every time we had come away from a case there had followed a period of bleak, hungry restlessness, characterised by shortness of temper, an inability to settle to a task, and the need for distraction – for which long, difficult walks or hard physical labour, experience taught me, were the only relief. And now, following not one but two back-to-back cases, with the client of the summer's case long dead and that of the autumn now taken to his Dartmoor deathbed, this looked to be a grim time indeed. To this point, the worst such dark mood that I had experienced was that same joyless period just under five years before, when I was nineteen and we had returned from two months of glorious, exhilarating freedom wandering Palestine under the unwilling tutelage of a pair of infuriating Arabs, Ali and Mahmoud Hazr, only to return to an English winter, a foe after our skins, and a necessary pretence of emotional divorcement from Holmes. I am no potential suicide, but I will say that acting one at the time would not have proved difficult.

Hard work, as I say, helped; intense experiences helped, too: scalding baths, swims through an icy sea, spicy food (such as the curry Mrs Hudson had given us: How well she knew Holmes!), bright colours. My skin still tingled from the hot water, and I had donned a robe of brilliant crimson, but the coffee in my cup was suddenly insipid. I jumped up and went into the kitchen, coming back ten minutes later with two cups of steaming hot sludge that had caused Mrs Hudson to look askance, although she had said nothing. I put one cup beside Holmes' brandy glass and settled down on a cushion in front of the fire with the other, wrapping both hands around it and breathing in the powerful fragrance.

'What do you call this?' Holmes asked sharply.

'A weak imitation of Arab coffee,' I told him. 'Although I think Mahmoud used cardamom, and the closest Mrs Hudson had was cinnamon.'

He raised a thoughtful eyebrow at me, peered dubiously into the murky depths of the cup, and sipped tentatively. It was not the real thing, but it was strong and vivid on the palate, and for a moment the good English oak beams over our heads were replaced by the ghost of a goat's hair tent, and the murmur of the flames seemed to hold the ebb and flow of a foreign tongue. New flavours, new dangers, and the sun of an ancient land, the land of my people; trials and a time of great personal discovery; our Bedu companions, Mahmoud the rock and Ali the flame. Odd, I thought, how the taciturn older brother had possessed such a subtle hand at the cook-fire, and had made such an art of the coffee ritual.

No, the dark substance in our cups was by no means the real thing, but both of us drank to the dregs, while images from the weeks in Palestine flickered through the edges of my mind: dawn over the Holy City and midnight in its labyrinthine bazaar; the ancient stones of the Western Wall and the great cavern quarry undermining the city's northern quarter; Ali polishing the dust from his scarlet Egyptian boots; Mahmoud's odd, slow smile of approval; Holmes' bloody back when we rescued him from his tormentor; General Allenby and the well-suited Bentwiches and the fair head of T. E. Lawrence, and – and then Holmes rattled his newspaper and the images vanished. I fluffed my fingers through my drying hair and picked up my book. Silence reigned, but for the crackle of logs and the turn of pages. After a few minutes, I chuckled involuntarily. Holmes looked up, startled.

'What on earth are you reading?' he demanded.

'It's not the book, Holmes, it's the situation. All you need is an aged retriever lying across your slippers, we'd be a portrait of family life. The artist could call it *After a Long Day*; he'd sell hundreds of copies.'

'We've had a fair number of long days,' he noted, although without complaint. 'And I was just reflecting how very pleasant it was, to be without demands. For a short time,' he added, as aware as I that the respite would be brief between easy fatigue and the onset of bleak boredom. I smiled at him.

'It is nice, Holmes, I agree.'

'I find myself particularly enjoying the delusory and fleeting impression that my wife spends any time at all seated at the feet of her husband. One might almost be led to think of the word "subservient",' he added, 'seeing your position at the moment.'

'Don't push it, Holmes,' I growled. 'In a few more minutes my hair will be—'

My words and the moment were chopped short by the crash of a fist against the front door. The entire house seemed to shudder convulsively in reaction, and then Holmes sighed, called to Mrs Hudson that he would answer it, and leant over to deposit his newspaper on the table. However, I was already on my feet; it is one thing to relax in the presence of one's husband and his long-time housekeeper, but quite another to have one's neighbour or farm manager walk in and find one in dishabille upon the floor.

'I'll see who it is, Holmes,' I said. He rose, maintaining the pipe in his hand as a clear message to our intruder that he had no intention of interrupting his evening's rest, and tightening the belt of his smoking jacket with a gesture of securing defences, but he stayed where he was while I went to repel boarders at our door.

The intruder was neither a neighbour nor a lost and benighted Downs rambler, nor even Patrick come for assistance with an escaped cow or a chimney fire. It was a stranger dressed for Town, a thick-set, clean-shaven, unevenly swarthy figure in an ill-fitting and out-of-date city suit that exuded the odour of mothballs, wearing a stiff collar such as even Holmes no longer used and a brilliant emerald green necktie that had been sampled by moths. The hat on his head was an equally ancient bowler, and his right hand was in the process of extending itself to me – not to shake, but open-handed, as a plea. A thin scar travelled up the side of the man's brown wrist to disappear under the frayed cuff of the shirt, a thin scar that caught at my gaze in a curious fashion.

'You must help me,' the stranger said. For some peculiar reason, my ears added a slight lisp to his pronunciation, which was not actually there.

'I beg your pardon, sir,' I began to say, and then my eyes went back to the darkness on his temple that in the shadowy doorway I had taken for hair oil. 'You are hurt!' I exclaimed, then turned to shout over my shoulder, 'Holmes!'

'You must come with me,' the man demanded, his command as urgent as his fist on the wood had been. Then to my confusion he added a name I had not heard in nearly five years. 'Amir,' he murmured, and his shoulder drifted sideways, to prop itself against the door-frame.

I stared at him, moving to one side so the interior light might fall more brightly on his features. I knew that face: Beardless as it was, its missing front teeth restored, the hair at its sides conventionally trimmed, and framed by an incongruous suit and an impossible hat, it was nonetheless the face of a man with whom I had travelled in close proximity and uneasy intimacy for a number of weeks. I had worked with him; shed blood with him. I was, in fact, responsible for that narrow scar on his wrist.

'Ali?' I said in disbelief. 'Ali Hazr?' His mouth came open as if to speak, but instead he stumbled, as if the door frame had abruptly given way; his right hand fluttered up towards his belt, but before his fingers could reach his waistcoat, his eyes rolled back in his head, his knees turned to water, and fourteen and a half stone of utterly limp intruder collapsed forward into my arms.

CHAPTER TWO

THE MAN LYING BETWEEN the crisp white sheets of the guest bed was very like Ali Hazr, but also distinctly unlike the Arab ruffian Holmes and I had known. In fact, I had nearly convinced myself that our visitor was merely a stranger with a strong resemblance to the man – a brother, perhaps – when a jab from the doctor's sewing needle brought him near to consciousness, and he growled a string of florid Arabic curses.

It was Ali, all right.

Before Holmes' pet medical man had clipped the thread from his half-dozen stitches, the patient had lapsed back into the restless swoon that had gripped him from the moment he fell through our door. Seeing his tossing head and hearing the apparent gibberish from his lips, the doctor reached back into his satchel for a hypodermic needle. With that, Ali finally succumbed to oblivion.

I adjusted the pad of clean towelling underneath his bandaged scalp and followed the two men out of the room, leaving the door ajar.

Downstairs in the kitchen, Dr Amberley was scrubbing the

blood from his hands and giving Holmes a set of unnecessary instructions.

'I'd say his concussion is a mild one, but you'd best keep an eye on him, and if his pupils become uneven, or if he seems over-lethargic, telephone to me immediately. The dose of morphia I gave him was small, because of the concussion – it ought to wear off in three or four hours, although he may well sleep longer than that. I suppose you wish me to say nothing about this visitor of yours?'

'I think not. At this point I have no idea why he's here or what happened to him, and I'd not want to invite an attacker to join us. Although by the appearance of his overcoat, I should say this happened far from here.'

It was true. Ali's incongruous city suit had been stiff with dried blood, his shirt collar saturated to the shoulders. Whatever had brought him here, desperation might well follow on his heels.

When the doctor had gone and Mrs Hudson was tut-tutting over the ruined clothing, Holmes picked up his hastily abandoned pipe, knocked it out, and began to tamp fresh tobacco into the bowl. I went through the house to secure the doors and windows and draw the curtains, just in case.

'It has to be something to do with Mahmoud,' I said when I came back. 'Ali would not have come to England without him, and would not have come to us for help except if Mahmoud were in grave danger.'

'It is difficult to imagine the one Hazr without the other,' Holmes agreed. He got the pipe going, then resumed his three-week-old newspaper.

'But, shouldn't we do something? He may sleep for hours.'

'What do you propose?'

'We could telephone to Mycroft.'

He did lower the paper a fraction to consider the proposition, then shook his head.

'My brother is in London, unless he's left since this morning. If Ali wanted Mycroft, he'd have stopped there. He wanted us, which meant that either he thought we would not respond to a mere telegraph or telephone message, or secrecy was foremost. No, Ali came from Berkshire to see us, not to speak with Mycroft. We shall have to be patient.'

The unused portion of a return ticket in Ali's pocket had revealed a journey from the farthest reaches of Berkshire, a rural station I'd never heard of called Arley Holt. It seemed likely that he had been injured during his journey's break in London. It was also more than possible that the wound had been not accident, but active threat; something, after all, had prevented him from seeking medical attention when he disembarked in Eastbourne, miles from our door.

Ignorance is always frustrating, never more so than when accompanied by the feeling that it obscures the need for action. Holmes and I wore our patience like a pair of horsehair shirts, prickly and ill-fitting, and while we kept our eyes on the printed word, our ears were turned towards the stairs, eager for the slightest sleep-befuddled query.

It did not come. Mrs Hudson abandoned her scrubbing brush and retired to her quarters. The fire burnt low. Midnight approached, with no movement from the guest room.

Finally, Holmes rattled his paper shut with an air of finality and fixed me with a gaze. 'And the cares that infest the day,' he pronounced, 'shall fold their tents like the Arabs, and as silently sleep away.'

We took ourselves to bed, but not to silent sleep; nor was the air filled with the music from the first part of his misquotation.

I had forgotten how emphatically Ali snored.

Two of us in the house slept little.

Morning came, the aroma of coffee trickled its way up the stairs, and still the Hazr snores rattled the windows. Not until after eight o'clock did they abruptly cease. Holmes and I looked at each other. Mrs Hudson came in from the kitchen, drying her hands on her apron and cocking her head at the ceiling.

'Shall I make another breakfast, then?' she asked.

'Either that or send for the undertaker,' I answered, but then a rattle of movement came from the bedstead over our heads, followed by the thump of feet hitting the floorboards. They stopped there, either through dizziness or because Ali noticed that he was more or less naked. Holmes folded his newspaper (he'd worked his way up to the previous week) and rose.

'If you would like to make a pot of tea, Mrs Hudson, Russell will bring it up. I'll find our guest a dressing gown. Give him a minute, Russell, to get his bearings.'

I was not certain whether Holmes was referring to the inevitable confusion following a head injury, or to the specific discomfort this man might feel after having tumbled into the arms of a woman he'd spent the better part of six weeks insulting, ignoring, and mistrusting. Our relationship had become considerably more jovial after I had come close to killing him a couple of times (accidents both, I hasten to say), but I might still not be the person Ali Hazr would have chosen to pick him up following a moment of vulnerability.

To be fair, I had to permit him to resume his mask of omnicompetence. Whatever had driven him to the extremity of seeking aid, it would only further complicate matters to begin with inequality. So I allowed Holmes to trot off upstairs without me. I did not even snatch the tray from Mrs Hudson's hands, but meekly waited for her to rearrange the biscuits into an aesthetic design before I took up the refreshment and carried it upstairs.

Holmes had built up the fire in the guest room and was seated on the low bench at the foot of the bed. The room's armchair held Ali, clad in a warm dressing gown and a pair of Holmes' pyjama trousers that extended past his toes. He looked up at my entrance and watched me set the tray down on the small table by his side. I poured him a cup. He added milk (rather to my surprise, as Arab tea is taken black) and two sugars, then drank thirstily. I refilled his cup and pulled the footstool up to the other side of the fireplace. A quick glance at the pillow confirmed that he'd bled, but not profusely, and none of the stains looked fresh.

The second cup followed the first down his throat, and he set it onto the saucer with the barest tap. Ali glanced at me briefly, and away.

'The English beverage,' he commented, which might have sounded like disparagement had he not drunk it so greedily. I decided this was his version of thank you. His hand went to his scalp, exploring the surface of the bandage. 'Someone has put in stitches.'

'Six,' Holmes told him. 'One of our neighbours is a retired surgeon. And in case you are concerned, he knows well how to keep a confidence.'

'Good. I . . . apologise for my state yesterday night. I do not remember too clearly, but I have the impression that my arrival was somewhat more . . . dramatic than I had intended.'

The drama of his arrival the previous evening, however, had been nowhere near as startling as the words he had just pronounced. And not only the words themselves (Ali Hazr, apologising?) but their delivery.

My first clear impression of Ali all those years before, seen by the light of a tiny oil lamp in a mud-brick hut near Jaffa, had been: Arab cut-throat. Glaring eyes and garish embroidery, knife as well as revolver decorating his belt, his very moustaches looking ferocious – from his flowered headdress to his red leather boots, Ali Hazr had been in that first moment what he remained the entire time: a Bedouin male, proud member of a haughty race, fiercely indisposed to tolerate anyone but Mahmoud, his brother in the deepest sense of the word. Touchy and arrogant, his hand reaching for his knife at the slightest provocation, in his attitude towards us Ali had veered between mortal threat and withering contempt. Passing the tests he and Mahmoud had set us, becoming a companion worthy of their trust, had been a profound source of pride that I had never acknowledged, even to Holmes. I had, in truth, been a different person when Ali and Mahmoud Hazr finished with me.

I looked at the man in the chair, and other than the colours of the tie draped over the bedstead, I could perceive little of that vivid personality now. His erect spine, and perhaps the darkness in his eyes, but the flash was missing from their depths, the aura of simmering violence well and truly damped down. With the gap in his front teeth bridged, even his oddly ominous lisp was gone, his once-heavy accent no more than a faint thickening of gutturals and a subtly non-English placement of the words on the tongue. Had Holmes not trained my ear, I might have thought our intruder merely an ordinary, tame English gentleman. Ali Hazr had shaved away far more than facial hair in transforming himself into this.

As I studied him, those black eyes glanced up at me again, and in that brief moment of contact I felt a spark in them, and read in his half-familiar mouth a distinct grimace. He knew what I was seeing – or rather, not seeing – and it was a face he was not happy about showing. His current appearance was no mere disguise.

'I think I should introduce myself,' he said. I had the impression he spoke through gritted teeth. 'My name is Alistair Hughenfort. Alistair Gordon St John Hughenfort. Although even as a child, my family called me Ali.'

Holmes' head jerked up and I, frankly, stared. Hughenfort? He must be joking. The Hughenfort name was a thing to conjure with, a noble name in the fullest sense of the word, one of a thin handful of the nation's families that had actually stepped onto England's shores at the side of William the Conqueror. Half the European wars had a Hughenfort leading some vital charge – and half the rebellions had a younger Hughenfort somewhere in there as well. But as an assumed name, it would have been like disguising himself as the Prince of Wales. It could only be the truth. Holmes shook off the historical details and went for the main issue.

'And Mahmoud?'

Our guest sat up sharply, scarcely wincing as the urgency of his mission overrode his ailments. 'He needs us. I need your help.'

This extraordinary confession passed straight over Holmes' head. 'I understood that to be so. My question was, what is Mahmoud's name?'

The wounded ex-Arab braced himself, took a soft breath, then answered in an even voice. 'The man you know as Mahmoud Hazr was born William Maurice Hughenfort.' He waited, his eyes on Holmes, to see what we would make of the statement.

It meant nothing to me, but Holmes' eyes assumed the faraway look that indicated a rapid search through his prodigiously stocked mental box rooms. 'Maurice Hughenfort. Known as Lord Marsh. Younger son of the Duke of Beauville. Good Lord. I should have suspected that family immediately when I saw where your ticket was issued last night.'

'I'm sorry?' I asked. Was this something from his accumulation of newspapers, a recent event we had missed while slogging through the depths of Dartmoor?

But Holmes waved a dismissive hand in the direction of the laboratory. 'Ancient history, Russell. He'll be in Debrett's. Unless . . . ?' He turned an eye to the man in the chair.

'The entry is still there,' Ali – Alistair? – confirmed. 'Incomplete, but there.'

Curious, I went down to Holmes' laboratory and took his Debrett's from its resting place on a shelf between an assortment of labelled coal samples and a massive and outdated treatise on Bertillonism. I went back down the corridor, flipping over the pages until I came to the name Beauville. It began with a crest of typically unlikely looking creatures and a snarl of heraldic devices above a motto of equally unlikely Latin, *Justitia fortitudo mea est.*

The Duke of Beauville, the list began, with the name of the (then-present) Duke, Henry Thomas Michael. I skimmed over the long paragraph of fine print that followed, packed with descending titles, education, and honours: *Earl of Calminster, Earl of Darlescote, baron of* this and *baron of* the other, *mayor of, secretary of, steward of,* so on and so forth.

I turned the page to find the Family of Hughenfort entry, where the dates began in the eleventh century, although details of the early barons were both few and heavily mythologised. Words jumped out: *knighted; liberal to his tenants and servants; high sheriff; chief justice; spirited debates in Parliament; battle of* various places and *service to king* so and so and *distinguished statesman.* Baron gave way to earl and eventually, in the early eighteenth century, to duke.

Finally I saw the name Maurice, and I slowed to read the entry of his father's generation:

Gerald Richard Adam, 5th Duke of Beauville, b. 14 May 1830, then the details of two marriages, with 'issue' given as:

1. *Henry Thomas Michael, Earl of Calminster, b. 1859, m. 1888 to his cousin Sarah, dau. Rev William Malverson, has issue: Gabriel Adrian Thomas b. 1899.*
2. *William Maurice, b. 1876 (whereabouts unknown since 1900)*
3. *Lionel Gerald b. 1882*
1. *Phillida Anne b. 1893*

I had to travel back up the lists to find Ali, but there he was, under a cousin of the fourth Duke's: *Alistair Gordon St John, b. 1881, Eton, Trinity. Badger Old Place, Arley Holt, Berks.* And again that odd notice, *whereabouts unknown*, although in his case it was *since 1902*.

The two Hughenfort cousins had slipped beneath the ken of Debrett's all-knowing eyes, into the king's service in the Middle East. Quite an accomplishment for a pair of Hons. So why had they come back?

Further queries were interrupted by Mrs Hudson and another tray, and although the man I was trying to think of as Alistair was reluctant to break off his quest even to take on nourishment, Mrs Hudson stood over him until she was satisfied that he was not about to let the buttery eggs go untended. Holmes, seeing that our guest's mouth was unavoidably occupied, stepped into the gap.

'Before your time, Russell. There was a mild sensation in the newspapers concerning a vanished baronet. Somehow a rumour got around that he had boarded a ship for New York and never arrived. 1896 or '97, as I recall.'

'Seven,' mumbled Alistair around his toast.

'The family denied the rumours, claimed their second son was merely travelling in Russia, but when Debrett's came out the following year it gave his address as "unknown", and Burke's followed. But – correct me if I am wrong – the son came home a few years later. For his father's funeral?' The bandage nodded. 'When he disappeared again after that, no one could work up much interest.'

Ali washed the toast down with the last of his tea; he had eaten all the eggs and the tomato, but left the bacon and sausage untouched. 'When I joined him in Palestine in 1902, my own family had learnt their lesson, and gave it out that we had mounted an expedition into the Himalayas and were not expected to return for years. I had my club forward letters, first to my home, and then later, when we became . . . associated with your brother Mycroft's organisation, to his office. It disarmed suspicion.'

The idea of Ali Hazr, Arab cut-throat and clandestine agent for His Majesty's government, as a clubman with noble blood in his veins made for an interesting picture. Holmes, however, returned to the question that had brooded over the house since the previous night.

'In what trouble is Mahmoud?'

Our guest looked down at his hands with a faint smile. 'It is good to hear my brother's name spoken. It gives me hope.' For one startling instant, Ali Hazr passed through the room, his hand creeping to the hilt of his wicked knife, ebony eyes flaring, the rhythm of a foreign tongue riding the English words. And then the ghost of a dramatic moustache faded, the swarthy skin became merely that of an outdoorsman, and we were looking again at Alistair Hughenfort.

'Four months ago, we received news that his brother was dying. Henry. His older brother. The funeral was in September.'

A picture began to take form out of the fog of ignorance.

'His older brother, the duke,' Holmes said. Ali nodded; Holmes settled his back against the end of the bench and allowed his eyelids to droop shut, the better to listen. He suggested to Ali, 'And the duke had no son.'

However, Ali shook his head. 'Henry – the sixth Duke – did have a son. Gabriel. The boy enlisted on the day of his eighteenth birthday, in August 1917. He was killed fifty-one weeks later. Gabriel was engaged, but not married. Henry had no other children.'

'Were there no other brothers?'

'Lionel, six years younger than Mah – than Marsh, but he died before the War. And there is a sister, Phillida, from the old duke's second wife. She is seventeen years younger than Marsh.'

Somehow, it was difficult to conceive of Mahmoud Hazr as one of a family of siblings going through the common lot of birth, teething pains, skinned knees, and all the other stages of human growth. I began to get an inkling of how absolute his own reinvention had been – more profound even than that of his relative Alistair. It was then the full picture hit me: Mahmoud Hazr, itinerant scribe for the illiterate Palestinian countryside, eyes and ears for General Edmund Allenby, the inadequately washed Bedouin who scratched his ribs and cursed his mules and roasted his coffee over a dried-dung fire in the dark confines of a goat's-hair tent, was also the seventh Duke of Beauville: his embroidered robes replaced by ermine, that dark, knife-scarred face topped not by *khufiyyah*, but by coronet.

It was a lot to absorb.

Holmes, as usual, kept to the essentials. 'I fail to see what I might be expected to do in this situation. If Mahmoud – if your cousin – Maurice – confound it! If Maurice Hughenfort feels it necessary to assume the duties that accompany his title, there is little I, or Russell, can do to dissuade him. If he does not so choose, he could always let the dukedom be in abeyance for his lifetime. Surely there must be another heir in the woodwork. Did the other brother, Lionel, have no heir?'

'There are . . . complications. You will understand when you see him. Will you come?'

I had known it would come down to this. With the mud from the last outing still damp on my boots, we were about to set out again. I must have sighed, because Ali pulled himself up, his face going dark in a way I remembered well.

'I ask you this—' he began, but Holmes put up one hand, saving a proud man from having to plead.

'We will of course come with you,' he said. Then he opened an eye, and added, in Arabic, a phrase translating roughly, 'One man's hunger makes his brother weak.' At the word 'brother', our guest froze; then he nodded, once, both as thanks and as acknowledgment of our right to claim that relationship.

Even I: I had, after all, been to all appearances a boy during the weeks in Palestine. I, too, might claim brotherhood to the formidable Mahmoud.

'You have neglected to tell us what happened to you on the way to Sussex,' Holmes pointed out, settling back into the bench.

'What happened – oh, you mean this.' Ali's hand went to the gauze on his head. 'Stupidity. This country makes a man soft. I imagined I was safe, and walked straight into a situation. It would never have happened in Palestine.'

Holmes abruptly abandoned his languid pose. 'You were attacked? Robbed?'

I fully understood the note of incredulity in Holmes' voice: It was hard to imagine a man with the lightning-fast responses of Ali Hazr falling victim to a common thief.

'No. Caught up in a riot.'

'In *London*?'

'A small riot. A Guy Fawkes celebration, I suppose – I had forgotten entirely about Guy Fawkes – that joined with a group of unemployed workers and got out of hand.' He saw our unwillingness to accept that truncated account, and reluctantly explained. 'When I got into Paddington I had an hour before the Sussex train, so I walked to Victoria instead of taking a taxi or the underground. Just before the station I came up to a knot of men with a pile of wood, as if they were about to light a bonfire on the street. They objected to the police clearing them off; bricks were thrown, truncheons raised. I thought the disturbance was behind me, then something struck me – truncheon or cobblestone, who knows? – and knocked me into the street in the path of a lorry. I managed to roll out of its way, and half fell into the nearest doorway. A pawnshop, as it turned out, where a handful of others took refuge as well. They wanted to take me to a doctor's surgery, but I could not risk missing the train.'

Riots in London? Ever since the War had ended, and especially in recent months, the unrest of common workers had steadily increased: Men who had spent four years in the trenches were ill-equipped to put up with dole queues. I had not known that open battle had broken out.

'It was nothing,' he insisted. 'Carelessness and a headache. We must go now.'

The man was in no condition to travel. Indeed, once on his feet he swayed dangerously, and would have fallen but for Holmes' hand on his shoulder, both supporting and holding him back.

'If we left now,' Holmes told him, 'we should merely find ourselves decorating an ill-heated waiting room for several hours. There is no service we can do for the Duke of Beauville that cannot be better done by going prepared.'

The room went abruptly cold as Ali Hazr drew himself up, no sign of weakness in him, his eyes dark with threat and his right hand fumbling at the sash of his borrowed gown as if to draw steel. 'You will not call him by that name,' he commanded. Neither of us breathed, and I fought down the urge to retreat at this sudden appearance of Fury in dressing gown and bandage.

'I see,' Holmes replied mildly, although I doubted that he did, any more than I. However, he decided to let pass for the moment what was clearly a basket of snakes, and said only, 'Perhaps you might allow Russell and me to pack our bags and take care of a few matters of urgent business. You rest here. I will enquire if Mrs Hudson can assemble you some clothing.'

We left him then, and although I half expected to hear the crash of his collapse onto the carpet, he must have succeeded in making his way to the bed. Only when we reached the main room, where Holmes dived into the heap of letters to extract those most pressing of reply, was I struck by the full scope of the undertaking: I was headed for the country house of a peer, no matter how unlikely a peer. We were full into the season of social weekend shoots, and Saturday loomed near. In something not far from horror, I turned to my husband.

'Holmes! Whatever shall I do? I haven't a thing to wear.'

CHAPTER THREE

IT WAS NOT STRICTLY accurate, of course, that I had nothing to wear. True, most of the garments hanging in my wardrobe were not exactly the thing for a country house Saturday-to-Monday, but I could pull together a sufficient number of quality garments (if in somewhat out-of-date styles and hem lengths) to remain presentable. I doubted that Mahmoud, even as the Duke of Beauville, would gather to his bosom the frothy cream of society.

Ten years earlier, my cry might have been more serious: Before wartime shortages had changed both fashion and social mores, even a three-day country house visit would have required a dozen changes of clothing, and more if one intended to venture out for a day's shooting or to sit a horse. With the relaxed standards of 1923, however, I thought I might be allowed to appear in the same skirt from breakfast until it was time to dress for dinner. Thus, two or three suitcases instead of that same number of trunks.

I piled a selection of clothing on my bed and, since I knew she would repack them anyway as soon as my back was turned, left Mrs Hudson to it. I found Holmes just closing up his single case, which I knew would contain everything from evening wear to heavy boots.

'You don't imagine dinner will be white tie, do you, Holmes?'

'If the possibility presents itself, we can have Mrs Hudson send a gown and your mother's emeralds.'

'I cannot imagine Mahmoud in white tie. But then, I can't imagine Mahmoud in anything but Arab skirts and *khufiyyah*.'

'The revelations have been thought-provoking,' he agreed, surveying the contents of his travelling-razor case and then slipping it into the bag's outer pocket. 'Although you may remember, I said at the time they were not native Arabs.'

'True, but I believe you identified their diphthongs as originating in Clapham.'

He raised his eyes from the trio of books he had taken up, and cocked one eyebrow at me. 'Surely you understood that to be a jest.'

'Oh, surely.'

He discarded two of the volumes and pushed the survivor in after the razors. 'By the way, Russell, our guest seemed anxious that we wipe those names from our tongues. Our Arab guides are now, I take it, Alistair and Maurice. Or possibly "Marsh".'

'Not Mr Hughenfort and the Duke of Beauville – or would it be Lord Maurice? Or, not Maurice, what was his first given name? William? What *is* the proper form of address for a duke who is refusing his title, anyway?'

'I believe the matter will be simplified when we are presented as old acquaintances.'

'Well, if he's changed as much in appearance as Ali has, it won't be difficult to call him by another name. You do realise, by the way, what his name means?'

'A pleasant irony, is it not?'

Maurice, which one might translate as 'The Dark-Skinned One,' has its origins in the word 'Moor'. Maurice: The Arab.

Patrick brought the motor to our door in time for the afternoon train. We loaded our cases in the boot and settled an ill-looking Alistair into the back, well swathed in furs and with two heated bricks at his feet. At the station, we had to help him up into the train carriage – his bruises had now stiffened, and the blood loss he had sustained made him quite vulnerable to the cold November air. We retained the heaviest travelling rug and wrapped him in it against the inadequate heat of the compartment; he was asleep before the train pulled out of Eastbourne.

I nestled down into my own fur-lined coat and, while I watched Alistair Hughenfort sleep, meditated on that peculiar human drive, loyalty.

On entering Palestine in the closing days of 1918, Holmes and I had been pushed into the vehemently unwilling arms of two apparently Arab agents for the British government intelligence service – that is, Holmes' elder brother, Mycroft. We had begun on a note – an entire chorus – of mistrust, resentment, and dislike, and only slowly had those abrasive feelings softened beneath the continuous rub of shared tribulation and danger. When I had proved that I would, if pushed to the extremity, kill to protect our band of four, Ali's eyes had finally held a degree of respect. When later we demonstrated our willingness to die for each other, we were forever bound, like it or not.

Five years or fifty, when people have sweated, suffered, and shed blood together, there can be no hesitation: If one calls, the other responds. We had shared salt and bread, those staples of Bedu life; now it appeared that we were about to share our combined strength. My blood family had been dead for nine years; however, in the interim I had acquired a most singular pair of brothers.

Darkness fell outside the windows long before we reached the tiny village of Arley Holt. We were the only passengers to disembark – as far as I could see, we had been the last passengers on the entire train.

Nonetheless, a figure trotted out from the warmth of the station to meet us, bowling along on legs too small for his stocky body and talking a streak from out of his bristling ginger whiskers, his gravelly voice comprising a delicious admixture of highland Scots, East End London, and Berkshire.

'There you are, Master Alistair, I was just going to spread my car rug out on a bench and stop the night here, meet the first train in the morning. Had a good trip did you? – I see you found your friends – no, miss, I'll carry those, the good Lord blessed me with strong shoulders and I'm happy to use them – watch your step here, should've brought a torch I should've, daft of me – oi, stop a mo',' he cautioned sharply, realising in the darkness that one of us was moving very slowly indeed. 'What've you done to yourself, young master? You're hurt!'

I expected Alistair to dismiss the servant's concern with a curt phrase – as Ali, he certainly would have – but he surprised me. 'It's nothing, Algy. I got bashed in Town yesterday and I've gone all stiff on the train. I'll be fine after a night's sleep.'

'Blimey,' Algy muttered. 'Let you out of me sight and you get yoursel' bashed, what will the Missus say, I can't think. Here now, you pack yourselves good and snug in the back, that'll warm you.' He wrestled from the boot an enormous bearskin rug that swallowed Alistair, with plenty left to cover the passengers on either side of him.

Holmes, without asking, went around to the front of the old motor and yanked the starter handle for the driver. When the engine had coughed and sputtered its way to life and Holmes was back inside (where 'snug' was indeed the word, as well as being redolent of large carnivores), the driver turned in his seat.

'Much obliged, sir, I'd've had a time getting 'er going in the cold. Name's Algernon, Edmund Algernon.' Ali roused himself enough to give the driver our names; Algernon touched his cap in response, then turned to shift the motorcar into motion.

The village died away in less than a minute; the night closed in. The tunnel of our headlamps revealed a well-kept track with hedgerows high on either side, so close that if I'd dropped the window I could have touched them without stretching, although our vehicle was narrow. Algernon kept up a running commentary, directed at his employer but with the occasional aside of explanation to us, concerning a flock of sheep, a neighbour's rick fire, another neighbour's newborn son, the relief when a villager's illness was deemed not after all to be the dreaded influenza, and half a dozen other topics, all of them rural and thus commonplace to me – although again, not the sort of thing I would have associated with the silent figure at my side.

After what seemed a long time, our headlamps illuminated a crossroads. Algernon prepared to go to the left. Alistair spoke up.

'Justice Hall, if you would, Algy.'

'Ah,' said our driver, allowing the motor to drift to a halt. 'Well, you see, sir, Lady Phillida arrived today.'

The normally effusive Algy let the flat statement stand with no further embroidery; indeed, from his master's reaction, none was needed.

'Damn. She wasn't due until Thursday. All right, home then.'

'Home' lay to the left. After a few minutes the hedgerows fell away, replaced by a brief stretch of wire fence, then stone walls, and finally a gate – not a grand ceremonial entrance, just something to keep out livestock. This was followed by half a mile of freshly laid gravel with centuries-old trees on either side, then another stonewall, with farm buildings, a heavily mulched herbaceous border, and a passage tunnelled through the ground floor of a long stone building. When we emerged, the headlamps played across a clear expanse of tidy, weed-free gravel as Algy pulled up to a stone building with high windows of ancient shape and numerous small panes. We came to a halt facing a wooden porch that was buried beneath a tangle of nearly bare rose vine.

The door at the back of the porch opened almost as soon as the handbrake was set, and out hurried Algernon's female twin. Her voice was high and lacked the influence of Scotland and London, but it was every bit as free-flowing as our driver's. I prayed that this was 'the Missus' Algernon had mentioned – a married Ali would be the final straw.

'Oh, Mr Alistair, you must be fair frozen, it's come so bitter out; let's have you in by the fire now – why, whatever's happened?'

These two had all the earmarks of old family retainers, riding a comfortable line between familiarity and servitude. In fact, for a moment I played with the idea that Algy and the Missus might be two more of Mycroft's peculiarly talented agents, placed here with Ali in a meticulously choreographed act – down to the very name Algernon, which meant 'The Whiskered One' – but no, I decided reluctantly; they were both too idiosyncratically perfect for artifice. The Missus bossed and fussed Ali (who cursed his infirmity beneath his breath, in Arabic and English) through the porch and into the low, oak-panelled entrance vestibule, while Algernon, reassuring us that he'd bring our suitcases from the motor, pushed us in after them and closed the heavy, time-blackened door at our backs.

With her hand under Alistair's arm (no mean feat, considering the ten-inch disparity in their height), the housekeeper led him into the adjoining room. A wave of warmth billowed out through the draught-excluding leather curtain, through which we gladly followed.

And there I stopped dead.

Had I been asked to place this man Alistair Hughenfort into an English setting, I might, after considerable thought, have described one of two extremes: It would either be the stark, bare surroundings of a man long accustomed to living within the limits of what a couple of mules can carry, or else ornate to the point of glut, both as overcompensation for the desert's forced austerity and as a means of evoking the richly coloured clothing, drapes, and carpets of the Arabic palette.

Instead, Ali Hazr was at home in the most perfect Elizabethan great hall I'd ever seen. Not a nobleman's hall – not huge, nor ornate, nor built to impress, just a room which for three hundred years had sheltered its family and dependents from the outside world's storm and strife.

The room was perhaps fifty feet long, half that in width and height. The walls were of beautifully fitted limestone blocks, aged to dark honey near the roof beams and above the fireplace, paler near the floor and in the corners. The beams arched black high overhead, all but invisible in the dim light, and the high, many-paned windows above our heads were black and uncurtained. Electric lamps shed an oasis of light before the crackling fire, illuminating the lower edges of the tapestries that covered the stonework, hangings so dim with the patina of generations, they might well have disintegrated with cleaning.

On the hall's end wall, opposite the wooden gallery under which I stood amazed, hung what after a moment's study I decided was the head of a boar, bristling furiously over the room. The huge and weirdly distorted shadow it cast up the wall made the head look like some enormous prehistoric creature brought forward in time. Perhaps it actually was as large as it appeared: The tusks, their ivory darkened along with the stones, looked longer than my outstretched hand.

'Shall I take your coat, ma'am?' enquired a voice at my elbow. The Missus had settled Ali to her satisfaction, stripping him down to Holmes' borrowed suit and propping his feet onto a cushioned rest, and she was now turning to his guests. Obediently, I took off my heavy coat and draped it over the one Holmes had lent Ali. The cold bit my shoulders, so I hastened down the room to join the men in front of the fire. Once there, I rather wished I'd kept my coat; warming one's self before a head-high fireplace in a large room involves one roasted side and one chilled, and the impulse to revolve slowly in compensation.

'Mrs Algernon,' Alistair called. 'Our guests might like a drink to keep out the cold.'

Mrs Algernon, having deposited our outer garments out of sight, had come back into the hall with her attention fixed on the bandage around her charge's head. His request was intended, I thought, to deflect her interest more than to provide us refreshment; if so, it had the desired effect. After a brief hesitation, she turned and left the room again. Alistair – I could almost think of him by that name, given the setting – closed his eyes for a moment, then removed his feet from the settee.

'Mrs Algernon will give us dinner shortly. Not as artful a meal as you would have got at Justice Hall, I grant you, but then again, the company won't sour your digestion.'

Holmes sat down on one end of the sofa and took out his tobacco pouch. 'You do not wish to encounter Lady Phillida?'

'Marsh's sister is not the problem, or not entirely. It's Phillida's husband, Sidney – known as 'Spinach' and just as likely to set your teeth on edge. They've been in Berlin, and weren't due to return until the end of the week. Having them back . . . makes matters more difficult. No matter,' he added, and gave a dismissive wave of the hand.

With that small gesture, Ali and Alistair came together before me for the first time. Had he been speaking Arabic, that final phrase would have been *ma'alesh*, the all-purpose verbal shrug that acknowledges how little control any of us have over our fates. *Ma'alesh*; no matter; never mind; what can one do but accept things as they are? *Ma'alesh*, your pot overturned in the fire; *ma'alesh*, your prize mare died; *ma'alesh*, you lost all your possessions and half your family. The word was the everyday essence of Islam – which itself, after all, means 'submission'.

Clean-shaven and bare-headed, his former long, bead-flecked plaits with *khufiyyah* and *agahl* transformed into a head of cropped and thinning English hair, Ali's ornate embroidered robes and high, crimson boots replaced by Holmes' old suit and well-worn brogues, the ivory-handled knife and mother-of-pearl-handled Colt revolver he had invariably worn now seeming as unlikely as a feather boa on a rhinoceros, and carrying with him an odour not of cheap scent but of mothballs and damp wool – nonetheless, that powerful and exotic figure was still there, a ghostly presence beneath the ordinary English skin. *Ma'alesh*.

Mrs Algernon broke my reverie, bustling in with a tray laden with her idea of warming drinks. The fumes of the hot whisky reached us before she did, and although the tray also held the makings for tea, there were three full mugs of her steaming mixture. She set one mug down within arm's reach of each of us; as soon as she had left the hall, Alistair put his back on the tray and poured himself a cup of tea. One thing that had not changed: Although the Bedu were not the most outwardly observant of Moslems, they did generally demur at pork and alcohol, and although I had once seen Ali eat bacon, I'd never seen either Ali or Mahmoud take strong drink. Alistair's diet, it seemed, remained as it had been.

The hot whisky did the trick for two of us (although I couldn't have sworn that the fumes did not affect the abstainer). Mrs Algernon came in before the cups were empty to say that dinner was ready when we wished, and although Holmes and I were impatient to hear more of the teeth-on-edge Sidney, Alistair obediently put down his teacup and forced himself to his feet, raising his weight more by willpower than by the strength of his muscles. His first steps were supported by the chair back, and Holmes and I exchanged a glance. The man was in no shape to be questioned.

The dining room, fortunately, was low of ceiling and therefore made positively cosy by its fire. It smelt heavenly – a heaven made not of subtle foreign spices and delicate sauces, but of earthy comfort and, oddly, childhood pleasures. I sat down to my plate and allowed Mrs Algernon to ladle out my soup. At the first spoonful, Alistair's description of the cuisine was justified: Plain-looking, it tasted of root vegetables and peasant grains, herbs rather than spices, chicken rather than the beef tea it resembled.

Under the warmth of the room (and the fumes of the drink,

perhaps) our host's social instincts were aroused, and when the housekeeper had left, he came out with an unexpectedly chatty explanation of the substance in our bowls. 'This is Mrs Algernon's patented cure-all. For all the years I've known her, she's kept a pot on the back of the cook stove and tosses in whatever she has at hand. It never goes cold, never goes empty. Somewhere in here are atomic particles of the beef from my twenty-first birthday, and the carrot I brought my mother in a bouquet when I was four, and for all I know, the duck served at my parents' wedding breakfast.'

'My grandmother did the same thing,' I told him with a smile. 'Her pot was always bubbling away – she'd give a bowl to tramps who came to the door, to workmen, to us when we were hungry.' Which explained why the room's odour had reminded me of childhood comforts.

'I could never figure out why it doesn't taste like the bottom of a dust bin,' he remarked, sipping from his spoon. 'Mrs Algernon says it's because she seasons it with love. I suspect her of using brandy. It is, I have no doubt, massively unhygienic. If we all die in our beds tonight, you will know who is to blame.'

Holmes and I glanced at each other over our unhygienic but satisfying soup, and I could see the same thought in his mind: In removing himself from Palestine, our host had discovered not only a streak of garrulousness, but a sense of mild social humour as well; Ali's Bedouin humour had tended to involve either bloodshed or heavy burlesque.

Mrs Algernon's dinner was, as Alistair had said, simple but substantial, if showing signs of a hasty preparation. By the time the pudding course had been cleared, however, the remarkably genial man at the end of the table was fading fast, exhausted by his efforts at sociability. When he attempted to rise, intending to lead the way back into the hall for coffee, he leant hard on the table, then sat down again abruptly. Holmes leapt to his aid while I hurried to fetch Mrs Algernon; we caught up with the two men on the curving stone staircase, Holmes half carrying the younger man upwards. I took Alistair's other arm, expecting him to throw me off, but he did not.

Mrs Algernon directed us into a wood-panelled chamber with a fire in the grate, a room lifted straight out of a Mediaeval manuscript. We deposited him on a bed not much younger than the house and left him to the scolding ministrations of his housekeeper.

Back downstairs, with fresh logs on the fire, fresh coffee warming in front of it, and a dusty bottle of far-from-fresh brandy standing to one side, I studied my surroundings again, looking for I knew not what clue.

'What are we seeing here, Holmes?' I asked. 'If you'd told me that Ali's past was . . . this, I'd never have believed you. How do you explain the complete shift in the man – not just his speech patterns and how he moves, but his basic personality? The Ali we knew was short-tempered and as stand-offish as a cat. He'd have been at death's door before he allowed us to carry him up a flight of stairs – or for that matter, before he'd have come to us for help in the first place. This is a completely different man.'

Holmes nodded. 'One can only assume that when he went to Palestine, Alistair Hughenfort created the image of an entirely new person, and then stepped into that image. Now he is home, his original persona has taken over again. You've done it yourself, Russell, when you are in disguise. It is akin to complete fluency in two languages; one moves from one to another with no pause to consider the changes.'

'Holmes, I realise that clothing makes the man, but this is a bit . . . extreme. To assume a disguise for days, even weeks, is one thing. He was Ali Hazr for, what? Twenty years? And it wasn't as if he went out to Palestine as a disguised government agent in the first place – he and his cousin must have been out there for some time before Mycroft claimed them. What could drive a man to tear up what are quite obviously deep roots in order to become a foreign nomad?'

At that question, however, Holmes could only shake his head.

CHAPTER FOUR

M OST UNUSUALLY, I WAS awake the next morning before both Holmes and the sun. Before anyone, I thought as I padded down the time-worn steps with my boots in my hand – but no; once in the panelled vestibule beneath the minstrels' gallery, kitchen noises of clatter and conversation came from behind the doors on the other side of the dining room. I hesitated, mulling over the appeal of a cup of tea, but decided my thirst for solitude was greater.

Frustration had awakened me, had in fact been my restless companion all the night, an impatience to act, or even to know what it was that we were being called upon to do. I had, I realised, been working for ten weeks straight at this profession I still thought of as Holmes'; like a turning flywheel, the momentum of activity was hard to slow.

The massive bolt on the front door slid easily back, and a wash of frost-tinged air poured in. As near as I could see in the half-light, the porch and yard beyond were free of people and slumbering dogs. I slipped out, eased the door shut behind me, sat on the porch bench to lace on my boots, and set out into the fresh, pre-dawn twilight.

Traces of mist hung over the land, but it was high enough that it did not obscure my half-seen surroundings. My boots crunched over tightly packed gravel to a break in the walls between the corner of the house and a small building I took to be a church. Once I was through the gap, the surface changed from gravel to grass, and my footsteps ceased to jar the air.

I wandered among the half-bare trees of a walled orchard, enjoying the ancient, sleeping garden, my feet raising the scent of fermenting apples from the slick, black blanket of fallen leaves. I crossed into a large kitchen garden, also walled, of which less than half seemed to be actively under cultivation, and saw a wooden door on the far wall. This opened onto a water meadow, the stream at its bottom bridged by a small structure that shuddered, but did not collapse, beneath my weight. The air lay so still on the land, it was like walking out into a painting.

I made my way through the soft pearl of gathering light, heading in the direction of a tree-capped rise glimpsed in outline perhaps half a mile away. The air smelt of grass and sheep and earth: no sea breath here, as at Sussex, no peat tang as in Devon. This was the growing heart of England, deep black soil that had been nourishing crops and cattle for thousands upon thousands of years, before Normans, or Romans, or even Saxon horde. As the sun's rays began to touch the high mist overhead, I noticed what appeared to be a bench at the top of the hill, just under the edge of the cow-cropped branches. I clambered over a stile and trotted up the side of the hill, brushed a layer of fallen leaves from the rustic bench, and settled onto the damp wood to watch the sun come into the fold of earth that held Alistair Hughenfort's quintessentially English house.

The cool streaks of mist shied away at the merest hint of sun; soon my hilltop was fully lit. After a minute, the first rays lighted on the tips of three Tudor chimneys, easing like cool honey down the lumpy brickwork to the neatly thatched peaks. The many-paned windows set into the half-timbered upper level of the house flared now into a mosaic of light; when the line of the sun made a neat division between the house's two storeys, an upstairs window flew unexpectedly open. The depths of the walls kept the light from falling on the figure inside, but I felt that someone stood for a few moments in whatever room lay behind the window, looking out, and then went away.

The house was stirring, but I did not. The sun felt delicious on the side of my face, bright with promise and the illusion of warmth. The vista before me, this intimate and timeless marriage of stone and wood, plaster and thatch, was too near perfection for me to wish to break away. The balance of golden buildings and green field, tree and rock, water and sky made the impatience retreat and my heart begin to sing. I wanted it, all of it: not just the house – I could have bought half a dozen sixteenth-century houses if I wished – but everything the house was, had been, would be. My mother's family had migrated to England in the last century; my father's people were rootless Californians; everything I owned that had been in my family for longer than two generations could be packed into a small travelling case.

Of course, for all I knew, Alistair's people (those who were not Hughenforts) could have come here as recently as my own. But I thought not. The way he had moved in the house, his manner of speech to the two servants, evoked a sense of bone-deep kin with house and land. In Palestine, the man had been edgy and aggressive; here his testiness was gentled by the landscape.

45

Movement caught my eye in the formal garden behind the house: a black-and-white cat, picking its way through the wet grass, heading to the stables to hunt its breakfast. Down the valley, a cow complained; in the yard, a cock crew; on my hill, I sat, spellbound.

Had the house been more deliberately planned, if there had been the faintest air of artifice about the view, the perfection would have been cloying. As it was, the house and its outbuildings were uneven enough, the materials sufficiently varied to make it apparent that the man-made objects had grown up as organically as the trees. Badger Old Place, the Debrett's listing had called it – and indeed, it even resembled the animal: low to the earth, shaggy and somewhat unkempt, its exterior giving little hint of the power and potential ferocity sheltering within.

I envied Alistair Hughenfort his home. I badly wanted to know what force had wrenched him away from it. I wished I could reconcile the two sides of the man. But above all, I wished that I had paused before coming out here to take a cup of tea.

Then as if the universe had heard my string of desires and chosen to grant me at least one, a figure emerged from the house, and near-perfection shimmered into absolute: The figure carried a tray, and what is more, the tray was coming in my direction.

The bearer, I realised, was neither servant nor husband, but host. Alistair negotiated the stream via a series of rocks I had not noticed, scorning the shaky bridge, and strolled easily up the rise, the silver tray balanced on the fingers of one hand as if he were a waiter in a crowded café, a waiter dressed in a knit jumper of shades which would make a peacock proud.

He nodded as he drew near, but placed the tray on the bench beside me without a word. He then stepped back and turned to face the house, looking wan, but rested.

'Good morning,' I said.

'Mrs Algernon was about to send a tray up. I told her I would take it. I did not tell her you were not in the house, so it will be cold.'

It was cool, but welcome. I poured and sipped; he stood and looked over his home, then pulled off his cloth cap and slapped it against his knee. I remembered clearly that of the two, Mahmoud had been the dour, rocklike one, Ali the volatile, always itching for action.

'The last time you brought me a cup of tea,' I told him, 'was the morning before we reached Acre.'

'That was Mahmoud,' he responded automatically, without stopping to think. I had known it was Mahmoud; I merely wanted to hear him say his cousin's name. 'Marsh,' he corrected himself.

'It was Palestine, so I should say that "Mahmoud" is correct.' I sipped my drink, wondering what had brought him up here.

'You and Holmes,' he began abruptly, 'you were good at what you did. Mah – my cousin was impressed. He is not impressed by many. He may listen to you.'

'What are we to tell him?'

'He must leave this place. He no longer belongs here. It is laying its golden ropes around him, and choking him to death.' He glanced down to judge my reaction to this flight of fancy. When the side of my face told him nothing, he went on. 'He thinks it a task required of him by his ancestors. A noble service. A sacrifice. It is not, I tell him, but his ears are deaf.' Stress had, I was interested to hear, brought the Arabic rhythm back into his speech.

'If your cousin has decided that family responsibilities require him to remain in this country, I can't imagine that anything Holmes or I have to say will dissuade him.'

'Not say – but no, it is no good for me to tell you. You must see for yourselves, listen to him, draw your own conclusions.'

'Very well,' I told him. Then, since clearly he was not about to explain himself further, I changed the subject. 'Where does the house name come from?'

'Not its appearance, if that is your question. You saw the boar's head in the Hall? My ancestor who laid the foundations was hunting boar one afternoon in the year 1243 when the animal turned on him, and caught him unprepared. The tusks you saw on the head are real,' he added, 'although the fur has been patched over the years. The animal would have gutted him in seconds, but for a badger's den that gave way beneath the weight of the boar as it pivoted. That moment's delay allowed Sir Guy de Hasard to set his spear and catch the charge. The boar died, Sir Guy lived, and the house he'd planned to build was moved half a mile up the valley to leave the badger in peace. There's still a den there, in that copse you can just see over the hill.'

'Your people have lived here since 1243?'

'The first Badger Place was built shortly after that, although I should say the family had been here more or less forever. Seven generations of my ancestors have been born in the bed where now I sleep. I myself was born there. Half of them have died in that same bed. My people lived right here when the Doomsday Book was compiled, not under the name Hughenfort – that came in by marriage during the last century – but the same family. Generation after generation farmed the land, reared their children, served the king, came home from the wars, and died in the bed where they were born.'

He seemed suddenly to notice the ever-so-faint air of wistfulness in his answer and the intensity of his gaze, because he blinked, then turned to me and added unexpectedly, 'My sister's son lives in the next valley. He farms this land; he will inherit it. He will move into the house, and die in that bed an old and happy man.'

'While Mrs Algernon's pot of soup simmers away on the back of the stove.'

He granted me a quick smile, which made years fall away from him. 'That I do not know. The old ways are disappearing. I have been away for twenty years, and the only thing I recognise is the land. The old order is gone. My nephew will not have a Mrs Algernon in his life.' He gave a last glance at his ancestral home, black and white and golden in the sun, then slapped the soft cap against his leg again and tugged it cautiously over his bandaged head. 'However, if we don't present ourselves to be fed, I may not have a Mrs Algernon for long, either.'

He gathered up the tray and led the way down the hill. I followed, thoughtful. Had he merely come to fetch me? Or to tell me that he trusted in the skills of the partnership Holmes and Russell? Or – odd thought – had he seen me sitting on the hilltop bench and been struck by a sudden desire for companionship?

Mahmoud – Marsh – at Justice Hall, Alistair here; it could not, I reflected, be an easy thing to be set apart from the day-to-day companion of two decades.

Breakfast was fortifying, the fuel of labourers. Afterwards, Holmes and Mrs Algernon bent over the scalp of an encouragingly irritable Alistair, pronounced themselves well pleased with the healing process, and replaced the bandage with a smaller plaster. Their patient stalked away, and Holmes and I went up to our rooms.

'We are to stay with Mah – with our old friend Marsh, then?'

'So it would appear. If nothing else, Alistair seems to have a minimum of servants at his disposal here.'

'He walked up the hill to tell me that Marsh was impressed by our skills, and that he might listen to us telling him to go back to Palestine.'

'So that is what Ali wants?'

'It sounded like it.'

'Should be a brief visit, then.'

So, our sojourn in the land of the gentry was to be a brief one. The thought cheered me considerably.

With the sun actually generating a trace of warmth, the motorcar's bearskin remained in hibernation. Alistair sat in the front beside Algernon, although there was none of the easy banter of the night before. Our host had also shed his colourful pullover, although around his neck was draped a brilliant purple scarf with lemon-yellow fringes, topping the handsome grey suit he wore beneath a trim alpaca overcoat. Both of the latter garments were considerably newer in cut than the formal garb he'd worn to Sussex. On his head was an equally stylish soft felt hat, although he did not appear to have bothered having new shoes made during the four months he'd been in the country. His cheeks were smooth, his hair combed over the plaster, and from where I sat I could see his right leg jogging continuously up and down, the body's attempt to release the tension that clenched his jaw and held his shoulders rigid. When threatened in Palestine, Ali had generally responded with a drawn knife; I couldn't help speculating what the country house equivalent might be. Cutting insults at forty paces? Charades to the death?

We moved along the unmetalled road in the glorious autumnal morning, keeping straight when we reached the signpost of the night before. 'Justice Hall' was an interesting name for a ducal seat, I thought, and made a mental note to ask for an explanation.

The roads improved as we went on. Soon we were running alongside a stone wall far too high to see or even climb over; it went for what seemed like miles, high, secure, and blank. I was beginning to wonder if we were circling the estate rather than following one side when Algernon slowed and the wall dropped away towards a gate.

This was a very grand gate indeed, ornately worked iron hanging from twin stone pillars on which coats of arms melted into obscurity and atop which unidentifiable creatures perched. There was a snug, tidy lodge house at one side, from which a boy of about twelve scrambled, pulling on a cap as he ran, to throw himself hard against the weight of all that iron to get it open. He came to attention as we drove past, tugging briefly at his cap brim. Alistair raised a hand to him, but Algernon said loudly, 'Thank you, young Tom,' receiving a gap-toothed grin in return.

The wide, straight drive that rose gently from the gate was flanked by fifty feet of close-cropped lawn on either side, behind which stood twin walls of vegetation – huge rhododendrons, for the most part; the entrance drive would be a pageant come spring. Taller trees, most of them deciduous, grew above the shrubs, to protect them from the summer sun.

We travelled steadily towards an open summit; as we neared the top, Alistair instructed Algernon, 'Stop for a moment when we've cleared the hill.'

Obediently, the driver slowed, timing it so that as we reached the highest point we were nearly at a stop already. The bonnet tipped a fraction, and then Algy set the brake and turned off the engine.

Alistair climbed out; Holmes and I did not hesitate to join him at the front of the car. The view was, quite simply and literally, stunning.

As far as the eye could see, Paradise as a cultivated garden. A vast sweep of greensward, undulating with delicate dips and rises, dropping to the long curve of a lake with a glorious jet of fountain spouting to the heavens, the whole set with centuries-old trees as a ring is set with diamonds. It was far too perfect to be natural, but so achingly lovely that the eye did not care.

'One can say this for Capability Brown,' Holmes drawled. 'He knew how to think on a grand scale.'

'Mostly Humphry Repton, actually,' Alistair told him. 'Not that it matters, except down near the water.'

But the house; oh, the house.

I was, truth to tell, quite set to detest the place. Whatever its age, no matter its architectural or historical importance, Justice Hall was keeping Mahmoud Hazr from his rightful and chosen place in the world. No pile of stones or family tree justified the disruption of a man's life – of the lives of two men. Two good, righteous, valuable men who had been happy doing hard and important work, until a brother had died and a title descended on one. I had no illusions that anything Holmes and I could say might prise Mahmoud from his perceived duty, but I had come here intending to try my damnedest.

But oh, the house.

I had thought Alistair's small mansion near to perfection, had found its human scale and diversity deeply satisfying. Justice Hall was another measure of human endeavour entirely.

The house was composed of three main blocks, with the largest, central portion set back between the two wings like a lion welcoming visitors between its enormous outstretched paws. Or like a sphinx; yes, there was something distinctly feminine about the Hall, its strength delicate rather than muscular. The drive crossed a stream that merged with the beautifully curved pond, and came to its end in a circle between the two paws; from where we stood, the drive looked remarkably like a ball of yarn stretched taut, awaiting the great feline's attention and amusement.

Too symmetrical and unadorned to be called Baroque, too richly varied for a Palladian label, its stone some indeterminate shade between warm gold and cool pewter, with crenellations and domes and a wealth of windows that hovered just on the safe edge of excessive, Justice Hall was unlike any building I had ever seen. Rather, I corrected myself, it resembled other grand houses of the nobility, but in the way that a woman of strikingly original beauty resembles her inevitable crowd of imitators – the similarity is in one direction only. I felt I had never truly seen a country house before. It was almost improper to think of it as a mere 'building'; this was an entity whose signal characteristic was its unearthly perfection.

The sun did not shine on Justice Hall so much as Justice Hall called forth the sun's rays to fall at such and such an angle. We did not look upon it; rather, it invited our eyes to admire. It sat in its exquisitely shaped bowl and smiled gently on the careful arrangement of dappled deer on its slopes, the fall of shadows from its trees, the play of the breeze on the water at its base. In the summer it would glow; in the rain, its face would appear pensive; under a blanket of snow it would be a fairy-tale castle; in the moonlight, this would be the dwelling place of the gods.

Justice Hall was the most self-centred house I had ever seen. My heart went out to the man at my side: If Justice Hall wanted Mahmoud, I did not believe Ali had a chance.

As if he had read the thought on the side of my face, Alistair made a small sound, a grunt of disgust, or perhaps of despair.

'You see?' he said.

I do not know why it took me so long to consider that Alistair's motives in seeking us out might not be purely philanthropic, but it was only at that moment that I perceived the stain of jealousy beneath his philadelphic goals.

Maybe, I thought, just maybe we will find that Marsh Hughenfort actually wanted to come home. Perhaps his eyes viewed the panorama before us with all the love and devotion of his Norman ancestors. His blood and bones, after all, were bred here; more than eight centuries of his people had devoted their lives to holding the land against all comers. Mahmoud must be nearing fifty, the time when a man's eyes might well begin to tire of the dry, grey, comfortless, and infinitely treacherous desert and to seek the relief of green hills and childhood shapes. Perhaps Justice Hall's seventh Duke had chosen to come home from the wars, to die as an old man in the bed where he had been born.

With that, I was no longer so sure of the coming discussion with the man I had called Mahmoud Hazr. I was bound by loyalty, without question; but there were two of my brothers here, and what suited the one might not, I now saw, suit the other.

Silent and thoughtful, I followed Holmes into the back of the motorcar, to continue our short journey into the glittering heart of perfection.

CHAPTER FIVE

T HE DRIVE UP FROM the main road had been perfectly straight, but once the summit was reached, its path began to curve with the contour of the hillside, less from necessity, since the descent was a gradual one, than to present a more dramatic approach. The track curved at the base of the hill, then dropped a fraction, so that for the last half mile one not only faced the house straight on, but felt as if the house lay above. I could not help speculating on the quantity of soil Humphry Repton had caused to be moved in order to create that subtly humbling approach.

As it was, Justice Hall waited foursquare at the head of her drive, occupying her terraces with the patient air of a queen awaiting obeisance. A wide bridge crossed the artificial lake that separated the house from the world outside the gates; as we drove over it, I happened to glance up at the roofline. A flag flew above the front portico, and below its gently undulating colours stood a figure, nearly hidden by the crenellations. A man, I thought, briefly glimpsed, and then we were circling around and coming to a halt before the house.

One clear indicator of an establishment's degree of affluence, in 1923 as in 1723, was the number of unnecessary individuals it maintained. Messengers and footmen, rendered all but superfluous by modern methods of communication and transport, were nonetheless kept on by the grandest houses, for show more than any actual convenience they might provide. So I was curious to see how many persons would be required to recognise our arrival.

Two, it seemed (in addition to young Tom at the entrance gates). Before I could make a move towards the car door, it opened, held for me by a rigid-spined young man who stared off with proper fixity at the distant hillside. On the other side of the car an older man in a formal cutaway coat was aiding Alistair and Holmes. Alistair greeted him as Ogilby; this would be the butler.

When I was safely freed from the motorcar, I half expected the discreet young man to climb into the motor and direct Algernon in an entire circuit of the house in order to offload our bags at the service entrance, but instead Algernon merely handed them over, and the footman disappeared promptly in the direction of the house.

While Alistair was telling Algernon that he'd ring to Badger Old Place when he wanted to go home, I looked over the top of the motorcar at the ornate fountain that formed the centre of the circle. It had not yet been drained for the winter, and the low sun collected in a million diamonds, the water playing and dripping off the bronze figures. Pelicans, I saw, and nearly laughed aloud at the unlikely frieze of beaks and outstretched wings that intertwined and emitted jets of water into the bronze sea-cliffs at their base. I did not think I had ever seen such an ornate fountain incorporating such whimsy. Certainly it did not have much in common with the immense dignity of the house itself.

A throat cleared, and I tore my eyes away from the Baroque

splendour to join Holmes. We made our scrupulously escorted way up the seven wide steps of a brief but psychologically distancing terrace. A vestigial portico sheltered us; an ornate door swung wide of its carven stone surrounds; Justice Hall permitted us entrance.

Just inside the door, some surprisingly indulgent past master had built a small vestibule for the guardian of the door. The butler even had some heat source, the brush of warmth on my face informed me, and I could see a chair and footstool accompanying the more usual front-door implements of waiting umbrellas, a house telephone, and the all-essential silver salver for accepting the cards of callers. Once past this private oasis of comfort, the interior hall was freezing cold, but as unremittingly impressive as any duke could have asked – or many kings, for that matter. A hundred visitors might collect beneath that frescoed dome, under those arched colonnades, among those acres of echoing marble both real and faux; the grandeur would still dwarf them all. Three guests, a butler, and the housemaid receiving our outer garments made for a human element that was insignificant indeed.

I told the maid that I would keep my coat, thank you. She bobbed her response and went away with the garments of Alistair and Holmes over her arm. The butler admitted he would have to enquire as to His Grace's whereabouts, and suggested that we follow him into the drawing room, but Alistair said we would wait in the Great Hall. Ogilby too slipped away, leaving Alistair to pick up a copy of *Country Life* from the top of an exquisite scagliola sideboard while Holmes and I craned our necks and gawked like a pair of museum patrons.

I had seen grander entrance halls – huge halls, halls whose every inch was encrusted with gilt and mirrors, halls dizzying with the sheer accumulation of beauty – but I had never known a room with a stronger sense of what I can only term *personality*. The room was a cube of marble and alabaster, the black-and-white tiles of its floor giving birth to a pale stairway slightly narrower at the top than the bottom. Near the foot of the stairway stood a larger-than-life statue of a Greek athlete, the outstretched right arm that had once held a javelin now empty; at first glance, he seemed to be preparing to stab any unwary passerby. Fluted columns of a heavily veined alabaster tapered up to support first an upper galley and then the side-lit dome above. The veins of chocolate and cream in the columns were peculiarly symmetrical, with a heavy streak in one leading the eye to a similar stain in the next column twelve feet away. As one studied them, the sensation grew that they had actually been cut from a single contiguous piece, the remnants of an original alabaster monolith left when the rest of the room was carved away, as if Justice Hall had been whittled from a huge block of living stone. The image was disorientating, and I tore my eyes from the fluted columns to look up.

It took a while for me to decide what the fresco on the dome depicted. Normally such paintings are either of battles – the ceiling at Blenheim, for example, created for the Duke of Marlborough to commemorate his victory at the battle of that name – or allegorical, with classical gods and illustrated stories. This one showed robed figures reclining at a feast, with dancers playing tambourines and musicians with harps and a variety of unlikely-looking woodwinds in the background. A cluster of remarkably serious greybeards stood to one side, looking for all the world like barristers discussing their briefs. Farther around the dome's circle, a wood sprang up, with birds and wild animals decorating the dark and gnarled trees, and a single man, running from a tawny creature that I thought might represent a lion. The man was making for a small hut, looking back over his shoulder at the lion and thus not noticing the bear (this animal quite realistic) standing at the corner of the hut, nor the snake dangling from the eaves.

The combination of animals was unexpected in this setting, but as soon as I saw them I knew what the painter was illustrating – and indeed, in the remaining space of the dome's bowl, in what I knew would be the eastern quarter, the sun was rising over an idealised English landscape of green fields and tidy hedgerows. Its rays illuminated the lower sides of a great and gathering darkness, crimson and black and awesome across the innocent land.

'Good Lord,' I said involuntarily.

Alistair glanced up from a *Country Life* article on improving one's backhand in tennis. 'Cheerful, is it not?'

'Do you see it, Holmes?' I asked. He shook his head, admitting ignorance. 'From the Book of Amos. A description of Armageddon – the end of the world. "The Day of the Lord", the prophet calls it, which some desire as the time when the Lord comes to set human affairs straight, but which, Amos says, we ought to dread for just that reason. "Why would you want the Day of the Lord"?' I recited. '"It is darkness, and not light. As if a man ran from a lion"' – here I pointed up at the unlikely beast – '"and a bear met him; or went into a house to lean against the wall, and a serpent bit him." The Lord goes on, "I hate, I despise your feasts, I take no joy in your solemn conclaves." He accepts neither burnt offerings nor sacrifices, will not listen to the singing and music given Him. "But," He says, "let justice roll down like waters, righteousness like an ever-flowing stream." You see? It's even written along the bottom, over and over again in Latin.' This alternated, I saw, with another phrase: *Justitia fortitudo mea est*, the Mediaeval Latin quaintly corrupt. 'Righteousness is my strength.'

We stared at the scene overhead, at the huge black clouds flecked with crimson, at the unheeding feast-goers and the single doomed man, and at the rich blue splash in the centre of the dome, which depicted the very instant in which the dammed-up waters of justice were loosed, to roll down across the feasts and the solemn assemblies and flood the world in a torrent, that when it had passed, the stream of righteousness might flow undisturbed.

Then, between one breath and another, the master of Justice Hall was there, standing in the centre of the gallery at the top of that great staircase, framed perfectly by the arch of the doorway behind him, hands in his pockets, looking as if he'd been occupying the spot for an hour. Alistair threw the magazine down and trotted up the stairway; something about the way he swept upwards evoked the swirl of robes about his person.

Mahmoud – Marsh – remained where he was, so immobile he might have been unaware of his companion's approach, might have believed that the objects of his gaze – Holmes and I – did not know he was there, although we were looking straight at him. He might have thought himself all alone in the hall, but for his reaction when his cousin gained the top step and reached out to embrace him in the Arab fashion: The duke pulled back. Very slightly, a mere fraction of an inch, but it cut off the embrace more effectively than a fist. Alistair stuttered awkwardly to a halt; only when he had taken his hand from the ducal arm did Maurice Hughenfort come to life. He took his hands from his pockets, turned to look into his cousin's face, said a few words in a voice too low to hear, and reached out to grasp the younger man's shoulder briefly. He then started down the long staircase.

Watching him descend, my first impression was that five years had turned Mahmoud into an old man, deliberate in his every movement, going grey (had I even seen his hair before?). As he drew nearer, it seemed more that he was in some deep and chronic pain, the kind that only iron control can keep at bay. But then he came off the stairs and was crossing the marble floor towards us, and the knowledge came stark into my mind: *This man is dying.*

He moved with the ease of health and shook Holmes' hand with no sign of discomfort, but the look on his face was one I had seen too often during the War, when one of the wounded soldiers I was nursing gave up his fight, and let go. Such was the expression on the man now taking my hand, bending over it with old-fashioned formality, calling me Mary, a name he had never used: The man was one of the walking dead, a person who had made the decision to die, who in complete peace and bemused detachment watched the antics of his neighbours and his would-be saviours, awaiting only the day when he would be permitted to leave them behind. The wounds of some of those dying soldiers had been relatively mild, just as, other than the old scar down the side of his face, this man seemed whole and psychologically undamaged. And yet, the look was unmistakable.

'Mahmoud!' I cried out – or began to. I had only let out the first pain-filled syllable when he shot me a glare that shrivelled the name on my tongue. Dying he might be, but he could definitely summon the old air of command when he needed to.

'We are such old friends, Mary,' he pronounced, his dark eyes boring into me. 'Despite the change in circumstances, I insist that you continue to call me Marsh.'

The moment he saw that he had achieved my obedience, he withdrew – like that; in an instant he was once more bland and polite, his real self back inside that distant waiting room where he alone dwelt. He told Ogilby that we would be in the library, then ushered us out of the echoing hall and down chilly corridors crowded with marble busts, Regency cartoons, display cabinets bursting with priceless knick-knacks, and paintings of ancestors stamped from the Hughenfort mould – dark hair, dark eyes, proud lift to the chin. We turned into an older wing of the house, and two doors down entered a sort of masculine sitting room next to a billiards room that reeked of cigars.

It was a library with few books, and most of those dealing with the breeding lines of horses, but it was deliciously warm. As I removed my coat, hat, and gloves, I studied my surroundings. It was a big room made intimate by the placement of furniture and the apparently haphazard arrangement of objects, as if some family member had deposited his Greek souvenir in a corner as he came in the door in 1829 and nobody had bothered to move the ancient statue ever since. The walls were a combination of warm beech linen-fold panelling and faded red silk wallpaper, half hidden behind a variety of landscape paintings and a plethora of glass-fronted cabinets containing stuffed wildlife and casual archaeological discoveries, the sorts of things dug up by boys and turned over by ploughs: coins and spearheads, scraps of Samian ware from third-century Romans and blue-figured porcelain from nineteenth-century Victorians, a pair of dusty kingfishers perching on a twist of rusty metal that might once have been a blade, and a filthy-looking object that could have been a shoe or someone's scalp – I did not care to look too closely. The objects appeared to have been placed on the shelves willy-nilly and the doors then locked behind them, and I was quite certain the house residents never actually saw them when they were in the room. The family photographs on the mantel and desk looked similarly abandoned to become a sort of three-dimensional wallpaper, with the exception of a group of three silver frames towards the right end of the mantel. These included a handsome young lad in the uniform of a second lieutenant of the recent war, whose eyes and chin declared him a Hughenfort, a slimmer, younger Marsh.

I became aware that the butler had materialised silently, in that manner of excellent manservants, waiting for his orders.

'Tea?' the scarred duke asked us. 'Coffee? Something cold? No? That will be all, Ogilby.'

Ogilby faded away. The door was shut, and Marsh Hughenfort stood before the fire, concentrating on removing a cigarette from a silver case and lighting it with a spill taken from a Chinese bowl on the mantelpiece. When the cigarette was going, he flicked the half-burnt paper fan into the flames and walked over to splash whisky and a shot from a soda-siphon into a glass. He held it out as an offer – which Holmes accepted and Alistair and I refused – and then to my astonishment he made one for himself and took it back to the fire.

I glanced at Alistair, seated with his knees crossed and his hands clasped together on his lap. It struck me then, how unusual it was to see those hands empty and unoccupied. In Palestine, Ali always had some project to hand: patching the tent, mending a buckle, working oil into the mules' leather traces, or – first, last, and at all moments in between – whittling. He had whittled endlessly, using the deadly blade he wore at his belt to carve unexpectedly delicate and whimsical figures of donkeys and lizards and long-haired goats. Whittling, it would seem, was not an occupation for the drawing room.

The man at the fireplace did not look at his cousin, but turned instead to us, and remarked, 'You two are looking well.'

The sheer conventionality of the opening took my

breath away: It had been astonishing enough to see the man hold a drink to his lips, but Mahmoud Hazr, making polite conversation? The changes in Ali ought to have warned me, but the Englishness of Alistair was nothing to that of his cousin.

There was no trace of Mahmoud's heavy accent, no accent at all apart from that of his class and education. His movements evoked no swirl of ghostly robes; nothing in his demeanour indicated that this duke had ever held something as crass as a handgun, far less a killing blade; his eyes betrayed no hint of the watchful authority that had been the very essence of the man. His voice was lighter, his eyes seemed a lesser shade of brown, his stance was that of an amiable if distracted English nobleman. Had it not been for his scar, and for that brief flash of command when I was about to speak his Arab name, I should have thought him a different man. He even held his cigarette differently.

'And you, sir,' Holmes replied, always ready to turn conventionality to his own purposes. 'You are looking somewhat . . . changed.'

'They say change is inevitable.' The duke raised his gaze to face Holmes squarely.

'I find folk wisdom to be a somewhat overrated commodity,' Holmes retorted. 'It generally fails to take into account the workings of cause and effect.'

Rather than bristle, or retreat, at this confrontation, Marsh Hughenfort seemed to relax, just a fraction, and opened his mouth, but before he could respond some distant sound reached him. He paused in an attitude of listening; Alistair too cocked his head; then, as one, the two men slumped into gloom. Alistair even muttered a mild oath. Marsh retreated until his back was to the fireplace, and waited.

Children's voices, of all things. Two high-pitched excited chatterers, growing and then fading as they turned into another part of the house, giving way to the sound of a woman in monologue. The library door opened; Holmes and Alistair rose automatically to their feet.

'—just pop my head in to see if he's in here, p'raps you'd better inform Mrs Butter that we'll be here for luncheon after all, just too terribly tiresome of them, truly it is. Oh, hello. I didn't know you had company, Marsh. Good morning, Alistair.'

She was a small, elegant, expensive woman in her early thirties, plucked, pencilled, and pampered, working a pair of silver-grey gloves from her thin hands as she came through the door. In her case, the ebony Hughenfort curls had been tamed, by nature or art, into a sleek shingle, but the chin and eyebrow were instantly recognisable. She radiated a natural superiority; her clothing was too perfect to be anything but Paris; I felt instantly a frump.

'My sister,' said Marsh. 'Phillida Darling.'

For a startling moment, I thought he was using a term of endearment in detached irony, but I realised it had to be the surname of the teeth-on-edge Sidney. 'Phillida, this is Mr Holmes and his wife, Miss Russell. They are friends.'

Her eyes lit up. She glided across the room, dropping the gloves and her cloche hat on an exquisite marquetry end-table in passing, and held out her hand to Holmes. 'What a splendid surprise, to encounter not just one, but two of my brother's friends in a single day. Any relation to the Duke of Bedford, Miss Russell? No? Well, to think one might have missed you, if the Garritsons' two brats hadn't broke out in horrid spots this morning. We thought we'd lunch with them,' she explained, settling onto the divan beside me and taking out a cigarette case and ivory holder, 'and we'd already set out before their nanny came down to tell them about the spots, stupid girl, and although usually I'd just have let my two in – children have to get these things some time, don't they? – it's really not a terribly convenient time. Thank you,' she told Holmes, who had applied a light to her cigarette. 'I mean, one has a party here this weekend, and a ball in a month's time, wouldn't it be tiresome if half the housemaids came down in spots, too? It happened to a dear friend of mine, had to cancel the evening, the food all delivered and all. So tell me,' she said, having softened us up with the flow of trivia, 'where did you two meet my brother?'

Here in your entrance hall, I nearly said. I caught back the impulse, presented her with a cheerful smile, and answered, 'Aleppo, wasn't it, Marsh?' I swivelled my head around as if to consult with him, and read not so much relief as approval, and that quiet humour in the back of his gaze that made my heart leap with pleasure: Mahmoud *was* there, somewhere. 'That tawdry little café that your friend Joshua dragged everyone to, plying us with muffins toasted over a paraffin stove? Or was that Greece, the year before? One of those grubby but romantic spots,' I told her.

'But what was he *doing* there?' She could see I was going to be useless as a source of information, so she turned to confide in Holmes, arching her pencilled eyebrows in appeal. 'He vanishes utterly for years and years, sends us a letter every six or eight months – postmarked in London, although one *knows* he can't be in London, one's friends would have seen him – and then back he comes, positively *bristling* with mysteries and secrets. A person might think he'd been in prison or something – I mean, just look at his poor face. He didn't have *that* when he left.' Referring to the scar, of course.

'Those Heidelberg duelling academies could be quite rough,

nicht wahr, Marsh?' This was from Holmes, contributing his own obfuscation.

'Of course,' I added, 'the Carpathian shepherds who took him in couldn't have helped the healing any. Health care in the mountains is still quite rudimentary.'

I was interested to see a flash of real irritation beneath Lady Phillida's sisterly exasperation. Understandable, I supposed – if nothing else, the family would want to know if the heir had a string of warrants, a pile of debts, or a wife and six sons trailing behind from some foreign land. However, if Marsh had not told her where and how he had spent the last twenty years, it was not up to me to fill the gaps.

She pouted prettily, stubbed out her cigarette, and lounged upright. 'You two are as bad as my brother. Shall we see you at luncheon?'

'They may be stopping here for a day or two. Perhaps more,' Marsh told her.

Her eyes went wide in dismay. 'What, over the weekend? Oh, Marsh, why didn't you tell me earlier we were having additional guests?'

'It was just now decided.'

'Well, next time you must let Mrs Butter know in advance.' It was a gentle scold, for the sake of keeping face before guests, but she must have heard the edge to it because she turned to me with a little laugh. 'Men – they just don't understand the servant problem, do they? We have to coddle Mrs Butter – where would we be if she upped and left? Anyway, lovely to know you won't be leaving right away, do feel free to stay on until Monday – we'll have to get together for a nice long girlish chat. And at least we won't have to worry about thirteen at the table on Saturday night.'

She stepped over and kissed the air near her brother's cheek, which gesture he accepted without a flinch, and then she swept from the room. Alistair slowly let out a gusty breath, and reached for his cigarettes. All four of us twitched, like a group of hens settling their ruffled feathers, and I reflected that my own visceral response to the accents of power and privilege had at least become more controllable over the years. I was still intimidated by women like Phillida Darling, but I did not show it outwardly.

'We were, I believe,' Holmes said, recalling us to our state before Lady Phillida had entered, 'speaking of the nature of change.'

Alistair shook out his match and cut into any response his cousin might have made. 'Not here. Not with that woman and her husband listening in at the windows. I even caught the daughter with her eye to a keyhole last week.'

'This afternoon,' Marsh said, sounding resigned. 'After lunch we will put on our boots and remove ourselves from windows and keyholes.'

The lack of hope or even interest in his voice stung me into speech. 'We did come here to help,' I told the duke sharply.

As if I had not spoken, he flicked his cigarette into the fire and left the room.

Luncheon was every bit as difficult as we had been led to anticipate, with Marsh silent, Alistair monosyllabic, and Lady Phillida making constant gay forays in her quest for information. Sidney Darling appeared after the rest of us had settled to our first course, full of apologies ('Trunk call to London; business couldn't wait'), bonhomie ('Alistair old man, been a while'), and charm ('Perfectly splendid to meet friends of my brother-in-law; what a perfectly lovely frock on you, Miss Russell. I say, any relation to Bedford?').

Sidney Darling was a tall, thin, languid, inbred aristocrat with protruding blue eyes and the pencil-thin moustache and sleek light hair of a film star, dressed in a height-of-fashion dove-grey lounge suit with Prince of Wales turn-ups. His topics of conversation ran the narrow gamut from horse racing and shotgun makers to the best spots to winter along the Riviera. His response to our lack of interest in those accepted passions of the leisured class was mild surprise followed by a pitying smile. Sidney Darling did indeed set one's teeth on edge.

Despite their traditional interests, however, I could see that the Darlings were not cut to the peer's age-old pattern. Certainly, they were the very definition of old money – at least, the wife was; nonetheless, the Darlings moved in a social milieu that included film directors, the sons and daughters of American tycoons, progressive European novelists, and the sorts of artists more often seen in newspaper columns than on museum walls. This was, I thought, the new generation of the entitled, whose traditional studied lack of interest in the getting of money, the dictates of fashion, or human beings outside their circle was being modified to include the people and places, music and talk of the West End, Europe, and even brazen America. Indeed, Lady Phillida's own speech reflected this, wavering as it did between the lady's compulsory 'one' and the blunt and egalitarian 'I'; she had even used the vulgar term 'weekend' without a hint of coyness.

Eventually, at the conclusion of one long recitation of the personal history of a prized shotgun, it registered on Darling that the rest of the table was not participating in the narrative with any degree of enthusiasm. He dabbed at his thin moustache and turned dutifully to Holmes.

'Tell me, Mr Holmes, what do you do?'

'I raise bees.'

The slightly pop blue eyes blinked. 'Ah: How int'resting.'

'Very.'

Seeing her husband foundering on the rock of Holmes' avocation, Lady Phillida decided to give me a try.

'And you, Miss Russell. Do you also keep bees?'

'I read theology. At Oxford.'

'Oh. Well. That's rather . . . interesting as well,' she replied dubiously, her mind, no doubt, filled with furious speculation concerning the private dinner conversations that took place between the spectacularly mismatched married couple which her brother had inflicted on her for the weekend.

Alistair gave a small choking sound and reached to retrieve a hastily dropped table napkin. For the rest of the meal, we spoke about gardens.

CHAPTER SIX

SIX PEOPLE ESCAPED WITH gratitude from the lunch table, scattering in all directions to marshal thoughts, and energies, before the dinner hour would bring us inexorably back together. Holmes and I went up to the rooms we had been given, which were in the oldest, western wing of the house but which had been made comfortable by efficient fires and an actual modern bathroom between them. My own room was a festivity of blue and gold, with a froth of silken drapes on its four posters, a counterpane of delicately embroidered silk, and terrifyingly pale carpets on the floor. Mahmoud would have given it me as a joke; of Marsh, or his sister, I could not be sure. Holmes was given the King's room, all heavy red velvet and massive carved bed; the king had been George I, whose visit had no doubt precipitated a large part of the grand rebuilding and propelled the Hughenforts to the brink of penury.

Marsh's suite was down the corridor in the same wing, we had been informed by Ogilby, although I thought it had pained him to admit that the new duke was sleeping down here rather than taking up rooms in the grander central block. I thought Marsh had probably kept room he'd occupied as a schoolboy, and decided to interpret that as an encouraging sign: Making a large space over to his taste would have been a declaration of permanence.

When we had boots on our feet and coats over our arms, we descended the noble stairway into the Great Hall, beneath the dome where the waters of Justice were poised to spill. A young housemaid broke off polishing a spotless display cabinet to accompany us to the so-called library. It was empty, but we followed the crack of billiards to the next room.

The library might be neutral ground for the family, but this was a male enclave, heavily masculine with dim Victorian colours, a smattering of animal heads, and the patina of ten thousand cigars over the velvet drapes and leather sofas. And dark: Other than the lamp-lit table itself, the brightest spots in the room were the areas of pink female flesh in the paintings decorating the walls and the unusually luminous ceiling, where light seemed to shift and play. Over the elephantine fringed table I glimpsed the waters of Justice Pond, the low, wintry sunlight sparkling off its fountain-stirred surface onto the plaster and beams above us.

How, I wondered, could I ever have mistaken Alistair for an Englishman? Dressed in plus-fours and boots he might be, with a Norwich jacket belted around his stocky frame and a soft cap on the sofa waiting to go onto his head; nonetheless, everything about him shouted 'foreigner.' His stance, his scowl, the way his fingers tugged at his lower lip in the absence of moustaches – he looked like Feisal in fancy dress.

His cousin, on the other hand, presented the very essence of English Lord. He was bent over the green table, studying the lay of the balls, and ignored our entrance as assiduously as he was ignoring his fidgeting companion. The birch-and-ivory cue rocked three times over the prop of his fingers, then with a sharp crack his ball flew over the green felt and into its pocket. Two more followed, one of those a complicated ricochet shot, and then the table was clear. He replaced the cue in its rack, picked up a smouldering cigar from its rest on a small table and took a last draw before circling the burning end off in the bowl, then picked up a squat glass with half an inch of amber liquid in it and swallowed it down. He caught up a heavy tweed jacket tossed over the back of a leather armchair and strode towards the French doors, giving a short whistle between his teeth. A pair of retrievers scrambled out from under the billiards table and shot out in front of us. Marsh held the door for us; as I went past him, I smelt whisky.

He set a brisk pace through the formal terraces and around the western wing. The perfect lawns stretched away in all directions, nestling around the Pond and gardens, speckled with deer and broken by enormous oaks and beeches, set here and there with buildings – a Gothic-style boathouse on the lake, a Palladian music house surrounded by trim gravel nearby, and a picturesque ruin atop a distant hilltop. As we marched up the grassy slopes, I kept an eye on Alistair, but he was not about to admit to weakness by being left behind. Past the layered centuries of stonework we went, along the path that followed the northern bank of the stream, and up the parkland until the house and lake had disappeared and we were in the park proper.

There, Marsh's pace slowed. He glanced over his shoulder at the lagging Alistair, and for the first time noticed his cousin's infirmity. However, he did not then exclaim, as the Algernons had, 'What happened to you?' Instead, he watched Alistair approach, then stepped forward to tug the injured man's shoulder down and squint at the plaster. One brief look, and he stood away.

Alistair met his eyes, and shrugged. 'An accident. In London.'

Marsh's gaze lingered on the other man's; emotion moved not so much across the duke's face as in the muscle beneath it, an emotion composed of apology and bewilderment, that he'd spent hours in his cousin's company without taking notice. I saw Marsh's hand come up to trace the scar on his face, a thing Mahmoud had done when deeply troubled. Marsh was no more aware of his gesture than Mahmoud had been, and I clasped to myself this sign of Mahmoud's presence beneath the unknown exterior. Then Marsh turned away, and we were walking again across the manicured landscape as if nothing had happened – although this time at a slow stroll.

'You two have been busy?' Marsh asked us.

'Reasonably so,' Holmes replied. 'We have just returned from Dartmoor, a somewhat interesting case involving land fraud and family inheritance. Why do you ask?'

'No reason. You look tired, is all.'

'Nonsense. You, on the other hand, look distinctly unwell.'

'I have put on nearly a stone and taught myself to sleep in a feather bed again. How could I be unwell?'

'Mahmoud, we—'

'Do not use that name here.'

Holmes caught his arm and forced him to stand still. Deliberately, he said again, 'Mahmoud,' and followed it with an Arabic quotation: 'A man feels shame at the mistreatment of his brother.'

He might have been speaking Mandarin Chinese; Marsh reacted not at all to the guttural syllables. He, merely said, 'In Palestine, you may have known a man of that name. You may even have considered yourself to be his brother. Here, there is no such man.'

'Whatever the trouble, it would be best if you were to permit us to help.'

'Trouble? What trouble can I possibly have? I own more land than a man can walk in a day, possess more works of timeless art than many museums, occupy a position at the right ear of the nation's power. I have men to cook my food and polish my shoes, women to lay my fire and starch my collars. Nine hundred years of British authority is in my bones, and I have returned to the land of my family. How could that possibly be construed as "trouble"?'

I tried to hear a bitterness in his voice that would match the worn expression on his face, but I heard only a mild, inescapable litany of fact. I could not bear it.

'You once said to me,' I told him, 'after we were ambushed on the road to Jericho and Holmes taken captive, that trouble came because you neglected your rightful state. That you were a man who went about on foot, and permitting yourself to ride in a ruler's motorcar was a foolish thing. You do not belong here, with your mouth at the ear of power. You are a scribe, and belong in Palestine, with your ear to the mouths of others. That is where you are happy.'

'Happiness is nothing. And another man said those words,' was his implacable reply.

Holmes tried again. 'Mahmoud—'

Before any of us could react, Holmes was sprawled on the ground with a furious English duke standing over him, right arm drawn back for a second blow. 'You will not use that name!' he roared.

'Then tell me why!' Holmes bellowed back. He clambered to his feet and stuck his face into Marsh's. 'Explain to me why . . . that man has ceased to exist!'

Marsh teetered on the edge of his fury, and I made ready to leap on his shoulders and pull him off Holmes. Then, in the blink of an eye, the shutters slammed down, the homicidal rage was folded back into its cage; control was regained. In that brief instant of transition, Mahmoud looked out from those dark eyes, but he was gone in a flash, and a middle-aged Englishman was studying the reddening jaw of the man before him. His own flush faded, and he nodded.

'It is true, I owe you that much. The man you speak of is not here, but his debts remain. I will explain, and then you and Mary can pack your bags and be safely home in Sussex before my sister's friends begin to arrive.'

The two dogs that had skittered away in a panic at his outburst were now back, shrinking at his knees and grinning nervously until he thumped their ribs and sent them off in search of throwing sticks. We drifted after the dogs, and Marsh began to explain.

'One cannot begin to speak of the seventh Duke of Beauville and the state of his affairs without looking first at how the family's history has shaped him. That, after all, is the entire point of the English aristocracy: continuity, and responsibility. If you wish to understand the current duke, you will have to permit a lesson in history.

'The family presence in this country begins with Hastings in 1066. When William came to claim the crown of England, among his nobles was a man barely twenty named Richard de Hughfort. The younger son of a minor landholder, he had nothing but the sword in his hands, the horse between his knees, and the head on his shoulders. He acquitted himself well on the field of battle, won the eye of the Conqueror, and was given responsibilities.

'Some months later, with the Conqueror's forces well established in the south, young Richard happened upon three armed knights entertaining themselves with a farmer's wife. The farmer lay dead, the twelve-year-old boy who had tried to defend his parents lay in a heap, the other children fled, and the wife . . . Well.

'Unfortunately, the three knights were William's men. And not just any men, but knights who had brought with them men-at-arms and full purses. Richard, as I said, had no name and had joined with little more than his sword. Which he raised without hesitation to come to the defence of a peasant woman and her family.

'He killed two of the knights and drove the other off – three experienced, armed fighting men. Richard received a wound in his breast, from the point of a sword that slipped under his armour. He helped the woman bury her husband, accepted a drink of water – the family records are quite meticulous about noting that, for some reason – and left her to nurse her injured boy.

'He rode into William's camp leading two horses with knights slung over their backs, and knelt in front of the Conqueror, sword offered, to receive his punishment. They were important men, after all, and William could not afford to let their deaths – over a mere peasant – go unavenged.

'But he did. He looked down at Hugh's bare neck, bent before him, but instead of using the edge of the sword, he used the flat, and knighted Richard. You've never heard this story?'

'In its outline alone,' Holmes told him.

'What William said then became the family motto, drilled into successive generations of impressionable minds: *Justitia fortitudo mea est*. "Righteousness is my strength."

'I will not force on you the next eight and a half centuries of family history; if you're interested, look for it yourself in the green library. Richard was not given a high degree of authority – William was no fool; he well knew that any man who would place righteousness over common sense was no person to command an army – but he gave him a degree of trust, and more to the point, some land.

'Which is where my family has stood ever since, both on the land and in the attitude. We are loyal unto death to our monarch – except for those odd occasions when a strain of fanatic comes to the surface, and makes us see the king's cause as unjust. This, as you might expect, has led the family into trouble once or twice. For the most part it has been hothead younger brothers who chose righteousness over loyalty, but once or twice it was the earl, or later the duke, who made his stand, and then the foundations shook. The second earl wavered onto Mary's side, and Elizabeth took his head for it, stripped the family of its lands, and declared the title attainted. By great good fortune, however, the earl's son had already proved himself to be a queen's man, and the title was soon restored. Then in Monmouth's Rebellion the seventh earl took his men and marched on London. He, too, lost his head; and again, had his younger brother not already proved himself a trustworthy friend to James II, we should not be standing here today.

'My father, Gerald Richard Adam Hughenfort, was the fifth Duke. I was his second surviving son. My elder brother, Henry, was seventeen years older than I, with two stillbirths in between us. Our brother Lionel was born when I was six. Mother died a few weeks after his birth, and five years later Father remarried. Phillida was born the year I went to university.

'My elder brother married when he was thirty. Henry was the perfect heir – did an adequate degree, took a responsible and interested view of the land, wasn't too wild in his trips into London and the Continent. He didn't even gamble much, which is the thing that usually brings down houses like Justice.

'What's that fool dog into?' he asked, and interrupted his narrative to investigate. When the putrid rabbit had been removed from its adoring finder and buried, we turned back to the path, and to Marsh's tale.

'So it did not matter all that much to Father that his second son, Maurice, found Justice dull, detested farming, and was interested only in the study of history and language and foreign peoples. I was, as they say, "the spare", but since the heir himself was healthy, strong, and sensible, there was no cause for concern.

'I made the grand tour as most young men did after university. However, when I reached Venice, my eyes went east, not south to Rome. I crossed the Adriatic, worked my way through Yugoslavia and Turkey, then sailed from Rhodes to Alexandria and Cairo. I saw the pyramids, the Nile, the beginnings of the African continent, but the only thing that truly called out to me was the desert to the east.

'I joined up with a group of ragged and corrupt nomads crossing the Sinai – not Bedu, just traders. When I laid eyes on the Judean hills, I was home.

'I lived there for ten months that first time, before my cousin was sent to fetch me back to England. I stayed here, the obedient son, for over a year. At the end of it, Henry's son Gabriel was born and thriving, my younger brother, Lionel, was seventeen and by all appearances on a straight course, and I was both superfluous and smothering.' Alistair glanced at Marsh and then swiftly away again, and walked on with his eyes glued to the countryside ahead; I wondered what Marsh had left out, or lied about.

'You may have an idea how terribly tight-knit a stratum of the social order we are even now – and the higher, the tighter. We're an entire society of in-laws and cousins: Our sisters go to balls on the arms of the brothers of boys we went to school with; members of our fathers' clubs command our Guards regiments. Holidays would be at an uncle's hunting lodge, our Saturdays-to-Mondays spent at the country house of a mother's childhood friend who was also a second cousin; our chaperones—'

He caught himself. 'You see the picture. After the desert, the stultifying drawing-room air was killing me. It was certainly driving me mad; I used to dream about the desert, about dry warm sand trickling down across my face and burying me, and would wake happy at the thought.'

This self-revelation was more than he had intended; he veered away, to look over a herd of the spotted deer that had caught his attention, and it was a while before he resumed.

'After a year here, my parents eventually had to admit that I was a lost cause, and permitted me to return to my life in Palestine. My cousin spent his long vacations with me for the years of his university, which made them think that they were keeping track of me. When my cousin finished his degree, he joined me permanently.

'And all was well. Until my brother's son Gabriel died.'

The control in his voice held, but with the last word, we could hear the effort. Not, I thought, because of any particular affection he felt for the boy as a person – how old had the child been when his uncle left the country? A few months? – but because his nephew Gabriel had been the foundation stone on which the entire weight of a noble family rested. With the heir snatched away, unmarried and with no son of his own, the order of succession took a very different track. But Marsh was going on with the story.

'My other brother, Lionel, was as I said six years younger than I. Lionel was sickly as a child. Every nursery ailment laid him low, every cold threatened pneumonia. When I entered Cambridge, just after his twelfth birthday, he had some foul illness the doctors thought might well carry him away. Instead, it seemed to burn him clean, and when I came home for Christmas I found him outside, building a snowman in the freezing cold, with Ogilby fretting nearby.

'He grew stronger physically, went off to school, did sports, even. All seemed well, until he entered Cambridge.

'There he did what is called "falling in with a bad lot". That is the other side of an incestuously tight society: Once a young man falls in with a group of young men interested only in gambling and drink, there is no escape.

'He was sent down, of course. Rather than coming here, he went to London. Shortly before my cousin came out to Palestine for good, Lionel was involved in some huge scandal, and had to leave the country. He spent the next twelve years in Europe, moving from place to place with his friends, wintering in the south of France. He only came back to England once during the following years, when Father died in 1903. Lionel himself died in the spring before the War – his lungs, apparently, weakened by drugs and drink and an accumulation of careless living.'

Marsh took a deep breath. 'However. Just after the new year of 1914 Lionel wrote to our brother – the head of the family, of course – to say that he had married and his wife was expecting a child. He asked Henry – told him, actually, in no uncertain terms; I've seen the letter – to increase his monthly stipend to account for his wife and the child. Henry went immediately to see this for himself, and found Lionel living in Montmartre with an older woman who looked little more than an amateur whore. But they had a marriage licence, and the woman's condition was obvious, so he came away. What could he do?

'Henry and his wife Sarah wrote to me, of course. I might have tried to do something about it, but by the time the letter caught up with me, it was accompanied by a telegram informing me of Lionel's death.

'The child was born three months after the marriage, six weeks before Lionel died. A boy; Thomas is his name. He is now nine and a half, has lived his whole life in France, and none of us has ever set eyes on him. None of us has any idea what kind of person he will be.'

He took another careful breath. 'Which is why he and his mother are coming to London on Tuesday. Phillida and I will go down to meet them the following day. I need to look at the child. It's not that I mind in the least supporting the two of them – Lionel wished it, after all – but since Thomas is next in the line of succession after me, I must at least find out if he bears any resemblance to my brother.'

Marsh had been studying his boots as he talked, but now he looked up, first at me, then at Holmes, one dark eyebrow raised quizzically.

'I for one should be rather surprised if he does. You see, by all accounts, from the time he left Justice to take up his place at Cambridge, Lionel was what you might call flamboyantly disinterested when it came to women.'

CHAPTER SEVEN

MARSH'S AMBULATORY TALE HAD taken a fair time in the telling, interrupted as it was by the antics of the dogs, the side-trip to inspect the herd of deer, another diversion to see the state of the sheep, and occasional stretches when Marsh had simply pulled away to gather his thoughts, or his strength. We had trudged more or less continuously cross-country for a good two hours, although we had only travelled three or four miles in a straight line from where we had begun. The sun was not far from the horizon, Alistair looked ready to drop, and I really thought it time to turn back. Even the dogs had ceased to bounce.

Marsh, however, had other plans. We had for some time been coming up at an oblique angle on the high wall that surrounded Justice; as we entered into its very shadow, the duke dug into his pocket and brought out a key the length of his hand.

'I need a drink,' he stated, and made for a stout iron gate set into the stones.

I could only stare at his back, hunched over the lock. Holmes was every bit as bemused as I.

'Not a statement I'd have expected to hear coming from that man,' he murmured. Then he added, 'However, I can agree with the sentiment.'

The iron gate debouched on a narrow, overgrown path leading through some decidedly unmanicured woods. Sunlight glinted sporadically through the trees, and I wondered if we were planning to negotiate the return journey by torchlight. Sunset came early, in November.

The narrow swath of woods ended at a wooden fence and its flimsy gate, both of them shaggy with lichen. The gate's hinges, however, opened without so much as a squeak; I deduced that this was a regular escape for the seventh Duke of Beauville. The lane we found on the other side of the gate led into a village; Marsh, a man of his word, led us straight to the public house.

It was an inn, two storeys of ancient, leaning ramble with a faded sign proclaiming DUKE'S ARMS hanging over the door through which we all, even Marsh, had to duck our heads. The room inside was warm and smoky, low of ceiling and even dimmer than the dusk outside. Brass gleamed around the bar, however, and the rush-scattered stones beneath our feet had none of the reek of long-spilt beer.

Half a dozen patrons sat in two groups; judging by the nods and greetings they exchanged with our leader, this was by no means his first visit here in his four months of residence at Justice. I, the only woman in the place, created more of a stir than the entrance of the duke himself, and the only curious looks were directed at Holmes and me. The dogs made a beeline for the enormous fireplace and collapsed into a satisfied heap on the black hearthstones, quite obviously at home there.

Marsh turned to us. 'A pint? Sherry? They could probably do you a cocktail, if it wasn't anything too complicated.'

Holmes agreed to a pint, I said I'd have a half, Alistair merely shook his head, and Marsh gave our orders to the ruddy-faced man behind the bar, ending with, 'And I'll have my usual, Mr Franks.'

Marsh Hughenfort's 'usual' turned out to be a double measure of whisky, downed at a toss, followed by an only slightly more leisurely pint. A fairly committed regimen for a man who had spent twenty years a teetotaller.

For Alistair, the innkeeper's wife came through with a pot of tea. He, too, had clearly been here before. As she approached our table in the corner of the low-ceilinged room, Marsh picked up his pint glass, cradling it to his chest as if to warm himself.

'Evening, Mrs Franks. How's Rosie today?'

'Worlds better, Your Grace, bless you. That syrup you sent down tastes like the devil's brew, she says, but she sleeps just fine, and the cough's clearing up.'

'Mind you don't give her too much.'

'I measure it out like you said, Your Grace. And I watch the clock, every four hours, no sooner. I'll be ever so careful. Anything else for you now?'

'In ten minutes you can have your husband bring us the same, thank you.'

'Opiates for the masses, Marsh?' Holmes asked when the woman was out of earshot, referring to the soporific effects of the cough potion. None of us mentioned Mahmoud's generous dose of pure opium paste that had nearly been the death of Holmes a few years before, but all of us had it in mind.

'The child's cough was painful to listen to; customers were staying away. I thought a night's sleep might make everyone feel better.'

Holmes set down his glass, and it was clear that he had dismissed the plight of little Rosie Franks from his mind. 'How did your—' he began, then stopped.

A man carrying with him the palpable aura of cow barn stood a few feet from our table, hat in hand. Literally so, but also figuratively.

'Beggin' your pardon, Your Grace, but I was out the—oh.' His gaze had fallen from Marsh to the empty glass before him; his face fell as well. 'Missed me chance, have I? Sorry to bother you, Your Grace. Another time.'

'Tomorrow morning, Hendricks? When you've finished the milking, come and see me.'

The man's face brightened. He pulled on his cap, rubbed his palm against his trousers (which improved the state of neither), thought the better of shaking any aristocratic palms, and tugged his hat instead, wishing us all a happy evening as he retreated.

Holmes, for once, was side-tracked. 'What was the significance of the glass?' he enquired.

Marsh very nearly smiled. 'When I first started coming in, once they grew accustomed to me, they began to bring me their problems and disputes. Not that I mind – it's part of what you might call the job – but it looked to dominate my visits here. So I let it be known that if they could catch me before I'd finished my first drink, I'd help them; otherwise they'd have to wait until my mind was clear. It's become a sort of game between us. They're considerably more scrupulous about following the rules than I am – I would have gone ahead with whatever is troubling Hendricks, but he'd have been uncomfortable.'

In his life as an itinerant scribe, Mahmoud had observed the Arab rules of hospitality with his clients, although in that land the rituals had centred around coffee rather than alcohol: When coffee ceased to be offered, or accepted, business was concluded. The unlikely parallel amused me; Holmes, however, was back on the scent.

'Does that rule apply to any guests you might bring here? Is our conversation now limited to record bags of grouse and the breeding lines of retrievers?'

Marsh shrugged – and even that was an English shrug, not the eloquent, full-shouldered gesture of Palestine. 'I've not brought a guest here before. Other than my cousin,' he added, making it clear that Alistair was not guest, but family.

'In that case,' said Holmes, 'I should like to ask how your nephew Gabriel was killed.'

The question took me by surprise. I had thought the cause behind Marsh's tension when he pronounced the words *Until my brother's son Gabriel died* was the upheaval that death had inflicted on the family, particularly on Marsh's own future. Holmes, on the other hand, had traced the tension further back, to the boy's death itself, and indeed, he seemed to have hit it on the head: The bleak, dying-man look settled back onto Marsh's face; his right hand crept up to finger the scar on his face, which the sudden clamp of tension had drawn into a sunken gash. He drained his glass, looked around to catch the landlord's attention, and waited until the next round was on the table. He ignored the beer, picking up the smaller glass and looking into it.

'They said, "died in service",' he told us at last, but he had to throw the fiery contents of the small glass down his throat before he could get the rest of it out. 'I think he was killed by a firing squad.'

I do not know which of his companions let out the sound, something between pain and disbelief, but it could have been any of the three of us – even Alistair, who must have heard the story before. Alistair squirmed in his chair and dug a penknife out of his pocket, eyeing the pile of logs on the hearth, but after a minute, he folded the knife away. Holmes slumped down into the hard chair and prepared to listen, fingers steepled over his waistcoat, eyes half closed and glittering in the firelight like those of an observant snake.

'I only began to suspect it a few weeks ago,' Marsh resumed. 'My brother Henry had been ill for a long time before he died, so that I found his affairs in chaos. I have to say, Sidney did his best, but Henry tended to take back certain responsibilities, and then not carry through. There were unpaid feed bills from three years ago, notifications from the builders concerning urgent roof repairs set aside. Last month, among a collection of papers concerning the local hunt, I happened across an envelope with some things belonging to Gabriel. An identity disc, half a dozen field postcards, a couple of letters addressed to Henry. And the death notifications.'

His fingers started to go back to the scar, then he caught the movement and changed it to run the hand over his face, rasping the stubble with his callused palm. 'Have you ever seen an official notification? Of course you have; who hasn't? Well, in the first years of the war the notifications of executions were apparently blunt to the point of being brutal. And to top matters off, they stopped the family's pension payments. But after an awful lot of these came through the War Offices, and local councils started having to provide support for the survivors, and questions began to be asked in Parliament, the powers that be began to think it might be considered punishing the innocent, that it might prove more politic to act humanely towards the families left behind. So they disguised the truth and reinstated the war pensions.

'Gabriel's notification says "died in service" like all the others, but the wording is different, more ambiguous. And the sympathy of the King and Queen is pointedly omitted.'

'That is hardly conclusive,' I objected.

'I think it is. And I think my brother knew. Henry kept a diary, although it's for the most part simply a list of where the hunt went this day or how many birds were taken on that, with the occasional farm details. But he wrote one entry, in August of the year Gabriel was killed, in which he reflects on the nature of bravery and cowardice. Only a few lines, but it's as if he was bleeding onto the page. Add to that the fact that he wouldn't let his wife send out memorials. Sarah wrote to me about that one; she couldn't understand. She was a gentle thing – ill a lot, but a good mother to the boy. My brother wouldn't have told her that Gabriel's death was anything but honourable, for fear of her health. As it was, Sarah died the following winter in the influenza epidemic. Other than Henry, and the four of us sitting here, no one knows. I suppose Ogilby might suspect the truth; Ogilby knows everything that goes on in the house, but he won't have breathed a word.'

'But . . . why?' Why would a young aristocrat, so eager that he signed up the very day he turned eighteen, commit a capital offence a year later? Why would a boy of noble birth not have received a lesser sentence? Why would a Hughenfort . . . ?

'I don't know. I do know he was blown up in February, when a shell hit his trench and buried him in the mud along with half a dozen others. He nearly died before they dug him out, and spent the better part of a month in hospital and on leave. And then as soon as he went back up the line he was in heavy action – even in the desert we knew that the Germans were on the very edge of breaking through, so all hell must have been loose in France. I should suppose the boy's nerves must have been dicier than anyone imagined, otherwise his commanding officer would have pulled him out.'

Marsh dropped his head into his hands, both elbows on the scarred wooden table. 'He wrote a last letter to Henry. "Dearest Pater", it begins, but it doesn't say anything of substance, only some memories of summer evenings at the Hall and the hope that he can remain—' Marsh's voice wavered, then caught, '—remain brave. Ah, sod it all, I wish I'd known the poor little bastard.' He stood up so fast he nearly upended the heavy table and hurled his half-empty glass into the fireplace. 'Sorry, I need to . . .' he began, and waved in the direction of the public house's back door. His stride showed little indication of the four measures of strong drink and the pint and a half of ale he'd put away in a short time. The inn went deathly still; when he had passed through the door, I felt the villagers' resentful eyes settle on us: What had we done to their duke?

When he came back past the bar, the duke stopped to have a word with Franks before resuming his place. More drinks soon joined the collection, although a number of the glasses on the table were nearly full. Before we'd had more than a couple of swallows, however, Marsh got to his feet again, more circumspectly this time.

'We shall miss the dinner gong if we do not leave, and that will make my sister cross. Not that I mind making Phillida cross, but I prefer to choose my fields of battle instead of declaring outright warfare.' As he told us this, his pronunciation deliberate, he took up his overcoat and began to button it on with equally deliberate fingers. We followed his example, and the dogs, familiar with the sequence of events, rose, shook themselves, stretched with eager yawns, and trotted over to put their noses at the door.

When the cold air outside hit Marsh, he stumbled against

Alistair, but recovered immediately. I was glad to see that we were not about to attempt the now completely invisible path through the wall and into the parkland; instead, we turned up the road, which, though equally difficult to see, was identifiable by the surface underfoot and the occasional lighted cottage along its length, and which presented no brambles at our legs.

Marsh began to recount the history of the Franks family – the arrival of the publican's grandfather during the third Duke's time, the family's losses during the War, and an elder son in trade down in London, but I did not listen much, being more interested in keeping my feet on the track and wondering just how late the Hughenfort family took dinner. It would take us at least an hour and a half, even at a brisk pace, to circle the wall and follow the entrance drive, and our pace could hardly be termed brisk.

It would appear, however, that part of the evening's sequence involved a telephone call from village to Hall, because before we reached the metalled main road, a set of powerful headlamps approached from the direction of the Justice gates. They turned into our track, caught our figures, and halted. The driver's door opened; Holmes and I piled into the back, followed by the dogs.

Marsh came last, Alistair's surreptitious hand on his elbow. He dropped hard into the seat, but before the hand could retreat, he seized it and gripped it hard for a moment before letting go. 'Goodnight, my brother,' he said, and Alistair shut the door.

Marsh closed his eyes, smiled to himself, and muttered something under his breath. I realised with surprise that it had been in Arabic: 'Eyes like a cat,' he had murmured. A phrase I had once heard him apply to Ali when we were crossing the desert by night.

With this phrase two things became clear. One, that despite

his recent injuries, Alistair would be walking alone to Badger Old Place through the moonless night. And two, that Marsh was very drunk indeed.

He sobered during the drive back to Justice Hall, and went up the steps with straight back and steady pace.

'Have you rung the gong yet, Ogilby?' he asked that gentleman.

'Not yet, Your Grace. Lady Phillida suggested they might wait awhile longer.'

'I can't be bothered changing, Ogilby. And I'm sure my guests are famished. Give us five minutes, and ring.'

I scurried up to my room to rid myself of overcoat and muddy shoes, and was straightening the pins in my hair when a hollow reverberation began to rise through the house. We reached the drawing room before the Darlings, and were thus witness to the astonishment followed by vexed disapproval with which Lady Phillida greeted the sight of her brother, still dressed in mud-spattered tweeds and holding what was clearly not his first drink of the evening. She then glanced at us, saw that we were similarly underdressed, and her face went polite again.

'We'd have been happy to wait – but it does not matter in the least. In fact, it's rather fun to be Bohemian; the business of changing is so stuffy, don't you think?'

Bohemian or not, Sidney Darling stepped forward to present his properly clad black arm for me to go into the dining room upon, leaving the rest to sort themselves out as best they would. He deposited me at Marsh's right hand.

We were seated at one end of a table that could have accommodated thirty with ease. As it was, a great deal of empty wood stretched out to one side, and only two of the room's forest of candelabra had been lit for us, a pair of Baroque silver objects that reminded me of the fountain outside, although I could not make out any pelicans in the tangle of figures. A display of plate glinted on a side table, and the walls glimmered here and there with gilt. Three footmen and Ogilby were on hand to ensure we did not starve, die of thirst, or pull a muscle in reaching for the salt.

I wondered if the family dined in such lonely splendour every night, and on the whole imagined not. There would be a smaller family parlour, or the breakfast room put to dual purpose. I was honoured, if uncomfortable, not only because my two-year-old walking skirt was so severely below the standards of the room, and our dinner companions so out of sorts: The room was also physically chill, without a few dozen warm companions to supplement the fires, and it was probably just as well that I was wearing wool and not silk.

After several false starts, and eschewing both beekeeping and theology as unpromising, we embarked on a conversation concerning opera. Darling with relief seized on the stage as a point of communication with the guests – or half of them, at any rate, since my passion for warbling sopranos is fairly cool. Holmes, however, admitted to an interest, and so the two men kept the conversational ball in motion, aided by the occasional remark from Lady Phillida or myself.

Marsh drank steadily.

Tenors and librettos, set design and the acoustics of various halls kept the silence at bay, although after ninety minutes of it, Darling was beginning to repeat himself and any real interest was long since exhausted. Lady Phillida and I had a chatty moment over the meat course about fashion, when she asked where my skirt had come from. I was tempted to tell her that Gordon Selfridge's had a good selection of them on the rack, but instead gave her the truth, and the name of the married couple who made most of my clothes. She raised an eyebrow, but not, it transpired, a disapproving one.

'They're quite well known,' she told me, as if I might be unaware of this fact.

'Yes, they do beautiful work. And she has an extraordinary eye for fabric.'

'It's rather surprising,' she said, then hastened to explain. 'That they would take you on, I mean. I understand they have quite a long waiting list of clients.'

And I, clearly, was not quite up to snuff. The extraordinary thing was, I reflected, she had not intended an insult. 'They were my mother's tailors,' I told her. 'And relatives of hers. Cousins or something.'

I could feel Lady Phillida's shock from across the table, although she was too well bred to allow it onto her face. That one would admit to blood ties with tailors was perhaps forgivable, but – *Jewish* tailors? She gaped at me for a moment as if I'd demonstrated an unsavoury habit, and then pulled herself together. *Funny*, I thought, taking up my fork again, *she doesn't look Jewish*.

Oh, this was going to be a long weekend.

In vino veritas, or so it is said. I did not expect to prise a great deal of *veritas* out of our host while he was in his cups, but it was worth listening to whatever flotsam might wash up from the depths of his ducal mind on the flood of whisky, ale, and claret he was consuming.

Unless he simply passed out on the hearth.

However, he continued to hold his various liquors well, simply becoming ever more taciturn as the meal wound to its close. With such a small gathering, I hoped we might overlook the ritualistic segregation of women and the subsequent reassembly in the drawing room, and to my relief it was so. In fact, Lady Phillida excused herself with a headache, and although her husband hesitated, in the end he came down on the side of joining her and leaving us three to finish the evening.

The library was cosy. A pair of decanters stood on a tray with the appropriate glasses for port and brandy. Marsh picked up the nearest decanter, which happened to be the port, splashed some in three of the glasses, and handed us each one without asking if we wanted it. He sank into an armchair and stared into the flames; I thought he had forgotten we were there until he spoke.

'I've never been shot, myself,' he informed us, sounding reflective. 'Stabbed, yes; cut by a broken bottle, run down by a lorry, beaten, burnt, even trampled by an enraged camel once, but never shot. I wonder how it feels.'

'It doesn't feel,' I responded. 'The body ceases to communicate with the mind; all the person registers is a profound sense of shock. That was my experience, at any rate.'

He took his eyes from the fire. 'You? You've been shot?'

'With a pistol. A few weeks after we left you – the same case we came to you to avoid, in fact.'

'Where? Where did he shoot you?'

'It was a she. In my shoulder.' I rested my hand on the fabric over the puckered scar, and was startled when Marsh laughed merrily.

'Never had I met a woman such as you. Do you remember when Ali—'

He froze over the name, and at the intrusion of a life that was over. Then he set about retracing the thread of his thoughts.

'So, being shot resembles a deep stab wound. Not the surface cuts – at those the body screams from violation. The mortal wounds are too terrible for the mind to acknowledge, so it retreats. Interesting. That is encouraging. You see, I find myself wondering sometimes what young Gabriel felt. Knowing it was coming, having to stand upright and proud despite the state of his nerves, waiting for his men – his own men – to raise their rifles and take aim at his chest. What a death, for a boy of eighteen. Poor bloody little bastard.' The picture in his mind had gone far beyond suspicion: He clearly had no doubts concerning his nephew's fate.

He downed the wine in his glass and went to the tray again. This time his hand fell on the other decanter, and brought back a glass with enough brandy in it to stupefy an elephant. He drank half of it straight down as if it had been water, fingered the scar on his face, and then noticed what he was doing and shifted the glass to his right hand.

'When Alistair and I were boys,' he said, his voice just beginning to slur, 'we would meet at a hut old man Bloom the gamekeeper kept in the woods, and listen to his stories. There was one day . . .' Tales of boyhood foolishness carried him along until he had reached his goal of insensibility, until his voice faded and he sat as if he'd been clubbed, far beyond speech, veritable or otherwise. Holmes stubbed out his half-smoked cigar, removed the glass from Marsh's senseless fingers, and went to fetch Ogilby.

They came back with a muscular young man who looked enough like the morning's footman to be a brother. Between them, the footman and Ogilby got Marsh upright and supported him out of the library. Holmes and I stood and listened to the muttering, bumping progress of the men.

To my surprise, however, Holmes made no move to follow

them. Instead, he went to the tray and dashed into a glass a smaller dose of Marsh's anaesthetic. He then paced to the end of the room and back, took a cigarette from the box on the table and lit it with sharp, tight movements, then sucked in only two or three deep draughts before flicking it irritably into the fire. He returned to his glass, topped it up with a harsh clatter of crystal, and stalked off into the adjoining billiards room.

I found him outside the French doors, glaring across the garden, sat the darkness with a fresh cigarette between his fingers. There was no moon and the terrace lights had been shut down, but the distant patter of the Pond's fountain reached our ears, and a faint breeze stirred the nearby leaves. I was conscious, however, only of the waves of emotion pouring out of the silent man beside me.

Holmes was in a rage.

I knew Holmes as a man of great passions, but they tended to be volatile – or at least, swiftly brought to rein by force of will. I had only occasionally felt in him the deep, burning pulses of an uncontrolled fury; the sensation inevitably made me wish to creep silently away, far away.

Instead, I waited in the open doorway, listening to the falling water and the sharp whistle of breath through his taut nostrils, until he had smoked his cigarette to the end. Only then did I speak.

'What is troubling you, Holmes?'

He flung the near-flat butt to the ground and ground it beneath a vicious boot-heel, then went back into the house.

'Fools and butchers, all of them,' he stormed. 'Sitting in their offices and deciding that an example must be made, that the men won't fight without a threat hanging over their heads. The Romans practised decimation – line up one in ten and stab them to death to encourage the others. Pah! Idiocy.' He became aware that I was staring at him as he paced, and made an effort to pull himself together. When yet another cigarette was going, his voice came, taut with control.

'I was once asked by a family to investigate the death of their son. This was in the first year of fighting, when the War Offices just flatly told the families that their son, husband, whatever had been executed. In this case, for cowardice. Can you picture what news like that does to a family, already grieving? The father committed suicide. The mother wanted to know.

'Russell, he'd been scarcely more than an infant! A schoolboy, who'd lied about his age. Barely seventeen and at his third relentless rolling barrage his nerve broke. He dropped his rifle and ran, straight through deadly fire, over the tops of trenches, anything to get away from the ungodly noise. Desertion, cowardice – shell shock, for which the official cure was a hail of bullets. He couldn't even stand upright, his nerves were so bad; they had to bring out a kitchen chair—'

He broke off, unable to continue the sentence. The old house waited in silence; when he resumed, his voice was deceptively quiet and reasonable. 'Do you know, Russell, when I asked to see the boy's file, I was told that only the individual involved had the right to see closed records. When I pointed out that the "individual involved" was dead, I was informed that the records were therefore closed, full stop. The logic of the bureaucrat. I had to have Mycroft steal the file for me. That trial was a farce: no defence, no medical testimony as to the state he was in, two of the four witnesses had only hearsay evidence, a third was a personal enemy. And his wasn't the only such; there have been outraged questions asked in Parliament. One October, in 1917 I believe it was, only one of the twenty-five soldiers executed that month had anything resembling a defence. There was effectively no right of appeal, no sending or receiving of letters, no mechanism for bringing in witnesses who weren't immediately to hand. The entire system was a travesty, and ripe for abuse.'

Abuse, I thought: *murder*. After a while I said, 'And you think . . .'

'Come, Russell; can you honestly believe that a son of this house could act the coward without reason? *Justitia fortitudo mea est*; it's all but tattooed on their foreheads at birth.'

Abruptly, the rage loosed its hold on him, leaving him looking ill. He gazed at the dregs in his glass, then dashed them into the dying flames. A convulsion of blue-tinged fire reached up the chimney, and subsided. Without another word we followed in the direction that Marsh had been carried a short time earlier.

Holmes and I went to the end of the corridor, and there found the most ornate set of servants' stairs I'd ever seen – except that they were doubtless the original central stairway of the house before its eighteenth-century transformation. The stairs were lit by a pair of electric bulbs, weak but sufficient for safety, and enough to give us an impression of dark colours and rich textures. It was a tapestry of a room, far more than just a means of changing levels in the house, from a time when the social life of the great families had begun to move up, away from the servant-populated Hall.

Pelicans had alighted here, too, I saw: carved atop the newel posts, painted into the walls, even incorporated into the plasterwork ceiling. I stopped to study the unlikely, ungainly, big-beaked creature brooding over the newel post; when it occurred to me that the nearly amorphous granite shapes guarding the main gates had originally been pelicans as well, my mind suddenly made the connection.

'Sacrifice!' I said aloud. 'Of course.'

'Sorry?' Holmes asked.

'The pelican. It's an odd choice as the heraldic beast of a great house – I mean, they're positively comical except when they're actually in the air. But the pelican is a symbol of ultimate self-sacrifice – piercing its breast to feed its young. Zoologically inaccurate, of course, but it goes very deep in Christian mythology. The symbol was applied to the Christ, and later used in Mediaeval alchemy. See, you can even make out the painted blood on this one.'

Holmes stopped to peer with me at the red stream flowing down the breast beside the carved beak. Mutely, we both glanced upwards in the direction of Marsh's rooms.

Self-sacrifice could take many forms; the only common characteristic was the high cost to the giver.

No wonder Marsh Hughenfort looked like a dying man, ripping out his own heart for the sake of his family.

CHAPTER EIGHT

I WOKE DURING THE NIGHT with the feeling that I had heard voices raised, but when I came fully awake and identified my surroundings, all I heard was silence, and after a time a clock striking four. I settled back into my feather pillows and pulled the thick bedclothes back over my ears, grateful that I was not a housemaid whose job it was to lay fires before dawn.

(Although my ears persisted in thinking it had not sounded much like a housemaid; that it had in fact sounded like Ali. An invention from the recesses of memory, no doubt, summoning the rise and fall of long conversations overheard through walls of canvas and goat's hair.)

In the morning, I was alone in the tapestried bed. The sky was an expanse of grey, although it was not yet raining. I washed (calling down blessings on whichever duke it had been whose sense of luxury extended to hot water taps in the guest bathrooms) and dressed, taking myself down the back stairway so that I might have another look at it. This time, with the electric light supplemented by that seeping through the mullioned windows, I noticed that one of the carved pelicans was standing on a knob set with the date 1612. Its builder had either been to Knole or had been responsible for that stairway as well, I thought as I continued slowly down the stairs, studying the chipped, faded, glorious walls, until I was nearly flattened by an oncoming maid intent on her burden. I dived to one side, so surprising her with my sudden movement that the tea tray nearly came to grief despite her concentration.

'Ooh!' she squeaked. 'Oh, you didn't half give me a turn. That is to say, begging your pardon, mum, I didn't see you there. Was there something I could do for you?'

'The breakfast room,' I said. 'I forgot to ask directions last night – no, no; just tell me which way it is. If you take me there, that tea will get cold. But first, tell me your name?'

'It's Emma, mum. And you're sure you don't want me to take you? Well, when you get to the foot of these stairs you go through that door there, and straight down the corridor for just a little way and then to your right. Then—'

Her instructions seemed to send me in a circle and the tea was probably cold anyway when she had finished, but I thanked her and went on. How hard could it be?

Had I depended on her verbal map, I might have found the breakfast room in time for luncheon, but by following the odours instead of her directions I had no great trouble.

The room was, as I had expected, a more intimate chamber than the formal dining room of the night before, although no less ornate in its way. It was on a more human scale, for one thing, so that one could crackle toast without being intimidated by echoes, and although the ceiling was thick with gilded grapevines from which swung an exuberance of frescoed putti, and the walls were more than half mirror, the fat cherubs seemed happy enough to oversee the meals taking place below, and the silver in the mirrors had tarnished to a comfortable dimness.

Alistair was there, bent over a plate with a folded newspaper beside it; Holmes presented a similar figure across the table from him. Both men looked up at my arrival, and Alistair rose to pour me a coffee from the steaming samovar-style pot.

'Arc ladies permitted in this club, gentlemen?' I asked.

'Difficult to keep them out, I should think,' Holmes answered, holding my chair for me. He was his usual self again, last night's rage well concealed.

'What excitement is occupying the world today?'

'One Lady Diana Hamilton was sent to prison for stealing two rings and three brooches from friends who had rescued her from an "unfortunate and distressing situation" in a Paddington hotel. And the Chancellor of the Exchequer acknowledges the receipt of two pounds sixteen shillings' conscience money from "X. Y. Z." The world of crime is, I fear, not only singularly dull, but not even terribly remunerative.'

The usual complaint. 'Is Marsh down yet?' I expected to be told he was still abed, nursing a pounding head, but apparently not.

'Here and gone,' his cousin replied. 'I believe he is interviewing the cow-man Hendricks in the estate offices.' I could not but wonder if a hungover Marsh Hughenfort would be an ill-tempered creature or an exquisitely silent and sensitive one, but I did not see that I could enquire. I should, no doubt, see for myself before the day was through. Alistair went on. 'Phillida and Sidney are in London for the day. Marsh asked me to show you the house this morning. If you wish.'

'I should love to see Justice Hall,' I said with pleasure.

He looked taken aback at the enthusiasm in my voice, and

retreated into his newspaper, leaving me to ladle out a bowl of porridge and reflect on, as Holmes had put it, the workings of cause and effect. In Palestine, Ali had kept me – Holmes, too, but particularly me – at arm's length, if not at actual knife's point. He resented my presence, grumbled at the extra work we created, refused to grudge me an iota more responsibility than was absolutely necessary. He would happily have abandoned us in the desert, had it not been that Mahmoud developed an inexplicable interest in us.

Now, the basis of our relationship was turned upside-down. He had actively sought us out to ask for help; his present identity, though to all appearances a comfortable fit, left him stranded on unfamiliar territory when it came to action. In Palestine, he had deferred only to Mahmoud; in England, his bone-deep yeoman nature demanded a banner to follow. He was not exactly lost, but with Mahmoud so vehemently refusing to lead anyone anywhere, Alistair was definitely casting around for familiar landmarks. To put himself into a friendly footing with 'Amir' was jarring, but if it helped move Marsh a few inches more in the direction of Palestine, he was willing to try. In Palestine, he had willingly walked thousands of miles on foot in the service of king and country; he had baked and frozen and scratched at flea bites; killed, spied, defused bombs, and even committed torture when it proved necessary; in England, it would seem, he was willing to bring me a cup of pallid coffee and offer us a tour of Justice Hall.

Holmes, however, demurred. With Alistair's warning about the eye-to-the-keyhole propensities of the Darling clan, to say nothing of servants, clearly in mind, he folded his newspaper onto the table and said, 'I too shall venture into London for the day. A matter regarding the young man of whom we were speaking yesterday afternoon. Solid information concerning his actions has become a priority.'

'Do you want—' I began, but he was already dismissing my offer.

'I shouldn't dream of cutting short your weekend, Russell. You enjoy yourself while I expend shoe-leather on the dirty cobblestones.'

'Thank you, Holmes,' I said dryly.

I made haste to finish my toast, then followed him up the stairs and helped him pack a few things in a rucksack. He still maintained his secret boltholes across London, and would no doubt retrieve from them anything else he needed, from false moustaches to armament.

'I should really rather come with you, Holmes,' I told him in a voice too low to be heard beyond the door.

'Of course you would. But I believe the cause will be better served by dividing our forces.'

'And inevitably I must be the one to remain behind and make tedious conversation over the dinner table.'

'My dear Russell, had you spent the last few years nurturing informants and contacts in the less salubrious portions of London instead of frittering away your time in lecture halls and libraries . . .'

'I know, I know. When will you return?'

'Saturday, or perhaps the following morning.'

Which only indicated that he planned to be away for less than a week. Unless, that is, something came up. Which it generally did. I handed him his shaving case.

'I'll let Marsh know. Will you go as yourself?'

'I think not,' he replied. 'This investigation needs to remain *sub rosa*. The combined drawing power of the names Hughenfort and Holmes would start a fox before the hounds. We wouldn't be able to hear ourselves think, for the "view halloo" of the tabloid journalists.' He did up the buckles on the rucksack, then paused. 'See what you can turn up about the boy yourself. Ask to see the letter she wrote his father, particularly that last one. Look closely at any belongings he may have left. I should be particularly interested if he left a diary, papers, whatever. You know the drill.'

I did indeed.

'And over the weekend, particularly when the house guests arrive, listen and watch closely. Map out currents, as it were. And before you protest that you do not know what we are looking for, I am aware of that minor problem, and can only trust that you have sufficient mental flexibility to work a case that is not yet a case.' He swung the rucksack over his shoulder, and then, with his hand on the doorknob, paused. 'But, Russell? Watch yourself. I believe that as the investigation develops, we will find that these placid waters have been concealing any number of powerful tides.'

He closed the door on my 'goodbye', leaving me alone with Justice and her populace.

When Holmes had driven off for the day – or the week – Alistair and I descended the decorated stairway and passed through a door set into the wall opposite the foot of the stairs, nearly at the end of the old, western wing. It led to a tiny room, little more than three doors and a scrap of wall. Alistair closed the first door behind us, then sidled past me to that on our right, which was tiny, off-square, and locked. He had the key, an object no more than a century old.

The door opened onto another set of stairs, although these were of stone, narrow and steep and treacherously uneven, spiralling down into the depths beneath the house. Electric light bulbs had been strung from metal staples along the wall.

The wall against my right shoulder was worn smooth by ten

thousand passing shoulders before me. The stairs ended at a corridor with an arched roof and a floor so worn, the dip in the centre nearly duplicated the ceiling in reverse. The walls brushed our shoulders as we passed, single file, then turned to the right, and the narrow passage opened into a room.

In the recent past, it had been used as a cool storage room for barrels of wine and kegs of beer, but it had not been built for that purpose, and no doubt the servants were relieved to have given it up. It had been a chapel, I thought; its groined arches still bore traces of a plaster finish, and beyond it the dark maw of a tunnel, suitable for the passage of individuals less than five and a half feet tall.

Alistair stood and allowed me to explore the space without comment. I stepped behind one of the dusty barrels; when I spoke, my voice rang hollowly against the stones.

'This part of the foundation is old,' I observed in surprise. 'Those arches have to be Norman.'

'This part of Justice is built on the foundations of a Mediaeval abbey,' my guide told me. 'The family owned the land adjoining the abbey; after Dissolution, the second earl, who was a friend of the king, arranged to have the abbey grounds added to his. Seems the abbot had spoken treason against Henry, so they hung him from one of the trees in the park. He was actually a relation of the family – nice irony. The monks would have had a mill on Justice stream, and taken fish from the Pond. Marsh thinks this was the crypt. Within a few years, it was in use again as a chapel, only this time in secret, for the earl's wife remained a Roman Catholic. But before it was an abbey—'

'—it was Roman,' I exclaimed.

Alistair came around the corner into the adjoining room and

joined me in staring down at the scrap of mosaic flooring revealed when a small patch of the cracked Mediaeval tiles had been rucked up.

'Before that, Roman,' Alistair confirmed.

'How on earth did this just stay here?' I couldn't believe some renovator or antiquarian had not got his hands on it – heavens, if *my* fingers itched to see what lay beneath those tiles, why hadn't some duke along the way decided to have a look?

'The stairs were bricked over, sometime in the early nineteenth century. It wasn't until about thirty years ago that Marsh's father had the bricks down – some project Phillida's mother had in mind for the stillroom near the kitchens. That tunnel was built by the second Duke in the 1750s. Seems he had a peculiar aversion to the continual passing of servants through the main rooms. This was his attempt to cut down the traffic. It comes out in the kitchens, or did, until it was blocked off. I remember when they had the bricks down; it was just before Marsh went off to Cambridge, so I must have been eleven or twelve at the time. I was here a lot, then, even though no one much liked his stepmother. But they didn't use the tunnel very long; after two housemaids fell on the stairs, the duke had the wine moved and locked it up again. It was probably the same reason that the end was bricked up in the first place, even though servants were cheap then.'

I could well believe those stairs would bring brisk-moving housemaids to grief. They were soldiers' stairs, narrow and turning so as to be defensible by a single swordsman. Not that the original builders could have anticipated much swordplay, against enemies pouring into the house from the depths of the crypt.

With a last reluctant glance at the enticing fragments of Roman mosaic, I followed my guide up the steep stairway. At the top, Alistair shut down the lights and let me pass so he could lock the small door.

As I reached for the latch on the door through which we had entered, I glanced at the smaller door's twin and asked him where it went.

'Up,' he said, unnecessarily. 'To the roof, eventually. Justice is riddled with nooks and crannies. When Marsh and I were children, we used to crawl all over the place – lock each other in obscure rooms, hold pitched battles in the tunnel, stage duels up on the roof leads. It's a wonder we weren't killed a hundred times. Once I was climbing these stairs and Marsh was waiting on the next level with a claymore in his hand. Another time he rigged a trap that would have shot me out over the battlements if I hadn't seen it.'

'Good training exercises,' I commented. I ducked my head under the outer door frame to get back into the hallway at the end of the 1612 staircase; when I straightened, I found myself the target of two pairs of pale and accusing eyes.

They belonged to a boy of perhaps eight and a girl a couple of years older; between their haughty expressions and the shape of their facial bones, there was no doubting their parentage: These were the Darling children. By the looks of them, no name could be less appropriate.

'What were you doing down there?' the girl demanded.

'Who are you?' the boy chimed in.

'You're the friend of Uncle Marsh,' the girl said to me, and then to her brother, 'She's one of the friends of Uncle Marsh.'

'She doesn't look like a friend of Uncle Marsh.'

'How would you know?' she retorted. 'The only friend he's ever invited here was that small man with the yellow hair who came when Mother and Father were in London.'

'He had a motorcycle,' the boy informed me, sounding impressed.

Alistair had finally got the key to work and came out of the broom closet to rescue me. 'What are you two doing here?' he grumbled. 'Where is your nurse?'

'Miss Paul's a governess, and she's lying down with a headache.'

'I am not surprised. You go along back to the schoolroom and play.'

'Aren't you going to introduce us?' The child even sounded like her mother.

Alistair glared at her, then gave in. Turning to me, he said, 'Lenore and Walter Darling.' It sounded less an introduction than the identification of two possibly noxious varieties of local wildlife. 'This is Miss Russell. Now be gone.'

Lenore Darling ignored him imperiously. 'Are you of the—'

'The Bedfordshire Russells?' I finished for her, rather fed up with the question. 'Do I look like a Woburn Russell?' The family had been called 'grander than God'.

'Actually, no,' the girl admitted, and went on before Alistair could resume control. 'I ought to warn you not to say anything about *Peter Pan*. My brother might kick you.'

'I beg your pardon?'

'*Peter Pan*. The play by Mr Barrie?'

'I don't know it, sorry.'

'Oh, that's all right, then. It's just that the family in the story is named Darling and my brother thinks Mr Barrie should have been stopped from using the name. Walter gets quite cross when someone makes a joke about Tinker Bell or the Lost Boys.'

Characters from a children's play, I deduced, and wondered how we were to be rid of these two. Alistair's flat commands fell on deaf ears. Perhaps he proposed to bind them to a newel post?

He turned down the corridor leading up the wing towards the front, and when the two children stepped off the stairs to follow, he whirled and went back to loom over them.

'I. Said. No.' It was like speaking to a pair of stubborn puppies. They dropped their eyes to study the toes of their shoes; Alistair took this as a sign of obedience, and gestured for me to continue. I thought, however, the meekness was an act, and indeed, as we went along our way we could occasionally hear a stealthy step, trailing a safe distance behind.

This evidence of insurrection annoyed Alistair, enough to distract him from his lectures on Justice Hall's history and architectural styles. We moved rather rapidly through a drawing room done in pale, chilly blues, then a trophy room packed with the stuffed heads of large animals, the stuffed bodies of smaller creatures, and case after case of exterminated butterflies and beetles. This room opened onto an orangery, with tiled floor and murals of picnicking black-haired aristocrats, and then a conservatory, inhabited by one enormous tropical vine with huge yellowed leaves pressing up to the glass, a dying palm tree, and not a lot else. We pushed our way through the dank, deserted glass house to the far end, where a door opened into the billiards room.

There Alistair prepared to lay in wait for our persistent tail, standing terrible and stern with arms folded, ready to explode when they crept through the door.

I touched his arm. 'They're doing us no harm. They must be restless for distraction here.'

'I do not like to be followed.'

Or disobeyed. 'Of course not. But think about it: If you don't allow children to practise following and watching, or to rig traps out over the battlements, where will your friend Joshua get his next generation of spies?'

He reared back, stared at me in astonishment, stared at

the still-vacant doorway, then gave a loud bark of unexpected laughter and reached out to clout me hard on the shoulder.

'That is good, Mary,' he said, chuckling. 'I do like the idea of two generations working for Joshua. Very well; we shall permit the brats to practise their skills on us. Just so you remember never to say a thing in this house that you do not want to find its way into nursery and servants' hall before nightfall.'

Much cheered and able now to concentrate on his task, he led me through the public rooms on the ground floor, tossing out tit-bits about the various dukes, duchesses, and powers-that-be of their times. The Prince of Wales had descended on Marsh's father for a few days of slaughtering birds, bringing with him half the court and despoiling the countryside of anything with feathers (to judge by the photographs commemorating the occasion). The current King had dropped in for tea on the terrace one sunny summer afternoon, which as obligatory social events go must have proved a bargain by comparison.

One long corridor, wrapping around the back of the dining room, chronicled a period of about ten years during which Justice Hall had stepped into the centre of the social whirl. Dozens of photographs, all eight inches by twelve and identically framed, recorded one weekend after another. The guests were assembled on croquet courts or picnic grounds, arranged up the great staircase in the Hall or around a leaping bonfire in the out-of-doors, posed with artificial spontaneity around a card table or with the day's tally of birds laid out in neat lines at their feet. Some gatherings were as few as eight or ten guests, others a dozen times that, but all the groups looked as if they were having a good time.

'Marsh's stepmother enjoyed entertaining,' Alistair said, seeing me stopped in front of one panorama of at least fifty people in fancy dress, masks in hand. Professional beauties, members of

Parliament, one well-known tycoon, and three royals, with a handful of actors for leavening.

'Must have been quite a time.'

'We were already in – we were out of the country by then,' Alistair amended, mindful of cars. 'This particular one, I believe Phillida wrote to Marsh about. Yes – there's Darling.' Indeed, the handsome young man, tall and slim and blond in the fancy dress costume of Napoleon, was standing at her side. We went through the dining room, Alistair pointing out the Cellini ewers and the Adam plasterwork, a fairly uninhibited painting by Caravaggio and a somewhat dim one on the opposite wall by Van Eyck, a huge cabinet displaying several hundred weight of identical Sevres porcelain, and an attractive but incongruous inlaid screen taking up one corner of the room, no doubt the booty of some family member who'd spent time in India. At the moment it was screening from our eyes two fledgling spies, which fact Alistair either did not notice or, considerably more likely, chose to overlook.

The dining room gave way to a music room of Jacobean plasterwork painted in orange and white, rather like plunging into an enormous bowl of apricot cream; then another drawing room, its walls completely taken up with a series of paintings depicting some momentous historical event that appeared to have involved a landing on a storm-swept beach followed by a lot of red-clad men riding horses with huge hindquarters up a hill towards a vaguely Germanic castle. After this room came the Great Hall, and up its stairway we went, to pass through the columns of chocolate-and-cream alabaster into an absolutely stunning long gallery.

The gallery glowed with light and felt warmer than its actual temperature. Its walls combined a pale yellow silk with white detailing and a collection of family portraits that somehow contrived to look like affectionate friends rather than the stern eyes of a disapproving past. One could almost imagine them joining in the conversations of family members taking their exercise beneath that densely intricate plaster ceiling, strolling up and down the whole bright length of the room while the rain or snow came down on the terraced gardens outside of the mullioned windows, turning the curve of Justice Pond to a thing of pewter solidity. There was even, I saw, a folly on the top of the distant hill, crumbling artistically.

One of the primary reasons for country houses of this sort, I reflected, has always been intimidation. Less a family home than an assertion of power, the country house was the focus of the estate's energies: the more powerful the landholder, the grander the house. Badger Old Place might be an organic extension of the countryside – its roots old as the hills themselves – but where it was an essentially domestic piece of architecture, Justice Hall was military history in stone and mortar, a weapon from battlement to Great Hall, intended to keep the peasants and all potential enemies in their place. Well, it was certainly working on me: I was well and truly intimidated, and feeling more and more like a country cousin with cow dung on her boots. Since the invention of Culture in the sixteenth century, these people had been skimming the cream off European art and artistry, bringing it here for the pleasure of the few, perfecting the art of being first and foremost. Lady Phillida drew to herself an aura of privilege in the same way the long gallery drew light; I crept along its edge, feeling every inch the mongrel parvenue.

Holmes came from country squires – minor squires, true, but at least he spoke the same language. I, on the other hand, was the result of a cross between Jewish merchants and American tycoons:

half outsider, half nouveau riche, completely beyond redemption.

I escaped the beautiful room wondering how many more priceless works of art and exquisite vistas were going to sear themselves onto my soul before the tour was over. We entered a state bedroom hung with silk hand-painted chinoiserie wall covering and the matching silk bed hangings; from the door came the brief sound of footsteps crossing the bare boards at the side of the carpet down the centre of the long gallery. Alistair came to a halt and raised his voice.

'Were a person to wish to follow another without being noticed, he might do well to remove his shoes.'

Utter silence radiated from the long gallery. Then a small voice called back, 'We're not allowed to remove our shoes. It makes Miss Paul quite cross.'

'Life is full of decisions,' Alistair commented. Having delivered himself of this philosophical dictum, he went cheerfully on into the next room.

The sound of footsteps ceased to dog our heels.

CHAPTER NINE

THE SKIRMISH WITH THE two children had restored Alistair to something approaching good humour. As we wended our way through the state bedrooms of the central block he would pause for a moment, then continue with a look of amused satisfaction. It came back to me that one of the man's quirks had been the occasional pleasure he took at being bested, especially in the areas of his own expertise. He had once laughed aloud when my thrown knife had nearly taken him in the throat – a reaction I attributed at the time to astonishment, but which was now looking like a sort of generosity of spirit that I had not suspected.

At the turn of the corridor that led into the east wing, he stopped. 'These are the family's rooms. Nothing of interest.'

I could hardly insist on poking my nose into private bedrooms, although I should have been interested to look at Lady Phillida's dressing room. One can learn a great deal by studying a woman's cosmetics and medicine cabinet.

Instead, we doubled back (causing a short flurry of panicked whispers and hasty movement) to retrace our steps through the gallery (ostentatiously ignoring the unnatural bulge of the curtains in one room) and past the genial ancestors to a door at the other end. This opened into the room Marsh had referred to as the 'green library', although there was nothing particularly green about it.

But it was certainly a library, rather than a room with decorative books and well-used sofas. Shelves lined the walls, unbroken but for five windows, two doors, and a fireplace with a portrait above it. Free-standing bookshelves of a subtly newer appearance extended into one end of the room, creating three bays that filled a third of the library's floor space. On the other end, under the windows, were two long mahogany worktables and a trio of leather armchairs, all of which were equipped with reading lamps.

I felt instantly at home, and wanted only to dismiss Alistair, along with the rest of Justice Hall, that I might have a closer look at the shelves. I had to content myself instead with a strolling perusal, my hands locked together behind my back to keep them from reaching out for *Le Morte d'Arthur, Caxton 148*5 or the delicious little red-and-gilt *Bestiary, MS Circa 1250* or . . . If I took one down, I should be lost. So I looked, like a hungry child in a sweet shop, and trailed out on my guide's heels with one longing backward glance.

A boudoir, a schoolroom with battered ink-stained tables and a lot of out-of-date equipment, a similarly disused nursery (explaining the children's lack of enthusiasm), then the suite of rooms Holmes and I had been given, followed by a smaller, unoccupied suite. Marsh's rooms were at the end of the wing, overlooking the terraces and the end of the long, curving Justice Pond; then we were at the carved stairway again, with Alistair leading the way down.

Back on the ground floor we passed through the strung-together salons and dining rooms behind the Great Hall, working our way through the central block to its north eastern corner, where it connected with the stable wing. The estate offices were located here. Marsh was still occupied – not with Hendricks the cow-man, but with an authoritative voice connected to a ruddy face, whose lack of deference placed him as the estate steward. The voice – something about a low pasture wanting drainage – broke off when Alistair put his head in.

'Give us twenty minutes,' said Marsh's voice, and Alistair withdrew, to continue into the block of stables. This was little more than a hollow square, with a quarter acre of cobbled courtyard flanked on three and a half sides by the enclosed stables. Most of the boxes were scrubbed and empty, but the rich odours of straw, ammonia, and dubbin pulled us down the row to the remainder of Justice Hall's equine populace, to the hunters and hacks and the huge, placid draught horse with the leather boots for lawn-mowing hanging over its stall, and a pair of fat ponies so venerable they might have carried Lady Phillida as a child.

We had lost our pair of spies, I was glad to see. Probably they had decided that the current surface was not suited for stockinged feet, and been unwilling to risk the wrath of Miss Paul. In any case, the back of my neck ceased to itch, and we could relax our tongues a fraction as we made our way down the spacious, old-fashioned horseboxes.

'I should like to see the effects left by Marsh's nephew,' I told my companion, although I kept my voice low.

'Why?'

A reasonable enough question, to which I had no ready answer. 'Holmes asked me to look at them,' I replied, which seemed to satisfy Alistair. More than it did me.

The last box was filled by a great gorgeous stallion, his bay coat as polished as one of the tables in the Hall, haughty and unwilling to give us mere humans more than a glance. He filled the eye, the epitome of *Horse*, and he well knew it. I wondered uneasily if this was a recent acquisition; horse-breeding is a long-term occupation.

'Does it belong to Marsh?' I asked Alistair.

'No. Darling intends to build up a stud here. Or he did; things are somewhat uncertain now.' The thwarting of 'Spinach' Darling was clearly cause for satisfaction. I had to admit, however, that as gentlemen's occupations went, this at least was well timed. The wholesale slaughter of innocents in the trenches had extended to England's requisitioned horseflesh as well; four years of loss had still not been overcome. Any offspring of this gleaming animal would bring a good price at auction.

I said something of the sort to Alistair. He snorted.

'Oh yes. Darling has many plans for Justice. He stands about wringing his hands, fearing his agreements with Henry will be as dust.'

'A place like this wants working industries, if it's to survive. Agricultural revenues won't support it, not with capital taxation.'

Those last two words would have sparked a tirade in most gentlemen of his generation, men who saw a way of life being sucked dry by the viciously ruinous taxes imposed in recent years, men faced with the impossible choice of selling off the land that kept the house going, or tearing down the house itself. Alistair, however, merely shrugged.

'It should be worked, yes.' But he was not about to admit that the man to do so was Sidney Darling.

This wing of the block was now ended, and we had the option

of either turning up our collars and sprinting across the wide cobbles to the end of the other arm, or retracing our steps. I waited to see what Alistair would do. In Palestine, he would not have hesitated in walking out into the downpour – or rather, he would have done so with all deliberation, hoping this irritating female would wilt, or melt. But we were in England, and Ali was Alistair. He shot a quick glance at my footwear (which was nearly as sturdy as his own) and chivalrously turned back.

Marsh was there, one elbow on the half door of a pony box. Alistair's head went up and he strode forward vigorously; I went more slowly, to study their greeting and to better look at Marsh Hughenfort.

Alistair's Englishness I had grown more comfortable with, as enough of Ali remained there to see the man I had known behind the unlikely disguise, but Marsh was proving more difficult. My mind continued to search for similarities between him and Mahmoud, struggling to meld the two faces into one. It was like doing a jigsaw puzzle without the picture, with scraps of pattern from which the eyes could decipher no image. His dignity and authority remained the same in tweed or robe – he could no more shed his aristocratic origins than he could stop his lungs from drawing air. And the stealth of his movements, that too seemed as much a part of him as the shape of his bones. Perhaps the slight droop of his eyelids, the sense that they veiled a great deal from the outside world, perhaps that remained, exaggerated by the effects of what he'd consumed the night before.

It would be easiest, I reflected, if I were to tell myself this was my old friend Mahmoud's brother, a new character in my life. But to do so, I was certain, would be a disservice to us all.

I was suddenly hit by one of those memories, so vivid that for a moment I was there: Holmes addressing Ali across a cook-fire in the desert, commanding with razor-sharp scorn, 'Think of Russell as Amir, picture "him" as a beardless youth, and you just might succeed in not giving us away.'

I blinked, and there were two Englishmen with greying hair, gazing with affection at a fat pony. One of them, the older one, turned a pair of impenetrable eyes on me.

'Has my cousin showed you the house?'

'It's an amazing place,' I answered him.

Marsh looked at me sideways, causing a brief stir of familiarity. 'You liked the library?'

'It was all I could do to keep her from bolting herself inside,' Alistair told him.

With mock indignation, I protested, 'I never even touched a book. I walked through and walked out.'

'Her eyes were filled with an unnatural light,' Alistair confided in his cousin. 'I feared for my safety.'

'No violence can ever take place in that room,' Marsh said seriously. 'Mr Greene would not permit it.'

Was this one of the house staff responsible for quelling riots? I wondered. Marsh saw the question on my face.

'You noticed the portrait over the fire?'

'Thin man with large ears? Yes.'

'Mr Obediah Greene, hired by the second Duke to assemble a library suitable for a gentleman. I doubt that particular ancestor ever picked up a book himself, but Mr Greene laid the foundations, and furthermore bullied his employer to set aside a permanent portion of the estate budget for acquisition and maintenance. As children, we were convinced that to dog-ear a page would bring down the wrath of Mr Greene's ghost.'

'I shall offer him obeisance when next I am there.'

'He is said to savour the odour of rosemary,' Marsh replied. 'If you are moved to take an offering.'

He gave the pony a final pat and moved away, leaving me to wonder if he had just made a joke.

We strolled around to the other end of the stable wing, trading the aromas of hay and horses for those of oil and petrol. Gleaming generating engines were joined by rank after rank of the batteries that lit the great house at night, and were followed by the Justice motorcar collection, eight vehicles, including a Model T with leather seats the same crimson as the Egyptian boots that Ali had worn, a Hispano Suiza that would be blinding on a sunny day, a Rolls Royce Silver Ghost touring car, an electrical cart with a handle in place of a wheel for steering, and several others I did not recognise but which were all as thoroughly polished as the Hispano.

'My brother's,' Marsh noted, without much interest. 'Ringle can't bear to part with them – Ringle is the estate manager,' he explained. 'It tortures him that we don't have the staff we did when he came in 1890. I brought up the possibility of selling two of the smaller farms to pay the taxes; he looked at me as if I were coming after him with a bone-saw. Capital tax will be the death of us. Still, it makes for a change, to have the government take it back systematically – traditionally they've had to wait for the families to throw up a wastrel duke who would lose it all at the card table. When I was a child, we had sixty horses in this wing – and God knows how many servants worked here. The economy of this entire corner of Berkshire rested squarely on Justice. Now it's a narrow step from becoming a tourist attraction or a girls' school. You're fortunate to have seen the place in its glory, Mary, even if at its twilight.'

He sounded more matter-of-fact than wistful, and I had to remind myself that to a man whose chosen way of life was that of a scribe, and beneath that a spy, who lived in a tent with neither dependent nor permanent fixtures, Justice Hall might not be an object of adoration.

'We did not get to the chapel,' Alistair told him.

'Oh, we must show Mary the chapel. People come from Scandinavia and the Balkans just to see the chapel. And – what's the time?'

Alistair made a show of pulling a watch from his pocket and popping it open. 'It's just gone eleven.'

'Dare we risk the kitchen? Oh, I think we must.'

'We could go by way of the Armoury, put on a bit of chain mail first. Mary might fit into Long Tim's suit of armour.'

They *were* joking, by God, like a pair of idiot schoolboys. Marsh's frivolity was somewhat forced, either from disinclination or hangover, but he was trying hard to act the mischief-maker – and making not a bad go of it. It was the first sign of life I'd seen in him, and I did not know if I should rejoice, or fear that the summoning of good cheer was just one more kind of sacrificial blood-letting.

'It would take too long,' Marsh told Alistair. 'We'll have to chance it. Have you been shriven, Mary – or whatever Jewish girls do to meet their Maker?'

'This sounds quite alarming,' I told him.

'Mrs Butter in a rage is a sight to behold.'

'The War would have been over in months if Mrs Butter had been willing to cross the Channel,' Alistair assured me. 'As it was, the government held her in reserve as their secret weapon, should the Kaiser reach Dover.'

We passed the offices, where a man (Mr Ringle) was shouting down the telephone about a disputed bill, then entered the Hall, heading for the old, western wing. Marsh paused, and asked me, 'Are you acquainted with Vetruvius?'

I gazed blankly for a moment at the nearest object, the marble bust of a handsome young rake with a plaque attributing it to Christopher Hewetson. 'Vetruvius. Classical writer? Architecture?'

'*Aedium compositio constat ex symmetria, cuius rationem diligentissime architecti tenere debent,*' Marsh intoned. "The composition of temples is based upon symmetry, the principles of which architects must most diligently master." The first Duke seems to have picked the idea up on his travels – he himself was probably as illiterate as his son later was – and instructed his builder to emulate it.' Among other things I tended to forget – that Marsh Hughenfort had absorbed a Cambridge undergraduate degree.

As we strode through the gorgeous marble cavern, Marsh's voice playing among the upper gallery and rising to join the figures inhabiting the dome, our private world was suddenly shattered by the sounds of scurrying feet and urgent conversation.

Startled and unable at first to tell where the reverberations originated, I swivelled my head around, searching for the source of the noises, until the footsteps cleared the end of the upper gallery and became localised: Phillida and Sidney Darling, flying down the stairs in a confusion of garments and snatched phrases. I had thought them long gone – they had not come to breakfast and Alistair had said they were in London for the day – but clearly I was mistaken. Words tumbled down the staircase and we held ourselves back so as not to be flattened.

Sidney was clutching a telegram flimsy; Phillida was trying to settle her hat as she descended, half-listening to Sidney.

'—don't know why they think the march is still necessary, the police will be waiting for them and they won't hesitate to shoot, not with the way things are.'

'Perhaps Ludendorff will talk him out of it.'

'Not bloody likely, not if I know—Marsh!' he broke off to exclaim as his gaze lifted from the marble steps and he saw us gathered there. 'I, er . . .'

'Trouble?' Marsh enquired.

'Nothing, no, just a friend – or not a friend, actually, a business acquaintance I—Yes, Ogilby?'

The butler had glided up with his silver tray, on which lay another telegram. Sidney stuffed the one he held into his pocket and snatched at the fresh one.

'Shall I go ahead?' Phillida asked her husband.

'Yes, my dear, I'll be there in a moment. Is the car here, Ogilby?'

'Certainly, sir.'

'I'll just . . .' Sidney tossed the shredded envelope in the direction of the silver tray and frowned down at the telegraphist's words, which he had sheltered automatically from our view. He read it through twice, then shoved it unceremoniously into the pocket after the first one; without another word, he scurried out of the door, moving too fast for the attentive footman to get it fully open in front of him.

'Well,' Marsh said.

'What do you suppose that was about?' Alistair asked.

I turned to Ogilby for enlightenment. 'Mr Darling seemed to think there was to be a march that might turn violent. I hope not in London?'

'I believe the news originated in Germany, madam.'

'The national socialists are about to stage a *putsch*,' Marsh explained. 'General Ludendorff is one of the leaders, he and a young firebrand by the name of Hitler. Sidney is trying to decide if a change in the government would bode well or ill for British interests. He gave me some pamphlets to read; I found them dangerous nonsense.'

I let my gaze climb to the scene on the dome. *Who would wish the Day of the Lord?* And although Sidney might be depending on the Justice coffers to lay the foundations of an international manufacturing project, Marsh did not sound overeager to become involved in the country's considerable problems.

With a last thoughtful look upwards at the man about to lay his hand on a serpent, I joined Marsh and Alistair, as we continued our tour.

Quitting the Hall for the western wing, we turned to the right, away from the decorated staircase at the back of the house. Marsh pushed open a door; I looked, then stepped in: the Armoury.

This would have been the banqueting hall of the original house, massive stone walls topped by a fourteenth-century timber roof and inset with ancient warped windows illustrating the family's history. A sixteenth-century painted screen lay across one end of the hall, a huge fireplace dominated the other, and the arms of ages occupied the walls and corners. Four full suits of armour – one of which had been for a man standing nearly seven feet high, no doubt Long Tim – guarded the fireplace and the door opposite, pikes in their sheathed hands. A sunburst of broadswords and a wider one of pikestaffs faced each other across the southern end of the room. Plumed helmets, faded banners hanging free and behind glass, knives, longbows, and half the armament known to man. There was even a long row of matched blunderbusses, whose recoil would knock an unwary man down.

'A person could mount a small war out of this room,' I commented.

'When the eighth earl, who was to be the first Duke, built the new block beginning in 1710, he couldn't quite bring himself to tear this out. It vexed his architect no end. But truly, it had to stay; it's the heart of the place. Before the second earl got his hands on it and raised the roof a few yards, this was the abbey's hall.'

The room had changed since brown-clad monks gathered here for soup and Scripture, but it took little imagination to conjure up a long feasting board filled with loud, heavily scarred fighting men, women carrying trenchers across a rush-strewn floor, huge pale dogs gnawing bones underfoot. Henry VIII, or either of his daughters, would have felt right at home in this room. It carried the history of this house as the Great Hall and the long gallery did not, and I circumnavigated its lumpy whitewashed walls with respect, taking in the window (*Justitia fortitudo mea est*, at the top of each branch of the tree with its names: Henry the Unwary, fourth earl; Robert the Unwashed, seventh earl), the captured banners of defeated enemies, and the gargoyle at the corner of the fireplace, which bore a startling resemblance to a bewigged Marsh.

As I turned to go, my eye travelled up from a massive wooden chest big enough to act as coffin for half a dozen Long Tims to a third sunburst, this of curving Saracen sabres alternating with smaller knives. Ironic, I thought – and then I noticed the smaller blade that marked the centre of the radiating steel. I looked more closely, then glanced at Marsh and Alistair. Their faces were just a bit too expressionless, which instantly confirmed my suspicion: I had last seen that particular knife decorating the belt of Mahmoud Hazr.

I wondered if the children's dressing-up costume box held the remainder of the costume.

The chapel was located in a quiet niche of the kitchen block. Perhaps if I were a Christian, I might have found the small, melancholy little church more compelling. Since I am not, it just seemed to me unnecessarily crowded, as if the builder had laboured to distract the worshipper from the chill solitude of the ornate memorials set into the walls and standing out in the floor. Certainly between the angels, the saints, and the flocks of pelicans inserting their ungainly beaks into everything, one would think the afterlife a busy time indeed. Prominently displayed was the effigy of a young boy, its alabaster purity gleaming with innocence, the naked feet beneath its stone drapes pathetic in their vulnerability. However, I had no opportunity to peruse it or any of the myriad statues, busts, plaques, or inscriptions at leisure; the cousins had other things on their minds.

We passed the butler's pantry, its outer door standing open to reveal a comfortable chair before a fireplace, a locked safe door the height of a man, and a desk with neatly folded newspapers on one corner and a telephone in its precise centre. The long row of old-fashioned bells stretched along the wall outside Ogilby's sanctum, and then a wide door whose much-bashed sides testified to long years of fast-moving food trolleys.

I will admit that I dragged my feet somewhat as we approached the clatter and tumult of a kitchen coming around to luncheon. The sound of chopping and a billow of steam, a crash of pans and the crackle of an open fire, a strange, rhythmic clanking sound that called to mind a Mediaeval instrument of torture, and above it all a woman's loud voice raised, in command and chastisement and question. I put my head cautiously around the door.

The tiny woman with her back to us could only have been the Justice housekeeper, Mrs Butter. There was a cook as well, a cowed-looking Frenchman in a white toque, who might normally have expected to reign supreme in this his rightful kingdom; but here the woman ruled. One of the under-cooks saw us and straightened abruptly. Mrs Butter whirled about to see what had so distracted her assistant, a terrible fury gathering in her pink face until she saw who the intruders were. Pleasure flashed briefly across her face before the scowl descended again, but although she struggled to maintain her disapproval of any invasion of her realm, it was a losing battle. Marsh and Alistair stood meekly studying their toes, two schoolboys acknowledging their wrongdoing without a word being said; the sight was so ridiculous, after a moment her mouth twitched, and the rigid, apprehensive workers who filled the kitchen relaxed as one and returned to their sauces, their roasting spit, and their scullery duties.

Mrs Butter folded her arms. 'I suppose you've come down to tell me nobody served you breakfast and you'd like some bread and dripping, please, Mrs Butter.'

'No, mum,' said Lord Marsh the schoolboy. 'My cousin wanted to pay his respects.'

She eyed Alistair, a foot taller than she and a generation younger. 'Good day to you, young man. By the looks of you, you've been feeding better now that you've left those foreign parts.'

Alistair stepped forward and kissed her firmly on the cheek, which astonished her almost as much as it did me. She became flustered, which I thought was probably why he had done it, a part of the ritual of their kitchen visit. Alistair grinned at her, she scolded and bustled off, but only as far as the morning's baking cooling fragrantly on a scrubbed wooden shelf. She brought back a loaf, along with butter and a knife, and set about sawing off generous slices.

'Mrs Butter,' Marsh told her, 'this is Miss Russell, visiting from Sussex for a few days. You must be nice to her, and let her have a slice of bread. She saved my life once.' Which was an exaggeration, although it impressed the servants.

'And nearly took mine,' Alistair added, which was not, and impressed them even more.

'You probably deserved it,' she retorted, and slapped an inch of buttery brown bread into his hand. 'Pleased to meet you, miss.' My bread came on a plate, as did Marsh's. She stood over us until the bread was no more than oil on our lips, then she took back the plates.

'If you'll excuse me, Your Grace, luncheon isn't going to cook itself,' although to my eyes the work had gone on unabated. She, however, whirled around and started snapping out commands. Obediently, we faded away.

'There can't be too many kitchens like that left in England,' I said, referring as much to the organisation as to the facility itself. Marsh chose to apply my remark to the latter.

'My stepmother tried to renovate the kitchen in the nineties. It is, after all, essentially a Mediaeval room – the only thing that's changed is the motor running the spit, which I clearly remember in my childhood being harnessed to a dog.'

After the steam room of the kitchen, the cold November house bit at us. We'd walked back past the chapel and turned into the hall, with an eye to going upstairs for a proper introduction to Mr Greene's library, when Marsh glanced out the window overlooking the drive and fountain. Whatever he saw there first rooted him to the spot, then sent him running – *running* – along the bust-filled corridor to the Great Hall and out of the front door, passing the sedate Ogilby in a couple of bounds. Alistair and I reached the door in time to see Marsh slow, then halt on the step above the drive. The approaching car circled the fountain and came to a halt in front of him. The driver's door opened, and a woman unfolded herself.

Ogilby hastened to lift his umbrella over the newcomer, but she seemed not to notice. She had eyes only for Marsh, and he, it seemed, for her. He descended the last step, opened his arms wide, and wrapped them around the woman.

I couldn't help an involuntary glance sideways to see Alistair's reaction; astonishingly enough, the man so jealous of his cousin's energies and attentions had a smile on his face, and strode forward into the rain to greet her as well.

She looked remarkably ordinary for this extreme response, I thought as I watched them come up the steps (Ogilby fretting at the impossibility of keeping all three of his charges dry at once, despite the large umbrella and the closeness of the three walkers). Tall and slim, her hair cut short but not in the fashionable shingle style, wearing a skirt and coat the colour of milky coffee, with a common wool overcoat across her shoulders (not even fur trim). She looked a bit like me, in fact, had my hair been cropped short and dark – with, I saw as she entered the porch, threads of white here and there. Mahmoud's age, more or less, in her mid-forties. No powder or lipstick, her only jewellery a gold wristwatch and a silver band on the ring finger of her left hand; she had cornflower-blue eyes with laugh lines around them, the vigorous step of a tennis player and, I found in a moment, a strong and calloused grip.

Marsh gave her my name, which she seemed to recognise. Then Marsh withdrew very slightly from me, to put his hand on the woman's shoulder.

'This is Iris Sutherland,' he told me. 'My . . .' He paused to glance at her, and they exchanged an expression of mischief, as at a private joke shared. He turned back to me and completed his sentence.

'My wife.'

Chapter Ten

I'M AFRAID I GAPED at the woman. For couple of seconds before my jaw snapped shut and my hand went out, I must have resembled a stunned fish.

'How do you do?' I managed.

'Quite well, thank you. Despite the foul weather. It wasn't raining in Paris; it began halfway across the Channel, like walking through a curtain. Alistair, you look marvellous.'

She was English, but had lived long enough in France to have a fairly pronounced accent, and she presented her cheek for Alistair to salute as a European would have done. She then noticed a damp but formal presence lingering in the background.

'Ogilby, that *is* you, isn't it? Good heavens, you haven't changed a whit since I was in pigtails! What *is* your secret? I'll sell it and make us a fortune.'

Torn between pleasure and professional dignity, Ogilby allowed himself a personal response, inadvertently revealing a great deal about Iris Sutherland's one-time popularity in the house. 'No secret, Your Grace, just clean living.'

She shook her head sadly. 'Oh, dear, that will never catch on, not in Paris. But, you want to know what to do with my machine, yes? I wonder, Marsh, if you might put me up for couple of days?'

'Of course – there's always a place for you at Justice, you know that. But I should warn you that Phillida and Sidney are here, and there's to be a weekend party.'

'Oh, how very jolly,' she said, not sounding jolly in the least. 'Birds, drink, dancing to the gramophone, and a lot of terribly British conversation. If I'm very lucky, we'll even have charades. Ah well, if I'd wished for civilisation, I'd have stayed in France. So yes, Ogilby, if you'd be so good as to store my machine under cover. My bags are in the boot, keys are in the ignition. It's a self-starter,' she added. 'You shouldn't need the handle.'

Ogilby headed off to summon motorcar-movers and luggage-carriers. The woman's blue gaze watched his retreat, and she leant close to murmur, 'Marsh, that man is ancient – he was old when I knew him; he must be a hundred by now. Why haven't you let the poor thing retire?'

'I offered, he refused. And he's not even seventy. Give me your coat.' He transferred the garment to the arms of a handy housemaid, added gloves and hat, and offered the newcomer his arm for the stroll to the so-called library. 'What will it be?' he asked her. 'Something hot or something strong, or both?'

'Oh, both would be a life-saver. One can either drive a motor or be warm in it, not the two at once.' Inside the warmth, she went straight to the fire, standing practically in it and moving not at all as Marsh bent to throw more logs onto the low-burning flames.

He had to brush past her silk-stockinged legs to do so; it came to me that I had never seen him as comfortable with a woman, not even his sister. It also came to me, more or less simultaneously, that the framed pictures on the right end of the mantelpiece had been rearranged, that the handsome young second lieutenant was missing, and that a younger version of this woman was in the family group that remained.

Marsh told the maid – Emma, the young woman I had encountered on the stairway – to bring hot coffee made strong in the French manner. Iris gave her hands a last brisk rub over the flames and said she'd be back in a moment, then marched out of the warm library. No one had to tell her where the cloakroom was, I noticed.

Marsh dropped into a chair and lit a thoughtful cigarette. His first reaction to her appearance on the Justice front steps had been surprise and the pleasure of greeting an old friend. Now that reaction was retreating, to be replaced by a sort of concern over what her arrival meant.

It was nothing to the speculation that was racing through my own mind. His wife, clearly long estranged, yet welcomed back as a comfortable, long-time companion? Alistair, as ferocious in his protection of Marsh as he had been of Mahmoud, without a trace of jealousy? (And I was watching for it, you can be sure.) And Ogilby – in my experience, a man's servants were often more vigorous in their efforts to safeguard their master than even the man's friends, and yet Ogilby, too, reacted to her as a long-absent member of the family, not as a wife living shamefully, even scandalously apart from her husband.

I cursed my own absent husband: This was no time to be away in London.

'You know why she's here?' Alistair asked Marsh in a low voice.

'I suppose so. She has the right, certainly. She might even have something to contribute.'

'Your sister will not be pleased.'

'Then Phillida can remain behind.'

The door opened and Iris Sutherland came back in. 'My God, Marsh, what mad and profligate genius thought to place a radiator in the lavatory?'

'Henry put them all over the house, when he and Sarah came back to England after Father died. He said it was an attempt to keep Sarah from freezing, after all the winters she'd spent in Italy. Actually, I think it was make-work to keep the estate builders employed over the winter. I don't believe he ever expected the things to work.'

'It's glorious in there; I'm surprised you don't lose guests regularly, find them camping between the fixtures. Is it possible I may escape England without a case of chilblains?'

'That,' replied Marsh carefully, 'will depend on how long you stay.'

'Well,' said his wife, with equal care, 'I rather thought I might go to Town with you on Wednesday. To meet the boy.'

It made sense that Iris Sutherland would wish to lay eyes on young Thomas Hughenfort, her husband's nine-year-old nephew and heir, the boy who might keep her from inhabiting Justice Hall as its duchess. And if, as it seemed, she had been close to the family before Marsh and his cousin decamped to Palestine and left her to her life in Paris, she might indeed have something to contribute to the discussion. If nothing else – and despite any irregularities in this marriage – the lady had a good head on her shoulders.

The coffee came, steaming hot and the consistency of India ink. Marsh pawed through a cabinet, brought out a bottle of Calvados brandy, and held it up for approval.

'Oh Marsh, you remembered! Yes, that would be absolutely perfect. Do you know, I believe that's the very bottle we drank from after your father's funeral. Could that have been—Good Lord, twenty years ago?'

'I'm afraid so. And it probably is the same bottle. Does it taste poisonous?'

'It tastes heavenly.'

I expected him to add a dollop to his own cup, as a hair-of-the-dog, but instead he added from the jug of hot milk. Alistair took his black; I had milk in mine. With a cup in my hand, it was difficult to fade quickly and politely away, but I was very interested to see more of this new Marsh – yet another unsuspected side to the man.

When we were settled again, Marsh took out his cigarette case and offered one to his wife and me, then to Alistair. When they were all three lit, he resumed his cup and said to her, 'How's Dan?'

I seized on the name. Aha! – Iris has a man in Paris, and this marriage, as I thought, was of convenience only. No wonder they were friends; no wonder Alistair wasn't worried.

But: 'She's fine. Sends her greetings, says I should scold you for passing through Paris and not stopping with us.'

'We were in a hurry.'

'Yes. I was sorry to hear about your brother – but I wrote to you already about that. Henry was a good man, in his stolid British way. Would that he had lived a long time.'

If he had (all four of us no doubt were thinking), we should not be gathered here. Had Henry, Lord Beauville, lived long, or even had he remarried and fathered a son or two, Marsh could have returned to Palestine following the funeral. I put down my half-empty cup and stood to go; these people had many things to communicate, and I was definitely superfluous to requirement.

'If you don't mind too much, I'd like to sneak a look at the Greene Library,' I said.

'You needn't go,' Marsh told me ('No, do stay,' urged Iris), but I assured them I would see them at luncheon, and I went.

Half an hour later, comfortably set in the intoxicating Greene Library with a stack of books and an armchair near the window, I glanced up to see three figures draped in voluminous waterproofs and rubber galoshes, walking in a line off into the park, the dogs gambolling ahead. Half an hour after that, a single figure, the tallest of the three, came back down the hill with two sopping dogs at his heel. Another forty minutes, and Marsh and Iris reappeared, arm in arm and heads bent together against the noise of the rain on their waterproof hats. After a while, the gong went, and I folded up my books to see what Mrs Butter had caused to be made for us.

Alistair was downstairs already. Marsh and Iris came in together, their colour high from the onslaught of fresh air, their good cheer somewhat modulated from the earlier high spirits, but with an element now of unity of purpose.

And still Alistair was not troubled.

When we were served and drinking our soup, Marsh said to his cousin, 'Iris agrees that we need to know more about Lionel's wife and the boy.'

'Of course she does.'

'Perhaps you ought to come down with us on Wednesday, and tail the woman back to her house in Lyons? It would be nice to know where she and the boy live, if they live alone, or . . . you know.'

'Marsh,' I interrupted, but he took no notice.

'It's a vulnerable age,' he continued, 'nine, and if she's living as she shouldn't, it could give us a clear—'

'Marsh,' I said again, sharply. He turned his eyes to mine.

'Let me follow her. Alistair would stick out, and there's a hundred places he couldn't go.' And it would make me feel as if I were doing *something*, I did not say aloud.

'My cousin will manage. He is very good at it.'

'He's very good in . . . other places, but in London, following a woman and a child? Marsh, I am trained to this. There are few better.' No time for false modesty.

He looked surprised, Iris puzzled, Alistair relieved. The two men consulted without words – the first time I'd seen them do that, here – then Marsh nodded. 'Very well; you and Alistair. You can act the happy pair, and follow her into crowds or the cloakroom.'

Not what I had in mind, but the compromise was acceptable, and we finished the meal in peace.

Afterwards, Marsh announced that he and Iris were going for another walk (I refrained from glancing at the streaming window) and Alistair said that he was due to meet his nephew for a discussion of the Badger farms. This left me either to interview children and servants, or to take to the Greene Library.

It was no difficult decision.

Before retreating up the stairs to the sanctuary of the library, I made a quick dash through the rain to a rosemary bush I had noticed growing outside of the billiards room. Feeling more than a little silly, I dutifully laid the wet sprig onto the mantel below the portrait of Obediah Greene, and although I cannot know if it pleased his shade, it certainly made the air sweet.

I went to my room to fetch my pen and a block of writing paper. When I got back to the library I found Alistair standing in the middle of the library, gazing up at Mr Greene. When he turned, I saw the large, lumpy file envelope he carried. Wordlessly, he held it out, and watched me carry it to the table I had mentally chosen for my own. I loosed the tie and poured the contents onto the pad of clean blotting paper.

Three fat journals filled with boyish handwriting, five letters, a pair of identity discs (one the standard fibre tag on a neck-cord, the other a brass disc on a chain bracelet), a silver pocket watch, a much-used penknife, several field postcards, and a leather-bound Testament with the salty tide-marks of sweat staining its cover.

'When you have finished, Marsh asks that you give them back to him.'

'I will. Thank you.'

He turned to leave, but paused in the doorway. 'There is a magnifying glass in the desk below the window. Should you need one.' Then he was gone, leaving me to paw through the personal effects of Sub-Lieutenant Gabriel Hughenfort, Earl of Calminster, ducal heir, enigma of the moment.

The identity discs might have been of value for a psychic reading, but all the necklace told me was that it had ridden on a man for longer than some I had seen, and not as long as others. The bracelet showed signs of dried mud, or possibly blood, but I did not see that laboratory attentions would tell me any more than that a man had worn it in mud, and possibly to die. The sweat-stained Testament had been given to Gabriel by his mother, on his eighteenth birthday according to the inscription. The penknife looked to be a boy's treasure taken to a man's job. The letters GATH were scratched crudely into the side, and the shorter blade was bent so badly it was difficult to open. It also had a chip in the blade, I saw when I had finally prised it open. The longer blade was freckled with rust but was still razor-sharp.

I folded the knife away and took up the pocket watch. Its cover popped easily, showing me hands stopped at 3:18 (How long after its owner's death? I wondered). On the inside of the cover was engraved *Justitia fortitudo mea est* – the Hughenfort motto, carried with him always. I prised open the back of the watch, saw that the works would need some attention before it would run again, and put the timepiece with the other things.

The artefacts had taught me nothing, only that their owner had lived hard in a damp place, which was no surprise. I was left with his written legacy, and with a grimace, I picked up the more difficult first: the letters from the Front.

The field postcards were the usual thing, their laconic printed phrases sending the message that their soldier was alive and fit enough to wield a pencil – or at least, to direct the pencil of an aide. *I am quite well*, Gabriel had ticked off, along with *I have received your letter dated/parcel dated*, after which he had written in a strong, tidy script: 29 December. The checked spaces on one card informed his parents: *I have been admitted into hospital [wounded]/ and am going on well/and hope to be discharged soon/Letter follows at first opportunity.*

On that card, the signature was shaky, from nerves or injury I could not know.

The three letters written in Gabriel's neat hand were another matter. All had come via the Field Post Office, so their envelopes were stamped with the usual black postal circle as well as the red triangle of the censor. The earliest was dated 27 December 1917, sent from France, and contained four pages of news that sounded very like an extended attempt to whistle in the dark – aimed at reassuring not them, but himself. The next was from early April, although it did not seem to be the *Letter follows* that was promised by the postcard, since it made only passing reference to his time in hospital, saying merely that he was recovered but for his twisted knee and an irritating (his word) sensitivity to falling mortars. He sounded, truth to tell, not only recovered but positively bursting with optimism and good cheer. There were jokes about lice and cold tea, stories about his fellows, a matter-of-fact report on a gas attack, and one wistful passage about the Justice parkland in April. Compared with his earlier letter, Gabriel quite clearly had his feet beneath him, and looked to be having what survivors called a 'good war'. I was certain there had been other letters between these two, but taking them as the only representatives, I found the change in his attitude and self-assurance striking.

I then took up his third envelope. This was thinner, and contained but a single sheet of paper. It had also had a much harder journey to reach Justice than the other two: a worn crease across the middle, one edge crushed in, the back of it looking as if it had ridden about in a filthy pocket for days, if not weeks. The glass showed me several thumbprint-sized smudges and the remains of no fewer than three crushed body lice. Sub-Lieutenant Hughenfort had carried this letter a long time before it had been posted. The sheet inside was undated. It read:

Dearest Pater, Beloved Mama,

I write from a nice dry dugout left behind by Jerry, who shall, with any luck, not be needing it again. I trust that you are well and safe within Justice Hall. I think often of the peace inside the Park walls, of how sweet the air smells after a mowing, the dash of swallows in the spring and the loud geese that ride the autumn winds. We have received orders for the morning, and although this has been a quiet section of Front recently, there is always the chance that a German bullet will find your son. If that were to happen, please know that I love you, that I would happily give my life ten times over if it served to keep the enemy from Justice Hall. My men feel the same, willing to give their all for their little patch of England, and I am proud of every one of them.

For your sakes, I shall try to keep my head down on the morrow, but if I fail, please know that death found me strong and happy to serve my King and country. You formed me well, and I will do my best to remain brave, that I might live up to my name. Righteousness is my strength.

Your loving son,
Gabriel

Lies, I thought, all of it pretty lies to comfort the mother and bereft father, just as families were told of clean bullets and instant death even if their boy had hung for agonised hours on the barbed wire of No-Man's-Land. I only hoped it brought his parents some scrap of comfort, when it reached their hands.

The last letter was addressed by a different hand. It read:

7th August 1918

Dear Sir and Madame,

By the time this letter reaches you, you will have received the foulest news any parent could have, the death of your beloved son. I did not know Gabriel well, but over the few months of our acquaintance, he impressed me profoundly, as

*a soldier and as a man. The men under his command, too,
had come to respect him far more deeply than they did many
officers of longer experience and greater years. I do not claim
to understand the forces that conspired to bring your son to his
end, but I am convinced that as an officer, your son inspired
nothing but loyalty and courage in those under his command,
and that at the end, all that he did was for their sakes.*

Joining you in your sorrow, I am

*Very truly yours,
Rev. F. A. Hastings*

This last letter I read several times. Taken in conjunction with
the alternate wording of the official death notification, I began to
see what had led Marsh to the conviction that Gabriel had been
executed. 'I do not claim to understand the forces that conspired'
sounded awfully like a lament for a loved deserter. I could only
wish that the Reverend Mr Hastings had gone into a bit more
detail concerning 'all that he did'.

With relief, I slid the letters back into the large envelope and
turned to the youthful journals with a lighter heart. They had all
been written before Gabriel Hughenfort went to soldier; their
sorrow and bloodshed would be limited to anguish for a dead pet
and the slaughter of game birds.

I read long, grasping for the essence of the boy and finding a
degree of sweetness and nobility that was hard for my cynical mind
to comprehend. Afternoon tea inserted itself on my awareness as
nothing more than a cup at my elbow and a sudden brightness
as the maid turned on the light. The next thing I knew, it was a
quarter past seven and a woman's ringing voice startled me from
my page: The Darlings had returned.

I looked down at my tweed-covered lap and dusty hands, and knew it was unlikely that we should be excused from changing two nights running. I closed my books and shut down the lamps. After returning the envelope into Marsh's hands, without comment from either of us, I went to don the hair-shirt of civilisation.

My perusal of the two dinner frocks in the wardrobe was interrupted by a knock at the door. I tightened the belt of my dressing gown and went to see who it was, opening the door to find Emma, the housemaid whom I had nearly sent flying on the 1612 staircase.

'Beg pardon, mum, but Mrs Butter sent me to see if you'd like a hand with your hair. I was a ladies' maid at my last position,' she added, as if Mrs Butter might send a scullery maid for the purpose. I stepped back to let her in.

She chose my dress, rejected the wrap I had chosen in favour of the other, picked a necklace and combs, wrapped my hair into a slick chignon, and finally produced a powder compact and lip-gloss. The ugly duckling thus transformed into a higher species, the gong sounded as if she had made some signal giving permission.

'I thank you, Emma, you're an artist. Before you go, tell me, how formal is Saturday dinner?'

'Oh, it'll be black tie, mum. There's one or two might wear white tie, but that'll be only the older guests.'

'In either case, I'll need to send for a dress. If I put a letter near the door, will it go in the morning?'

'Certainly, or you could ring, and someone will come for it.'

I had discovered writing materials and stamps in the table under the window. Mrs Hudson would not receive the letter until Saturday morning, but I felt sure she would rise to the challenge of getting evening apparel here to Justice by the afternoon.

And if it did not arrive, I should have a good excuse to plead a headache.

I very nearly used that excuse to avoid that evening's demands on sociability. Following my afternoon's reading, aware that the tragedy of Gabriel Hughenfort would be moving restlessly through the back of my mind, the thought of spending two or three hours making light conversation was a torment.

But when the gong sounded, I went.

Dinner was in the parlour where we had taken breakfast, and more comfortable it was than the formal dining room. Sidney Darling had spent the day at his club with friends; Lady Phillida had spent the day at a lecture and the shops with friends. He began the evening superciliously amiable, she determinedly cheerful; both of them detested Iris Sutherland.

I could not tell if their palpable dislike was due to the potential for rivalry she represented, or to Iris herself. Phillida kept glancing irritably at Iris's dress, a subtle construction of heavy chocolate-brown crepe with flame-coloured kid trim that fit Iris like an old shirt and made her sister-in-law's ornate velvet-and-beads look like dressing up. Sidney seemed particularly irked by Iris's arrival; he found the soup cold, the bird tough, the fish going off, and the wine inadequate.

Marsh watched these undercurrents with lidded eyes, and then over the meat course rolled his little bomb into the room. 'Iris will be coming with us to London on Wednesday, Phillida.'

Lady Phillida's upbringing held, and she managed to confine her reaction to a blink of the eyes and a brief contraction of the lips before saying merely, 'How pleasant.'

Sidney, however, betrayed a less stringent upbringing. His fork clattered to his plate in protest, although he managed to contain his words to a strangled, 'You feel that necessary?'

'Not necessary,' Marsh replied equably, 'but she offered, and I accepted. Do you disapprove?'

Sidney was in no position to disapprove of any of the duke's actions, but he could not quite rein in his vexation. He burst out, 'I truly cannot see why you chose to handle this situation in such a formal manner. Surely we could have made them welcome at Justice. The poor old girl'll feel as if she's on show, like some . . . agricultural creature on the auction block.' That being a fairly accurate representation of the position in which Mme Hughenfort and her son were being placed, none of us tried to argue with Sidney. He went on, stabbing and sawing at his succulent roast. 'I do not know why we couldn't have had them here. I'm sure the child is housebroken. And I'm sure his mother is charming; most French women are. It is hardly a welcoming attitude. I need more gravy,' he ended petulantly. The footman leapt to attention, and we continued our meal with close concentration.

I glanced at Iris to see how she had taken this blatant lack of welcome; she shot me a look of quiet amusement, and went on placidly with her vegetables. I found myself liking Marsh's wife more and more. She was intelligent, clear-spoken, interested in everything, and possessed of a sufficient degree of self-confidence to regard the waves of disapproval coming down the table at her with equanimity, even humour.

It was she who pushed away the increasingly heavy blanket of silence. 'How was London today, Phillida?'

The lady of the house had clearly felt the blanket more than the rest of us, for she seized the question with relief. When we had ridden out the blow-by-blow account of the lecture Lady Phillida had attended on auto-suggestion rendered by a disciple of Coué, and before we could get to her shopping triumphs, Iris turned to me and asked how I'd spent my afternoon.

'I've been exploring the library – the proper library, upstairs.'

'You spend a great part of your life in libraries, I am led to believe.'

'Guilty as charged, I'm afraid.'

'Why afraid?'

'Oh, it's just that most people haven't much use for academics. I freely admit it's a fairly strange way to spend one's life, burrowing through dusty tomes.'

'What are you working on at the moment?'

Phrased in that manner, the question had to be taken seriously. I thought, however, that I might give the room a general answer rather than what I had actually been doing in the Greene Library that very afternoon. 'I'm putting together an article for an American journal. I met the editor last spring at a function in Oxford, and he asked me to write something for it.'

'What is the subject?' she pressed.

'"The Science of Deduction in the Bible",' I told her. It was the sort of title that tended to cause conversation to grind somewhat until people had chewed their way through it, and indeed the two Darlings had that familiar How-does-one-approach-this? look on their faces. Iris, however, looked only interested.

'"The Science of Deduction" – do you mean, when people in the Bible work things out? Like Susannah and the Elders?'

Full points for Iris Sutherland, I thought. 'Exactly. Or psychological deduction such as Joseph used in interpreting the Pharaoh's dreams.'

We turned this topic over for a while, with Marsh listening and the Darlings frowning, until I thought that we had inflicted the room with enough theology, and I asked Iris what she found of interest in Paris. (In other words: And what do *you* do?)

'The immense wealth of its artistic life. Writers and painters are coming back, now that the worst of the damage is patched up, and musicians. Music somehow sounds better in Paris, don't you think?'

This was no rhetorical question; she expected an answer. I had to disappoint her.

'My husband would no doubt have an opinion, but I'm afraid that I have what could only be called a tin ear.'

'Ah.' She looked down at her plate, a smile tugging at her lips. 'I, on the other hand, teach music.'

Our eyes met in shared recognition of a brick wall. I could only spread both hands in a rueful admission of inadequacy; she laughed aloud, a rich, deep sound that seemed to startle the painted figures on the walls.

'Well,' she said. 'That puts paid to any discussion of modern composers.'

'I met Debussy once,' I offered. 'When I was a child.'

'I said "modern."'

'Under what circumstances did you meet Debussy?' This from Darling, who either suspected me of prevarication or simply did not wish to be left out of the conversation. I gave the room a version of the encounter which seemed to satisfy him, particularly because at the end of my narrative the door stood open to his own tale of an episode involving Jean Sibelius.

Marsh was silent and watchful; he drank but a single glass of wine with his meal.

CHAPTER ELEVEN

IN THE MORNING WHEN I came into the breakfast room, I thought
for a moment the first of the weekend guests had arrived: A slim
young man in an attractive herringbone suit sat with his back to
me, chatting amiably with Marsh and Alistair. Then 'he' turned at
my entrance, and I was looking at Iris Sutherland, yesterday's skirt
exchanged for trousers.

'Good morning, Mary,' she said. 'May I call you Mary, by the
way? I feel as if I've known you for years.'

'Do, please.' This morning I helped myself to coffee, and settled
into a chair without assistance.

'I'm trying to talk these two males into a walk to The Circles,
but they'd rather sit by the fire and do needlework.'

'It is six miles away and I have a morning full of appointments,'
Marsh answered.

'What are The Circles?' I asked.

'Prehistoric stone circles, concentric, and one simply cannot
cheat and motor over there. Part of the experience is the effort.'

'If you're looking for a companion, I'd be willing,' I told her.

The sky was grey but not actually raining, and it was cold enough that perhaps it would stay dry.

'Lovely! And,' she added, 'if one walks, one is justified in indulging in a nice, stodgy luncheon in the village. To strengthen one for the return trip.'

'Sounds excellent,' I agreed, helping myself to a second breakfast – to strengthen me for the trip out. Fortunately, among the clothing I had brought were some old but comfortable woollen trousers, which looked to be the uniform of the day. Before I had finished, Phillida bustled in, a sheaf of notes in one hand.

'Marsh,' she said without preamble, 'I need to go over the day's schedule with you. I've sent Lenore and Walter off to the Cowleys'; no spots there and they owe me a favour. They'll stop there until Sunday, let Miss Paul have a rest. Now, about the rooms. I need to see if—'

I escaped before she could put me to work. As I went upstairs to change into my trousers, I was aware that the house was humming with energy, the final, manic spurt of preparation before the London trains began to pull into Arley Holt. Not even Marsh would dare venture into Mrs Butter's realm today. With luck, Iris and I would be gone until teatime.

Thoroughly bundled from hat to boots, I presented myself at the library door, received Iris's critical but approving glance, and followed her out into the cold air.

I half wondered if Marsh and Alistair had chosen to occupy themselves elsewhere in order to give Iris and me a chance to speak, at length and undisturbed, and so it proved. After the first mile we no longer felt the house looking over our shoulders, we had each other's pace for walking, and we could settle into the morning.

'You must be curious,' Iris opened. 'About me and Marsh.'

'It is not the usual situation,' I agreed, deliberately vague – although by this time there was not much left to speculate about, other than the degree of amity in the so-called marriage.

'I'm a lesbian,' she said bluntly. After a few steps she looked out of the corner of her eye at me; when she saw that I was not shrinking away in horror or even particularly surprised, she went on. 'I've always known it, from the time I was a girl, and I dreaded marriage. Not the physical side necessarily, but the sense of bondage, a thing that ate at my mother until—no, let's, not go into that. Suffice to say that I was left with something of what we might now term a "phobia" about marriage. And because I was my parents' only child, it was going to be very difficult not to marry. These days, it might be easier; then, and especially with my parents, a spinster daughter would have been cause for a family war.

'I'd known Marsh since we were both eight or ten – our mothers were second cousins. I always liked him, always recognised in him a kindred streak of unconventionality. When he went off to the Middle East after university, we kept in touch, exchanged letters every few weeks. I used him as a sounding board – you know how it is, it's easier sometimes to speak of things on paper than in person, so Marsh knew all about my situation.

'His parents dragged him back home after a few months off the leash. This would have been in the autumn of '98, because I'd just turned twenty-one. I'd gone to live in London; he came down to see me, took me for a long walk on Hampstead Heath, and he proposed.

'It was, quite simply, a business proposition. He, too, was being pressured to marry, particularly because after ten years of marriage, the heir's wife – Henry and Sarah were living in Italy – showed no signs of a successful pregnancy, and the old duke was getting nervous. Marriage with Marsh would be a sham, of course, but it would take away a lot of pressure, and make both our parents happier. It would also give us considerably more independence, being married people. And, I had an inheritance riding on getting married.

'So we married, in a very quiet ceremony in the Justice chapel. It was so quiet, in fact, that nobody knew about it. Marsh couldn't bear the thought of engagement announcements and photographs in *The Times* and the long, drawn-out accounts in the society pages – all the nonsense. And since his mother was dead, and his stepmother didn't give a fig, and I was a legal adult, I just told my own parents after it was done.'

'You even managed to slip it past Debrett's,' I commented.

'I know. That was very clever of Marsh, wasn't it? And then as luck would have it, Henry's wife got pregnant. Personally, I think having the family's intense scrutiny off Sarah's reproductive cycle for a while was what did it, although Sarah claimed it was the warmer climate agreeing with her. Marsh and I moved to Paris – well away from my family, and an easy trip for Marsh to Cairo and Jerusalem. Gradually his trips lengthened, and I met Dan – Danella is her name; I'm still with her – and things settled down into what they have remained for twenty years now. I've seen Marsh half a dozen times over the years, I like him, he likes Dan, and there you have it. The portrait of a marriage.'

It explained a lot, including the brother/sister sort of affection between the two conspirators. I'd be happy to see someone, too, if my freedom had been won through her.

'Thank you for telling me.'

'Marsh thought you should know. You and your husband.'

'You know who my husband is?'

'Marsh explained. He also tried to explain what you were doing in Palestine, five years ago.'

'That would have taken some doing, since we were none too sure ourselves, at the time.'

She laughed. 'But you stumbled into something important, which seems to be what Marsh does there generally – poke his nose into things until something bites back.'

She did indeed know everything of importance about her husband, this sham wife.

Seldom have I enjoyed myself more with another person than on that long day's hike across the hills with the lesbian wife of the seventh Duke of Beauville. We would talk for a while – about Oxford, academics, and the life of an Oxford scholar-cum-detective, Paris, the art world, and the life of a frustrated pianist – and then we would drift into an easy silence, listening only to the day, each of us deep in our own thoughts. I felt the restless exhaustion that had come on me in Sussex, which Alistair's arrival had interrupted but not displaced, shrink and fade, to be replaced by a degree of serenity rare in me.

Two hours later we were standing in front of a small forest of jagged, lichen-encrusted granite chunks thrusting up from the pastureland, and I couldn't think at first why we had stopped. Then I remembered: The Circles. The reason for our excursion.

Prehistoric monuments are invariably lonely, if for no other reason than a group of standing stones near habitations will not last long before being hauled away and incorporated in someone's wall. Their solitude, and their combination of crude workmanship with clear deliberation, make objects such as The Circles puzzling and evocative; they seem to occupy a portion of the universe apart from daily life, and appear to have been fashioned by hands other than ordinary human ones. The breath of God – or perhaps of the gods – has brushed these sites, and changed the very ground from which they rise.

'Extraordinary place, isn't it?' Iris was circumnavigating the outer stones, her right hand tapping each one as she passed.

'I was just thinking how otherworldly these sites are. Have you seen Stonehenge?'

'Once, briefly.'

'I spent the night there, one winter solstice.'

'The cold must have been excruciating.'

'It was that,' I agreed, with feeling. 'But the sunrise on the stones was glorious.'

'The three of us came out here to see the summer solstice one year. Marsh had some theory that this was orientated towards the sun, too. Either it isn't, or else too many of the stones are worn away. It was a nice sunrise, though – warmer than yours, I don't doubt. He caught hell for keeping Alistair out all night. We were, oh, thirteen maybe. Ali would have been seven or eight.'

Ali, his childhood nickname – it took me aback to hear Iris use what I thought of as Alistair's real name. I watched Iris complete her circuit of the outer circle, then step inside to perform the same touching ritual with the inner stones. These were in better condition – either that, or had started out taller – because she did not have to stoop as often to reach them. When the second round was fulfilled, she walked straight uphill from the monument, then stopped, turned, and sat down on a low boulder overgrown with grass and dead nettles.

There were three stones in a row – placed there, I thought, not buried in the ground by ancient Britons. I envisioned these three childhood friends, of disparate ages and peculiarly entwined futures, laboriously hauling the river-smoothed boulders here for viewing. I sat on the end rock, then looked at the one between us.

'Who generally sat in the middle?' I asked her.

'Marsh. Marsh was always in the centre.'

'He still is.'

'Do you know how he came by that scar?' she asked abruptly. 'He fingers it, when he's troubled – I'm sure you've noticed. I don't know why.'

To feel his shame, I thought, but bit my tongue hard against the words. When Mahmoud's fingertips traced that shiny brown welt, they had been recalling the shame of capture and torture, the abject humiliation of a proud spirit at the hands of a Turkish madman. Marsh's fingers, I thought, were reminding him that he was a Hughenfort for whom righteousness had not been strength enough.

'War injury,' I merely told her.

'It changed him,' she said. 'When first he came to France with it, he was not the same man.' She sighed. 'Poor, poor man. He's going to be so unhappy if he stays.'

'Will it affect you?'

'I'll not move here, if that's what you're asking. But I should think it will require regular visits from Paris, in order to keep up appearances.'

It was peaceful in that lonely place populated only by a stand of gnarled stones and abandoned trees. I thought perhaps the reason Marsh had excused himself from the outing was not the pressure of work, but his unwillingness to encounter these mute reminders of uncomplicated youth and its long, free days beneath the summer sun.

'You haven't met this boy Thomas who's coming over on Wednesday? Lionel's son?'

'I haven't. The mother lives in France – Lyons, isn't it? During the War, I could never see a reason to go out of my way and introduce myself, and since then, no one seems to know where she lives.'

'Did you ever meet the other nephew, Gabriel?'

'Him I did meet, yes.'

'When was that?'

'When he was an infant, the first time; then when Marsh's father died and we all came here for the funeral. He must have been about four. And a few times when Henry and Sarah were passing through France. But the last time was just a few months before he died, when he came to see me for two days.'

I looked at her, startled by the raw grief in her voice. Her face gave nothing away, but I had not mistaken the depth of emotion. 'You liked him?'

'Gabriel was a lovely, lovely boy. Intelligent, beautifully mannered – the sort of manners that come from within, from being thoughtful. Not tall but well made, with a grace that made me think he would be a good dancer. Quiet. Passionate. Deeply loyal. Gabriel reminded me of his father at that age.'

'Henry must have been devastated.'

She blinked, as if she'd been suddenly pulled back from a place far away and infinitely kinder. 'Henry. You never met him, did you? No, of course not. Poor man. He was so proud of Gabriel. Marsh thinks he suspected that his son had been executed. I hope not. I pray that Henry went to his grave believing that Gabriel died honourably. It would have mattered terribly to him.'

'Marsh seems fairly sure of Gabriel's fate,' I commented.

'You've seen the letters?'

'Alistair gave them me, yesterday,' was all I would say. She took it as agreement.

'Then you'll have seen. Once the thought occurs, it is hard to read the Hastings letter in any other way.' She sounded bleak; the boy had made quite an impression on her in a short time. A lovely boy who, I had come privately to agree, would end his life with a blindfold over his eyes, lest his cowardice prove infectious. 'When Marsh showed them to me, all I could think was, "Why didn't Gabriel write to me when he was first charged?" Surely he must have had some time before – If I had known, I'd have had your brother-in-law step in. It must have been some tragic, God-awful piece of military blunder.'

'My brother-in-law,' I repeated in astonishment. Did she mean Mycroft? Could Marsh Hughenfort possibly have told his estranged wife about Mycroft Holmes?

'Mr Holmes,' she said. 'Ah – I see. You are concerned that Marsh spoke too freely. I myself have had dealings with Mr Holmes' organisation too, Mary, although in a minor role. Many of us were in a position to pass on information about the Kaiser's army; I did so three or four times. Nothing more. And I do not speak of it where there are ears to hear.'

'Mycroft would be relieved to know that,' I told her, and allowed my mind to return to the incongruity of the impressive young soldier and his catastrophic end.

'Tell me, did Gabriel seem disturbed when you met him in Paris? Shell-shocked, perhaps?'

'It was just two days' leave between getting out of hospital and returning to the Front, and he was a rather quiet young man meeting an aunt for the first time since he'd put on long trousers. He was hardly going to pour his heart out. Too, the Hughenforts all excel at self-control. I will say that I saw that kind of quiet in other soldiers, men who'd spent too long a time at the Front and were not far from the breaking point. Gabriel had only been in the trenches for a couple of months, but they'd been hellish months.'

Like the men with minor wounds who gave themselves over to death, I thought; strong men were shattered, weak men survived, with no knowing the why of either.

'What would you say to a meat pie down at the Green Man?' Iris asked me.

'I'd say that was a fine idea,' I answered.

The pie was mostly pheasant, the beer kept by a true craftsman, and we were well content when we left the small public house with the mythic name. We followed a hilltop path back that was every bit as ancient as stone circles and the Green Man, a prehistoric highway worn deep by the feet of folk with none of the foreign Roman passion for straight lines.

The grey cloud layer thinned as the sun neared the horizon. We dropped away from the ancient ridgeway to branch off in the direction of Justice Hall. A dip and a rise, a dip with the early stages of a stream and another rise, and just as we crested this last hill, the sun broke beneath the clouds. The wide valley was transformed into a place of vibrant colours and deep, perfect shadows; Justice Hall basked therein, like a cat on a warm ledge. The long curve of the Pond sparkled; a trio of black swans floated on the surface. It was not possible to pass on without stopping to admire.

After a minute, Iris said, 'I wish I could simply hate the place and have done with it.'

'One cannot help equating beauty with goodness, and feeling the impulse to serve, can one?'

'The impulse takes a lot of killing,' she agreed, sounding grim. 'Marsh told me once he'd documented forty-three violent deaths within these walls.'

'Forty-three? That seems a lot, even considering its age.'

'More than half of those were a massacre during the Civil War. The Armoury must have run ankle-deep with blood.'

'How did Gabriel feel about Justice Hall?' I wondered.

'He adored it. Funny, that, considering that he was born in Italy and spent his first years there. Every rock and blade of grass; he lived and breathed the place. Walked every inch of every farm, knew every tenant and his children by name.'

So much for the faint thought that I had played with, an agreeable fantasy of Gabriel's faking his death and deserting, waiting in France to be restored to his family. Not if he lived for this house. Well, it hadn't been much of a thought, anyway.

'He was engaged, before he enlisted, wasn't he?'

'Not formally,' she said. 'The girl was too young, I think.'

'What happened to her?'

'I heard she married, after the War. Susan, her name was. Susan Bridges, now Edgerton. But even if Gabriel hadn't died, they would not have wed. When he came to see me in Paris, one of the things he talked about was how to break it off without hurting her. So even then he realised that they'd grown too far apart.'

'What else did he talk about?'

'Do you mind telling me why you're so interested in the boy?'

I hesitated. To anyone else, I would have given some song-and-dance about innocence destroyed, or constructed an imaginary brother whom Gabriel resembled, but I did not wish to do that to her. 'You know that the reason Holmes and I came here was because Alistair thought we might help free Marsh from Justice Hall?'

'So Ali told me, although not in such direct terms. What does Gabriel have to do with that?'

'Frankly, I don't know. But then neither Holmes nor I have the faintest idea where to begin with Marsh. The threads that tie Marsh to Justice Hall are so numerous.' Indeed, the man was like the giant Gulliver, bound into immobility by the countless tiny threads of the Lilliputians. I shook off my fancy. 'If we can snip through a few of them, it might free him to make decisions unencumbered, instead of allowing himself to be bound. He may not, in the end, choose to go back to Palestine, but we owe it to him as a friend' (as a brother, my mind added) 'to give him that choice. Gabriel's death, which seems to trouble him deeply, was simply the first loose end to present itself.' I felt I ought to apologise for such a feeble explanation, but I had none better. 'Any action, even completely peripheral, is better than feeling useless.'

'I know what you mean,' she surprised me by saying. 'I suppose it's why I've come back, to help him look at this French son of Lionel's, even though there's not much I can do except offer support.'

'Which is a thing he would never ask for himself.'

'Which is why Ali brought you in, I suppose, because Marsh himself never would.'

'Did Gabriel keep a war diary, do you know?' I asked.

'He always used to keep one, when he was a boy. I sent him a very grown-up journal from Venice once, for his twelfth birthday; you will have seen that among his things. But a lot of things change in a boy, especially when he puts on a uniform. He may have grown out of diaries.'

'What about his possessions? Did his father keep any of his books, or those treasures boys tend to keep? I don't even know where his room was.'

She looked at me oddly. 'He had the room where Marsh is now. It used to be Marsh's when he was a boy, but as he had no intention of returning here, he had no objections to Gabriel taking it over. You know, you sound as if you and your husband are actually investigating this death. As if there was something criminal about it.'

'Strictly speaking, there must have been: He must have had a court martial to convict him of a crime, even if we haven't found the trial records yet. But yes, Holmes seems to feel that there may be something odd about the death. Please, though, don't say anything to Marsh about it.'

She turned away to look down at the lovely, ghost-ridden house, chewing at her lip with a strong white incisor. 'All right,' she said finally. 'I won't say anything yet. And in fact, I am glad someone is looking more closely. I find it hard to believe in the picture of Gabriel as a coward.'

She cast a last glance at the house and then concentrated on the slippery ground. But this time, I thought, she had looked at Justice Hall with loathing.

The proud beauty basking in the glow of the sun hid a number of secrets behind her ancient façade, it would seem. The strength of the sun faltered; with that sudden reminder that we had brought no torches, we did not pause again.

Before we had taken more than a couple of dozen strides, however, a vehicle appeared on the other side of the valley: the house Daimler, returning from the station, laden with weekend merrymakers. There would be no peaceful cup of tea before the fire for us.

'I have an idea,' Iris said. 'If it's still open. This way.' I followed willingly, since she clearly had a plan that did not include inserting our wind-blown and mud-bespattered selves into London Society.

We kept to the backs of the hedges and the far reaches of the formal garden, coming past stone gladiators and goddesses to the oldest part of the house. Iris led the way to a door, which she opened cautiously; deciding the voices were at a safe distance, we slipped inside. I thought we should be making a break for the carved stairway a third of the way down the corridor, but instead she turned immediately left, to dive into a sort of mudroom filled with old boots and waterproofs. Not the sort of place I might have chosen to inhabit until the coast was clear, I thought, but Iris pressed farther back, pawing aside coats that might have hung there since the fourth Duke's day, if not the third. All I could see of my companion was the back of her herringbone trousers, and I was beginning to wonder how on earth we would explain ourselves if one of the servants happened upon us when I heard a click, followed by a low exclamation of relief.

'In here,' she whispered.

I picked my way into the musty clothing, rendered half-blind by the combined darkness and steaming-up of spectacles. Iris seized my outstretched hand and pulled me in; then to my consternation she shut the door, cutting off what light there had been and losing the first tendrils of claustrophobia.

'Hold on,' she murmured. I could hear her shuffling about, her hand patting across some part of our tiny enclosure. I shifted away from the unexpected intimacy of her leg against mine, and then she spoke again: 'Here we are.'

The rattle of a matchbox warned me what to expect; on the third try, the head ignited and was held under the wick of a candle stub. There were several such, I saw, arranged on top of the doorsill, all of them furry with dust. She took a second one down, blew it clean, lit it from the one already going, then handed it to me.

I had thought the stairs down to the crypt were snug. This was more like a spiralling ladder. I had to take care not to set Iris's coat tails on fire, so nearly directly above me did she climb; my free hand rested on the steps in front of me for support, in the absence of anything resembling a rail.

We climbed a full circuit, then stopped at a narrow landing; the stairs continued their spiral up into the darkness. Iris's candle illuminated a tiny door, its frame topped by another collection of candles and matchboxes. The latch seemed to be little more than a stiff wire jabbed into a tiny hole, but it gave Iris some difficulty. She poked and prodded away, experimenting with marginally different angles and degrees of force, until one finally worked. With a click like that of the first door, the wall gave. She pushed, leant out to survey the room beyond, hopped down, and turned to help me climb out.

It was a jib door, I saw when it was shut again, its seams rendered invisible by a square of wood trim, the same as any of those mounted decoratively atop the wallpaper all around the room.

We were in a bedroom – Marsh's quarters before and now after his nephew's time, bearing traces of an undergraduate's personality. The room felt old, as the library and the billiards room below had not, all stone and rough-hewn black beams. One of the two Hughenforts had liked art deco, as testified the four lamps in the shapes of vines, leaves, and nymphs, although the wallpaper and Turkey carpet were probably half a century older. It was a shadowy chamber, in spite of the two windows: black wood, burgundy-coloured velvet drapes, and gloomy paintings.

Oddly like the interior of a Bedouin tent, in fact.

Iris swept the room with a disapproving gaze. 'It was certainly more cheerful when Marsh was an undergraduate. And I can't imagine Gabriel living with those paintings – Phillida must have moved them in here to get them out of the way. And those curtains! This was a sort of lumber-room when we were children. Marsh claimed it for his day-room as soon as he discovered the stairs, although his mother wouldn't allow him to sleep here.'

'Because of the stairs?'

'Actually, I don't think she knew they were there. No one did – that was the appeal. I think it was simply that the room was not appropriate in her eyes for a child. One can rather see her point, although at the time we all thought her terribly unreasonable.'

'As far as you know, this stairway is not common knowledge?'

'I shouldn't think so. You saw the candles – those have sat there gathering dust for a long time. Our generation knew, but we also knew if we told, it would have been blocked up. Gabriel may not even have discovered the door's existence.'

'Well, I should be quite careful about using the stairway when the Darling children are about the place, if you wish it to remain a secret. They are highly inquisitive, not terribly well supervised, and fond of hiding in odd places.'

'I'll keep that in mind.'

With a final glance to see that the jib door was invisible, Iris crossed the room and put an eye to the more ordinary door leading into the corridor. Satisfied, she pulled it open, and in a moment we were at our own rooms, hers on the other side of Marsh's dressing room, mine next from hers.

'I'll ring and ask that tea be sent up for us both,' she told me. 'We can be naughty and hide out in our rooms until dinner. Enjoy your bath,' she added, and like two truant schoolgirls, we evaded our social obligations until the clamour of the gong recalled us.

CHAPTER TWELVE

I GIRDED MYSELF FOR THE dinner as grimly as any young knight girding for a tournament – and as painfully aware of my inferior equipage and relative inexperience.

To make matters worse, the only members of the party absent when I reached the drawing room were Marsh and Iris. I stood in the doorway, alone in my second-best dress, looking up at the furious murals of battle on the walls and feeling eleven sets of eyes come around, to rest on me. My fervent impulse was to turn and sprint for the safety of the Greene Library; instead I stiffened my spine, put on a smile that Holmes would have admired, and went forward to greet my hosts and their guests.

Lady Phillida's introductions were, for my purposes, woefully inadequate. Not that she was trying to exclude or patronise me – indeed, I believe it was the opposite, that her casual, first-name introductions were an attempt to make me feel welcome, as if I were already on the inside of her circle and she was merely reminding me of people I already knew. In fact, her method had the opposite effect, leaving me uncomfortable about addressing anyone by name, yet incapable of asking who they were and what they did. The structures of traditional formality have their uses.

By the time Iris and Marsh arrived, I had met Bobo, Peebles, Annabelle, Jessamyn, and the seven others, and knew nothing whatsoever about any of them beyond what I could glean by my own senses.

'Peebles', for example, was a dissipated individual with artificially blackened hair and moustaches whose compulsive double-entendres and caressing lips against the back of my hand at introduction made clear his devotion to the sensuous life, even as the chemical odour his pores exuded told me that champagne was not the strongest stimulant in which he indulged. *Aristocrat*, I mentally added when one of the men addressed him as 'Purbeck'; there was a Marquis of Purbeck, I remembered.

'Bobo' was clearly an actor, as theatrical here beneath the chandeliers as he would be under spotlights. There were also two watchful London businessmen (who winced slightly at being presented as 'Johnny' and 'Richard') and a pair of German immigrants in expensive suits.

The three remaining guests were women, but not quite ladies. Their accents wandered up and down the social scale, and even before Marsh came in with Iris and fixed them with an icy glare, I had already decided that they were there to entertain the gentlemen. In one manner or another. (And, watching the actor circle around Peebles, I suspected that he had been brought for essentially the same purpose.)

When we went in to dinner, I was cut off from my two comrades, and found myself seated between Bobo and one of the Germans. As I tipped my head to permit an arm to snake forward and fill my glass, it occurred to me that, four years earlier, I would never have believed that I might one day positively crave the presence of Ali Hazr as a dinner companion.

Because the actor spent the entire meal talking across the table at the Marquis, and the German on my right was more interested in his countryman to his own right, I spent the meal in isolated splendour. Drinking rather more than I ought, true, but listening as well, and watching everything.

The seating arrangements were wildly unconventional and most provocative. Marsh and Iris were at one end, with Sidney and Phillida at the other: Which end, a person was left to speculate, was the superior? And Marsh played along with it: When the wine was brought to the table, he diverted its steward to the other end with a nod, leaving Sidney to taste and approve. Iris glanced at him, saw the hidden amusement behind his face, and relaxed.

The servants, however, were clear as to where authority lay, so that when a footman entered with a message, he went first to his duke for permission before circling the table to where Sidney Darling sat. Darling excused himself and followed the man from the room, returning with the faint bulge of a crumpled telegram distorting his elegant pocket and a thoughtful look distorting his elegant features. He went to the two Germans and bent to tell them something in a voice too low for me to hear, then straightened and was heading for his pair of London businessmen when Marsh's voice stopped him.

'Have you news, Sidney?'

Darling hesitated, glanced at Johnny and Richard, then returned to his vacant chair to sit down beneath the concerted gaze of the table before answering his brother-in-law.

'There was a demonstration today in Munich, an attempt to proclaim a national dictatorship. Police fired on the crowd, a dozen or more people were killed. General Ludendorff gave himself up for arrest. Herr Hitler was injured and has escaped.'

'What will all this mean for your business interests?' Marsh asked, all friendly interest on the surface.

Darling's answer had too much frustration in it to be anything but the truth. 'I don't honestly know. We have friends on both sides.'

'So you intend to wait and see who comes out on top, then make your arrangements with them, trying in the meantime to avoid creating enemies inside either camp.'

Darling flushed, more at Marsh's tone than the actual words, but he did not argue with the analysis, merely clenched his jaw, inclined his head, and picked up his fork. The German on my far right, however, was disturbed by this exchange, and he turned to my neighbour to whisper urgently in their native tongue, 'But he told us the duke would support the project, that—'

I don't know if the man to my right kicked him or gestured him into abrupt silence, but the question cut off in the middle, and the table talk was wrenched back into innocuous paths. But the quick protest had given me something to think about: As I had suspected, Darling's plans in Germany rested on the financial support of Justice Hall. Marsh not only knew this, I saw, but had just declared that although Darling might perform as the master of Justice Hall, master was he not. The duke had publicly and knowingly cut Darling's legs out from under him; Darling responded with a brief inner fury followed by a summoning of civility, and the party went on.

Marsh's taste for mischief was awakened, however, so that when eventually the interminable meal had wound to its end and Phillida was rising to lead us ladies out, a pair of bright ducal eyes flicked between me and Iris, and he said, 'I imagine my two feminist companions will choose to stay for the port?'

It was command, not question; we stayed. Phillida could do nothing but usher her three entertaining ladies from the room, leaving behind seven variously startled men, two highly amused women, and a trouble-making duke.

The port was waiting in the library, a pair of noble and cobwebby bottles with the equipment to decant them laid out like an array of surgical tools. As we came into the room, Marsh waved at the display and said, 'Sidney? You care to do the honours?'

Another man, with another voice, might have been restoring his sister's husband to authority, with a tacit apology. Or with a slightly different emphasis, might have been condemning Sidney to the humiliating position of mere wine steward. With Marsh, it could have been either, or both. It might only have been a simple admission that Sidney would do a better job of it – and even I could not tell which attitude he intended. Sidney certainly had no idea. I could see the moment when the man decided that there was no point in taking umbrage, that making the most of an uncertain situation would impart the most dignity. He nodded graciously and took up the tongs, to heat them in the glowing coals (although the emphasis with which he thrust the long-handled implement into the fire made me suspect that he was visualising applying their prongs to the neck of his brother-in-law, not the neck of the bottle).

Red-hot tongs, cold wet cloth, the clean snap of the bottle's neck, and the painstaking decanting of the dark liquid through a silver sieve: Men have more rituals than women have hairpins. Then the cigar ritual followed, and talk made awkward by the presence of two ladies and a duke who was not One of Us; it was no wonder the men drifted away to the billiards table and left us in possession of port and fire. Long before the women rejoined us, the limits of conversational topics among the men had been firmly established, enforced by sharp, eloquent silences during which stern looks and gestures were exchanged, and by the occasional clearing of throats. Germany's politics were forbidden, its art and music allowed (although the Marquis's knowing reference to some nightclub elicited two simultaneous throat-clearings); business of any kind was out, which meant that horses and horseracing were permitted, whereas stud fees and auction houses were not.

We three sat listening through the open doors to this verbal dance as it smoothed out from its stilted beginnings, and I could see that any opportunity for learning more about the Darling situation was probably gone for the night. I was just about to take my leave of the duke and his unlikely duchess when Marsh's head came around and he fixed me with a look in which swirled meaning and mischief.

'What would you say to a game of darts, Mary?'

I puzzled for a moment at the overtones behind the question; when I caught his meaning, the surprise of it knocked a sharp laugh out of me.

Once upon a time, Marsh and I had teamed up to cheat an unsuspecting village of their hard-earned savings, linking his gift for smooth patter with the unexpected accuracy of my throwing arm. If I understood him right, he was proposing to set up his brother-in-law's friends for a similar fleecing. I was sorely tempted, not only for the pleasure of the thing in itself but for the joy of forging an alliance with Marsh Hughenfort; reluctantly, I had to decline.

'Marsh, I would absolutely adore playing such a game with

you, but I think I had better put it off for the moment. Perhaps at the end of this weekend, when everyone is more . . . relaxed?'

His eyes were dancing when he agreed, and I went to bed, well pleased.

Saturday dawned clear – and I do mean dawned. The house broke its fast early, despite the late night, with a breakfast that would have done a Victorian household proud. The previous night's quartet of entertainers were conspicuously absent, either allowed to sleep in or, I thought more likely, already bundled up and got out of the way. Nonetheless, their numbers over the groaning buffet table were more than made up for by friends and neighbours – and, I saw to my amusement, by the wives of the gentlemen in our party of the night before – gathered to spend the day trudging across frozen hillsides and firing expensive shotguns at our host's carefully raised and artfully driven birds.

I have, I hasten to say, nothing against a shoot. As an enterprise, it is no more silly or time-consuming than many. The objective viewer may find it incongruous for a landowner to rear, coddle, and set free hundreds of birds just for the challenge of shooting them out of the sky and picking lead shot out of one's food; however, one could argue that (other than the occasional cracked molar) it is little different from raising chickens for the family plate, with the additional benefit of fresh air and open skies for bird and shooter alike. There even exists the narrow – very well: minuscule – chance that some of the nurtured birds may escape the flying lead to assume their ordained state in nature. Even the man with the gun appreciates a crafty escape.

I say 'man' advisedly, for generally speaking, women were permitted to spend the day of a shoot at their leisure, perhaps joining the shooting party for a picnic lunch alfresco and lingering to witness the next drive before being packed off home for tea, a long bath, and preparation for the travails of dinner. Certainly Phillida and the visiting wives planned such a calendar, along with a number of the morning's newcomers who were hardly dressed for a day in the open.

I was waiting my turn at the buffet, smiling absently at strangers and anticipating a day of literary pleasures under the watchful eye of Obediah Greene. (What to wallow in first? A folio today: *The bybble in Englyshe, 1540* with the signature 'O. Cromwell' inside? Or perhaps the 1624 *Donne's Devotions upon Emergent Occasions, and Severall Steps in my Sicknes?* Or—) I looked up, startled, as my name pronounced by Marsh's voice cut through both my distraction and the clatter of forks and knives.

'Mary,' he called. 'Will you be joining us today?'

I looked across the room, saw the expression on his face, and decided that the intensity of his gaze indicated that the question had taken the form of the Latin 'question expecting the answer yes'. I spooned another egg onto my plate, and kept the surprise (and, I hoped, disappointment) from my face.

'I shall be happy to, if the gentlemen don't mind,' I answered.

'We'll pair you with Iris then, shall we? Put the ladies together? She's a formidable shot.'

'I'm sure that Iris is formidable at anything she sets her hand to,' I said easily, which answer seemed to please him. I took my plate to the table and bolted my hearty breakfast, then trotted upstairs to change from my decorous skirt into the tightly woven trousers I'd worn the day before. At least it looked to be dry again today. Freezing, but dry.

Downstairs, I found the shooting party beginning to drift out of the front door and down the steps to the drive. Neither Marsh nor Iris seemed to be among them, although another motor had just driven up and was off-loading yet more newcomers. The two males of the party retrieved guns from the boot and went to join the other warmly clad gentlemen; the females darted up the steps, clutching the sorts of bags used for knitting or needlework. The men were all involved in hearty greetings and introductions, followed by the inspection of weapons, so I went back inside. On the other side of the Great Hall I spotted the multitalented Emma, walking coquettishly at the side of an unfamiliar figure with a crooked nose and the dress of a manservant. Unwilling to shout across the echoing space to attract her attention, I speeded up to catch her before she vanished into the house. Before I could do so, Ogilby emerged from the same doorway towards which Emma and the stranger were heading. She went immediately demure under the butler's glare, leaving me to reflect on the scant opportunities for romance among the staff of a country house.

'Mr Ogilby,' I said, when that good gentleman was in earshot. 'Have you seen the duke or duchess?'

'Her Grace suggests that you join her in the gun room,' he replied, and led me there himself, to a room in the stables wing not far from the estate offices.

'Quite a lively gathering,' I commented to his shoulder.

'Indeed,' he agreed, sounding more gratified than harassed.

'Does Lady Phillida do a lot of entertaining?'

'This time of year, we are a busy house.'

'Makes for a lot of work.'

'It is satisfying to see the house full,' he explained, formal but I thought honest.

'Not as full as some of the weekends before the War,' I said. 'I saw the photographs.'

'The sixth Duke and his wife were great entertainers,' the butler agreed, sounding proud of the fact. 'The gun room,' he announced, and opened the door.

'Ah, Mary,' said Iris, lowering a gun from her shoulder. 'What kind of weapon do you fancy?'

'The one I use at home is an American make, my father's old gun. What do you recommend?'

'How good a shot are you?'

'Passable.'

'Is that modesty or honest judgment?'

'Well, better than passable, I suppose.'

'Thought so.'

'Not quite in the formidable class, though.'

She grinned at me. 'Men take pride in such odd things, don't they?' She held out the gun she'd been examining, and suggested, 'Let's see how this one suits you.'

I automatically broke it and checked that it was unloaded, then set it to my shoulder while she watched critically.

'You're left-handed, aren't you?'

'Yes, but I shoot the usual way. I don't seem to have a dominant eye.'

'That one's too short for you. Try this.'

She took back the first one and exchanged it for one slightly longer in the stock, squinted at my technique with that one, and reached for a third.

At the fifth gun, I had to ask about the size of this arsenal, which was nowhere near depletion. 'Who was the gun collector here?'

'Oh, there's always been a big collection. Marsh's father and brother were both fine shots.'

'But some of these are new.'

'Sidney,' she said succinctly. 'Look, I don't suppose you can shoot without the glasses?'

'Not unless we place everyone else behind me.'

'Right. Well, try this one; it tucks under a bit closer.'

I tried that one, and then another, a sweetly balanced Purdey that nestled into my shoulder like an infant's head.

'Sidney seems very much at home here,' I commented as I dry-fired at the various stuffed heads poking out of the walls.

'Marsh's brother turned a lot over to him, especially after the War.'

'Alistair showed me Sidney's future stud farm.'

'He's done some good work around here,' she said, meaning Sidney and sounding reluctantly approving. 'He's a hard man to like, but I'll admit that without Phillida and Sidney, Justice Hall would be in sad condition. Is that one all right, then?'

'It's a beauty. You're sure you don't want it?'

'I've got my gun. Marsh wanted to know if we want two loaders each, or one, or none.'

'What do you like?'

'Truthfully? I prefer to be on my own. It means I only get a handful of birds at each stand, but I'm not out to feed the district. I let the men do rapid-fire volleys and get the high count.'

'That sounds good to me.'

'Are you sure? We'll end up fetching a fair number of our own birds.'

'All in a day's exercise,' I told her cheerfully. Apart from which, servants at one's shoulders did inhibit conversation so.

We joined the others in the terraced front drive. I was apprehensive that they might have been waiting for us, but it appeared that although Sidney Darling was there, Marsh and Alistair were not. We did receive a couple of disapproving glares from the older guests, either because of our clothing or our mere presence, but Iris blithely ignored them, and set about the introductions like one who had been participating in these events for years. As indeed, in a way, she had.

The oldest gun was a judge and former member of Parliament in his early sixties, Sir James Carmichael (grey hair, pale blue eyes, and a rigid posture that spoke of spinal problems rather than discipline). He was paired with Peebles, who indeed turned out to be the Marquis of Purbeck; both men had brought their own loaders and dogs. There was a cousin of Alistair's named Ivo Hughenfort (thirty-five, intense, dismissive of introductions and interested only in getting the day started), and two young men, boys really, who turned out to be non-identical twins out for their first day's shoot. They were with their father, Sir Victor Gerard, another business acquaintance of Sidney Darling's, who walked with a limp that would grow worse as the day went on.

Iris even included a few of the hired men in her greetings, men she had known when they had heads full of hair not yet grey. 'Webster – I'd know you anywhere. How have the years treated you? That can't be your son? He's changed a bit since he was two. And you're . . . no, no, don't tell me, you caught us damming up the trout stream one time, I thought I'd die of terror: Doyle? No – Dayle, that's right. You still raise ferrets?'

Childhood knowledge of the country and its people, intimate and too deeply implanted to be worn away by twenty years of living abroad. The men looked at her sideways – they could not help being aware that her marriage to the current duke was somehow irregular, even if they didn't know the details – but they responded to her as to one of their own, going so far as to venture a joke or two. It was a thing they would not do with Sidney Darling.

Marsh finally appeared, carrying a gun, with an unarmed Alistair trailing behind and looking resolute. Shooting, I guessed, was not a favourite with Alistair. We were twelve guns in all, it would seem, with the twins and their father holding one gun between them, and Alistair just out for the air. Iris and I were the only women. Twelve guns, plus loaders and dogs and however many men had been hired to drive the birds to us.

The drivers were, of course, already deployed in the fields and woods. A day such as this was a carefully choreographed affair; a well-conducted shoot was a work of art, balancing the timing and presentation of the birds with the number and abilities of the guns. I knew within seconds of Marsh's appearance on the steps that the day's planning was not his, but that of Darling in conjunction with the head gamekeeper, a short, taciturn countryman by the name of Bloom. After a brief consultation, Bloom gathered together his loaders and their dogs, and in two groups, the well dressed and the working man, we moved out into the parkland.

In addition to the men introduced by Iris, our party included Sidney's four business partners from the night before. The two Germans were called Freiburg and Stein, and were looked upon with mistrust by the others: They might dress like Englishmen and speak the language fluently, but the War was too fresh for easy acceptance of the enemy, even when he had lived here long enough to smooth out everything but his Rs and Vs. The Londoners Johnny and Richard were more formally a banker named Matheson and an industrialist by the name of Radley, who had made a major fortune on armaments during the War. These two were as thick as the proverbial thieves they probably in fact were, and spent most of their time talking about the American stock market.

Iris talked with Dayle for a while about ferrets; when he was called away by the chief gamekeeper, I turned to her.

'I was led to understand that the Darlings moved inside the London social whirl. These guests of theirs seem fairly staid.'

'Apparently they alternate their social circles. After one weekend when a trio of experimental artists sabotaged the shoot, got roaring drunk, and offended a magistrate, Phillida decided the two sorts were best kept apart.'

'Pity,' I said. The party looked as if it could use a bit of livening up.

'I don't know. The Marquis and the twins look as if they might have some fun in them.'

I gave a snort of laughter, then nearly leapt out of my boots as a figure appeared at my shoulder – but it was only Marsh, silent as always in his approach.

'You found a gun to your satisfaction?' he asked.

'Iris found one for me, yes. Will you tell me why you wanted me to come shooting today?'

His answer was oblique to an extreme. 'You have not heard from your Holmes?'

In a house crawling with servants, one could hardly expect that a message from London would go unnoted. I took his answer to indicate that my presence was required in Holmes' absence.

'If I do not hear from him by tomorrow, I shall make enquiries. What is it you want?'

'This is an interesting group of professional men my brother-in-law has brought together. I should be interested to know if you perceive a particular . . . link between any two or three.'

'You think this may be a business meeting, then?' I had thought the same myself, the night before.

'I do not know. You and Holmes, you are perceptive. I should like to hear your thoughts when the guests have left on Monday.'

'They won't speak freely in front of me.'

'Neither would they before Holmes. I wish the wisdom of your eyes, from the distance that will be placed upon you.'

'Very well. I will watch.'

'Thank you. You are good with that gun?'

'I am an adequate shot.'

'Better if you would be allowed to bring the birds down with a knife; I think?' There was a smile deep in the back of his eyes, but he turned away before it could reach his mouth. I, however, laughed aloud.

'What did that last comment mean?' Iris asked curiously, when he had left us alone.

'He's referring to this odd skill I have with a throwing knife,' I told her – clear indication of how I had come to trust her in the few hours I had known her: This was not an admission one would make to a casual acquaintance.

'When did he witness this skill?'

I met her eyes. 'In Palestine.'

'Do you know,' she said, shifting her gaze to Marsh's retreating back, 'that's the first time I've heard him refer to his time there, even obliquely, since I came. In France he would talk about it freely, the handful of times he came to visit me, but every time I say anything about it here, he just looks blank. He said that Phillida isn't to know, but even when we're out of hearing of the house, he won't talk.'

And to think that I had speculated that he might actually

have wanted to return home from Palestine, I thought wryly. 'I believe,' I said slowly, 'that the possibility of having to remain here permanently is so painful, the only way he can accept it is to cut himself off completely from that life.'

'He calls Ali "my cousin",' she agreed ruefully.

'Yes, and he punched Holmes – my husband – for using the name Mahmoud.'

'Good heavens.'

'Yes. Of course, he'd been drinking at the time.'

'Who? Marsh? *Marsh?*'

'He seemed to be drinking more or less continuously until you arrived.'

She stared at me, disbelief struggling with the unlikelihood of my being mistaken, until acceptance asserted itself.

While we had been talking, we were following the others without paying much attention to them, other than making sure to keep a safe distance from other ears. Now we found that we had come to a halt on a rough patch of open ground between two long fingers of woodlands. The coppice to the right was alive with untoward sounds, the cries of alarmed birds punctuating the approaching racket of the beaters: their whistles and calls, the crackle of their boots, and the *thwack* of sticks against tree-trunks. Anticipation mounted; cartridges slid into place; dogs quivered on their haunches; shoulders grew ready for guns.

Twelve guns seemed to me an unwieldy number; at any rate, it was more than I'd ever shot with before. I had been on organised drives any number of times, although I preferred the informal method of flushing birds out one or two at a time; I braced myself for the noise, and glanced down the line at the others. Twelve in all: Freiburg and Stein had been placed nearest the wood, followed by Iris and myself, then Sidney Darling with Alistair's cousin, Ivo, on his left. The banker Matheson and the industrialist Radley came next, then Sir James and the Marquis; on the far end, nearly a third of a mile from Freiburg, stood a cluster consisting of Marsh and Alistair with Sir Victor and his two boys. The twins were taking turns under their father's tutelage, while Marsh looked as if he had little intention of pulling a trigger. Yes, twelve was a lot of guns; I couldn't help wondering if the head-keeper Bloom had been given any say in the matter.

The first pheasant of the day broke from the woods, taking off high in an effort to escape the pressure of the strange noises closing in so inexorably. It took me by surprise, but Iris had her gun up and fired, and the bird dropped to the ground with a soft thud. She took the next one too, then I got one, and then the sky was full of fleeing birds and deadly lead shot. The roar of the pair at our left was nearly continuous, since Darling and Ivo Hughenfort had two loaders each and both were aggressive shots. Unnecessarily so, I thought, on the part of Darling, who was for all intents and purposes the host here. Iris and I plucked birds from their flight selectively; Darling and Hughenfort sent a killing cloud of pellets out before them; the rest did as best they could with the birds that got through. The doctrine of Ladies First was acceptable, particularly when the ladies loaded for themselves, but I could not see that the boys on the far end would get much practise today with this arrangement. Rabbits, perhaps: they'd got two already.

The pale smocks of the beaters began to be visible through the final trees; the last wily birds launched themselves into the air; the guns fell silent. The first drive of the day was over, with forty-seven limp bodies to hang on the game-cart. Three of them were mine, six Iris's, a round dozen went to Darling, and ten to his partner.

I reckoned six for a one-woman show counted as top score, and going by Darling's dark looks, he was aware of her superiority as well. Iris seemed oblivious, merely collecting her bag with her own hands, but on the way back to the cart she gave me a wink, making it clear how conscious she was of offended male pride. I stifled a smile, and wondered if Darling would move us down the line a bit for the next drive.

Sure enough, at the next stand, which was a lightly wooded area through which a stream wandered, Darling suggested positions in a slightly different order. My inexperienced eye could see no difference between our deciduous copse and that of Freiburg and Stein fifty yards away, but either the drive or the location meant that our birds came high and fast. I pruned any number of high branches, but only brought down two birds, despite the overall superiority of numbers: fifty-three this time, two of them woodcock. Darling and Ivo Hughenfort were engaged in a mild rivalry, with fourteen each – until, that is, Iris came happily up and thanked Darling for suggesting that she stand where she had.

He looked confused, and blurted out, 'But you only got five.'

'And all of them deliciously tricky,' she responded, all enthusiasm. 'One of them straight overhead – I have bits of shot in my hair. No, five birds like those are worth twenty in the open. I shall thank Bloom for them.'

Darling watched her troop off to fetch another pair of birds, frowning in an attempt to decide if she was serious. I nearly laughed aloud, and when our paths coincided, I said to her, 'You're being wicked to that poor man.'

'That poor man is stacking the decks.'

'Shall I load for you on the next drive, get your numbers up a bit?'

'You don't need to do that – if I wanted loaders, I'd have asked for them.'

'Just one drive?'

'Well, all right. It's very naughty, though.'

'What, to stack our own deck?'

She shot me a grin of pure mischief. 'I shall have a word with Bloom.'

Our third stand, near to midday, was in open ground again. We spread ourselves out across the rolling hillside, each of us backed by one or two loaders and their dogs. Except Iris and me. She took my gun and snapped it to her shoulder two or three times. She would have to compensate each time to the differences in make, length, and weight, hardly an ideal situation when the goal was a quick fire. At least hers took the same cartridge as the Purdey – I wouldn't have to fumble too much in my loading.

The others, naturally, saw the change. Alistair abandoned Marsh and his family group to stroll back the line in our direction.

'Do you wish me to assist?' he asked.

'No,' said Iris briskly. 'Thanks, old boy, but we're fine.'

As a loader I was far from professional, but we quickly reached a rhythm, Iris thrusting the hot gun back to me without looking, me slapping the full one back into her hand, the stock leaving my grasp in an easy, continuous motion. The drive was a heavy one, and it seemed to me a larger percentage came our way this time than the last, but I had little time to look up or even note the birds falling. I dashed the hot barrel open, knocked the spent cartridges to the ground, shoved the fresh ones in, and snapped it shut in time to exchange it for the other gun. Around and around the guns went. I was vaguely aware of birds raining down, but it seemed a long time before the continual roar along the line slowed to a sporadic bang. One last bird broke, overhead and behind Iris; she spun around and took it.

Triumphant, panting with exertion, she was transformed, very near beautiful. I was sweating myself and felt it fair to join in the triumph.

'Twenty-five,' said Alistair. Even his eyes gleamed. Iris threw back her head and laughed aloud.

Darling, with two loaders and perfectly matched guns, had got twenty-three.

CHAPTER THIRTEEN

WHILE WE WERE BUSY decimating the avian population of the parkland, a luncheon had been transported for us over hill and dale, so that at the next rise we came upon a mirage of folding tables and snowy linen laid out on the upper lawns. The dog carts and Daimler in the background helped account for the phenomenon, but the redoubtable Ogilby, standing beside a tray of crystal goblets with a bottle of wine already in his hand, appeared to have summoned our meal from the faeries of the wood.

The wine was white and slightly fizzy; the temperature of the food the only concession to the distance from the Justice kitchens. I was suddenly ravenous, and even the presence of half a dozen beautifully coiffed and clad women did not stay me from my plate. Phillida made introductions, and I dutifully nodded and murmured acknowledgments around my mouthfuls of food, but it was not until Ogilby had begun to produce coffee on an elaborate machine over a spirit flame that I began to put them together.

The two German women were as unmistakable, and as inseparable, as their husbands. The tall horsey sort of woman was attached to Sir Victor and the twins, and was dutifully bent over a blow-by-blow account of their bag, which had come to a brace of pheasants each, a hare, and three rabbits. Sir James was linked with a rather exotic looking dark-haired beauty named Costanza, who spoke with an American accent; the Marquis seemed unattached; a conventionally pretty blonde woman losing the battle with her frown lines was the wife of Alistair's cousin Ivo; and a flighty, flirty girl of about my own age, a friend of Phillida's, was I thought there on her own but later decided had a male left back at the house.

Inevitably, the talk was of the shoot – the birds, the near misses, the triumphs, and underneath it all, the numbers. It would not do to boast too openly, but everyone knew before the plates were before them how many Darling and Ivo Hughenfort had taken. It was Alistair, with Marsh playing the role of audience, who introduced the subtly superior bag of Marsh's wife. By the time he finished telling Marsh about her shooting, no one there, even the two German wives, retained the illusion that numbers were of any importance when it came to judging skill. Alistair was, in a manner both polite and devastating, very nearly contemptuous of the two men's superior numbers – and, by implication, of the two men themselves. He was eating an apple, and his voice carried as he spoke to Marsh, until by the end, everyone including Ogilby was glued to him.

'—and I am quite certain it was twenty-five, because I was behind her watching the birds fall, so that when that dog of Spinach's carried one of Iris's in, I brought it to his attention. I don't know if he counted it as his or not.' All innocence, he popped a slice of apple into his mouth and carved another one off.

Sidney Darling had gone pale with anger. 'I hardly think I need to steal someone else's birds to pad out my count,' he objected, truthfully enough.

Alistair looked around, surprised. 'Oh, hullo, Darling. Did you think I was talking about you? Don't know why you'd assume that. No, I was telling Marsh about Ivo's numbers. Ivo always has a way of looking good at whatever he's about.'

Everyone there looked to see the cousin's reaction. It was the first time I had really focused on the man, who was something of a nonentity physically, and I had no idea if Alistair's words were meant – or would be taken – as a friendly jest or a deadly insult. For a heartbeat, Ivo Hughenfort just looked at his cousin, without expression but for the abrupt tightening of his hand around his cup frozen mid-air. Then he put on a smile – a rather forced one, indicating that the jest had not been altogether friendly. 'My cousin Ali has a way of looking too superior to join in at any competition. Saves face, don't you know? Not having to lose.'

Before Alistair could react (Ali would have had his apple slicing knife at Ivo's throat), Darling was on his feet, signalling the end of the meal – and of hostilities. 'Good thing there's no competition here, then, wouldn't you say?'

To my interest, he was addressing Ivo, staring him down until the Hughenfort hackles subsided.

'I agree,' Hughenfort said after a moment, trying to sound hearty. 'Couldn't agree more. And honestly, Iris, I'd never have deliberately taken off with one of your birds. My man may have been overly zealous. I'll have a word with him.'

'Heavens, Ivo, take all you like,' Iris replied sweetly. 'I'm only here for the hard ones; that's where the fun lies.'

If Alistair had set the man up for an insult, Iris had bowled him down, all but accusing him of choosing easy numbers over skilled challenge. And this from a woman, to whom he could hardly retort in kind.

I thought Marsh and Alistair would burst from the effort of containing their glee. It was the most cheerful I'd seen Marsh yet.

We abandoned Ogilby and his assistants to their dishes and scraps, and made our way, with our numbers now swollen by a captive gallery of females, across the stretch of the high lawns and onto the other side of the park. The ground here was lower and spotted with bog plants, with a small lake glittering below.

'Mrs Butter likes duck,' Iris told me in explanation, although I could also hear the beaters starting up in the woods across the lake from us. We worked our way up the end of the wet area, where a tiny stream trickled clear and cold over a tumble of water-rounded stones. Waiting for the action to begin, I picked up a handful of the smaller stones, thinking to skip them over the face of the lake; then I realised that the others might look disapprovingly on such a frivolous, and potentially bird-distracting, entertainment. I slipped the stones into my pocket and took up my gun.

This drive was not as untarnished a success as the previous one. Some of the birds, faced with open water before the safety of the next trees, even managed to double back over the beaters' heads. Bloom's voice rang out harshly, berating his hapless men, and the birds when they came flew raggedly, in fits and starts.

Which did not stop them from dying. The two Gerard boys, both of them now armed and Marsh behind one of them looking on, had great success. At the end of the firing the dogs were loosed to retrieve in the water.

One of Marsh's retrievers swam eagerly past me, its whole being focused on the wet lump of fallen pheasant at Iris's feet. I watched the sleek thing pass, marvelling at the propensity of dogs to go with joy into ice cold water to fetch a bird they would not be allowed to eat. Then I thought of the humans, arrayed across the half-frozen ground for the opportunity of shooting birds that might as easily have been raised in a pen, which would not in any case be on the table until long after their shooters had left, and I decided that we were not far removed from the dogs, after all. I thrust my free hand into my pocket to warm it; just as my fingers came into contact with the smooth rocks I had gathered and forgotten, a bird exploded up from a patch of reeds, panicked by the retriever's passing. Without thinking – as a joke more than anything else – I pulled out a stone and sent it flying after the bird.

The two splashes were nearly simultaneous, rock and bird, dropping into the water at the same place. They were followed an instant later by a flash of brown and white and a larger splash, and then Marsh's other dog was paddling energetically out into the lake. Half the men and women there were gaping at me, the other half at the bird or each other, and I tried furiously to decide whether throwing objects at game birds might be considered more, or less, sporting than using a firearm. Should I apologise and creep away, or claim a rather queer triumph?

The dog had the bird now, and turned to swim back with it to his master. Every eye watched as the dog gained the bank, paused to shake off a spray of drops, then trotted up to drop the feather bundle at Marsh's boots. The thing lay there, well stunned by my rock. This was too much for Darling; he shoved his gun at one of the loaders and stalked over to examine the bird. As did we all.

It was not just stunned, it was dead, without a mark on it but with its neck neatly snapped.

'Now, that's a first for me,' Sir Victor said. 'You boys ever seen anything like that?'

The two boys looked as stunned as the duck had. The adults did as well, until Iris, coming up behind me, took one look at the bemused duke with the dripping, limp-necked duck cradled in his hands, and began to chuckle. Soon the rest joined in, pressing forward to see what must be one of the odder kills a shoot has produced.

It was not, I noticed, strung up with the other birds on the game cart, but was carefully set apart for the appreciation of the below-the-stairs residents of Justice. I sighed: The whole county would know of my feat by the end of church tomorrow. So much for Marsh's proposed darts match.

We finally dispersed, most of the women towards the house, the rest of us heading to the next and no doubt final drive of the afternoon. Before we had left the bog ground, however, Bloom came up to consult with Marsh. Darling quickly joined them. I could not make out their words, but Bloom gestured with his thumb at the sky, which I noticed was not only taking on the purple shades of early dusk but was also showing signs of mist. Darling shook his head and made calming gestures with his hands. Marsh stood figuratively back from the discussion, nearly an argument, until Bloom turned physically away from Darling to appeal to the master of Justice. Who shrugged, opting out of authority.

Immediately, Darling turned to signal to his loaders, and Bloom, disapproving but obedient, jogged off to urge his beaters towards their last drive of the day, leaving behind him two men and their dogs to gather the remaining birds.

We guns followed at a more leisurely pace, since it would take the men a while to drive the birds to us. As we went, I had to admit that the conditions were fast becoming far from ideal. The evening air was drawing moisture from the wet ground, the mist coalescing in patches and drifts which the low angle of the fitful sun caught here and there. Visibility was tricky in these circumstances, and the mixed woodland, cedars, firs and the occasional dark holly interspersed with deciduous trees, contributed its own share of half-light. Darling placed us, then Marsh came through and shifted each gun farther apart from its neighbour, for greater safety. He and Alistair disappeared down the line in the direction of the boys and Sir Victor, and I heard the first whistle of the beaters drawing near.

Bloom must have ordered them to sacrifice artistry and numbers for the sake of speed, because the whoops and crackles came towards us at a brisk walk rather than a controlled stroll. The peculiar noises, the weird light, the near dusk, and the culmination of the day's competitive excitement into this last drive had us all kneading our gunstocks with tension. Iris, again off to my right, coughed with the damp; the Germans and Londoners beyond her had gone quiet; to my left, strung out unevenly, were the twins with Sir Victor, then Darling and Ivo Hughenfort, and invisible to me at the far end, the Marquis and Sir James. I could hear men moving off in the woods behind our line – not the loaders, who would be gripping the spare guns at the shooters' elbows, but probably unneeded beaters, here to watch the final event of the day, or a couple of the women who had stuck it out. It might even be Marsh and Alistair coming back up the line, having spread the guns to their satisfaction.

The birds broke over our heads, and I ceased to speculate. I was pleased to notice that Bloom's men had, by accident or intent, concentrated the birds along our end of the woods. Iris's gun sounded steadily, and I was kept busy as well, although to my left the normal continuous fire of the two top-scoring men seemed sparser than it had been.

The cold, wet air was filled with the sound of shouts and shot, with rising lead and falling birds, cordite smoke blending with drifting mist. The pheasants seemed to burst out of a white curtain. They were nearly impossible to track, requiring hair's breadth reactions, the finger jerking the trigger before the eyes had a chance to register what they saw. Mist and the smell of guns and autumn leaves; death and an extraordinary sense of vitality and challenge; competition and camaraderie.

And then down the line out of a sudden volley of shots rose an eerie cry and simultaneous bellow that froze every person in earshot, raising the hair up the backs of our necks. Before the sound faded, I had broken my gun, clawed the cartridges out, dropped it to the ground, and set off running through the trees. Branches snatched at my clothing; people moved around me, bent on the same task; men's voices shouted, nearby and at a distance, as the birds were forgotten.

Half hidden in a clump of holly, two men huddled together. The colour of blood was shockingly bright amidst the grey light and the dull green foliage; brilliant spatters had travelled all the way up – but no, those were berries, the same startling crimson as the stuff on Alistair's coat.

Marsh half lay in his cousin's arms, bleeding freely and grimacing with pain, but not dead. From the sound of his curses, he was far from death, and I felt suddenly faint with relief.

Darling reached them first, put his hand out to seize Marsh, and found himself looking cross-eyed at the shiny blade of a knife. Not the long and wicked blade Ali had carried in Palestine, but still plenty sharp enough to slit a man's throat.

'You touch him,' Ali snarled at Darling – and it was Ali, even to the accent – 'you die.'

CHAPTER FOURTEEN

ARLING STUMBLED BACK; THE others began to collect in a wide circle around the fallen man. Alistair looked like a mother wolf, teeth drawn back and murder in his eyes. It took a deliberate effort to approach him, but I did, warily.

Iris had no such hesitation. She elbowed the men aside and dropped to her knees in front of the bloody tableau. I joined her, moving deliberately so Alistair would not feel threatened. Only when her outstretched hand was inches from it did she notice the knife.

'Ali! Put that away,' she commanded, and pushed his wrist away in order to peel back Marsh's thick jacket. Alistair hesitated, then the knife was gone.

'Are you shot, too?' I asked him. 'Or just Marsh?' He had blood on him, but I couldn't tell whose it was.

'No. A few pellets, maybe. He walked in front of me just as the gun went off.'

'Whose gun?'

After a moment, he tore his eyes from mine to look over my

shoulder at the others, then back to me. 'I did not see.'

Iris had excavated the clothing layers enough to determine that the pellets had buried themselves into Marsh's left side fairly evenly but that there were no torrents or spurting wounds; his injuries would be painful, but not life-threatening. She turned her head to look for Darling, but just then Bloom came pounding up, white faced and gasping. She spoke to him instead.

'We need to get him to the house, and to ring for the doctor. He'll be all right – nothing vital seems to have been hit.'

I thought Bloom would collapse at the news, but he pulled himself straight and then leapt to do her bidding. I caught up with him before he reached his men, still drifting in confusion from the woods. 'Mr Bloom,' I said. 'Don't let any of your men go home yet. The police will want a word.'

He stared at me. 'The police? But it was an accident.'

'Of course it was. But they will want to be thorough.'

'I need to let my men go home before it gets dark.'

'Yes. Well, do what you can. At least write down the name of anyone who has to leave. Please?'

'Very well, mum.' He trotted off, summoning runners as he went.

Back at the holly trees, Iris had wrapped Marsh back into his clothing and was in the process of extricating him from his cousin and checking Alistair's 'few pellets'. She was trying to, anyway. Alistair was none too pleased at being prised from his wounded comrade. Not until Marsh spoke quietly in his ear did Alistair allow himself to be pulled away and given a cursory examination.

I was close enough to hear Marsh's low words, and although my Arabic had gone rusty with disuse, I had no doubt that it was in that forbidden language that Marsh had spoken. The key word, my mind eventually translated, was 'accident' – but the phrase in which it was embedded had not, I thought, been merely 'It was an accident'. As I turned the words over in my mind, the conviction grew, underscored by the uncharacteristic and blatant relaxation of suspicion on Alistair's part, that Marsh's actual phrase had been, 'It must appear an accident.'

I glanced up again at the audience, and noticed how many guns there were, all pointing in our general direction.

'Are those weapons unloaded?' I snapped. Most were, but the Marquis and one of the twins flushed with oddly identical embarrassment, broke their guns, and emptied them.

'Did anyone see what happened?' I asked more mildly.

My answer was in the small movement the embarrassed boy made away from his father and brother. Sir Victor's arm was across the boy's shoulders, and looking at them, I noticed for the first time that the lad was rigid with something more than the general horror. When he felt my eyes on him, he began to tremble; his father's arm tightened. I stood up and went over to have a quiet word with them, but the boy spilled out words for the benefit of the entire gathering. He looked terribly young.

'I was on the end, just next to a clump of trees, and I knew this would be my last chance for a bird, and then I saw one out of the corner of my eye – I saw movement in the branches.' I must have winced in anticipation of an admission of carelessness, of firing blindly into a moving bush, because he began to protest. 'I didn't shoot – I wouldn't want to hit one of the beaters – but I started to bring my gun around and this pheasant took off, beautiful and low. I think it must have been winged earlier, because it was clumsy and slow enough for me. I'm not a very good shot,' he confided painfully. 'I came around and pulled the trigger, and then out of the corner of my eye I saw His Grace and Mr Hughenfort. Even when I saw them, I thought I was all right – that is, they were all right – because I thought my shot was well clear. I just didn't know how wide the spread was, I suppose. And I'm sorry, I'm really awfully sorry.'

In a moment he would begin to sob, and humiliation would anneal itself to horror to make this day a burden for the rest of his life. I bent to look him in the eye, desperately trying to recall his name (Roger – or was that the brother? Damn, I thought, I'll have to go for formality, pretend I'm a schoolmaster).

'Mr Gerard, His Grace is going to be all right. If there weren't ladies in earshot he'd be swearing up a storm, and I can only hope the doctor who has to dig the shot out is very hard of hearing. But he's going to be fine in a week or so, and perhaps you've taught him a valuable lesson concerning the stupidity of wandering about where men are shooting.'

The reference to cursing, the suggestion that the duke might have had some responsibility for his own injury, and the inclusion of this teary boy among the 'men' made the tears recede and had him standing a fraction away from the comfort of his father.

'Show me where it happened,' I suggested.

He glanced at his father, but readily led me to one side to illustrate how the mishap had come about. 'I was here, you see? Father and Roger were by that log.' Discarded cartridges still marked both boys' positions.

'Which way were you standing?' I asked.

He planted his feet, then stepped a little to one side. 'About here. It's hard to tell – it's getting so dark.'

'And you heard something from those bushes?'

'A rattle. Like a bird panicking through the undergrowth.'

'And you turned . . .'

'I took a couple of steps, and then the bird flew out.'

'From the bottom, near the ground?'

'About halfway up. Sort of where that dead branch is.'

'And you brought up your gun.'

'I counted two. It helps, to count. Steadies the gun on the bird's path.'

'One thousand one, one thousand two, is that how you count?'

'Faster. One. Two. Bang.'

I picked my way in the direction of the holly clump, where Marsh was fighting to get to his feet (cursing all the while, in English now, ladies or no). The pheasant lay tumbled on the forest litter; I knelt beside it, trying to tell if there might indeed be blood of two different ages on the feathers, but it was impossible to tell. That on the wing might have been marginally more dried, and thus indicate, as the boy thought, an earlier injury that had made the bird both clumsy and nervous enough to flush from what was actually a safe haven. There was no telling. I left the bird there and went back to the boy.

'Did you use both barrels?'

'I just had one. I'd tried for a bird a minute before, and missed. Father was loading for Roger. We didn't need a loader before His Grace lent me his gun.'

We both looked down at the elegant weapon the boy still carried, his face gone stark with renewed horror, mine no doubt fighting a rueful smile: Marsh had been shot with his own gun.

The beaters devised a rough pallet to carry their wounded duke off the field of battle. While dogs and men scurried to retrieve the birds before darkness rendered them invisible, one of the motorcars that had been waiting to transport us back to Justice was pressed into service as an ambulance. Alistair and Iris rode with Marsh; the women who had stayed on piled into the other vehicles; I walked a ways apart from the men trailing cross-country back to the house; they, in turn, kept their distance from the grimly limping Sir Victor and his two silent sons. There was little of the merriment that normally accompanies a returning shoot, and I for one had much to think about, as I trudged tiredly through the swirls of fog towards the glow of Justice Hall.

As we approached the house, I fell behind to allow the others to enter before me. In fact, I sat at the foot of the pelican fountain for a while, allowing my thoughts to quiet, considering what had happened that day, the effects and implications. When finally I stood up to brush off my trousers, the drive and entrance were empty. I went up the steps, and had my hand on the elaborate brass latch when the door was jerked open from within. Ogilby held the door, his professional calm worn so thin he looked almost harried. As I entered the Hall, I understood why: Our staid little party had expanded exponentially. The Hall was a tumult of colour and motion. And sound – voices shouting over what sounded like two gramophones playing different songs at full throttle.

'What on earth is this?' I asked the Justice butler.

'It would appear that some friends of Mrs Darling were in the neighbourhood and decided to drop in.' Ogilby's face gave nothing away, but I could just imagine the state of the kitchen at the moment, with what looked to be thirty unexpected dinner guests.

I gave the butler a look of commiseration, and stepped inside. The very air seemed to push out of the doors past me, fleeing for the still terraces.

'Where did they take the duke?' I asked him.

'His Grace was taken up to his apartment, madam. The doctor is with him.' Beyond the temporary confusion of sheer numbers, I thought, the butler seemed distracted, even distraught.

'He'll be all right,' I tried to reassure him. 'Very uncomfortable, but all right.'

'Thank you, madam,' he replied, so clearly unconvinced that I had to wonder if something further had happened on the trip here. I hurried off to see for myself.

I had no intention of getting caught up in the fray, and made along the front wall of the Great Hall in the direction of the western wing, but even that backwater was pulsing with full-throated conversation. I edged around a three-sided argument involving a woman wearing a sort of Romanian peasant gown with a multitude of scarves over it, a tall, cadaverous man with a handful of turquoise chips hanging from his right ear lobe, and a short, plump individual in a man's lounge suit who might have been male or female. This last person wore a small, ill-tempered spider monkey on the left shoulder of the suit; the creature was plucking irritably at the jewelled collar and gold chain that kept it from leaping to the heights. I gave the monkey wide berth, nearly knocked into a huge betasselled sombrero someone had perched on a marble bust of the third Duke, avoided the peculiar green drink thrust in my direction by a woman dressed predominantly in beads and fringe, and escaped.

Standing outside of the heavy door to Marsh's rooms, I could hear voices. I knocked, then turned the knob to open the door a few inches.

'May I enter?' I asked.

'Come in,' Iris answered.

The tableau that greeted my eyes was like some dramatic canvas depicting the aftermath of battle: doctor in rolled-up shirtsleeves with blood to his elbows, his assistant (Alistair) holding up a lamp to throw strong light on the victim, a worried nurse (played by Iris) clasping her hands. Except that none of them were dressed for the part, the victim was more furious than suffering, the surgical table was a vast high bed covered in velvet, and the worried nurse on closer examination seemed rather to be clasping her hands to keep back laughter as the grizzled Scots doctor mumbled on and on about the foolishness of walking out in front of bairns with guns. I shook my head to dispel the images of paint on canvas (Justice Hall was having a powerful influence on my imagination, I thought in irritation) and stepped forward to offer succour to the wounded. Or distraction, at the least.

With the blood cleaned away, the injury became a matter less of gore and carnage than of a myriad of oozing punctures gone angry with reaction. The doctor, working his way methodically from cheek to thigh, was currently prodding away at the upper arm. A small saucer of dugout shot lay to one side, and Iris reached out with the sticking plaster to cover one trickling but empty hole in her husband's shoulder.

The doctor's digging produced another tiny lump, which he dropped into the saucer with a wet *clink*.

'You're certain you won't have a wee bit of morphia, are ye?' he asked. 'You'll find it goes ever so much easier.'

'No morphia,' Marsh grunted.

'Very well,' the doctor said in an It's-your-funeral sort of voice, and picked up his probe.

Sweat was running freely down Marsh's taut face, the only indication of what had to have been agony.

'Can I get you a drink?' I asked him. 'Water? Whisky?'

His answer was a flicker of the eyes in the direction of the bedside jug near the doctor's elbows. I took the glass to the lavatory and filled it with water from the tap. When the next piece of shot was in the saucer, he propped himself on his right elbow and drank thirstily.

A rat-a-tat of knuckles on wood interrupted us, and a sudden increase of noise indicated the door being opened.

'Yoo-hoo,' came Phillida's voice. 'Anyone here? There you are – Marsh, you poor boy, are you all right? How terribly awful for you—er.' Her cheerful air did not survive the sight of the doctor's bloody hands or the small plate of gory lead pellets, but she did not flee. 'Marsh, dear. You must hurt like the blazes. Do you want me to put my friends back on the road so we won't disturb you?'

'That won't be necessary,' he told her, his eyes narrowed against the probe in his ribs. 'Just keep them in the centre block and I won't hear you.'

'Are you sure, my dear? I don't mind if you—'

'Phillida, please. Go back to your party.' She started to say something, but in the end just turned and left the room.

After a while, I told Marsh, for distraction more than anything, 'The boy – not Roger, but the other one – is devastated. He thought he'd killed you.'

'I thought he had too, for a moment,' he said with a glimmer of dark humour. 'I'll see him when this butcher is finished.'

The doctor seemed unoffended. Perhaps he actually was deaf, I speculated, but his next words proved he was not. 'When I'm finished, you will rest. No interviews with guilt-ridden laddies.'

Marsh acted as if the medical man had not spoken. 'Would you also ask Ogilby to send trays up for us? I don't imagine either Iris or my cousin will much care for a formal dinner. Have yours sent up too, if you like.'

The annoyed doctor bent to his task again, and Marsh withdrew into himself. Distraction, I saw, was clearly impossible; I might as well go and try the hot water supply for a bath. Even if I succumbed to the temptation of dinner on a tray, I should prefer to be clean for it.

First, though, a responsibility: I tapped Alistair on the arm and gestured with my head towards the door. He handed the bright light to Iris, and followed.

I spoke in a low murmur, for his ears only. 'This looks like an accident.'

He looked back steadily. 'That is how it appears.'

'Still, it might be good for you to remain in this room tonight. And, if a tray comes with food for him alone . . .'

There was no need to finish the sentence, I saw. However: 'It would also be as well for you to watch your own back, too. You and he were standing side by side, after all.'

He did not appear even to have heard what I was trying to say, but I did not push the issue. I could only trust that his protective alertness would extend out from Marsh's person to cover his own.

'I will see you in a little while,' I told him. 'I'll be in my room, if you need anything.'

Just before I left, a voice followed me. 'Peter,' Marsh said. 'The boy's name is Peter. Tell him to come and see me later.'

So before I retreated to hot water and privacy, I hunted down one worried boy to reassure him that his victim was well and had asked to see him after dinner. Both parents looked grateful, and I climbed the steps again, meditating on the powerful, potentially devastating commitment to the future made by parents.

Until I had my hand on the doorknob of my room, I had forgotten about my letter to Mrs Hudson concerning the appropriate wear for a formal country house dinner. For about half a second, I thought about finding someone who might know whether she'd sent it, and whether in the confusion anyone had fetched it from the station, but then I decided not to bother. A tray would do me fine. I turned the knob and walked in.

And there the dress lay, tossed on the bed by a remarkably careless housemaid. I looked at the heap of crumpled grey silk, and knew in an instant that no Justice Hall housemaid could ever have abandoned such a dress in such a state. Which left only one possible culprit.

'Holmes?' I called.

'Russell,' answered the voice through the connecting door to the shared bathroom. 'What on earth is going on out there? The place sounds like an overturned beehive.'

I followed the voice through the steam-filled bathroom and found my partner and husband seated on the edge of the dressing table bench, threading studs through his shirt. I went and sat beside him, leaning into his shoulder with affection.

'Oh, Holmes, it's so very, very good to see you.'

'Why? What's happened?'

'Does something need to have happened for me to be glad to see you?'

'When it is said in that tone of voice, yes. You sound like a besieged subaltern seeing his lieutenant heave into view.'

'You're right. It is relief as well as pleasure. Someone shot Mah—Marsh.'

'*Shot* him?'

'Peppered him with bird shot. If he'd been ten feet closer or had his face turned towards the gun, it could have been serious. One of the inexperienced guns – a boy of fifteen – looks to be responsible. An accident.'

'But also not an accident?'

'It feels slightly wrong. Here – let me show you.' I went to paw through his writing desk for a sheet of the elegant Justice stationery and a pen, then began drawing, Holmes bent over my shoulder. 'We were here, strung out along the side of a hill lightly covered with bare trees and the odd clump of evergreens. The beaters were working their way towards us along this line.' The uneven row of twelve Xs was joined by a long squiggle indicating the front of the drivers. I drew in a couple of starbursts to show the clumps of evergreens. 'The two boys and their father, Sir Victor, were here. The boys each had guns – they started the day sharing one, with their father unarmed and coaching them, but Marsh gave his gun to one of the boys after lunch, so they could both shoot. Sir Victor must have been a front-line soldier,' I reflected aloud. 'And he must have been wounded at some point – he limps, and twitched at every shot.'

It was, in fact, proof of the man's will power that his body hadn't taken command and dived for cover at some of the louder volleys. I'd seen soldiers on the street do just that, leaping for doorways at the backfire of a lorry.

'This drive was to be the last,' I went on, 'since the mist was coming in and it was getting dark. In fact, the head-keeper and Marsh's brother-in-law had a disagreement over whether we had time to do one more drive. Darling insisted, but it meant that there was a bit of a rush on.' I described in some detail the ground, the placement of the guns, the movement of the beaters approaching, and the presence of a person or persons behind me.

Holmes leant over the desk, propped on the heel of his right hand, studs forgotten, all his attention on the rough sketch taking shape under my pen.

'The drive was probably more than half over – the thickest body of birds already out of the woods – when Peter Gerard heard movement in the shrubs to his left and turned his gun in that direction. It sounds as if his movements were sensible, to a point: He waited until the bird broke, followed it for a quick count of two before firing. Only, Alistair and Marsh were here behind him, moving up the line in the same direction the bird flew. Marsh had just stepped in front of Alistair when the gun went off.'

'What are the distances here?' He pointed to the marks for Peter Gerard and the two evergreen clumps.

I estimated as best I could, not having had a measuring tape with me in the field. The three marks – gun, bird, and Marsh – formed a lopsided triangle, the line between gun and victim being slightly the longest.

'And the bird – did you see where it lay?'

I drew a small X approximately halfway between the clumps, then turned the pen upside-down and used the end to trace the creature's path from its emergence at the clump to the point at which I had found it. As I moved the pen, I recited, 'One. Two. Bang.' The pen end halted at the small X.

Far short of the holly bush into which Marsh and Alistair had fallen.

'Could the boy be wrong?'

'Wrong, yes, but not, I think, deliberately lying.'

'I must speak with Marsh.'

'Not for at least another hour. The doctor is with him,' I explained.

He grunted his frustration, then returned to the drawing. 'All the guns will be here to dinner?'

Damn, I said to myself. 'As far as I know, dinner will go ahead without Marsh. Alistair and Iris will stay with him.'

'Who is Iris?' he asked absently, and the last two days suddenly flooded in on me.

'You did not interrogate the servants upon your arrival? That isn't like you.'

'I found a taxi at the station, and when I came in the servants were all frantically occupied. Why?'

'Iris, my dear Holmes, is the wife of Lord Maurice, the seventh Duke of Beauville. Mahmoud is married.'

His astonishment was instantly gratifying. He lowered himself onto the dressing-table bench. 'I appear to be lacking some fairly vital information,' he remarked.

'They kept it from Debrett's,' I told him.

'They kept it from Mycroft,' he said, and I had to agree that was the feat truly worthy of note.

'They were married—'

'Wait,' he interrupted. 'Tell me while you are getting ready for dinner.'

'Oh, Holmes, must we? It's chaos down there, they're all the most eccentric friends of the Darlings, and I've spent a full twenty-four hours being sociable. Marsh suggested a tray.'

'Sympathetic as I am to your plight, my dear Russell, I think dinner is potentially too rich a mine for data for us to miss. I shall draw you a bath while you shed your hunting gear.'

I first hung the crumpled silk dress above the steaming bath to relax it, then slid gratefully into the scented water.

Holmes drew up a stool. 'Now: Tell.'

I told.

No reason to dwell lovingly on the glories of Justice Hall: Holmes could see those for himself. The hidden stairway was worth a bit of detail, and I could see his interest rise at the hidden Roman floor (this from the man who had once told his friend Watson that he was not interested in useless knowledge!) before he deliberately pushed it aside as peripheral. The contents of the Greene Library pulled even more strongly at his imagination; that too was set aside. The Circles, the deep relationship shared by the three principals, the painful reading of the Gabriel Hughenfort documents, I summarised those and moved on.

The water in the bath was growing cool and the hour of the gong fast approaching when I finished with the previous evening's dinner party. That episode had demanded considerably more detail in the telling, and evoked a long, thoughtful silence while Holmes fiddled with the bath brush.

'Berlin is the centre of Darling's activities, you would judge?' he asked me.

'He spends a great deal of time there, and he knew of this escape by Mr Hitler before it was in the papers. He claims altruism as his chief interest in the rebuilding process, but at the same time, what industry starts up in the post-war years, he intends to have his hands on the controls.'

'A man worthy of Mycroft's attentions.'

'If Mycroft hasn't noticed him already.'

'It must be said, there is nothing criminal in foreign investments. If there were, we would all be in gaol. Not in the least my good wife. I should like to be able to give Mycroft more than a mere name, however. Did Darling give out the title of his company, or even precisely where it is?'

'No. I'm not even sure just *what* it is, other than some kind of heavy manufacturing.'

'Of course, a man in his position would not wish to appear too knowledgeable about his investments, too eager for them to succeed, lest his fellow club members suspect him of ungentle manly pastimes. I wonder if his business papers—'

'Holmes, we couldn't very well burgle our host's rooms. At least, not unless we get Marsh's permission.'

'It might be perceived as ungracious,' he agreed.

'And with all the servants around, we'd need spectacular luck not to have a maid walk in at the wrong moment. Or one of the children.'

'The children, yes,' he mused, a faraway look in his eye. 'Your Justice Hall Irregulars. Do you suppose . . . ?'

'Holmes! Absolutely not! One cannot use children to spy against their own parents – it would be – the ethics of the situation would demand—'

'I suppose it does go against the Rules of War,' he admitted reluctantly.

'Freiburg and Stein, on the other hand,' I had begun when we were interrupted by a knock at the door to my bedroom. I raised my voice to call permission to enter: It was Emma, maid of many talents, enquiring through the bathroom door if I wished assistance with my hair. I was impressed that anyone had thought to send her, considering the circumstances. I also wondered that anyone was bothering to dress. Perhaps Romanian peasant-dresses and monkey-capped lounge suits were considered formal dinner attire by that set.

'If you could return in ten minutes?' I called back. Emma gave me a 'Very well, madam' and the outer door closed again. I hurried to finish with the rest of the Friday and then the events of Saturday; Holmes did up my buttons as I finished.

'And the precise sequence of the shooters at the final drive?'

'I was in the middle, with the twins and their father to my left, followed by Darling, Alistair's cousin Ivo, the Marquis, and I think Sir James bringing up the end. Iris was directly to my right, with Matheson, Radley, Stein, and then Freiburg at that end. Twelve guns in all, with Alistair and Marsh just there for the company.'

'A long line of guns.'

'Bloom is a first rate gamekeeper. What a man with his talent for presenting birds is doing here, I can't think. He'd be taken on at Sandringham in an instant.'

He was about to ask me something else, and I was positively simmering with eagerness to know what he'd come up with in London, but we were out of time. With a knock on the door, the obligations of society took over. He slipped out to tell Marsh that he was back; Emma devoted herself to my hair for a feverish seven minutes; Holmes was back in time to clasp my mother's emeralds around my throat; we were gathered downstairs before the gong had ceased to vibrate.

Not that anyone could have heard it.

CHAPTER FIFTEEN

T HE LONG DAY HAD left me tired, troubled, and none too pleased with the prospects of an extended evening of merrymaking; at least, I thought as I walked down the formal Justice stairway on Holmes' elegant arm, my dress was up to the occasion. The grey silk had a faint green thread shimmering through it, and the heavy beadwork that wrapped my upper body also glinted with that occasional reference to the stones around my neck. Clothes might not make the woman, but they certainly can add starch to her spine.

Not until we were in the doorway to the drawing room did I realise that I needn't have bothered.

Oh, some of the party were dressed for dinner. The Darlings shone, and those of the shooting party who had stayed on, but the impromptu gatecrashers had come-as-they-were from their day's events. And a mixed lot of events those seemed to have been, since the participants were wearing everything from banker's black to a silk smoking costume with fur trim, belted with a string of carnelian and lapis lazuli stones and topped by a brilliant swatch of lapis-blue silk, a sort of cross between a bow and a turban. One woman had come in a riding outfit, although on closer look her jodhpurs were of velvet and her crop studded with seed pearls; another, who spoke a studied artificial Cockney and whom I mistook from the back for a maid, wore what appeared to be the uniform of a Lyons restaurant waitress, with the addition of blood-red lipstick, ivory cigarette holder, and immense diamonds at her throat and ears.

I turned to speak in my companion's ear. 'Holmes, do you truly expect to learn anything in this bean-feast? Half the men at the shoot appear to have gone home.'

'Who is here?'

'It's hard to be sure. That bewildered quartet in the corner is made up of Freiburg and Stein with their wives. The small gentleman at the punch bowl is the Marquis. I don't see the Londoners—no, there's Radley, although I don't know the person with him. Sir Victor and his family have probably left, for various reasons. I don't see Alistair's cousin Ivo either. I say! – Look, over by the windows; isn't that—Christ!'

My question concerning the identity of a famous face on the other side of the room was cut off when a small, cool, leathery hand insinuated itself into the hollow of my throat and wrapped its diminutive fingers around the necklace. I jerked away, dislodging the spider monkey from its shoulder perch and nearly throttling it on its own jewelled collar. It shrieked hideously, the owner cursed freely, and all hopes of a quiet entrance fled.

Three of the party greeted the introduction to Holmes with coy remarks about the unfortunate resemblance he bore to the Conan Doyle detective; one man heard the name and slunk rapidly away, never to appear again; one woman (she of the silk smoking costume) enquired earnestly if I thought it a fixation or a phobia that had driven me to marry a man more than twice my age; the man with the turquoise-chip earring whom I had seen earlier said they were getting up a game of mah-jongg after dinner and did I play, and if not would I care to learn? The man with the monkey poured some of his gin into a small glass for the creature, saying it would calm his familiar's nerves. Phillida laughed carelessly at the famous actor's jokes, acting like a woman ten years younger and two children lighter (and appearing remarkably unconcerned – for a woman who had been chary of upsetting the housekeeper with a mere pair of extraneous house guests – at the house's present inundation by a considerably larger party of gate-crashers). Sidney held his glass as if it and the house were his own; Marsh, Alistair, and Iris were conspicuous by their absence. I heard at least three versions of Marsh's shooting, the ill-concealed glee of gossips at their host's mishap. I accepted the glass that was put into my hand, not knowing if it held arsenic or champagne (and not much caring by that point), and allowed myself to be swatted to and fro by the conversations around me.

'Tristan? Oh, he's gone off to the Alps to study the chemical effects of prayer.'

'More likely the chemical effects of—'

'Do you have any idea how hard it's been to bring together decent breeding stock since the War? That poor old bitch of mine is nearly—'

'—recited the whole of Eliot's *Prufrock*, standing on the lion's head in Trafalgar—'

'—Matrimonial Causes Act came just in time for her.'

'Poor old Steed, found Her Ladyship with the gardener right there amongst the orchids, old boy hasn't been the same ever—'

'Dear Antony, such a lamb, but this nuts-and-berries diet he's embarked on to cleanse his cells is making him a touch pale.'

'—Serge and the divine Isadora on a stage, in the moonlight . . .'

'We're not on speakers at the moment, not since he brought that horrible female home and expected me to—'

'—Josephine Baker revue, the most extraordinary—'

'He'd been fine all these years, but he just collapsed, went into his club to read the *Daily Mail*, and just started sobbing, so they had to take him away and lock him in the attic; so sad.'

'The *Daily Mail* will have that effect on a man.'

'—want to play a few rounds of mah-jongg?'

'Stan, that damned monkey of yours has done something unspeakable on your jacket.'

'So tiresome, I know. Michael Arlen has the same trouble with—'

'—came a cropper on the hedge near the stream.'

'—Arabia, wasn't it, Miss Russell?'

The sound of my own name jolted me from my reverie. I blinked and looked into the sparkling, avid eyes of Marsh's sister. 'Arabia,' Phillida repeated. 'Where you met Marsh? Terry heard him cursing like the devil after he'd been shot, said my brother had a nice line in Arab gutter invective. And Terry should know.'

I went to sip from my glass, found it empty, found too that it was not the same glass I'd started with. How many drinks had I downed while my mind was wandering through green and quiet fields? I searched for a convenient surface and got rid of the glass, but when I had done so, Phillida was still there.

'It's a large area, where Arabic's spoken, isn't it?' I said. 'Although if you know your brother at all, you'd not expect him to settle in a place as unromantic as either Cairo or Damascus.'

'Baghdad!' she pounced. 'It was Baghdad, wasn't it?'

I answered not, just gave her an enigmatic smile that sent her away happy.

Dinner was too hugger-mugger to arrange a convenient, that is, knowledgeable dinner partner whose brains I might pick concerning the ties and habits of the Darlings. Of the men on either side of me, one was walking the edge of drunkenness, had no idea who his host was other than that he thought he might have been introduced to him at the door, and told me plaintively several times that he was only trying to get back to London in time for the final curtain of his girlfriend's play. The man on my other side was if anything drunker, and proceeded to tell me many apocryphal tales of that thrilling old detecting gentleman at the next table. I couldn't bring myself to tell him that I was married to the gentleman in question, nor that I knew for a fact that three of his stories were utter nonsense.

The dinner showed signs of having been hastily stretched to accommodate twice the number as originally planned for, the soup rather more liquid and the meat somewhat more thinly sliced than they might otherwise have been. When we were freed from our places, I made for Holmes.

'I am not going to be segregated with the ladies,' I informed him. 'If you wish to join the men at their cigars, you shall find me upstairs in Marsh's rooms.'

I was not surprised when he accompanied me from the room. Somewhere nearby, Gershwin was giving over to a painful attempt at 'Kitten on the Keys'.

Once outside the din, I leant up against the wall to catch my bearings. 'Did you notice,' I asked Holmes, 'the men in that room?' For a post-war gathering, there had been an astonishing percentage of whole and hearty young men.

'Not a missing limb or a gassed lung among them,' Holmes agreed, adding, 'and half the guests are using cocaine.' (I kicked myself for my innocence: I had thought it merely high spirits.) A raised shrieking and bellows of male laughter followed us from the Hall; Holmes grimaced. 'And these are the men for whom Gabriel Hughenfort died.'

I knocked lightly on Marsh's door and then opened it, following the call of 'We're in here' through to the sitting room, where we stepped into an utterly unexpected cosy domestic scene: Iris before the fire with a book on her knees, Alistair across from her, Marsh stretched out on his right side on a leather sofa. They had been listening to her read – from, I was amazed to see, *The Wind in the Willows.* Iris waited until we were inside, then calmly finished the section before placing a marker in the book and putting it to one side.

Alistair came over to shake Holmes' hand and to pull us up a couple of chairs. He had been out of the room earlier when Holmes stopped in and was, he said, glad to see him. Earlier, Alistair had still been too covered with Marsh's blood to determine if he'd been injured himself, but now I could see that some of the gore had indeed been his own. What he had dismissed as 'a few pellets' looked to have been closer to a score; one pellet had gouged a line across his forehead, missing both the eye and the soft temple by mere inches. His jaw had a pair of sticking plasters, but his left hand and forearm had received the brunt of the spray. Hand and wrist were bound in gauze, and although he tried to act as though nothing was wrong, he could not help favouring the arm. Holmes took the chair from him and set it in the circle; we all sat down. Holmes was, I knew, wary of the extra woman in our midst, and uncertain as to the extent to which we would include her in our knowledge and our discussions.

Marsh took care of that question right off. 'Iris is to be trusted,' he said bluntly. 'Anything you have to say, she may hear as well.'

Holmes dived in with equal bluntness. 'You are aware that this was no accident,' dipping his chin at Marsh's state – a curiously Bedouin gesture.

'I thought it unlikely. The boy is not a careless child, and two shots went off on top of each other. Even with the shock of being hit, it seemed wrong. Then when I saw the shot the butcher dug out of me, I was certain. Assuming that Peter was still using my gun.'

'It was in his hand when I saw him,' I answered. 'How is the shot different?'

'I always load my own cartridges for that gun. Its pellets are larger and smoother than those the doctor took out.'

'So. A gun, aimed at you, ready to go off as soon as the boy could be brought to shoot behind him,' Holmes said. 'Too far away, as it turned out, most fortunately. An opportunistic crime, not a meticulously planned one, and it went awry. Who could it have been? Two men, I think. Or one very quick one.'

'Well, it wasn't Iris, at any rate,' I joked. 'I could see her the whole time.'

'I had already assumed that,' Marsh replied.

'I should hope so,' Iris retorted.

'Had you been intending to murder me, you would not have missed,' he clarified, on his face a faint but welcome smile.

'And it wasn't Sir Victor – he had no gun, and I could hear him talking to his sons,' I went on more seriously. 'It could have been any of the four on the far side of the clump of trees. Then again, I heard someone moving behind the line, which could have been any of the four to my right, or the women who'd stayed on to watch, or any of a hundred men. Sorry, but between the distractions and the fog, it's an open field.'

Holmes brought out his pipe and assembled a contemplative smoke. 'What do we know about the two Germans?' he asked.

'They're Sidney's connection in the City,' Alistair answered. 'Sidney made a young mint during the War – profiteering, I'd call it, although nothing was proved. Freiburg and Stein did the same, smuggling black market goods into Germany. Luxury goods and foodstuffs, rumour has it, not guns. No one was much interested in prosecuting them, particularly as they had a certain amount of loot to offer in return. Small, portable works of art that were formerly in museums within Germany are now to be found on mantels across England.'

'And the others?'

'I don't know the Marquis; he's a newcomer. Sir Victor was a front-line soldier until '16, seconded to London after he lost some toes and got shell-shocked. He has at least two medals. Of the two Londoners, Matheson seems a good sort. I don't know Radley.'

'And Ivo Hughenfort?'

'My cousin?' Alistair said. 'He lives five miles from here, has always considered Justice his second home. His friendship with Darling does not recommend him, but it's hardly a criminal offence. I don't know him all that well – he's eleven or twelve years younger, and lives just beyond easy horse range from Badger. I do know he was a staff officer during the War, in northern France.'

'You don't say,' said Holmes thoughtfully.

'What do you mean by that?' Alistair demanded, but Holmes continued as if he had not spoken.

'We are agreed, then, that someone took a shot at the two of you, a more or less impulsive shot that took advantage of the mist, the concealing shrubbery, and the possibly wounded bird?'

We were all in agreement.

'It would be nice to know for certain who the target was,' Holmes mused.

'What do you mean?' Alistair said, sounding indignant. 'The gun was aimed at Marsh.'

'Who was moving across the line of fire at the time, and who could therefore have been the inadvertent recipient of a load of shot meant for you.'

This time Alistair could not miss the suggestion, but the very idea that someone would place him over Marsh, even as a candidate for murder, offended his yeoman's soul so deeply that he did not even deign to answer, merely moving off to rummage through Marsh's desk for a packet of cigarettes. Iris watched him; Marsh did not.

'You have information for us, I think,' Marsh said. His voice was a bit slurred, either by the effort of keeping the pain at bay or else from some drug one of the others had forced upon him. Holmes studied him closely, and I knew that this would be a long and demanding tale, since he was wondering if the telling had not better wait until the morning.

Marsh saw the look, too, and responded with the ghost of a smile. 'I'll not sleep for hours yet, Holmes; you may as well provide me with distraction.'

His lips pursed, Holmes slapped the still-burning contents of his pipe into the fire and dug the bowl into his tobacco pouch. 'You were correct in your suspicions,' he told Marsh. 'Your nephew was indeed executed.' Alistair grunted in pain, Iris closed her eyes, but Marsh sat, mutely braced for the rest. 'For refusing an order.'

Seeing that lack of reaction on the part of the wounded man, Holmes nodded, and began the tale of his time in London.

'You did not give me much to work with. I'm not complaining, you understand, merely making note of the fact that in general, a case begins with some starting point, be it a body or a missing necklace. Here, all we have is an untenable situation that wants straightening up. And as my housekeeper could tell you, straightening up is hardly my strong point. Therefore I resolved to approach the situation as if there was an actual case, knowing that sooner or later, a thread would appear and ask to be followed.

'The thread I chose, to fill the time until Wednesday's meeting in London with the heir apparent, was that of Gabriel Hughenfort.' Holmes paused to set a match to his pipe, then settled back into his chair.

'I began my search for your nephew's war record, logically enough, at the War Records Offices.'

'Under what name?' Iris asked.

The question rather confused me – how would she know that Holmes had been in disguise? – but Holmes shot her a sharp glance.

'Ah,' he said. 'You knew.'

'That Gabriel had enlisted under a pseudonym? He told me, yes.'

Holmes looked at Marsh. 'But you did not know this?'

'I had no idea. Why would he use a false name?'

'Because he wanted to be a soldier,' Iris told him simply. 'Not a Hughenfort.'

Marsh nodded, understanding. 'When I wrote him, I sent the letters through my brother,' he explained. 'My knowledge of his whereabouts was likely to be out of date. They never mentioned it. What name did he use, then?'

'Gabriel Hewetson,' Holmes answered.

'Hewetson?' I repeated. 'As in Christopher? Irish sculptor, eighteenth century?'

'You saw the Hewetson bust of the third Duke in the Hall?' Iris asked. 'It was one of Gabriel's favourites, looked a bit like him. He may have chosen the name because it hits the ear rather like "Hughenfort".'

'It might even appear like "Hughenfort" on an envelope at the Front,' Holmes said, and added, 'You'd have saved me half a night of pawing through filing cabinets, had you known. Still, it can't be helped.

'There is a clerk in the Records Offices for whom I once performed a discreet service, and who in return is happy to expedite any enquiries I might have concerning those who have worn a uniform. That Gabriel Hughenfort's was not a public record was apparent immediately I heard that members of the man's own family were unaware of his fate. A shameful end for a prominent name – records are sealed for much less than that. However, I had not expected that they might be removed entirely.

'All started well enough. I arrived in London, I found my man, arrangements were made for an after-hours rendezvous when we might read our files undisturbed, and I passed the intervening time in an afternoon concert. I am pleased to report that the cultural life of the great City is quite recovered from the losses during the War. However, you are not interested in my pleasures.

'I presented myself at the appointed hour, allowed myself to be escorted surreptitiously through a side-door, and gave my clerk the information I required. It was not with the general records, which was no surprise, but we pressed on.

'Eventually, we found a file with the name we sought, but as a soldier's service record, it left a great deal to be desired. His family history consisted of *Justice Hall, Berks*, full stop. There were medical records from his enlistment, height, weight, and childhood illnesses, but those contained nothing after October. The service record itself covered training and made note of where he was being sent, then that too stopped.'

'So his records from the Front were either lost or separated?' I suggested.

'So I'd have thought,' he said, 'except that his file also contained the standard typed notification of Gabriel Hughenfort's death.'

That, we all had to agree, was difficult to explain.

'My clerk was well and truly stymied. He'd never seen anything like it, he said – and then he corrected himself. He had, perhaps, once or twice, when he'd chanced upon the ill-concealed record of government agents. Spies, if you will.'

Holmes puffed his pipe and watched our reactions. Alistair and Iris sat up sharply; Marsh tried to, and grunted. Even I was startled – and here I'd thought I was joking when I speculated about the future Phillida's two children might find in the family espionage business.

Holmes was nodding. 'My ears pricked, as you can imagine. And then I noticed, written in faint pencil on the inside cover of the file, the name Hewetson.

'Under that name, however, there was little more, only the record of where he'd trained before being sent to France. No service record, no medical papers, not even a death notice.

'Of course, the Records Offices are in deplorable condition, and even the most straightforward of records go astray all the time. Assuming that this specific case of loss was due to malice would be leaping to conclusions – an exercise at which, as Russell could tell you, I have much practise, although I try to kerb the impulse.

'Still, I now had the unit with which he'd been sent to France. Assuming, that is, that he stayed with the original regiment.'

'Which he didn't,' Iris broke in. 'When I saw him in Paris in March, he was en route to a new posting.'

'My dear lady, I might as easily have remained here and had most of my work done for me by your arrival. However, in the end, rather than pursuing the boy through several million dusty bits of paper, we let ourselves out of the building and I caught a cab straight away for my brother Mycroft's.'

He paused to choose his words. 'My brother is a mine of information when it comes to the inner workings of the machinery of government.' This was a delicate way of explaining Mycroft's all-pervasive and enormously powerful role in, as Mycroft whimsically called it, 'accounting'.

'I know your brother,' Iris said. 'I did some work for him during the War.'

'You don't say? Well. In any case, after I'd turned Mycroft from his bed and confronted him with the name, he was no more forthcoming than the clerk's file had been. He'd never directed a man by that name. He did agree, however, that for a second lieutenant to have virtually no records was an unexplained irregularity, and it is my brother's function, certainly in his own mind, to explain the inexplicable, to account for the unaccountable. It took him the entire morning – which is an exceedingly long time for Mycroft – but he did follow young Gabriel's elusive tracks far enough to uncover the second regiment to which he was posted, following his release from hospital in March.

'Once I possessed that piece of information, the rest was footwork. The names of the demobbed from that regiment and their addresses allowed me to winnow out those men from London, as I could see no advantage to be had in seeking out names from far-flung villages. Time enough for that, if it proves necessary.

'From the score of names that immediately presented themselves, I chose half a dozen to begin with, all of them old enough to suggest that their survival was due to a degree of low cunning, rather than sheer luck. One captain, one sergeant, the rest privates.

'The four I located before the hour became too late for calling told me a story that interested me deeply. I began by showing them the photograph I had borrowed from the library downstairs, and although they were all uncertain about the name Hughenfort, they did know the face, and knew that "Angel" – their nickname for the lad – had been shot.

'Two things concerning the testimony of these soldiers interested me greatly. First and most obvious, that they knew the face and the first name, but none recognised the family name. This confirmed that your nephew used his *nom de guerre* exclusively, not just for the authorities.

'The other thing that interested me was not so much what the men knew, as how they felt about their "Angel" Gabriel. When I first brought up the subject, each was loath to speak of the lad at all. When they did, it was with an uncomfortable mixture of deep resentment and sorrow that quite obviously pained them. All felt considerable distress at what happened to the lad, and a kind of hurt bafflement, as if a friend had badly let them down, for reasons they could not comprehend.

'It was not shame. Nor was it the disappointment in a too-soft sprig of the aristocracy, a lad who had no business in the trenches and ran afoul of his own inadequacies. It was more a case of, There but for the grace of God might I have gone. They accepted Gabriel as one of their own, a fledgling soldier with a weakness none had foreseen, but none could condemn.'

'They mourned him,' Iris said in a soft voice.

'Precisely. And at a stage of the War when few souls had any capacity for mourning left in them.'

I looked at my companions, and found that the soldiers were not the only people to mourn this 'sprig of the aristocracy'. Iris was staring unseeing at the flames, her eyes dry but tragedy on her face – she'd been fond of the boy, this representative of a lost generation of golden youth. Alistair was scowling and kicking with his heel at the basket of logs. And Marsh—

One glance at Marsh, and I shot to my feet in confusion, exclaiming, 'Look at the time – after midnight already; I'll tumble into the fire with exhaustion. Holmes, surely we can continue this in the morning?'

I practically hauled at his ear lobe to get him out of the room; fortunately, he caught my urgency, if not its reason, and we made our hasty farewells.

But I knew that the image of Marsh Hughenfort, his face half covered by one hand and actual tears trembling in those black eyes, was one that would stay with me for a long, long time. The man looked decades older than Holmes, and far from any source of vitality or hope. We had no business inflicting the vivid reminder of an innocent's death on the man when he was in his current condition.

Let Iris drug him to sleep with the tale of Ratty and Toad.

CHAPTER SIXTEEN

In the morning, however, Marsh's rooms were silent, and I for one was reluctant to break into his rest. We continued downstairs to join those houseguests who were upright at this hour, a pair of unshaven young men still in dinner jackets, who seemed to have not bothered about going to bed at all, and who were in no condition to intrude on our peaceful enjoyment of eggs and toast. After breakfast, I gave Holmes a brief tour of the house (passing by the ancient stairway into the cellar-chapel, as I had no key) and ended up in the riches of the Greene Library. That was where Iris found us.

She was wearing a remarkably conventional wool dress and carried in her gloved hand a small, maroon-covered Book of Common Prayer. It took no great effort to discern her intent, although I was rather surprised at her willingness to attend the Sunday services; why, I do not know.

'Marsh is awake, having some breakfast; the doctor's coming in an hour, so we thought we might resume after that. You're welcome to join me in the chapel, if you like. Or not to join me – it is by no means compulsory.'

'Thank you,' I told her, 'but I think we'll commune with The Divine among the stacks.'

'I'm sure God dwells here as much as in the chapel. More, perhaps, since it's considerably warmer. Shall we meet in Marsh's rooms at noon?'

We agreed, and she left us to our reading.

Today was November the eleventh. At 10.58 the house gong sounded a brief warning. It went off again precisely at 11.00, somehow conjuring up a sombre sound, rather than the energetic crescendo it produced at mealtimes. We rose to our feet for the nation's two minutes' silence, and then returned to our books.

Holmes, appropriately if uncharacteristically enough, was poring over an immense and ancient family Bible. Not the printed section, but rather the generations of Hughenfort names, beginning with the eighteenth century.

'Write this down, Russell,' he ordered; I uncapped my pen. 'Ralph William Hughenfort, born 1690, eighth Earl of Calminster, made first Duke of Beauville in 1721. Probably lent some sage advice to the Crown and saved George I from losing his breeches over the South Sea Bubble. At any rate, duke he was. Sons William Thomas, born 1724, second Duke, died without issue, and Charles John, born 1732, third Duke. Charles' son Ralph Charles, born 1761, had three sons and two daughters, then died before his father. Those sons were Lionel Thomas Philip, born 1792; Charles Thomas, born 1798; and Gervase Thomas Richard, born 1802. Lionel became the fourth Duke in 1807 at the tender age of fifteen. His children were Gerald Richard, born 1830; Anne, in 1834; and Philip Peter, born in 1837, with four others who did not live to reach their majority. Anne died before she married; Philip Peter died in South Africa with no known issue. Gerald Richard was made fifth Duke in 1865, and had four living children: Henry Thomas, born 1859, with his son Gabriel born in 1899' (My pen paused briefly; I had been thinking of Gabriel as a dead boy, but in truth, he was a few months older than I); 'William Maurice – our Marsh – born 1876; Lionel Gerald, 1882; and Phillida Anne, 1893. Henry was made the sixth Duke in 1903, and Marsh the seventh.'

Long-lived and late to breed, I noted. Fairly typical for aristocrats.

'But to go back to the fourth Duke's generation. Lionel's brother Charles died without issue. The third brother, Gervase, had two sons, William, born 1842, and Louis, in 1847. William is the father of Alistair, his sister Rose, and his brother Ralph; Louis had one son, Ivo Michael – your shooting companion of yesterday.'

'All right,' I said. I scribbled and crossed out names, finally arranging the relevant generations (that is, minus most of the women) into a family tree. That gave me the following:

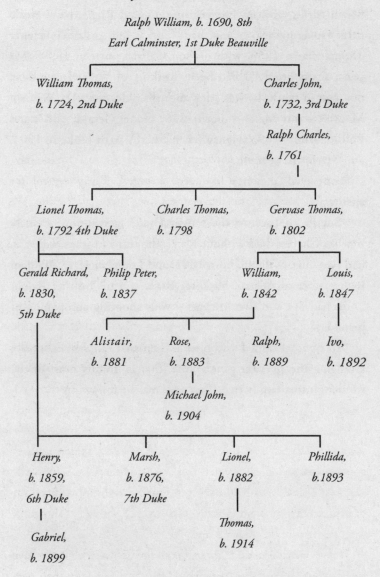

Ralph William, b. 1690, 8th
Earl Calminster, 1st Duke Beauville

William Thomas,
b. 1724, 2nd Duke

Charles John,
b. 1732, 3rd Duke

Ralph Charles,
b. 1761

Lionel Thomas,
b. 1792 4th Duke

Charles Thomas,
b. 1798

Gervase Thomas,
b. 1802

Gerald Richard,
b. 1830,
5th Duke

Philip Peter,
b. 1837

William,
b. 1842

Louis,
b. 1847

Alistair,
b. 1881

Rose,
b. 1883

Ralph,
b. 1889

Ivo,
b. 1892

Michael John,
b. 1904

Henry,
b. 1859,
6th Duke

Marsh,
b. 1876,
7th Duke

Lionel,
b. 1882

Phillida,
b.1893

Gabriel,
b. 1899

Thomas,
b. 1914

After Marsh, the seventh Duke, the future line of succession would be: Lionel's son Thomas; Alistair; Ralph; and Ivo. If Philip Peter had sons somewhere in South Africa, they would come after young Thomas and before Alistair; if Ralph had sons, they would come before Ivo. That no sons for Ralph were noted in the Bible meant little, since the latest date I could see recorded the death of a distant relative in 1910. Thomas's birth in 1914 was missing, as well as those of Lenore and Walter Darling.

'We can do nothing about the boy Thomas until Wednesday,' Holmes noted. 'I should like to have seen Gabriel Hughenfort's last effects, had you not dragged me away with such haste. We must also enquire about the fifth Duke's brother, Philip Peter, as well as Alistair's brother Ralph.'

'Are you going under the hypothesis that yesterday's shooting was an attempt to clear the succession?'

'The possibility cannot be ignored. See here: In January 1914, the sixth Duke – Henry – was alive and well, and could have made up the better part of a cricket team out of his heirs, with his brother Lionel's wife expecting a child in the springtime. By the end of 1918, heirs were getting a bit thin on the ground. The seventh Duke's heir is this boy Thomas, who has some doubts attached to him. At the beginning of the War Alistair, to take one possible candidate, was seventh from the strawberry leaves; yesterday there appears to have been only that one doubtful boy between Alistair and Marsh's title. When the seventh Duke and his immediate heir presented themselves in the close vicinity of a barrage of shotguns, well, temptation may have reared.'

'How ironic,' I mused, 'that after all the hazards those two have weathered over the years, they would very nearly die on their own doorstep in peaceable England.'

'Tell me your impressions of Sidney Darling,' Holmes said, not interested in irony at the moment.

'Languid gentleman on the surface, modern-day robber baron underneath.'

'Even twenty years ago he'd have had to conceal the latter, if he wanted to move in the levels of society his wife's name would open to him. Now, a little greed is looked upon as an amusing foible. O, saint-seducing gold!' he growled. 'That for which all virtue is sold, and almost every vice.'

'War seldom enters but where wealth allures,' I retorted, figuring that Dryden was at least as apposite a misquotation as Shakespeare or Jonson. 'And I don't know that you could in the least call Darling a saint. His greed lies deep, and I think he's sunk a fair bit of his own money into the stud, for one thing, and is worried about being suddenly left without a home.'

'Who came up with this boy, Thomas?' Holmes asked abruptly.

'According to what I've picked up, the mother herself wrote. She'd somehow heard of Henry's death in the summer and sent her condolences – and, rather pointedly, those of the new duke's nephew, Thomas. I don't know if it was Marsh's idea to bring them to London for inspection, or Lady Phillida's. In either case, both are going to Town in order to meet the boy. Or, they were both going to London. I don't know if Marsh will be fit enough.'

'I should think that man would have one boot firmly planted in the grave and still do what he deemed necessary.'

'I don't know, Holmes. If Alistair and Iris unite to keep him here, I'd not care to wager on the winning side.'

He smiled to himself. 'It is a rather interesting variation on a marriage, is it not?'

'Do you mean Marsh and Iris, or all three of them?'

But his smile only deepened.

Iris reappeared shortly thereafter, the odour of sanctity strong about her, but wearing an expression of worry.

'The doctor's seen Marsh,' she told us. 'Some of the wounds are festering, and he's running a fever. I think perhaps we should delay our meeting.'

'But of course,' Holmes said, hiding his irritation nobly. He scowled after her departing form, and turned to me. 'Let us use this opportunity to examine the ground where Marsh was shot. There may be some tiny piece of evidence not yet trampled or washed away.'

A change of clothing, a pair of walking sticks, and we were away.

Yesterday's mist had cleared, leaving the air frosty and dry. Setting a pace brisk enough to warm us, I led Holmes on a re-enactment of the shoot, from the first stand at the upper lawns to the lakeside where I had stoned a duck in full flight. There were men at the earlier sites, quartering the ground for unclaimed birds, as well as stray discarded cartridges, which not only looked untidy but did the stomachs of grazing animals no good.

Then to the final stand.

I walked the line of guns, pointing out roughly where each shooter had stood waiting. Holmes burrowed into the thick shrubs from which the bird, and possibly the murderous shot, had come, but it appeared that others had been in there since the shooting as well. He emerged, his clothing somewhat the worse for wear, after ten minutes of grubbing about.

'I'm very sorry, Holmes, I should have kept everyone out, but there was just too great a press. Bloom must have had fifty or sixty beaters, and they were all over.'

'I doubt there'd have been much evidence to begin with. The fallen leaves are too thick to show footprints, there is nothing that would take a fingerprint, and the only threads I could see are rough white cotton. I take it the beaters wore some kind of smock?' he asked, holding up the thread in question.

'Most of them.'

'Very well. You say the boy Peter and his father were here?'

'So the boy said. The other twin, Roger, was a little closer to me.'

Holmes squatted to examine the ground, tracing boot-marks with his long, gloved fingers. He shifted, lowered his head to gain a more extreme angle, and then stood up.

'And Marsh – if you would take up his position, Russell?'

I went to the holly clump where the two cousins had fallen, and faced Holmes. He settled his walking stick into his shoulder and sighted down it to the first stand of mixed evergreen shrubs.

'The bird breaks,' he said. 'One. Two. Bang.'

As my rough sketch the night before had suggested, he was now facing a point about halfway between the two evergreens. He repeated his motion, only this time faster, continuing until he was aiming at me. 'One-two-three-four-five-bang,' he got out, and nearly fell over as his feet corkscrewed around themselves.

'Unfortunately, Holmes, the bird was over there. In fact,' I said in surprise, 'the bird is still over there.'

We converged on the spot and looked at the twice-shot fowl.

'Why do you suppose they left this here?' I wondered.

'Overlooked in the dusk, or perhaps squeamishness. The bird was nearly the death of their duke, after all. However, I think it worth performing a cursory necropsy on the creature. Just to confirm a theory. How are you at plucking birds?'

I put my hands together behind my back. 'It takes me an hour and rips my fingers to bits,' I told him.

To my surprise, he sat down on a nearby log, removed his gloves, and proceeded to strip the bird of its feathers, with a practised jerk of the wrist such as I had seen Mrs Hudson perform. In a brief time a cloud of feathers spilt across his boots. I sat down – clear of the feathers – to observe. '*Birds in their little nest agree,*' he startled me by chanting in a singsong voice as he tugged at the feathers, '*it is a shameful sight, when children of one family, fall out and chide and fight.* So, Russell, what see you?'

Two distinct patches of shot were embedded in the rubbery skin. One followed the upper edge and tip of the right wing; the other, the shot that actually killed it, formed a cluster along the left side of the head and body.

'The bird could conceivably have got those two injuries at the same time,' I suggested, 'if the right wing was up in flight.'

'Russell, Russell,' he scolded, plopping the disgusting object into my lap and tugging at the half-frozen body until its wings were outstretched. 'Which way is the shot on the left side buried?'

I poked at the clammy skin, and hazarded an opinion that was half guess. 'As the bird flew, almost immediately below.'

'And the right wing?'

'Harder to tell.' Plucking a bird leaves it looking comprehensively raw.

'What about this?' His naked finger traced a half-inch welt along the wing that ended at a tiny hole in the body.

'That came from in front of the bird, level, and at a forty-five-degree angle.'

'I agree. Two shots, then.' Reaching into a pocket, he pulled out a folding knife and two wadded-up sheets of writing paper. He dug half a dozen small, rough pellets from the bird's wing, folding them into one sheet, then did the same with those in the body. I looked at the resulting large, smooth shot, and was glad: Peter

Gerard had brought down a bird, not a duke. Holmes cleaned his knife on some moss and folded it away, then rose and looked down dubiously at the mutilated pheasant.

'We can't very well carry it back with us, Holmes.'

'Pity. I've grown rather fond of it. Without that bird's testimony, a degree of uncertainty would remain.'

'Leave it here for the foxes, Holmes.'

'I suppose so.'

We arrived back at Justice in time for tea, to find the house guests still in residence and embarked on various pursuits of childhood, the two children returned from their weekend banishment looking on in adult disdain, and Marsh ill but demanding that we continue our consultation.

He was ensconced on an elaborately ornate brocade divan with fringes along its lower edge, propped into a great number of pillows in a room of tropical heat. Holmes and I stripped off as many layers as we could without impropriety, and fell on the tray of tea and sandwiches with enthusiasm.

Marsh waited with growing impatience, his face flushed with heat both internal and external, his eyes feverish but focused. Alistair did not look much better; between Monday's head injury and the scatter of shot in his own arm, I thought he wanted nursing himself. Holmes drank his tea, but when he reached for the pot, Marsh spoke up impatiently.

'You must have found out more, about Gabriel. What else did your four soldiers say?'

'Those four, and three more Saturday morning. Do you object to a composite – the statements of the men and what there is of an official record?'

'By all means,' Marsh growled. Holmes claimed an armchair with a nearby perch for his cup, and drew out his pipe.

'Gabriel Hughenfort sailed to France in December 1917, following a scant five months' training, and joined his regiment on the twentieth. They were occupying a supporting position, behind the lines, and moved back up to the Front in early January. By the time he first stood in the trenches, the young man had picked up enough common-sense knowledge to keep his head down. He acquitted himself honourably, and without mishap, during that period on the Front, then through the cycle behind the lines.

'His second front-line duty, he was not as lucky. His section of trench took a direct mortar hit, and he was buried – in, as one of my informants picturesquely described it, "a blast of mud that was thinner than some soups I've ate, and a lot richer in meat".'

'His fellows waded in and dug him out, scraped out his mouth and pummelled the breath back into him, then sent him to the rear – unconscious – with the next stretcher party. He spent three weeks in hospital, took a brief leave in Paris, then was sent to a new regiment farther up the line. Just in time to catch the March push.

'After that, the lad's story becomes more vague. The official records of his second regiment from that period are extremely spotty – some of them went down in the Channel, according to Mycroft's informant – and the evidence of his companions not much better. There was general agreement that the boy stood with them throughout March, including a period when they were fifteen straight days under fire in their waterlogged pits, unbathed, under-fed, and rotting inside their boots, but holding their ground as they'd been ordered. You'll recall General Haig's "back against the wall" speech: "Every position must be held to the last man; each of us must fight on to the end"; His fellows remembered Gabriel's presence during that time.'

The details of the boy's last weeks were not helping his uncle's state of mind. Iris, keeping an eye on Marsh's face, finally had to interrupt.

'Why does this matter?' she demanded. 'Of what earthly importance could it be where he was transferred and what the men knew about him?'

Holmes did not react to this heresy against the supremacy of knowledge; at least, he did not reveal a reaction. He also did not reveal in so many words the original assignment: to find a means of freeing the seventh Duke from his obligations. Instead, his answer walked a line between caution and clarity.

'We were asked to come here and assist Marsh in the decision he has to make. One of those decisions, concerning the paternity of the boy Thomas, will come into our ken on Wednesday. But, it appeared to me that there were other areas of uncertainty that cried out for clarification. The death of the sixth Duke's heir was one of those. The business practises of Sidney Darling may prove to be another. This shooting, particularly in view of Alistair's injury earlier in the week, may prove to be a third. I would not go so far as Schiller in asserting that there is no such thing as chance, but I would agree that what seems mere accident often springs from the deepest sources of cupidity.'

Alistair puffed up and began to protest that his had been a stupid accident, but Holmes merely put up a hand to stop him, and went on.

'The chaos of battle can hide many things. Rivalries explode; guns may find a mark short of the enemy. Without knowing Gabriel, I cannot know the likelihood that he was caught up in such a rivalry or resentment, but even before I began to investigate his life, I knew one thing: Had he survived, the boy would have become an extremely wealthy and influential man.'

'And if you didn't know Marsh as well as you do, you might be investigating him,' Iris interjected. By her expression, the thought worried her not in the least; seemed to amuse her, almost. And Holmes smiled as he nodded.

'If I did not know him, then yes, I would be looking closely at his whereabouts during July 1918.

'However, I do not think that will be necessary. On the other hand, I should very much like to know if the fifth Duke's brother, Philip Peter, had a son, and similarly Ralph Hughenfort.'

'Uncle Philip?' Marsh said, simultaneously with Alistair's. 'My brother Ralph, do you mean?'

'Yes,' Holmes said. 'To both.'

'Philip died a few years ago, in South Africa. He was a monk of some sort – not Catholic, but I've never heard of a marriage.'

'I can't imagine anyone marrying Ralph,' Alistair told us, pronouncing the name 'Rafe'. He went on, 'My brother had a fever when he was small; it left him uncontrollable. He ran away when he was nineteen, first to India and then Australia. Rose, our sister, used to get long, sorrowful letters from him, with requests for money, but they stopped during the War. His last one said he was thinking of joining the Anzacs. He probably lies in Gallipoli with all the others.'

'A degree of certainty in any of this would be a pleasant surprise,' Holmes complained, as if the Hughenfort family had conspired against the solution of his case. If, indeed, it could be considered a case.

'My brother began enquiries into his whereabouts after the War, but had not much luck,' Marsh told him.

'Another pair of assignments for my brother,' Holmes said

darkly. 'And now, I should like to see Gabriel's final letter, if you don't mind. And what diaries you may have.'

At Marsh's nod, Alistair went over to a third-rate nineteenth-century portrait on the wall, pulled it back, manipulated the dial behind it, and handed Holmes the packet that I had returned on Thursday afternoon.

Holmes glanced at the field postcards, then read all four letters, the three from Gabriel and the sympathy note from the Reverend Mr Hastings. When he was finished, he folded them into their envelopes and handed them back to Alistair; the leather-bound journals he retained. We watched Alistair lock the safe again as if he was performing some rite, and when he was back in his seat, Holmes asked Marsh, 'Very well; what can you tell me about your brother Lionel and his wife?'

Not much, it seemed. After Lionel had fled scandal to Paris, the only news Marsh had received was the occasional curt fact from their elder brother Henry or third-hand scandal through scandalised family friends. Marsh had seen Lionel once in Paris, finding himself consciously aesthetic and deliberately dissipated; he had a flock of beautiful young men. Marsh's voice showed how distasteful he had found the meeting. He had not tried to see Lionel again.

Of the woman, again he knew only what Henry had written, that she appeared a middle-aged whore. I wanted to ask how the sixth Duke could have believed the child to be Lionel's, if Lionel was known to prefer pretty young boys to ageing women, but in the present company, I thought the undercurrents quite complex enough already. And considering the variations in human relations, I supposed anything was possible.

We had been in Marsh's quarters little more than an hour and a half, but it was becoming obvious that the master of Justice was an ill man, increasingly feverish and unable to concentrate on the business at hand. There was nothing that could not wait until Marsh's head cleared, so we left him with Alistair. At the door to her room, Iris hesitated, then asked, 'I don't suppose you'd care to join me for Evensong? The rector remembered that I loved the service, and offered to say it for me.'

'Actually,' I said, 'I'd enjoy that. If he doesn't mind having an unbeliever in the congregation.'

'That would make two,' she said cheerfully, to my confusion. 'I'll meet you in the chapel in a quarter of an hour.'

I went to my room, meditating on the oddity of a self-described non-believer attending church services not once, but twice in a day.

The air in the ornate little chapel was as frigid as its marble walls and smelt of incense, but the rector possessed a pleasing sensitivity for the magnificent rhythms of the Evensong liturgy, and seemed to bring the three of us together as a congregation, along with the memorial plaques and statues that cluttered the walls. Iris had taken a seat near the naked feet of the ice-white alabaster boy who, I saw by the plaque, represented young Gabriel. The sculptor had swathed the sentimental figure in Roman toga, and caused the ethereal face to gaze down at the viewer in a disturbingly Christ-like manner, the calm, blank eyes seeming to focus on the pew where we were seated.

The rector chanted portions of the liturgy, said others, and at the end thanked us for permitting him to do the service there. Then he quietly departed, leaving us to the family ghosts.

Silence settled over the stones, the wood, the drapes and brasses. Without a fresh dose of incense, I now caught the honey smell of the beeswax, which transported me back to the Holy Land, and

Holmes the beekeeper tracking down our foe by a fragrant stub of stolen candle.

I found myself smiling at the unlikely memory, linked to this distant spot by a pair of cousins. I turned slightly to say something to Iris about it, and saw on her features the same tragic expression that I had glimpsed the previous night, when Holmes had described the sorrow of the battle-hardened soldiers.

She was looking up at the memorial to Gabriel with that very expression – naked loss and grief. In a burst of revelation that shook me to my bones, I comprehended why: the boy's foreign birth and its date; the regular letters Iris sent to a young soldier she scarcely knew; Marsh's near-tears and Iris's compulsive churchgoing at the effigy's feet; the devastation wrought on the family. And I understood why Marsh was not able to leave this place.

'My God!' I exclaimed, then caught myself and glanced over my shoulder to be sure we were alone before I continued in a lower voice. 'Henry wasn't Gabriel's father, was he? You and Marsh—Iris, you weren't the boy's aunt. You were his mother!'

CHAPTER SEVENTEEN

THE WOMAN ON THE bench beside me went as white as the marble boy above. I nearly seized her shoulders to keep her from collapsing to the floor, but then the blood swept back into her face with a flush. She turned to face the altar, showing me her ear and jaw-line.

'I don't know what you're talking about.'

'Iris, please.' She stared at the altar, unresponsive. 'I won't tell a soul. Not even Holmes, if you insist, although I suspect he'll figure it out on his own in another day or two. Just tell me the truth.'

I thought she would remain silent; after a few moments, however, her eyes were drawn to those of the alabaster boy, and she moaned. 'Oh, Lord. I was afraid this might happen. Well, I suppose you'll have to hear it – but not here, not with the children back and servants going past outside the door. Come, the garden.'

It was not a great deal colder out of doors than it had been in the chapel, although it was by now fully dark. I did not see that standing in the darkness for the conversation would offer any more security than would a warm room of the house – the dark hides listeners as well as walls do – but I had not reckoned with Iris's intimate knowledge of Justice. She strode down the paths as if she possessed a cat's vision, warning me of steps and turns. After a minute we crossed an expanse of crunchy gravel, took two steps up onto a wooden platform, and patted our way to seats on the bench that ran along the sides. We were in the Palladian music house I had noticed in the garden, set in a sea of pale gravel. If we kept our voices low, no one could approach close enough to hear us without warning, and there was no space in which two children might be hiding.

Besides, I thought: Some conversations are best held in the dark.

'Yes,' she began. 'You're right. Gabriel was my son, although I don't see how you could have known.'

'Your voice, when you speak of him as much as I've made you the last couple of days. It's not the voice of an aunt.'

'And yet I was. Scrupulously so. I sent him no more gifts than I sent any of the other children in my family, for Christmas and birthdays. I never gave him the faintest reason to think Henry and Sarah were not his parents; I'm positive of that.'

'I'm sure you're right that he never suspected. He'd never have written that last letter had he not thought of them as his true – and, I have to say, much loved – parents.'

'He was a loving boy. He deserved the home they gave him.'

'How . . . ?' I asked.

'How did it come about?' I was more interested in how they had got away with it, but this would do as a beginning. 'It was more or less as I told you – there weren't many lies in that story. Marsh's parents looked at Henry – approaching forty, married for ten years with no sign of a child – and they turned the pressure on Marsh. He and I had been friends since childhood, most of our friends and families thought we'd marry sooner or later, so why not do the thing now? Marsh and I had a long talk – at The Circles, in fact, not Hampstead Heath, although for once without Alistair – and we decided that if we both had to marry for the sake of our families, we might as well marry a friend.

'So we did. However, both of us drew the line at making a spectacle of a farce, so in the end we had a private ceremony, one October afternoon when we knew all the family would be away. There were no guests, just Alistair and a friend of mine as witnesses. *Fait accompli*; I thought my mother would die with disappointment. And although the physical side of things seemed fairly peculiar – I mean, Marsh was like a brother to me – we both had enough of a sense of humour, and a sufficiency of champagne, to legally consummate the marriage.

'And wouldn't you know it, once was all it took. By Christmas I was sure, and I was in a right state. I had a life I loved in London and Paris, and the thought of becoming a man's wife and a child's mother, everything that entailed, what it had done to my mother – it was driving me frantic. I had to tell Marsh, of course, even though I'd worked myself into such a state that I was convinced that this proof of virility would somehow transform him, turn him into his father. Or more to the point, into mine.

'But he surprised me. He could see that a child would kill us both – not literally, but *inside*. Selfish, but true. I was even considering an abortion, but then he pointed out that while we might have a child we didn't want, his brother wanted one he did not have. If I could bear to live with the thing for the remainder of the nine months and go through labour, two problems might be solved.

'It was like a light going on. I'd felt like I'd been shut into a trunk that was growing smaller and smaller, then suddenly the lid opened and the light poured in, and my panic was transformed into good will towards all.

'The only one who was not entirely happy about it was Sarah. I think, especially at first, she took it as a personal affront, she felt so keenly her own inability to bear Henry a child. Her "failure". But as soon as Gabriel was born, in the most remote Italian village we could find, I put him into her arms, and she just . . . melted. After that, Sarah *was* Gabriel's mother.'

'And you never regretted it?'

'Of course I regretted it! Never for long, but from time to time my arms longed for him, I'd find myself wishing I'd kept him so I could hold him, watch him grow up. Let Dan be a part of his life, you know. But Sarah was very generous with me – amazingly so, considering how she felt. She would let me know when they were passing through Paris, sent me photographs, never objected to my writing the occasional aunty letter. She was a fine woman. It was Gabriel's death that killed her, not the influenza.'

'Who else knows about all this?'

'The only person I've ever told is Dan. We met long after Gabriel was born, but I had to tell her. Some of the servants here may have suspected, when a few weeks after the wedding I went from feeling ill to bursting with happiness, then we left for Europe, and Henry and Sarah went away, too, shortly after that, only to return with a newborn in the autumn with no signs of milk or post-partum recovery. I assume that Marsh will have told Ali. And Sarah's doctor must have known – my own believes I had a stillbirth.

'But in general, society assumed that since they lived in Italy anyway, at least until the old duke died, it was not unusual that their child was born there. And since Henry looked like a taller version of Marsh, and Gabriel inherited my height, Henry appeared more like Gabriel's father than Marsh ever did.'

We sat in silence for several minutes, and then I sighed to myself. With his son's death unexplained, Marsh could not leave Justice, lest he be turning the family's honour over to someone who had in some way been responsible for that death. The death of a junior officer on the Front might easily have been arranged by someone a step or two down the line of succession, just as the accidental shooting of a duke could have been the work of the same hand. Or not by a direct heir, but by Sidney, who had proved himself more than ready to accept the candidate Thomas.

'Wouldn't it simplify matters,' I remarked, 'if the boy Thomas were kind-hearted and intelligent and physically the very image of Lionel at the age of nine?'

'It probably would. Oh dear, poor Marsh.' She fell silent for a moment, then gave a curt laugh. 'And to think, two weeks ago, Dan and I were sitting in a lovely noisy bar, getting pleasantly drunk with Djuna Barnes and Sinclair Lewis.'

'Two weeks ago Holmes and I were tramping in the rain across Dartmoor, getting horribly wet with the sheep and the ponies.'

She laughed again, her voice ringing out across the invisible terraces and cultivated shrubs, then shivered, as much from the relief of confession as from the cold. 'In that case, you deserve some warmth and a drink before dinner. And you will want to tell your Holmes about this conversation. Come.'

We stumbled back along the dark terraces to the house, its windows glowing and the noises of unsubdued merriment spilling from its long gallery upstairs. From the sound of it, the guests were practicing nine-pin bowling along the length of the floorboards, to the accompaniment of shrieks of hysterical laughter. The duke might be tossing in his fevered bed, but the guests would play, regardless. As we climbed the decorated staircase, Iris shot an irritated glance at the trompe l'oeil pelican from whose place on the wall the rumbles seemed to emanate, but she said nothing. At Marsh's door she said politely that she'd see me at dinner, and then slipped inside, but before I had my own door shut, she was back in the hallway, making grimly for the source of the sporadic rumble that vibrated through the bones of the house. I was not surprised when it ceased within minutes, not to resume.

I found Holmes before the fire in his room, the third of Gabriel Hughenfort's diaries in his hands and a scowl on his face.

'Now, Holmes,' I said. 'It isn't all that bad.'

'Sophomoric,' he muttered.

I glanced over his shoulder at the pages he was reading, and chuckled. 'Hardly surprising – he was seventeen. Everyone that age is consumed by earthshaking matters and philosophical speculations.' Holmes grunted and turned a page. 'You have to admit that his observations on the natural history and farming of Justice are quite perceptive.'

'One might wish he'd stuck with badgers and squirrels and left the French philosophers in their place,' he grumbled, tossing the volume onto the chair-side table.

'He'd have grown out of it. He'd have made Justice a fine master. What do you think of the letters?'

'The official notification is not that used for an honourable discharge, but that is hardly conclusive, as whoever was filling out the form could so easily have taken up the wrong one. The one from the Reverend F. A. Hastings is considerably more suggestive.'

'I wondered if I was imagining that air of "I don't care what anyone else says" in his praise for the boy.'

'You were not. I should say Hastings knows a great deal more than he was willing to set onto paper. We need to speak with him.'

'And the letter from Gabriel?'

'Undated, much travelled, long carried, thrice wet,' he judged succinctly. 'Written weeks in advance, then placed in his pack and either forgotten or else left there against the chance that he was caught without warning. Some soldiers had two or three such, lest one be lost in an attack.'

'Too ashamed, or too terrified, to write later?'

'There is no knowing. Yet,' he added, and reached for the journal again.

'Wait, Holmes. Put that down for a moment; I have something to tell you.'

He was surprised when I told him what I had discovered about Gabriel Hughenfort's true parentage, but by no means astonished, and I felt again that he'd have put it together as soon as he knew Iris better. He tapped his teeth with his pipe. 'An ideal solution, I agree, and not even much of a circumvention of the line of inheritance, since without a son Henry would have handed it over to Marsh in any case, and thence to Gabriel. Of course, had Henry had a son of his own after Gabriel, an ethical problem might have reared up. But he did not, and snipping Marsh out of the succession was neat indeed.'

'It is, however, by no means, common knowledge.'

'Obviously not. My lips are sealed, Russell.'

'Other than the romance of philosophy, what do you make of the journals?'

He looked down at the volume he had held on to, lying across his knee, then picked it up and laid it on top of the others. 'A son any man could be proud of,' he said painfully, and went to dress for dinner.

CHAPTER EIGHTEEN

IN JANUARY 1914, MARSH'S brother Lionel Hughenfort had married a woman named Terèse, who was at least five years older than he, and six months pregnant when they married. She gave birth in early April, and christened the boy Thomas. Lionel died of pneumonia in late May. For the past nine and a half years, the family bank in London had issued cheques twice each month to an accountant in Lyons. He in turn dealt with the distribution of funds to Mme Hughenfort, who moved house a great deal. Once a year, representatives of the London bank travelled to Paris to meet with Terèse and Thomas, in order to reassure themselves – and the family – that the boy and his mother were still alive and receiving their monies.

That was, according to what Alistair and Iris told us Sunday evening and Monday morning, the only contact the boy's mother would permit. No living Hughenfort had ever seen either member of this truncated branch of the family. This vacuum, inevitably, had been filled over the years by rumour and speculation, with the result that Terèse Hughenfort had become, in the collective mind of the English side, a raddled, aged harlot with bad teeth, hennaed hair, the wrong kind of lace on her garments, and a death-grip on her source of income, young Thomas. While the sixth Duke was alive, nothing further had been done about the boy, apart from an increase in the monies sent to cover the cost of schooling a duke's nephew. I had the impression that the boy, and Lionel before him, had been sore spots in Henry's mind, the less prodded the better.

When the title had passed to Marsh during the summer, locating the boy was one of his first tasks. Messages accompanied the next two cheques, and then a stern letter with the third. All three fell into the hole in Lyons. Finally, a bank employee was dispatched with the fourth cheque in hand, and an ultimatum to the Lyons accountant: There would be no further monies if the family did not hear from Mme Hughenfort herself with a suggestion for when and where the family might meet the boy.

She managed to drag the affair out several weeks, claiming a minor ailment, and the boy's schooling, until the threat was made good, and no cheque was sent on the first of October. She capitulated, but declared that she and the boy would come to London. The Hughenforts would foot the bill, naturally – and (her letter ended, on a spirited note) she expected both tickets and hotel to be first class; the heir deserved no less.

Phillida was piqued at the effrontery, and would have dumped mother and son in some second-rate establishment near Charing Cross, but Sidney, continuing his amiable support for the boy, had professed himself amused by Mme Hughenfort's transparent desire for a luxurious holiday, and suggested they grant it. In the end Marsh agreed. He would not, however, place them in one of the very top establishments: That would be a cruelty, to turn the raised eyebrows of staff on a woman with pretensions and a budget. The bank was directed to locate a hotel with ornate decorations and a heavy trade in foreigners who did not know any better, and to reserve a suite for the visitors there.

Terèse and Thomas Hughenfort were to arrive Tuesday, and meet their family for luncheon on Wednesday. Train tickets were sent, a letter of introduction for the hotel – and a supplemental cheque, for 'incidental expenses' such as a warm coat for the boy, or (more likely) a new dress for the mother.

We intended to be there when they arrived; in fact, we would be with them long before they arrived: Holmes and I planned to join their small party at the earliest possible moment, namely, when mother and son arrived at the Gare de Lyons in Paris to board the train for London.

The amount of organisation such an operation would require was not going to be possible within the well-populated walls of Justice Hall. Thus, early on Monday morning, Holmes, Iris (who was looking her age today, having ordered Alistair home and spent the night nursing her husband unaided), and I took our leave of Marsh, the Darlings, the remaining house guests, and the servants in the person of their representative, Ogilby.

We rode in demure silence to the station, allowed our bags to be carried inside, and watched the Justice Hall car slide away. Three minutes later, Algernon drove up; we loaded our bags into the car, and set off for Badger. This minor ruse merely saved explanation; the Darlings might hear that we had failed to board the train, but it hardly mattered. Why should we not choose to visit Alistair's home?

Badger Old Place welcomed us with all its run-down, shaggy magnificence, like an old friend shifting to make room on a bench. Iris was as at home here as she had been at Justice, and greeted Mrs

Algernon with cries of delight. When Alistair had extricated his cousin's wife from the conversational clutches of his housekeeper, he issued us upstairs to the solar, the Mediaeval sitting room located above the Great Hall for warmth, light, and privacy.

The solar was still, after three hundred years, a warm, light, private chamber. The furniture reflected the fashions of generations – spindly legs and thick, decorated and utilitarian, silk and linen and leather. All looked comfortable, the colours and shapes grown together in an unlikely but successful marriage of the ages. Alistair himself fit in nicely, dressed in another frumpy suit that had been the height of undergraduate fashion in 1900, decorated by a flamboyant crimson-and-emerald waistcoat. We settled into the circle of chairs and sofas clustered around the stone fireplace, with a tray of coffee and biscuits provided by Mrs Algernon.

'How are we going to work this?' Iris asked, when she had her coffee. 'Do I get to dress up in disguise and follow Terèse across London?'

Holmes and I did not comment on the difficulties in changing the face and posture of a woman such as she. He merely replied, 'I think it best if you and Alistair, in Marsh's absence, meet Mme Hughenfort and her son face to face. Along with Lady Phillida, of course. This means that most of the actual tailing exercise will fall to Russell and myself.'

Neither of them liked this division of labour, but both knew that if they were to dine with Mme Hughenfort, they could not be following her through the streets.

'We can take the night hours,' Alistair decreed.

Watching and, if necessary, following a person at night was a riskier proposition than loitering about a busy daytime street, since people in general are more wary in the dark. However, Holmes and I would have to sleep some time, and even if Madame were to encounter one of them, she would not as easily recognise her relatives when they later met by daylight. Holmes nodded his agreement.

And so it went through the morning, offers and counter-offers, criticism and suggestions, the four of us working out a plan by which we could keep a tight watch on the woman without being seen. If she had a confederate or a gentleman, we wanted to see any contact between the two.

We took an early luncheon beneath the solar's oriel window, then Holmes, Iris, and I caught the noon train to London, while Alistair returned to Justice Hall to sit with his feverish cousin.

The adventure of the duke's nephew – or purported nephew – looked to be one of those parts of an investigation that are necessary, but tedious. It was not entirely fair that Holmes and I were saddled with it, but still, it had to be done, and one cannot always choose for one's self the interesting, or even the comfortable, parts of a case. Or of life itself, for that matter. Thus in London we abandoned some of our bags to the left luggage office and boarded the boat train to Paris.

Mme Hughenfort had been sent tickets for a train that departed Paris just after nine o'clock on Tuesday morning. We bumped and splashed and rattled our way down to intercept her path, taking a hotel room late Monday night. We dined too well, slept ill, and returned to the Gare de Lyons to take up positions overlooking the entrance.

The family possessed no photograph of mother or son, and only the most general of physical descriptions of Lionel's widow. Still, we thought, surely there would not be an overabundance of women in their late forties travelling with nine-year-old boys. All we needed do was make note of the motor that left any such pair at the *gare*, and track down car and driver at our leisure.

Our optimism was unjustified: The taxi stand seemed filled with women of that description, as if Paris were about to hold a huge conference of mothers and sons. Here a blonde, there a redhead, there one brunette after another, following on the heels of a third.

I spied three who might be she, each with a black-haired boy at her side. I noted the numbers on each taxi, that the drivers might be interviewed later if need be, and waited until the last moment to climb onto the train. Holmes was even later than I, tumbling aboard as the doors were being shut. We went to our own first-class compartment to compare notes. He had seen four possible candidates, two arriving on foot, two in private motors. One of those had kissed her driver a passionate farewell.

When the train was under way, Holmes and I strolled in opposite directions to work our way through the first-class cars. I saw only one of my possibilities; he saw two of his, one of those the woman of the ardent goodbye. We kept all the women under sporadic watch, but none that we saw was approached by any person other than the ticket collector or other women with children.

It was on the boat that our vigilance paid off. We had narrowed our candidates down to two: a thin, sharp-eyed woman with a Parisian accent and a worn collar, or a short, round, brown-haired woman in a new, expensive, but subtly unfashionable frock. Both wore wedding rings and nervous expressions, but only the plump woman addressed her child as 'Thomas'.

We took turns in her vicinity, gathering impressions more than information. She grew more tense as England drew near, picking at her fingernails and pulling at her lips with her sharp yellow teeth – but I noticed that unlike many tense mothers I had seen, she did not take her vexation out on her boy. With him she was patient and attentive, occasionally reaching out to brush back a wayward lock of hair or to pat his arm for their mutual reassurance.

I was unreasonably pleased that she was not the one who had kissed the driver.

In London, I stayed close behind her while Holmes collected our bags. She gave the taxi driver the name of the hotel that had been arranged for her; I gave my driver the same, and rode on her heels to the door. There I took my time counting out the fare, lest she notice that the woman who'd been behind her at the station had also climbed out of a taxi behind her. When she was safely inside, I disembarked, then took up a position behind a potted palm until she had received her key and was being escorted to the lift.

In varying guises, alone and as a pair, Holmes and I kept the woman in view, from the moment when, rested and bathed, mother and son emerged to explore the park across from the hotel, until they took an early dinner at a café and then returned to their rooms. At ten o'clock, Holmes donned a uniform lent him by the management (between his name and that of Hughenfort, all things were made possible) and knocked on her door with 'a small welcome from her husband's family', namely, an enormous box of chocolates in gaudy wrapping. He found her with her hair down, preparing for bed, and speaking in a low whisper so as not to disturb her sleeping son.

Satisfied that Mme Hughenfort was not about to leave for a night amongst London's wilder clubs, we took ourselves to bed on the floor below hers. It was silent, all the night.

In the morning, Madame took breakfast in her room. By late morning, she could remain still no longer. At a quarter to eleven, Holmes, seated behind the *Times* in the lobby, spotted the pair coming out of the lift. He folded his paper and sauntered after them, hissing briefly to catch my attention as he passed. We followed them for the next two hours, alternating positions, changing hatbands and scarves and turning around our double-sided overcoats, exchanging parcels and carry-bags, slumping or striding out as the pace demanded. I was generally the one to follow her into shops, where I changed my hat brim and tilted the hat, or straightened to appear tall and aloof, before in the next shop becoming uncertain and dowdy.

They never spotted us, not even the boy, who had a bright eye. We stayed with them up to the door of the restaurant where they would take luncheon with their unknown in-laws. The door shut. As we stood on the other side of the street, watching Terèse Hughenfort hand her parcels over and straighten her son's collar and hair, Holmes asked me, 'Well?'

'He's not a Hughenfort. Wrong chin, wrong eyebrows, the eyes – everything.'

'The hair dye she used isn't even very good,' he agreed.

We took a quick lunch of our own, returned to the grand entrance well before five Hughenforts came out and then parted, and followed her back to the hotel.

Mme Hughenfort did not look terribly happy.

And she had not reappeared before Alistair and Iris came to compare notes, having seen Phillida safely back onto the train to Arley Holt. Alistair's hand was free of its gauze wrapping, although the arm seemed tender to movement. I assembled four chairs in front of the fire, and while Holmes perused the drinks tray, I telephoned down for tea. When I had finished with the instrument, Iris took it up and asked for a trunk call to Justice, in order to check on Marsh's condition.

'How was your luncheon?' I asked Alistair.

'The woman drank three gin fizzes,' he said with a shudder.

'Poor thing,' Iris said, modifying the condemnation. 'She was terrified.'

'She had a right to be,' Alistair growled, as ferocious a noise as ever Ali had come out with. 'She was trying to commit a fraud.'

'So you would agree?' Holmes asked. 'The boy was not fathered by Lionel Hughenfort?'

'Never,' Alistair declared.

'Lionel was built like Marsh,' Iris explained. 'Shorter even, dark, a muscular build even though he never took exercise and had a sickly childhood. Were it not for his hair, the child would look almost Scandinavian – his eyes are even blue.'

'The hair is dyed,' Holmes and Alistair said simultaneously. Iris looked at them, and frowned.

'You mean to say the *child* is in on the deception as well?'

I for one was not willing to go quite that far. 'He may regard it as a game. And I will say that he seems a keen enough lad, bright and well mannered, genuinely fond of his mother – and she of him.'

'So,' Alistair said, his voice dry. 'You are suggesting that the boy would make a suitable heir, were Marsh willing to overlook the small problem of the boy's paternity.'

Put like that, it was an unlikely scenario. Still, I registered a mild complaint. 'It really is a bit ridiculous, this whole business of preserving the male line, don't you think? And I'm sure that if you studied family portraits closely enough, you'd find anomalies in the noblest of families. Marsh needs an heir in order to feel that he can leave Justice: He could do worse than that child.'

I did not expect to convince them; I couldn't even convince

myself, since I knew that Marsh's determination to have the truth was all that counted.

'What did Lady Phillida make of them?' Holmes asked.

'That was interesting, didn't you think, Ali?' Iris answered. 'She seemed quite willing to clasp the child, if not his mother, to her breast. Started to talk about having them up to Justice until Ali cut her off.'

'Was she predisposed to accept the lad, would you say? Or did it only come about gradually?'

'The instant she laid eyes on him, she exclaimed how like Lionel he was. But here – Phillida brought these to show them, and Ali snagged them back for you.' Iris took an oversized envelope from her handbag, handing it to Holmes.

It held photographs of the family, in groups and alone. My eyes were drawn to one that showed most of the major players in our family saga, arranged on the steps before Justice Hall: Marsh as a man in his early twenties, standing between an undergraduate Alistair and a vibrant young Iris, the three friends looking as if they were repressing laughter at a shared joke; a taller, older version of the Hughenfort line had his arm dutifully around a thin, tense woman a few years his junior – the fifth Duke, Gerald, I knew from a portrait in the Hall – and between them a child of four or five who had the black curls and proud chin of Phillida. Then Iris pointed to the last figure in the group.

'That's Lionel, aged sixteen.' He resembled a washed-out Marsh. His eyes were too dark to be blue.

She sorted through the snapshots and studio portraits to show us a clearer picture of the man, slightly older and showing ominous signs of world-weary dissipation.

He looked nothing like the child we'd spent the last two days watching.

The other photos, of a grown Phillida at her wedding; of Marsh and Alistair at that same wedding, wearing English formal dress but with the beards of their Arab personas, neatly trimmed; of Marsh, Alistair, Iris, and two other young women seated at the base of the pelican fountain with champagne glasses in their hands; of Phillida and Sidney on a beach somewhere in France.

We were looking through the photographs when the telephone rang. I happened to be sitting closest the instrument, but on hearing that it was the trunk call come through, I held the receiver out in a direction halfway between Iris and Alistair.

'It's Justice,' I said.

Alistair allowed Iris to take it, which I thought showed remarkable restraint: He looked more likely to curse and rage than to listen to whatever servant or nurse had been dispatched to give news of the duke's state. Nonetheless, he hunched over Iris, their faces so close he must have heard every word that came over the line. I could tell by his darkening face that the news was not happy.

Iris hung the earpiece onto its rest, and gave us a small shake of the head. 'He's roaring at the nurses and throwing objects at the doctor. Ogilby asks when we are coming back. We'd best take the earlier train.'

Holmes, thoughtful, replaced the photographs in the envelope.

'Lady Phillida seems as eager as her husband that you all accept the boy,' he said. 'I believe we ought to know why. Or rather,' he corrected himself, 'what lies behind the "why". The "why" itself is fairly obvious: The Darlings being by English law unable to assert claim or control over Justice Hall, they see Thomas as their, shall we say, proxy duke. They know that Marsh longs to leave; they long for him to leave as well, to allow them to carry on as the de facto masters of Justice. Thomas is the means by which that goal might be attained, an heir, conveniently underaged, thus requiring regents to care properly for the house and farms. To say nothing of German industrial investments. What we do not know is if there is any criminal intent or deed behind the Darling sponsorship of Thomas. What was that you said, Russell?'

'Nothing, Holmes. It's just that I don't know that my simply continuing to change my hatbands and overcoat is going to keep the woman from noticing that the same woman has been following her from Paris to London and back again. It's all very well for a man – you all dress alike – but I can hear from your voice that we're headed back to France, and so I think I ought to replenish my wardrobe first.'

'You're right.'

'I should be back in a couple of hours,' I began, but he overrode me.

'I have a bolthole not far from this hotel,' he said. 'We'll find what we need there.'

I gave in. For one thing, he would have more make-up in one of his secret apartments than at my own London pied-à-terre, and with the right make-up, one person can be several.

We arranged with Iris and Alistair to stay behind in case Terèse and her son left the hotel. The manager would telephone to the room if the Hughenforts passed through the lobby, and Alistair would pursue them.

'Come, Russell,' my husband ordered.

I came.

To return two hours later, one of a pair of French priests.

CHAPTER NINETEEN

IN LONDON WE WOULD be noticeable; in France, invisible. We carried with us the odds and ends that would transform us into more ordinary citizens, since I had no intention of inhabiting the itchy cassock longer than necessary, but it was as priests that we left the hotel the next morning, as priests we boarded the train. We occupied our hard third-class benches as far as the French shore, when the newly boarded French conductor spotted us and led us up the train to first class and told us to be welcome. Properly speaking, we ought to have crouched with all humility in our luxurious seats. Holmes, however, had other ideas, and before I knew it he had found the Hughenforts, manoeuvred a change of seats, and was greeting Mme Terèse, bending forward to squint at her son through the thick glasses he wore, making admiring noises.

Thus we spent the last portion of the trip, with the rich French countryside passing our windows, in conversation with our quarry herself.

Holmes, at least, was in conversation with her, his fluent French with the accents of the south tumbling out like that of a priest on holiday, far from his parishioners and made free by the knowledge. I sat to one side, glumly reading my Testament and wafting a general air of disapproving youth over my elders.

And elder she was. Lionel Hughenfort had been born in 1882, and married when he was thirty-two. This woman must have been pushing forty then, if not actually past it – I could not help wondering how many other children she'd had before Thomas. She was now a buxom, comfortable fifty-year-old woman, well preserved but showing signs that her life had not been one of contemplation and ease. In her relief at escaping the judgmental English relations, she rattled on in garrulous abandon, proving not at all difficult to steer. She was unread but with a shrewd native intelligence, and hugely proud of her clever schoolboy of a son – although she made an effort not to gush, so as to save the child from embarrassment. She proved darkly suspicious of all things English, and revealed once a brief flash of Gallic pride at some unnamed but recent triumph over the citizens of that country, who were all of them – most of them, she corrected herself – sly behind their beefy grins. Had not her own husband been forced to flee to Paris, to escape his own family? And had not that same husband's brother come screaming and scheming to pull asunder what God Himself had joined? Oh, some Englishmen were true gentlemen, she would give us that, generous and fair – her poor dead husband's relation, for example, who had come to see her during the War to give her money for a new suit of clothes for the boy and sent gifts from time to time, now *he* was a true gentleman – but even they had their plans, and it would not do to put one's self too firmly into their hands, would it, Father?

And as for a mother's responsibility to her son, the sooner half of France lay between Those People and the boy, the better.

No, she would have nothing to do with British soil, not until her boy was old enough to view glitter and pomp with a certain detachment. Although their pounds, when translated into good clean francs, those were acceptable, wouldn't you agree, Father?

At this point, the child Thomas moved over from his mother's side to mine, either because he'd heard her opinions on the subject before, or because he had just got up his nerve to approach me. In either case, he decided to try for a conversation with the younger priest.

His '*Bonjour*' was friendly and not in the least tentative. I returned it, and then he asked what I was reading. I told him. He said it did not look like French, and I agreed that it was Latin. The ice being broken, it then appeared that he had a question.

'Father, someone told me that Jesus was not a Christian. Can this be true?'

Concealing my amusement, I explained to him that 'Christian' meant a follower of Jesus Christ, and that therefore the man himself could not, strictly speaking, have been one. 'In fact,' I added, 'Jesus himself was born into a Jewish family, worshipped in the Jewish temple, thought of himself as a Jew. It was only later that his followers decided that what he represented was a new thing.'

The boy's mind was supple and inquisitive, which I thought a remarkable pedagogic achievement for the son of a woman with no great intellect, and we talked for a time about the Old and New Testaments, about the kinds of stories each contained, about the differences between God and Jesus Christ. I could see him floundering at this last morass – no surprise, since many adult minds did the same – and turned him away with a question about his preferences in school.

I had to wonder who his actual father might have been.

On the outskirts of Paris it transpired – oh how astounding

and blessed a coincidence! – that we, too, were heading to Lyons, and we, too, not until tomorrow, in the afternoon! It was unlikely, of course, that we would again be moved up into first class by a devout conductor, but perhaps we would see Mme and the young scholar while boarding our respective cars? And perhaps, Holmes ventured piously, as we were to pass several days in that city, we might one afternoon call upon her? When the boy was home from his studies, say, and free to join us for a visit to the seller of ices?

Mme Hughenfort was a woman easily reached through an appreciation of her son. With no whisper of hesitation, she gave Holmes the address that no Hughenfort had been able to discover. He noted it down in a fussy hand, closed and tucked away his miniature notebook, and thanked her.

At the station, we retained our small, battered valises but assisted Madame in transferring her bags to the hands of a porter, and we stayed with our new friends, chatting amiably, until both were safely within a taxi. There we paused, ever polite, until she had given the driver her destination.

Her voice reached us clearly through the glass.

Holmes kept no bolthole in Paris, but he knew the city well enough to give our own taxi driver the name of a large, busy hotel frequented by commercial travellers, across the street from Mme Hughenfort's chosen accommodation. Our hotel occupied nearly half of a city block, and had entrances on three streets; no one would notice a couple of suddenly defrocked priests passing through the lobby, and no maid would unpack the younger priest's highly irregular female garments from the larger valise.

We took adjoining rooms, shed our identifying black garments, changed into more usual attire, and passed through the lobby separately to meet in a nearby brasserie, whose front windows just happened to overlook the front door of Mme Hughenfort's hotel.

We did not expect to see her. Digging up information on the woman's personal life was the purpose of accompanying her to Lyons, where there would be neighbours and shopkeepers to be questioned. However, less than twenty minutes later I glanced up from my *soupe a l'oignon* and nearly tipped the rising spoonful onto my shirtfront.

'Holmes – look!'

Strolling in our direction, looking the very essence of a French provincial family in the big city, came Mme and Thomas Hughenfort, accompanied by a swarthy man not much taller than she and equally stout. She did not look coquettish enough for it to be a recent friendship, and for a moment I thought the man might be a brother, come to fetch his sister and nephew home safely from the capital city. Certainly the boy seemed, if not overjoyed to see him, at least accepting of his presence, and even responded to one jovial folly with a grudging smile. But then the fingers of the two adults intertwined surreptitiously, in an exploration that was more foreplay than greeting, and I knew this was no brother.

'Russell,' Holmes said with an urgent note in his voice, 'I believe they are coming this way. The two of us might trigger a memory; I suggest one of us leave quickly.'

I was already on my feet and dropping my table napkin on my chair. 'I'll meet you back at the hotel,' I told him, and slipped out of the door while the trio was still crossing the street.

My own three-star luncheon was a baguette and some cheese in a park, feeding the crumbs to the pigeons. I then went into a few shops to add to my meagre possessions. Back in the hotel, with nothing at hand but the Testament, I had just reached the Book of Romans, and was struggling with Paul's arguments concerning justification by faith, when a key scraped in the lock of the next room. I lowered my book and waited. Holmes popped through the shared door.

'On your feet, Russell. The lady's decided that she was indiscreet, that the wicked English, being capable of anything, could have stooped to subverting the priesthood to prise her address out of her. She and the boy will take the train today; the good monsieur, about whom I know only that he calls himself Tony, will turn the tables and lie in wait for the priest, in order to follow him to Lyons on the afternoon train tomorrow.'

I burst into laughter at the convoluted plot. 'He didn't suspect the priest of being anything but?'

'Apparently not. Nor has it entered their heads that a person in a cassock may smile and smile and be a woman. Their innocence is, I have to say, both charming and encouraging.'

'What time is the train?'

He glanced at his pocket watch. 'You have twenty-three minutes to reach the station.'

I handed him the Testament and began throwing off one set of clothing and pulling on another, pinning my hair to support my new hat, dabbing on powder, colouring my lips, and generally changing into another woman. The cassock, men's shoes, heavy spectacles, and the rest of that persona were already in the valise I had brought here. My other clothing, English and French, went into my newly purchased leather suitcase. I turned my overcoat so the plain cloth was inside and the fur without, and dropped it nonchalantly over my shoulders. Holmes copied the address Terèse Hughenfort had given him and slipped it into my handbag along with a city map he'd picked up somewhere.

'Where shall I meet you?' I asked him.

'Take a room at the Hôtel Carlton. I'll find you there. And as an alternate, at noon in the new basilica. Now, be off.'

I had no trouble getting a ticket to Lyons, taking my seat in first class, and gazing out of the windows until Mme Hughenfort appeared, struggling with luggage and a foot-dragging son. Neither, I would guess, was happy to have their Parisian holiday cut short.

They sat in the second-class cars. Which was fine with me; all I intended to do was follow them, with luck to the address I had in my bag, and watch to see where they went next. I suspected they would merely gather a few things and retreat to a friend's house until Monsieur Tony caught them up, but it would be best if we did not lose them until we were certain.

When we were under way, I unfolded the map of Lyons that Holmes had put into my bag and located the address, then that of the hotel, and finally the tourist landmarks thoughtfully noted by the mapmaker. Would she believe the two priests intended to be on the next day's train? Or would she go straight to a safe place? I decided she would go home first. Else why go to Lyons at all, if outright disappearance was the goal? I did not think she was suspicious enough to panic, merely not to be at home when the two priests rang her bell. She would, no doubt, count on the ungentlemanly Tony to follow the scoundrels to their own lair and put the fear of a vengeful God into them. My mind's eye was taken up for a moment by the scene of Holmes in soutane and clouded spectacles blithely picking his way across the bustling *gare* while the prosperous and swarthy Monsieur Tony tip-toed along behind the pillars to keep him in view, taking up a hard third-class bench and settling in behind a newspaper so as never to take his eye off the dubious priest.

The vision faded, and I bent over the cartography of Lyons.

At the *gare* in Lyons, my first-class status and relative lack of bags meant that I was shut into my taxi before my quarry had joined the queue. I had the driver pull up, half a block away, and I gave him some story about my mentally disturbed sister-in-law who couldn't be trusted to find her way home but insisted on trying. He accepted this *blague* (men do, I've found, accept the most arrant nonsense from a well-dressed woman) and sat with the motor idling. Mme Hughenfort eventually got her taxi, and passed us, going towards the, city centre.

We pulled in behind her and followed her through the narrow Presqu'île and into the quiet area north of the busy centre, where her taxi pulled up in front of a block of flats with shops on the street level. I had my driver continue on slowly; when I saw the two travellers go through a door, I told him to take me to the Carlton.

Despite the hour, they had a room for me 'and my husband, who will be arriving tomorrow, or possibly Saturday'. I went up, washed the travel from my face and hands, turned my coat to present a bland cloth façade to the world, and went back down and through the dark streets to the Hughenforts' front door.

I had seen a brasserie across the street and up a bit – not ideally placed for my purposes, but seated at the window, I thought I should be able to see if a taxi pulled up in front of her building. It took the maître d' twenty minutes to produce the requested window table, but I did not think it likely their stop at home would be that brief.

So it proved. I no sooner took my seat than a glance out at the street showed a familiar dark-haired boy with a laden shopping bag coming out of a grocer's. The shopkeeper locked the door behind the boy and tugged down the shades; the boy walked up the steps and into the building.

The Hughenforts would, it seemed, be stopping the night at home. I ate my lamb cassoulet and drank two glasses of Moulin-a-Vent, then returned to my hotel, where I slept very well indeed.

In the morning I was back at my brasserie, its evening linen and herbs-and-garlic odours given way to scrubbed-bare tables and the aroma of coffee and croissants. I manoeuvred until I was at a window table, which I shared with several changes of patrons during my own extended breakfast. I drank more coffee than I had at any one time since the Palestine wanderings (with an unfortunate effect on my nerves) and ate the equivalent of a couple of large loaves of bread, presented in a variety of shapes and sizes, from brioche to baguette, all laden with butter and preserves. Feeling like a child at a birthday party, quivering with excitement and stuffed with sweet things, I paid my bill, abandoned my table, ducked in and out of an unfortunately maintained lavatory, and traded the restaurant for the now-open shops.

Two hours in the brasserie, two more examining each shop's wares with minute attention and a few purchases, and soon the noon hour would be upon me and I would be thrown out onto the street, to reclaim my window seat and eat yet more food. (I had, at least, left a good tip, by way of apology for my lengthy occupation.)

However, as the shopkeeper wrapped my parcel, too polite as he did so to point out that every other door on the street was closed tight and that all civilised persons were already seated at their tables, I saw a taxi pull up in front of the Hughenfort door. The driver got out to ring the bell, and I hastened to pay and scramble to find a taxi of my own.

Taxi drivers, too, are civilised people. It took me ten tense minutes

270

to find a man hungrier for cash than for *déjeuner* and to urge him back to my target. To his disgust, we then sat at the end of the road, the engine idling, while the other driver and the two Hughenforts pushed the last of their cases into the car and got in. Only when the other taxi was moving did I allow my driver to follow.

We travelled little more than a mile through the city, ending up not far from the railway station where we had begun on the previous day. The taxi turned into a quiet street and came to a halt before a run-down block of flats that were considerably less appealing, both aesthetically and in their local amenities, than the house we'd come from. Mme Hughenfort would not, I thought, wish to remain here for long, not with her young son in tow: The butcher's looked fly-blown, the nearest greengrocer's was two streets away, and there wasn't even a *boulangerie* in sight for their morning baguette.

'Hôtel Carlton,' I said to the driver. He swivelled around to stare at me, at this crowning instruction to the day's fare, but for once I couldn't be bothered coming up with a story.

He took me to the Carlton, accepted my money, and sped off to see what he could salvage of his lunch hour, shaking his head at the mad ways of foreigners.

Had I been in London, my next step would have been to discover who owned the building in which Mme Hughenfort had taken shelter. In this bastion of Gallic officialdom, however, it was a task I thought I would leave to Holmes, who was not only male but spoke better French than I. Instead, I thought I might go back to the woman's neighbourhood and show some photographs.

After the long lunchtime closure.

Besides which, I was growing quite fond of my brasserie's fare.

Following lunch, with my coat still turned to show honest cloth and the dumpiest of hats on my head, I took out the envelope of family photographs Alistair had given me and began to work my way up one side of the street and down the other. My basic story was that I was a second cousin of Mme Hughenfort, but the embroidery I tacked on to that thin beginning varied with my audience. In the brasserie, where I started my community interrogation, there was an inheritance involved, a solid pile of francs for Mme Hughenfort if she could prove, well, 'family concerns' (I let the precise nature of those concerns trail into speculation). To the good mistress of the flower stall there was a reference to a family madman; to the stout pair who ran the needlework shop a tinge of romance and scandal, and to the tobacconist a simple wager that had got complicated. And so it went, in the shops, among the neighbours. What I learnt, both through my deliberate efforts and through fortuitous accident, was most intriguing.

Her missing neighbours returned as darkness was setting in, and they contributed their own pieces to the puzzle.

Finally, as the rich odours of Lyonnais cooking crept into the evening air to mix with the damp from two rivers, I turned my steps back to the Carlton, where I was given, along with my key, the news that my husband had arrived. I held my breath as I inserted the key in the lock, knowing full well that with Holmes, arrival did not necessarily mean presence. But when I flung open the door, he was there, damp from the bath and working to get the cuff links through his shirt. He looked up in surprise at my abrupt entrance, his thinning hair still tousled from the towel and giving him an absurdly boyish look. I laughed aloud in sheer pleasure: the perfect end to a satisfying day.

CHAPTER TWENTY

SAY ONE THING FOR Holmes: Pompous he may occasionally be, but he does understand the need for physical expression when high spirits erupt, and he accepted my flinging myself into his arms and whirling around the room in a vigorous waltz with nary a repressive grumble. He even hummed an accompaniment for half a dozen twirls until I released him and subsided into a chair to loose my coat and free my tired feet.

'You have had a successful day, I perceive,' he commented.

'I know all about Madame Hughenfort and young Thomas,' I announced grandly.

'All?' he said, one eyebrow raised.

I waved away his scepticism. 'All of importance. But if I begin now we won't eat until ten o'clock, and considering the length of French meals, we shall still be at table when the café au lait appears on the bars.'

I had read rightly the sign of his crisp clean shirt: He, too, was ready to dine.

'An ascetic priest limits himself to thin soup and a prayer at midday,' he commented.

I turned to the dressing table to do my hair, and met his eyes in the glass.

'Did M Tony follow you all the way here?'

'Into Lyons, yes, although not, naturally, into this hotel, an institution not suited to a simple man of the cloth. I led him into the slums and lost him there. I spent three weeks here, back in the nineties,' he explained. 'That sort of neighbourhood changes little in three decades.'

My hair rescued from disarray, my day shoes changed for evening wear, a gossamer Kashmir wrap with silver beads transforming my plain dark dress into formality, I placed my arm through his and went to dine.

Subdued piano music and the distance between the tables made it safe to speak. After we made our choices and approved the sparkling young Rhône in our glasses, I recounted my day. When I had finished following our pair to their hideout near the *gare*, I paused to let the waiter clear our soup plates.

'It's so nice when things go as easily as that,' I remarked. 'It was as if nothing could go wrong: She couldn't see me behind her, she didn't leave while I was in the lavatory, her taxi didn't take off while I was still hunting for one. *Sometimes* things go right.'

'Too much so, you think?'

I began to protest indignantly, that I should certainly have noticed if the woman had been leading us by the nose, but instead I paused, to do his question justice, before I shook my head. 'She'd have had to know me, know my level of skills, in order to set it up so precisely. *You* might have been able to ensure I followed you without its seeming planned – *might* have – but not a stranger.'

He nodded, accepting my conclusion. We suspended my report long enough to appreciate properly my sole and his Coquilles St

Jacques, before I picked up with my tale in the afternoon. 'With her and the boy safely out of the way, I began the rounds of shopkeepers and neighbours, with a story for each of them that was more style than substance. You know the routine: indignation and a demanding of rights for the strong woman, the impression of tears and lace handkerchiefs for the older women, hints that somebody will get it in the eye for the young men drinking at the bar. Madame's only lived here for eight or nine months – came from Clermont-Ferrand, one of them thought; or Bourges, thought another; although a third swore he had seen her before, in the old city, a good two years ago.

'So I showed the photos, as we agreed, of the family she had either swindled or lost, depending on the story of the moment. No, no, they'd never seen any of those peculiar-looking English people.' I went into as much detail as I thought necessary – the delivery boy who thought Phillida resembled a woman who'd lived in the next street, the old man who believed Terèse Hughenfort a bad mother because the boy had once talked back to him, and a string of other statements that most likely meant nothing, but might potentially have some frail significance. The next course came and my duck was but a collection of bones and sauce by the time I came to the really interesting part.

'By this stage I was showing the pictures to anyone who would pause long enough to look. One mother in the fruiterer's took pity on me and glanced through them, told me sorry, and then her young son and his friend wanted to see what she'd been looking at. They recognised the house.'

'What, Justice Hall?'

'None other. It would seem that young master Thomas has a photograph of Justice Hall that he hides from his mother. The boys couldn't mistake that fountain.'

'He hides it from his mother?'

'A man gave it to him, they said, a month or two ago, along with a story that his father lived there, and some day would come and claim Thomas.'

'Which could be nothing more than the fantasy of a fatherless boy, but for the picture, which had to come from somewhere.'

'I thought you'd find that provocative. Particularly considering that shortly after that, Thomas's hair went dark. But half an hour after that interview, I found a man who could identify Sidney Darling.'

It was a night for being demonstrative: Holmes was seized by such glee that he snatched my hand from its resting place on the table and kissed it briefly, startling the waiter who was overseeing the respectful entrance of four noble cheeses.

'Tell me,' Holmes commanded, when the cheeses' trio of escorts had left us.

'It was about six weeks ago. He had purchased a piece of furniture from Mme Hughenfort – a cabinet or trunk of some sort, although the word he used was unfamiliar to me. Whatever it was, it was massive, such that he could not move it down the stairs on his own – that he made clear. One evening his wife's brother arrived, and the two men decided to go and fetch the thing. They went upstairs and knocked at her door. There were voices on the other side, and the woman's voice, which the customer recognised as that of Terèse Hughenfort, continued speaking as she came to the door.

'My informant gained the impression that she was expecting someone, possibly her son, who came up the stairs as they were going down again, so that she opened the door without asking who was there. She seemed startled at seeing her visitors, and

276

turned to look over her shoulder at the man in the room, but he was standing in plain view, so Madame merely allowed them to take the object and leave.

'The man was quite definite. He even thought the visitor was English, although he couldn't decide if the man had just looked that way, being tall, blond, and aloof, or if he'd said something and had an accent. He looked at the photograph of Sidney, and said it could have been him, although he wouldn't swear on his son's head that it was. All Englishmen look rather alike to him, it would seem.'

Our pleasure in the delicate cheeses was surpassed only by the savour of being able to tie Darling in with Mme Hughenfort. Still . . .

'It doesn't actually prove anything, though, does it?' I asked. 'Darling could easily say that he wanted to see the boy for himself, to try to save Marsh the trouble. There's no evidence that it was Darling who suggested that Madame dye the boy's hair, or that she insist on going to London rather than invite the family to her home ground. That is to say, if Darling was out to present Marsh with an adequate heir so that Marsh would clear out of Justice and leave it to the Darlings to run for him, he'd hardly have sent her a signed letter of instruction, would he?'

Holmes, looking ever more pleased, folded his table napkin and drained his glass. 'There is but one way of knowing.'

'Oh, Holmes. You don't intend—'

'A spot of burglary? But of course.' He looked over to catch the eye of the attentive waiter, and smiled. '*L'addition, s'il vous plaît.*'

We made a detour to our rooms so I might assume a more practical outfit for the role of burglar. When eleven o'clock had rung, we slipped out of the service entrance into the dark streets.

A light rain had begun, all the better for our purposes since it sent passers-by scurrying for shelter with their heads tucked down. I led Holmes up to my friendly brasserie, and nodded down the street at the house.

'The door between the florist's and the ironmonger's,' I told him. 'Their *appartement* is on the top floor, facing the street.' It was a three-storey building, flush to a taller building on one side and with a narrow alley on the other. 'I don't know if their flat goes all the way to the alley, or if the corner room is attached to the neighbour.' The entire floor was uniformly dark.

'I propose we find out,' Holmes said, and launched himself out across the street. Rather wishing that we'd remained disguised by the priests' robes, which might stay the gendarmes from actual assault, I followed.

I had been inside the building earlier that day, so I already knew which flats were inhabited by nervous dogs and which by deaf old ladies. The central vestibule was not locked, and we encountered no one on the stairs, although twice dogs began to yap frantically inside their doors and caused us to quicken our steps. Outside the Hughenfort door, Holmes took out his picklocks and bent to work.

The lock was old and simple, a matter of a few moments' nudging before we were inside. The curtains were shut tight, which made matters easier yet, and we divided up our attention, beginning at opposite ends of the flat.

This is what we learnt about Mme Hughenfort: She was an untidy housekeeper, although the rooms were clean beneath a layer of dust and clutter, and she had a frugal taste in foodstuffs and alcohol. Her furniture and clothing were serviceable but cheap, with the exception of a few items that might easily have been gifts.

The boy's room reflected more care than hers, his coats and shoes newer, his bedclothes thicker than hers.

We found no picture of Justice Hall among his things, although there was a dust-free gap on a shelf that might have held the sort of treasure-box valued even by boys who are not required to move house every few months: He might well have seized it to take into exile. The walls held awards from school, a letter of commendation from a teacher, and some drawings he had made, spare and surprisingly sophisticated. I spotted an essay the boy had been writing, glanced through it, and found that it too demonstrated an unexpected maturity in its language and its grasp of history. I put it back, thoughtful.

In her room we found nothing incriminating, until we reached the upper shelf of a built-in cupboard and saw an ornate enamelled music box, about four inches by nine, with a scene of some Bavarian village in the snow. The box was locked.

Holmes drew out his picklocks again.

She did not keep her legal papers in the box, but for our purposes something far better. Holmes slid his fingernail over the catch to keep the box from playing, and with his other hand took out the contents.

Love letters from three different men over a twenty-year period, none of which was signed 'Lionel' or written in an English hand. Snapshots of a younger, slimmer Terèse, mostly with friends, including one showing her dressed in a heavy winter coat, arm in arm with a tall Nordic-looking blond man. The dates had been pencilled onto the back of each in French schoolgirl writing; the one with the blond said, *'Pieter, novembre 1913.'*

One of the letters was signed with that name, the one that contained, along with a number of romantic lines I had just as soon not have read, the following admission (in French):

279

I will never cease loving you, my darling Terèse, but I cannot leave my wife. A divorce, with her in the state she is, would be the act of a scoundrel. So although I would give my life to be with you, I cannot in good conscience sacrifice hers. Farewell, my sweet girl. Think of me well.

The letter bore the date of early December 1913. A month before Terèse had married Lionel Hughenfort.

Did she snag him, or was she simply an old friend who needed a great favour? I thought the latter, that she was desperate, pregnant and abandoned; he was ill, in need of a housekeeper, generous with his family's money, and not unwilling to do his judgemental family in the eye by dragging in this unsuitable match.

There may even, I reflected, have been a degree of affection between them. The photograph of the pregnant Terèse and the worn-looking Lionel that occupied a place among the debris of her dressing table was an obligatory presence, since the man was her son's declared father, but it might also have a sentimental value to her. The pose, while hardly that of two newlyweds expecting a first child, nonetheless seemed to indicate friendship rather than a mere business transaction. They were leaning into one another, their faces at ease, as if each were taking a pause from the world's tumult with a similarly beset companion-at-arms. Neither seemed to place much trust in the other's strength, but at the same time, neither seemed to think it likely that the other was an active threat. And in the sort of life their faces testified to their having led, being safe from attack was nearly as good as being protected.

Holmes laid aside the photo of Terèse with Pieter and his last letter to her, put the rest back into the music box, then eased the lid down and locked it.

'She'll notice them missing,' I remarked, not meaning it as an objection. Holmes did not take it as such, either.

'That may be for the best,' he replied as he carried the box back to the cupboard.

I could see what he meant: that Terèse Hughenfort would take the missing objects as a declaration that the family was on to her scheme. However, when the monies continued to come (as I assumed they would, knowing Marsh), their arrival would send the further message that support would continue, so long as she did not attempt to foist her cuckoo's child into the family nest.

Out on the street again, doors locked behind us and dogs safely passed, I brought out the only real disappointment of the evening's excursion.

'It would have been nice to have some hard evidence of Sidney Darling's involvement in the attempt to place the boy in Justice.'

Holmes was shaking his head before I had finished. 'I believe you'd find that one of those occasions when the truth does more damage than a convenient lie, Russell. We still can't be certain if Darling was planning actual fraud, or if he was simply aiming at the easiest path for everyone: giving the duke an acceptable heir, a boy with the potential of being shaped to make a master for Justice when his time comes. Darling no doubt believes that such a situation would set Marsh's mind at rest, allowing a return to the status quo: Marsh and Alistair back to wherever they've been for the last twenty years, the Darlings back in charge of Justice. Nothing criminal there.'

He was right. The peculiar thing was, Darling's goal and ours were proving to be more or less the same thing. And as I'd said before, if I had to choose a commoner to train up as a duke, Thomas Hughenfort would be an ideal candidate: a supple mind, good manners, and an unspoilt upbringing by a caring mother.

Alistair's response to that, unfortunately, would dominate: The boy's blood was simply not that of the Hughenforts.

There was little more to be done in Lyons, short of confronting Mme Hughenfort, which was most definitely not in our brief. We spent an hour in the morning uncovering the owner of the flat to which the mother and son had fled, finding to our utter lack of surprise that the name was that of her long-time accountant to whom cheques were sent.

We were on the next train to Paris, where we spent the night, and arrived in London to the sound of church bells.

Holmes went into the first telegraph office we could find that was open on a Sunday, to dispatch a brief message to Justice Hall saying that we were back in the country and would report soon. Then we took ourselves to a small and inordinately luxurious hotel, where we were fed and pampered and could talk the whole matter through without being overheard.

In most investigations, Holmes aimed for the truth – no less, no more. In this case, we sought the truth, but perhaps not too much of it, and preferably truth of the right sort. Marsh was both client and brother, and his fate was in our hands.

Put simply, if we loved Mahmoud, we would lie to him. A simple declaration that, yes, the boy is your brother's son, and the huge weight of Justice would be lifted from Marsh's shoulders, allowing him and Ali to slip out from under that estate, those walls, that role of self-mutilating service, and resume the light existence of nomads. Marsh wished to trade stone walls for those of goat's hair as badly as his cousin did – of that we were both certain. All it would take was one word, a simple, unadorned 'yes', and our brothers would be free.

'I have, on occasion, lied to a client,' Holmes mused, addressing rather owlishly his several-times-emptied glass. 'It goes against my grain, rather, but particularly in my youth I hesitated not to play God.'

'But – with Marsh?'

'There's the rub,' he agreed. 'If it were merely a matter of backing Marsh up, I should happily lie to the prime minister himself, perhaps even the king. But to keep the facts from him, to make his decision for him? That is a far different matter.'

My initial objection had been founded more on the impossibility of deceiving the man than on the immorality of doing so, but I had to agree with this argument as well.

'What do you suggest?' I asked him.

'I propose to return to the scent I was working before Mme Hughenfort led us astray.'

'Interviewing soldiers?'

'One in particular, although not a soldier. The chaplain who wrote that letter of condolence to Gabriel's father. Hastings said he'd known Gabriel, and may well have sat with Gabriel his last night. I wrote to him before we left for France, and hope to collect his answer in the morning. Considering the bureaucratic tangle the boy appears to have been caught up in, the companion of his last hours may know more than the commanding officer.'

Chapter Twenty-One

In the morning, however, there was no letter waiting at the small tobacconist's shop that Holmes used for a convenience address. He scowled absently at the woman who ran the shop, then turned on his heel and left the cramped, fragrant little place. I threw a couple of soothing phrases at her and scurried after him; when I caught him up, he was deep in thought and I decided that he had been unaware both of his scowl and its effect.

'We may as well go to Sussex,' he declared. 'I left at least three vital letters unanswered, a week and a half ago.'

So we went to Sussex, to tidy up the many things left dangling by Alistair's arrival and precipitate demands. We spent the night under Mrs Hudson's care and returned to London, and the tobacconist, in the morning. She still had no letters, and she bristled and protested in florid Cockney that she couldn't be expected to produce a letter that never came. Holmes seemed not to think it an unreasonable expectation, and on that note we left the shop.

'I shall go to Dorking,' he declared.

'Even though the Reverend Mr Hastings may be absent?'

'The letter will have dropped through his letterbox more than a week ago. If he were away, a housekeeper would have sent it on to him. Of course, he may be ill, or out of the county; on the other hand, he may have had other, more subtle reasons for failing to respond.'

Such as being long dead, I thought, but did not say.

'Dorking is not so remote as to constitute an unreasonable waste of time,' he decided. 'Come, Russell,' and so saying, he threw up his hand to summon a passing taxicab.

The Reverend Mr Hastings' cottage was at the end of a lane that ran from the high street towards open down land. With a ruthless hand at the pruning shears the cottage might have presented a more friendly face, but between the untrimmed ivy and the overgrown bushes in the garden, the house windows looked dully out like the eyes of a long-unshaven prisoner of war. There appeared to be no one at home, but I thought it would look the same way even if the entire Women's Institute had been gathered inside. We picked our way up the weedy gravel path and rang the bell.

No sound followed the clamour, but the house seemed to grow watchful, and the image of a wary prisoner returned more strongly.

Holmes pulled the bell-knob again, and the sound died away a second time, but now there was something else: a scuffling noise, coming slowly down an uncarpeted hallway. The door opened, and we looked into the face of the prisoner himself.

Tall, so gaunt as to make Holmes seem fleshy, clean-shaven to reveal the furrows and hollows of his seven decades and more, he was dressed in an ordinary, old-fashioned suit gone shiny at the knees, but there was something about his stoop and his gaze that caused me to glance involuntarily at his ankles. He wore no shackles – at least, no tangible ones – but he stood nonetheless with the posture of an old lag at hard labour.

'The Reverend Mr Hastings?' Holmes asked. He took the man's silence for an answer. 'My name is Holmes. I wrote to you concerning—'

'I feared you would come,' the man interrupted. His voice was hoarse, either from injury or disuse. 'You should not have done so.'

'There are questions to which I must have answers,' Holmes replied, his tone gentle.

'Questions that ought to remain unasked.'

'Nonetheless, I must insist.'

Hastings neither denied Holmes' right to insist nor asserted his own right to refuse. Instead, the recognition that Holmes was not going to walk away settled over him like a weight, the latest of many, and his face aged another half decade. He turned away abruptly, leaving us to close the door and follow him down the dark hallway to the kitchen, where he filled the kettle from the tap and set it to heat.

The kitchen was pure Victorian, a gloomy servant's quarter without the servant. The shelves and cupboards had been painted a peculiar and unappetising shade of green long before Victoria died – perhaps even while Albert was still alive. The fluttering gas lamps reflected off that paint made our host look like a corpse, moving between hob and cupboards.

'Will you take coffee?' he asked over his shoulder, sounding as if he hoped the answer would be negative so he could drink in peace.

'Thank you,' Holmes answered for us both. Hastings had yet to acknowledge my presence; however, three cups appeared on the tray. In silence, he spooned and stirred and filtered the fragrant beverage into a dented silver pot gone black with tarnish, and carried the tray out of the room as if we were not there. Obediently, we trailed after.

The sitting room needed the gas up even in the middle of the morning. The coals in the grate smoked in a sullen fashion, as if they'd been put on wet, and the lamp on the wall behind me flickered badly. Hastings laid the tray on a low table, took what was obviously his customary chair beside a taller table piled high with books, and bent forward to pour into the three cups. He took his black, and left us to add sugar or milk as we wished. The milk in the jug looked dubious, so I satisfied myself with three sugars. I stirred, sipped, and coughed in astonishment.

For the first time, Hastings noted my presence enough to glance at me. 'Is there something wrong with it?'

'No, no – not at all,' I assured him. 'It's delicious.'

Actually, it was, but also powerful. The dim light and lack of cream had not prepared me for a brew nearly the equivalent of the thick Arabic stuff Mahmoud had made. It was not what I would have expected from such a frail creature.

'I drink it strong,' he told us. 'It keeps me from sleep.'

Holmes glanced up sharply, as the dread permeating the word 'sleep' slapped into the room. Hastings might as well have substituted the word 'nightmares'.

Holmes set down his cup and got the ordeal under way.

'Reverend Mr Hastings, as I told you in my letter, I am making enquiries for the Duke of Beauville into the death of his nephew, Gabriel Hughenfort. I was given your name as chaplain to the regiment in which Hughenfort was serving at the time of his execution.'

Hastings jerked so sharply at the last word that some of the coffee splashed out of the cup onto his knee. He did not notice.

'You can't—' he said. 'I can't—oh my dear Lord, he was only a child, nothing more than a child!'

And then he was weeping. An aged man carrying a burden of pain raw enough to reduce him to hard sobs is a terrifying thing to behold, and Holmes and I exchanged a horrified glance before he shot out one hand to rescue the cup. I reached for the throw on the back of my seat and draped it across Hastings' shoulders, a pointless gesture but the only sort of comfort I could come up with at the moment.

'Perhaps some tea, Russell?' Holmes murmured. 'If you can find some fresher milk?'

I slid away gratefully to the kitchen, located some more promising milk in the cooler portion of the pantry, and found that he had left the kettle simmering away. In bare minutes I was back, and Holmes thrust the hot, sweet tea into the man's hands.

The gentler stimulant did its work. When the cup held only a sludge of sugar at the bottom, Hastings drew a shaky breath and handed it over to be refilled. When that cup was halfway down, he summoned the strength to begin his tale.

'They were such children, by that point in the War – red-cheeked and frightened, trying so hard to keep a brave face, for themselves and the others. In the early days, of course, that wasn't the case. I offered my services as soon as war was declared, so I saw the first days of the Expeditionary Force. Those men, they were hard as rocks, with no more imagination than the mules that pulled the guns. Tommy Atkins at his best – Kipling would have known them in an instant.

'And then over the winter the new generation of Tommies began to arrive, in a trickle at first, then in numbers. Strong young men from factories and farms, undergraduates and lower clerks, idealistic and patriotic and oh, how they died. The government trained them for their fathers' wars, taught them how to handle themselves in honest battle, and then shipped them off to hell in the trenches.'

He blew out a breath, his eyes far away, seeing France nine years before. 'One boy I remember, he couldn't have been more than twenty-one, a shining example of English manhood. He arrived with his papers in October of '15, and instead of keeping him back until his regiment came off the front line they just passed him on. I was there when he reported for duty. The sergeant had just brewed tea, and was handing me a tin mug when we heard the noise of someone sloshing along the duckboards. We stuck our heads out from under the scrap of tarpaulin the sergeant had rigged as a shelter from the rain and saw this sopping-wet creature with a shiny new hat and mud to the thighs, stumbling up the trench. He spotted us under the flap and waded over to the dugout.

'And then the young fool stood to attention to return the sergeant's salute. Straightened his back, and a sniper took him, right through that pretty new officer's cap.

'And do you know, the sergeant laughed. It sounds utterly callous, but it was such an appalling irony, to see this fresh-faced, blue-eyed boy stand up proud to do his patriotic duty, before either of us could stop him. I still see it: The boy's hand comes up and – pop! God takes off the top of his head. What could the sergeant do but laugh? And God forgive me, it was such a shock, for a moment I couldn't help joining him. Twenty-one years of education and responsibility going into an erect spine at the wrong instant. God's sense of humour can be brutal.

'That was the volunteer army. It got so the sight of a newly applied set of officers' pips made my stomach heave, we lost so many young officers. It made me rage, that all their expensive training didn't include the basic skills of survival. Not a gentlemanly trait, I assume, self-interest. They sent us children, and we offered them up to Moloch, and they sent us more. I had a boy die in my arms whose cheeks had less down on them than a ripe peach. He was fourteen, and the recruiter who'd accepted the lie about his age should have been shot.'

Hastings' words had welled up like poison from a lanced boil, but at this last phrase he stumbled, remembering why we were here. After a minute he started again, the flow slower now but inexorable.

'We had three executions in the units I served with. I witnessed two of them. The first was a foul and bitter affair, a regular soldier in his late thirties who'd been drunk, got in an argument with his sergeant, and shot him. The man was charged with murder, and executed three weeks later. That was in April of 1915. Two of the men on the firing squad broke down during the summer, had to be transferred to less active duty before they were charged with some dereliction of duty as well. One of the men returned to the Front the next spring, the other I heard died of septicaemia from some minor wound left untreated, a year or so later.

'The second execution was in the winter of 1916. A private standing watch fell asleep on duty, and although he might have got away with ninety days' field punishment, he'd been warned twice before. So they shot him. *Pour encourager les autres*, you know. I was off having a couple of rotted toes sawn off, so I didn't have to sit with that one.' Hastings drew a shaky breath, and went on.

'Your duke's nephew came to my attention in the late spring of 1918. Not that anyone knew he was a duke's nephew – more than that, son and heir to one of the great dukedoms of the realm. Had

I but known, oh, had he but told me! If he'd given me the name, I could have stopped it in a moment. But I knew him as Hewetson, and only found out the other name later, long after he had died.'

'Why do you suppose he did not tell you?' Holmes asked, the first interruption to the narrative either of us had made.

'God!' Hastings cried out. 'I've asked myself that a thousand – ten thousand – times in the past five and a half years. Had I prodded him to tell me his story, had I performed my sworn duty as God's servant wholeheartedly instead of taking relief in the boy's lack of distress, he might have told me before it was too late. Instead of which I was a craven coward, pathetically grateful that he was not screaming and wetting himself with terror as my first executed prisoner had been.

'But I am getting ahead of myself.

'He joined the regiment in, oh, it must have been late March, a quiet boy with dark eyes and a limp. I was only too glad to see a bit of wear and tear on his uniform, since it meant I wouldn't have to wince in anticipation every time I heard a sniper's gun across the line. He knew enough to keep his head down, he wasn't burdened with all kinds of unnecessary equipment, he was oblivious to the stench and the rattle of guns beyond our range. He had the makings of a soldier, in other words, and the men responded in kind.

'He'd been wounded, that was clear, not only from the limp and the bits of rock embedded under the skin of his face and hands, but from the dark look that came into his eyes during a bombardment. The men were hunkered down in the trenches one long night, and I was working my way along the lines when I came upon him, tense as a humming wire but working hard to keep it from his men. I stopped to talk to him for a quarter-hour or so, which was when I learnt that he'd been raised in Berkshire, and that he'd already been buried once in a mud-soaked trench that took a direct hit. He dismissed it with a couple of brief but chilling phrases – "drowning in cream-of-man soup" is the one I still hear in the night – and said he thought it statistically unlikely that he'd take another direct hit, which was why his men were sticking so close to him.

'In truth, his men were near him because despite his youth, despite his apprehension, there was a core of steely authority in him that drew them like so many magnets. They clung to him, both protecting him and drawing strength from him. Hewetson and I talked for a short time – of birds' nests and fox hunting, I think it was – while the men pretended not to hear; when I moved on, the boy's tautness had eased a fraction and there was a greater degree of calm and unity of purpose in that one small section of trench. I could, you see,' Hastings added, 'perform the task that I had been placed there for.'

I thought that any chaplain who had volunteered for the trenches, at his age, to spend the entire four years in the mud with the common soldiers, had done a greater service than Hastings gave himself credit for. Some toes lost to trench foot or frostbite seemed to me the least of this man's wounds.

'I made it a point to seek him out from time to time over the next weeks. He never wanted my counsel – indeed, he seemed to cherish most our little talks about matters with no connection to our current circumstances – but he had much to say about the land, and our responsibility to it. One morning, marching back up the lines towards the Front, I happened upon him, standing at the side of the road to watch two old women trying to nurture a scrap of garden among the shelled fields. When he felt me beside him, he turned, nodded to me, and then gestured at the two bent figures in black. "If this war ever ends," he said, "anyone setting a plough to the entire north end of France is going to risk hitting a live shell. On the other hand, we've certainly enriched the soil for them." And then he settled his pack and walked on.'

'Dark humour for a young lad,' Holmes commented.

'The only sane response to the continuous, grinding brutality of living for weeks in that hell hole.'

'You would say, then, that Gabriel Hughenfort – or Gabriel Hewetson, as you knew him – was sane?'

'None of us was sane, not after we'd been there for more than a few weeks. But Gabriel was as balanced as any man I knew. He escaped into his memories of rural Berkshire, he read and he wrote for hours, then he returned to duty, strengthened.'

'He wrote, you say. What was he writing?'

'Letters, for the most part. And . . . a diary.'

Holmes and I looked at him, both of us thinking that the family's collection of letters could not have taken up a great deal of the young officer's time, and that diary had they none. Before we could ask, Reverend Mr Hastings was explaining, and his next words were even more of a revelation.

'He also had a young woman, I believe.'

'His fiancée in Berkshire, yes. Do we know her name, Russell?'

'Susan, Susan Bridges,' I told him. But Hastings shook his head.

'Not the same, not unless Gabriel's pet name for her was Hélène. Did this fiancée do VAD work in France?'

'I have no idea,' Holmes admitted.

'His young lady was an ambulance driver. She was taller than Gabriel and had bright green eyes, and that's all I know about her – that and the name. I assumed she was French, by her name, but fluent in English.'

'You met her?'

To my astonishment, Hastings turned red with what looked to be embarrassment.

'I—no, I never met her.'

'Then how—?'

'His letters – I never saw him write in anything but English. Perhaps he feared that the censors would have blacked out phrases in as foreign language.'

His skin returned to its former pallor, but the open manner in which he was meeting Holmes' eye had an element of defiance in it. For the first time, the old priest was hiding something.

Holmes saw it too, of course, and after a moment's reflection, decided on an oblique approach instead of direct assault.

'You say he wrote a great deal, to this Hélène person and in a diary. To anyone else that you noticed?'

'Someone in the government, a judge of some—Wait. If his name was Hughenfort, then . . . Not a judge. He was writing to the house. Justice Hall is the family seat, is it not?'

'It is. They received very few letters, however.'

'For some reason, I assumed they were dutiful missives to an aged judicial uncle who had retired to the country,' Hastings mused.

'The few I noticed – the men occasionally gave me their letters, to post behind the lines – were thin. I recall wondering once why it was this unnamed occupant of a judicial hall who received his letters and not his nearer family. I'd have thought him an orphan, but for one reference he made to his parents' difficulties in keeping the house warm. Had I known the size of the house,' he added with a glimmer of amusement, 'I might have been less sympathetic.'

'No one else that you noticed? Any letters he received from sources other than Hélène and Justice Hall?'

'None that I noticed, but then I was only occasionally present for mail call.'

'Do you know what happened to those letters?'

'He may have given them to the officer who visited him the night before he . . .'

'Lieutenant Hughenfort had a visitor?' Holmes asked sharply, then caught himself. 'Perhaps, Mr Hastings, you had best tell us what you know about Gabriel's final days.'

CHAPTER TWENTY-TWO

THE REVEREND MR HASTINGS settled back into his chair with an air of summoning his energies for the final push. He spread his hands out on the arms, where the upholstery was brown and shiny with wear.

'Gabriel joined us, as I said, in the middle of March, just in time to meet the full German assault. How he even got up the lines to the trenches I don't know, but he must have slipped in during a lull in the gas. The mortar fire was more or less continuous, but gas depends on which way the air is moving. At any rate, there he was, a fresh face – looking no less weary than the other men but a good deal less filthy. No one took much notice of him that first week, other than to see that he could hold his own, since we were all too busy with getting out the wounded and trying to keep from being pushed all the way to the sea. The Front retreated in a fifty-mile bulge in three weeks, then slowed, and in the second week of April we were laying down new trenches.

'That is when Gabriel Hewetson and I began to have our conversations about the natural history of Berkshire. When I became aware that we had a rather extraordinary young gentleman in our midst. When I began to regain a sense of my vocation. I've often thought that Gabriel gave me more spiritual guidance than I did him, without ever speaking about God.'

I did not know what to make of him as a man of religious sensibilities. His rage against God was powerful, yet the trenches had not killed his faith. I thought I might risk interrupting his flow of words with a question.

'I'm curious, Mr Hastings. I'd have thought that as a chaplain you would have spent more time behind the lines, and yet you seem to have been actually at the front line a great deal. Was this usual?'

'Jesus Christ was the Son of God, but He was also a man – a carpenter's son, a wandering preacher, a friend of the poor and the downtrodden. Jesus would not have spent that war comforting those already in the comfort of dry beds and hospital wards. When I volunteered, it was with the knowledge that I had to follow His example as long as my strength held out.

'Young Gabriel helped me maintain that strength, for a few vital weeks when I needed it most. And in the end, I failed him.

'We were among the armies transferred south in early May, to a quiet stretch of the Front on the west end of the Chemin des Dames, and it was as if we'd been lifted out of a cesspit during a riot and set down in Paradise. It was disorientating – there'd been heavy fighting there the year before, until the French mutiny, but the villages were still whole, church bells rang from intact steeples, old women went out to work the fields. Cows grazed, chickens scratched. We even slept to the song of nightingales.

'Three blissful weeks of this – broken by the occasional skirmish, of course, but with long stretches of silence to heal the soul. The air smelt of growing things, not of death. Bliss.

'And then, just after midnight on the twenty-seventh, the Germans decided that our patch was the one they wanted for their break-through, and we were back in the thick of it. Fast asleep, most of us, when the gas canisters landed, and almost before the sentry could get to the nearest shell casing and hammer out a warning, a thousand guns opened up. The ground heaved, trenches collapsed, the sky was aflame.' The memory was so raw in his face, for an instant I thought I saw the fires reflected in his wide-staring eyes.

'A ten-mile retreat that first day, thousands taken prisoner, utter confusion, equipment abandoned, men fleeing in the wrong direction. The next day was worse, with the men beginning to panic. By the time the Germans came up against the Americans at Belleau Wood the first week of June, we fully expected Paris to fall. We took one look at the Yanks, and despaired – they were far too shiny-new to be of any use.

'But by God they held, and the German offensive ground to a halt, and then it was time to march back up the line and dig in again, after our nice quiet holiday.

'Everyone knew now, after four years, this was it. The men had been fighting hard since March, but now the death-struggle began in earnest, every inch of ground bitterly contested. Our men were foot-sore and exhausted and ready to do it all again, and I've never been prouder of them.' He paused briefly to take a swallow of cold tea.

'We'd been jumbled in among the French this time, which made for a certain amount of confusion, but no doubt the rivalry helped maintain spirits on both sides. I was no longer in Gabriel's regiment, but as I was only a few miles up the road and padres were scarce, I saw him every two or three days. He had been badly shaken by the sudden bombardment down at the Chemin des

Dames in May, and spent a couple of weeks twitching and pale. I urged him to go back for medical rest, but he refused. His men needed him, he said. It may even have been true.

'His regiment had been set to hold a hill. One pitiful bump in a flat land, facing another insignificant rise half a mile off held by the Boches. More trenching, more sniping and waiting for orders.

'I wasn't there when his order came. I don't even know who issued it, but someone safely back in headquarters decided that Second Lieutenant Gabriel Hewetson needed to rouse his men into a wiring expedition that would show the French how it was done.

'The problem was, it was a full moon on a crystal-clear night. A rat couldn't have got through the wire unnoticed. Gabriel pointed this out, pointed out that the sniper opposite had a lethal aim, but the order stood.

'His men would have followed him. There was no question in his mind, or in theirs, or in that of the man giving the order. They would have followed him, and they would have died.' He looked down, studying his old man's hands; I wanted to stop his narrative to save him the reliving of it. Instead, we waited as he drew a shaky breath, and then went on.

'Gabriel said no. In fact, he specifically ordered his company to stand down.'

'Thus taking full personal responsibility,' Holmes said, to show the man that we understood. The image of the Justice mascot, the ungainly bird ripping its heart out for its young, flashed starkly before me. 'What was said at the trial? Did you attend?'

'I did not. It was so fast, by the time I heard about his arrest, he'd already been condemned.'

'What? How long was that?'

'Five days.'

'*Five days?* Surely that was an extraordinary rush?'

'It was judged to be a precarious time and place, and considering Gabriel's popularity, his insubordination threatened the discipline of that entire stretch of the Front. Instant punishment was seen as essential. He was executed ten days after his arrest.'

'Ten—' Holmes was without words.

'Did no one speak up for him?' I demanded.

'The opinion of his men was judged to be emotional attachment.'

'Surely his representative protested?'

'He had no defence.'

'No defence?' Holmes repeated, as appalled as I.

Hastings drew a deep breath. 'Normally, he'd have had some kind of advocate. Normally, for a man his age, an officer, and a first offence, he'd have been stripped of his rank, perhaps given field punishment; certainly that's what Gabriel expected. Normally, between arrest and execution there would have been at least two or three weeks, during which time appeals would be made. But in that part of the Front, in the summer of 1918, nothing was in the least normal. His court martial looked at his offence and heard him plead guilty. There was neither time nor inclination for leniency.'

'But he was an officer,' Holmes pointed out. 'I could find records of only two or three other officers executed during the whole War, and only one of those for refusing to fight.' It was, in truth, the most incomprehensible part of the whole affair: Gentlemen were simply not lined up and shot, and even as Gabriel Hewetson, the boy's class must have been instantly recognisable.

'It must have been the divisional commander's letter that did for him. "An example must be set," it said. "The regiment's unrest and growing unwillingness in the face of battle is a grave danger to us all," it said. "The cowardice of one young officer whose fighting skills have already been demonstrated to be of a low order must not be allowed to infect his fellows with the urge to mutiny."' Hastings rubbed his face with both hands, a dry rasp that made my own skin creep. 'The words of that letter are graven on my memory. But do you know, when I finally reached the man and confronted him with the result of his letter, in the first part of September, he could not even recall having written the thing.'

His aged voice trailed into the exhaustion of despair, and he did not need to tell us that this last betrayal had been the final blow. After a minute, he went on.

'They told him the day before, what his sentence was. That was common practise. I suppose it was hard on the other men, to hear the weeping and gnashing of teeth from their condemned comrade. The next morning they took him out and shot him at dawn. Marched him with a sack over his head so the eight men didn't have to see his face, and a square of white cloth pinned to his breast as the target. They stood him in front of a half-ruined house, with pock-holes where a previous man had been dispatched. Eight men picked up their rifles from the ground, each hoping that his held the blank. And do you know what that lad called out to his executioners when he heard the bullets going into their chambers?

"'Aim true, boys!" he said. "Don't let me down."'

And with that, Hastings finally buried his face in his hands and wept. I was not far from sobbing myself, and Holmes' stony features concealed little of his own emotion.

It would have been a mercy to end there, to offer the man our bleak thanks and leave him to his misery. Since that was not possible, we were obliged to regroup, to ply Hastings with food and drink until he had regained his equanimity. It was distressingly like the medical attention given a man to enable him to stand with his blindfold in place.

An hour later, with a degree of colour returned to those sallow cheeks, Holmes went after the last pieces.

'You told us he had a visitor.'

'The night before the execution, yes.'

'Only one?'

'Two, in addition to myself and his batman, but one was simply a representative from his men, offering their farewell greetings. The other was an officer, a staff major I had not seen before. He asked me to leave them alone, spent perhaps two hours with Gabriel, then left.'

'Did the boy tell you who this major was, what they said?'

'He was a friend, perhaps a family member. Some person of long acquaintance, to judge by the warmth of the handshake. And the man did seem to do some good. Before he arrived, Gabriel was growing increasingly agitated – pacing in his cell, unable to settle to prayer or conversation. He had been asking me if I would take a letter to the commanding officer. He had not written anything as yet, but he seemed to think that the letter might save him. I tried to press him – if there were mitigating circumstances, health problems, if he'd lied about his age, anything that might convert his sentence, that I could present in appeal – but before I could find out what he had in mind, this major arrived, and when he left, Gabriel's demeanour had altered entirely. Whatever they said to each other, the boy's fear had vanished, replaced by a calm acceptance that gave him a sort of wisdom beyond his years. He seemed to radiate holiness, if that doesn't sound like some foolish fancy of an old man. He was very beautiful.'

'And you have no idea who this red-tab major was?'

'I don't.'

'What did he look like? Tall, short, blond, what?'

'It was fully dark. The nights were brief then, but he came well after midnight. He was shorter than I, but not much. I didn't see his hair. If it is important, you might ask his family. They will almost certainly have saved the letter Gabriel wrote them.'

'It was brief and uninformative,' Holmes told him.

'No, no, I mean his last letter, the one he wrote and gave to the major.'

There was a moment's startled silence. Then Holmes said grimly, 'You had best tell us about this letter.'

'Do the family not have it? Perhaps they destroyed it. I can understand not wanting to have it as a reminder. It took Gabriel more than an hour to write, earlier that evening, before the visitor came. It came to several pages, I remember that, and was addressed to "Father". I did not ask to read it; I merely provided the paper and pen.'

'The only letter the family received was a rather grubby object of less than a page, informing them that he was going into battle on the morrow and that he loved them. It was undated.'

'Most of the soldiers carried similar notes, a final goodbye in case they were killed. But there was nothing else from the major?'

'There was no letter from any major.'

'Oh, dear Lord. It must have been lost. What a great pity. But he must have gone to see them, after the War. He was some sort of family, after all.'

'They had no word.'

'But . . . he was *staff*.' Meaning, staff officers, secure behind the lines, did not suddenly get themselves killed in the final months of fighting. Hastings assumed that we knew this, and continued with his narrative.

'I wrote to the family, of course. But then that is how you found me, so you know that. Writing letters to families was one of the main duties of officers. I found later that there'd been heated exchanges in the House of Commons over executing volunteers, particularly when they were not even legally adults. However, the Army deemed capital punishment a necessary tool in the maintenance of moral fibre, so instead of doing away with executions, they simply concealed them from the people at home. Death notifications became merely "died in active service". My own letter refrained from mentioning the manner of Gabriel's death, stressing instead the love his men had for him. I kept the details to myself, since I assumed the major would write and I did not wish to contradict whatever he chose to tell them. What a tragedy, that his parents did not have his final words to them. I suppose this means that Gabriel's own letters were lost as well?'

'Do you mean to say that this major appropriated the boy's letters?'

'Goodness. I always assumed he had. That same afternoon, I helped Gabriel's batman – McFarlane was his name; poor fellow, he was heartbroken – to pack up Gabriel's effects and return them to the family. There was a pretty biscuit tin where I'd once seen Gabriel put a letter from Hélène, and it was gone. I didn't have the heart to ask McFarlane about it – he was on the edge of tears the whole time. I thought that Gabriel had instructed his man to give them to the major, or perhaps to destroy them. They might have been too personal for him to wish his family to read.'

'Do you remember McFarlane's full name?'

'Jamie, I think it was – Jamie McFarlane. A gnarled stump of a man; looked as if he'd live to be a hundred and ten, but he died two days before Armistice. Not from injuries, either, but an illness. Pneumonia, as I recall.'

It was frustrating beyond belief, Hastings' tantalising bits of information that lacked any evidence to tie them together. The picture of Gabriel's last days had evolved into a ghostly sketch, but every possibility of adding colour and dimension – the major's name, the batman, the girlfriend's surname, Gabriel's letters and diary – was snatched out of our reach as soon as it appeared.

'And the diary, no doubt, went the same way,' Holmes complained bitterly.

But to our surprise, Hastings was again shaking his head. 'No. Gabriel kept that with him during the night, and wrote small notes in it from time to time.' And then, as Holmes was opening his mouth to demand what in God's name had happened to *that* piece of Gabriel Hughenfort's life, Hastings' next words dropped into the room with the impact of an unpinned grenade, tumbling over each other in his haste to explain, and justify. 'He gave it to me at dawn, just as they came for him, and said to keep it safe until someone came to ask me for it, and so I kept it, and I waited, and the War ended but no one came. No one came! That was when I learnt his true name – only then, nearly a year after his death, did I breach its pages to see if I could find . . . But when I discovered who he was, I didn't know what to do – I could not bring myself to write to such a family. No, Gabriel told me to keep it safe until someone came to ask me for it, so I kept it safe, and no one came. Until you.'

CHAPTER TWENTY-THREE

Holmes recovered his voice first.

'You *have* this diary?'

'Then you weren't sent to retrieve it?' Hastings said, which sounded more a confirmation of suspicions than a question.

'Why didn't you tell us you had it in the first place?' I demanded.

'I thought you would ask for it and then leave,' he answered slowly. 'When you did not immediately do so, I realised that I wanted you to hear the entire story. Would you have stopped here the afternoon if I'd offered you the diary the minute you arrived? Gabriel deserved having his eulogy delivered once, at least. Thank you for listening.'

With an effort, he pushed himself to his feet and tottered out of the door and up the hallway to the room at the front of the house. We followed, to a book-lined room whose clammy, stale air testified to the fact that its occupation was only occasional, probably in the summer months. Certainly the books looked well read; the desk was tidy but also showed signs of long use. He went around the desk, pulled open a drawer, and took from the top of it a volume about five inches by seven, bound in once-crimson leather, the edges folded in from a lengthy stay in its owner's pockets or pack. Hastings held it for a moment, then gave it to Holmes, who opened it just long enough to riffle through the pages before placing it in his pocket. Hastings' gaze followed the object until it had disappeared from view, then he reached down and slid shut the drawer.

Manners – and more, compassion – demanded that we allow Hastings to assert his hospitality by serving us more of his near-Arabic coffee. With pulses racing, we eventually took our leave, thanking him for all he had done, for us and for Gabriel.

'It is I who need to thank you,' he told us. 'For years I have longed to speak of that boy. It was good to say his name, even if your coming has meant that his name is now the only possession of his I have left.'

'The family will, I am sure, wish to thank you themselves.'

'They know where to find me.'

We shook hands and turned to go, but I hesitated, and looked back up at the old man.

'Will you be all right?' I asked. 'Is there anything we can do for you?'

'There is nothing you can do for me,' he answered gently, and the door closed against us, the house again a faceless presence.

'That is not entirely true,' Holmes muttered to himself, and stopped in the high street to send a long and carefully worded telegram to the parish's bishop, to the effect that one of his flock was in need of episcopy and succour.

We found the next London train to be in slightly less than an hour, and as one side of the waiting area was occupied by a weary woman with three small children and the other by an aged deaf couple, the noise precluded easy conversation. We retired to a nearby public house, ordered food and alcohol to modify the effects of the coffee that was coursing through our veins, and settled into a private corner with the musings of the young second lieutenant.

Both of us gave but a glancing look at the final pages. The agony of those entries demanded an attitude on the part of the reader that neither Holmes nor I felt capable of summoning at the moment; we were seeking facts, and although there were names there, none were immediately informative. Holmes turned to the entries dated February, skimmed through a self-consciously laconic account of battle and a rather more detailed description of the joys of the behind-the-lines delousing baths, and then went back to the front line to the night before a 'push.' The next entry was dated sixteen days later, with the notation, 'In hospital'.

Here we were introduced to Hélène, but as an introduction it left a great deal to be desired. The young man had spent a mere two weeks away from his journal, but during that time his life had changed so completely, it would seem that he could scarcely remember his previous existence. A good part of that, no doubt, was the consequence of having all but died in what he had so feelingly called 'cream-of-man soup'. His nerves were, as the diary put it, 'pretty funk', and the shaky handwriting, which I had seen earlier on the field postcard, reflected the state of his mind.

Gabriel Hughenfort's brush with death, however, was only a part of his transformation – or perhaps, was only the act of demolition that cleared the way for the next stage. For by the time he set indelible pencil to paper again, his mind and his heart had already grown up anew around the woman whose face he had first seen bent over his stretcher. He wrote:

It makes me smile, to think that at the first sight Hélène I thought she was a man. Her back was to me, of course – no one looking into her eyes would ever make that mistake, no matter how scrambled his brains! – and she was wearing a heavy leather jacket with sheepskin at the collar. Then she turned to me, checking that I wasn't going to be thrown to the floor when we hit a pothole, and thus undo all the work the bearers had gone to. I've never seen eyes like that, green as the hills she was raised in. Heaven only knows what she saw. I could've been a Chinaman for all she could tell, or old as her father or ugly as sin. I was clotted with France, hair to bootlace, and stinking of battle.

His description went on, the only references to her identity or appearance so obscured by infatuation as to be useless. She was green-eyed and tall, and strong enough to lift a grown man into the ambulance, but everything else was poetry and song. One could not even be certain that Hélène was her given name and not a lover's affectionate substitute for an unbearably ordinary, even ugly, true name.

Finding the VAD driver behind 'the face that launched a thousand ships' (the young man's rather hackneyed phrase which had made me suspicious of the woman's true name) was going to take some doing. I thought I might know where to begin, however, and as Holmes glanced at his watch and made to go, I proposed, 'Shall I take Hélène, and you the major?'

'As usual, Russell, you speak the very words on my tongue. And Simpson's at eight to compare notes?'

I glanced down at my travel-worn dress and the gloves that badly wanted cleaning. 'If we must, but I shall have to go by my flat to retrieve some clothes.'

'Give my regards to the Qs' was all he said. He, after all, should have to make a detour to one of his boltholes to exchange his own clothing, so I could not complain.

We took our seats on the train and spent the trip with the Hughenfort diary on our knees, but made few notes. We arrived in London, claimed the bags we'd left there, and went our separate ways.

My taxi deposited me in front of the modernistic block of flats in Bloomsbury in which I had taken a furnished suite of rooms several years before, and somehow never bothered to replace with a more permanent pied-à-terre. Or a more comfortable one – I always forgot, when I'd been away for a while, how awful the place actually was, all chrome tubes and glass. It had matched perfectly the persona I was assuming at the time of the original let, but was, I realised suddenly, a ridiculous place to maintain on the off chance I might need to act the social butterfly in the future. Too, the furniture the actual owners had chosen was beginning to look decidedly out of date. Time for a change, I thought, and dropped my bags on the floor.

A gentle knock followed by the rattle of a key in the lock told me the doorman had informed my housekeeping couple of my arrival. I greeted the Quimbys, husband and wife, and apologised for not warning them of my arrival.

'In fact,' I said, 'I asked the doorman to let you be. I'm only here for a change of clothing; no need to turn up the radiators and buy milk for that.'

But Mrs Q was already unloading a picnic hamper to make tea, and I submitted to her sense of propriety.

There was hot water for a bath, and the clothes hanging in the large and ornate bedroom were free of moth and must. I sorted through them, mildly grumbling at the change in hem-lengths over the past two years, and noticed that they had been recently gone over with brush and iron. Mrs Q had to be bored, caring for a household of ghosts, but I did not know that I could do much to change that, not with this place. I couldn't even ask how they spent their days, since both would be offended at my concern. It simply Wasn't Done.

The next time I passed through the kitchen I put my head around the corner into the portion given over to a butler's pantry. Q shot to his feet, a polishing cloth in one hand and one of my shoes in the other.

'Does your wife's cousin Freddy Bell still keep his finger on London properties?' I asked him.

'Well, yes, I believe he does, mum.'

'Good. I'd like to get out of this place, set up an establishment of my own. Maybe you and he could put your heads together – along with Mrs Quimby, of course – and see if there's anything on the market just now. House or flat, but larger than this, with quarters for you and Mrs Q. We'll probably decorate it ourselves – and *not* like this place.'

A whisper of approval slipped past his professional face at my final phrase; I gave him a sympathetic smile and left him to his polishing.

It took me a while on the telephone (an instrument of white and gilt) but I succeeded in locating the woman I sought. She was a dispatch rider in London at the time I had met her, a suffragette doing war service, but she had been a driver in Belgium until a stray shell had hit her ambulance, killing the other VAD attendant and the patients they were transporting. She herself had been made deaf by the explosion, and although a certain amount of hearing had returned, she blithely declared that near-deafness was an advantage to a London driver. Having ridden pillion with her once and been fully aware of the curses on our trail, I could only agree.

Gwyneth Claypool was, her colleague who answered the telephone told me, currently in a meeting with the head teachers of several schools, which was due to finish at four o'clock but would probably go on until closer to five. She gave me the address and rang off. I raided my wardrobe for a dress suitable both for confronting feminists and sitting in the women's dining room at Simpson's, had Q ring for a taxi, and left, promising to return for further discussions on the house question as soon as I could.

London was cold and inhospitable, a dreary rain splashing against the taxi's curtains and dribbling off of the passing hats and umbrellas. At the address I had been given, an assistant guarding the door refused to let me out of the freezing-cold entrance foyer and wouldn't think of disturbing the meeting with a message. So I took a seat in the least draughty corner I could find, and slowly congealed inside my fur-lined coat.

Gwyneth's voice half an hour later crackled through the building and rescued me from my icy perch. It had always been loud, I suspect even before her deafness set in, and the silent building quivered in reaction; the tinkle of shattering icicles seemed to follow it. She left the meeting as no doubt she had begun it, commanding action.

'—and I think you'll find the situation much improved. Girls that age need a goal, or they seek out all kinds of trouble. We'll meet again in the new year, see how it's coming along.'

I unfolded myself from my cramped huddle and stumbled forward on numb feet to intercept her. She spotted me, squinted in uncertainty; then her face opened in a wide smile and she boomed a greeting across the echoing space.

'Hello, Gwyn,' I returned.

'Mary! What are you doing here? Looking for me? But why in heaven's name didn't you come and find me – you must be in an advanced stage of ice cube-ism. Come along; we'll find a warm corner with drinks in it and bemoan the state of the world.'

Merely being in Gwyneth Claypool's presence tended to have a warming effect on a person, even before she thrust into my hand a drink she'd bullied the barman into constructing. It looked like pond scum, smelt of the Indies, and went down with a jolt that tingled the toes and lifted the scalp.

'Lord, Gwyn!' I gasped. 'What is this?'

'Rum butter. Does the trick, doesn't it? Wish I'd known about it in 1914 – if we'd issued the men rum in this form, they'd have overrun the Germans by Christmas.'

I loosened my coat and removed my gloves and hat, and set about getting the drink inside me, a quarter-teaspoon at a sip, while Gwyn and I caught each other up on our lives since we'd last met nearly three years earlier.

'Still married?' she shouted, raising the eyebrows of the other customers.

'Indeed I am. And you?'

'No time, no time for all the nonsense.'

So I asked her what she did have time for and she told me of her many projects related to the rights of women, and we talked of that and this and of times past and the feebleness of the present. No, she no longer sped around London on her racing motorcycle, she'd been run over by a lorry one day when she hadn't heard it coming and her mother made her stop. And no, she wasn't hurt, a broken wrist was all but Mum was seventy now and anxious, so the motorcycle resided in the country – or rather the original machine's replacement did – where she could roar up and down to her heart's content.

Eventually our drinks were empty, seconds refused, and she asked me what I'd wanted of her.

'I need to find one of the VAD drivers who was serving in France in 1918, somewhere west of Reims. She might've been French, although what she'd have been doing fetching our lot I can't think. The only name I have for her is Hélène, and even that may be a nickname. She had green eyes and was tall; that's all I know.'

'Green eyes sounds like Charlie, but she was a Scottish girl, or was she American?'

'French-Canadian, maybe?'

'She could have been. Yes, I think—no, I'm confusing her with another girl who was killed in an attack. Her name was something like Helen, but she had dark eyes. Pretty thing. Bled to death from a piece of shrapnel in the throat.'

The room cringed in reaction, and two customers beat a hasty retreat. Gwyn noticed, and lowered her voice.

'Sorry. I forget. Why do you need to find this driver?'

'A friend is trying to find what happened to a nephew of his who was killed in '18, not satisfied with the official story, and the boy's diary mentions this Hélène in a manner that indicates they knew each other. She drove him out to the first-aid post.'

'Love at first sight, eh?'

'So it seems. But because he changed regiments and moved around, it's hard to track down fellow soldiers who might have known him well. We thought he might've written this Hélène letters that gave an idea of his situation. The family just wants to know.'

'And the next step's a séance, is that it? Let me ask around, see

314

what I can come up with. She may've come after I had to leave – probably did, in fact, or I'd've met her. I'll give my replacement there a ring, see if green eyes mean anything to her.'

'That's great, Gwyn. Thanks so much.'

'So who's the family?'

I hesitated, then said, 'Can I tell you that after everything's cleared up? It's only, sometimes publicity raises dust and makes it hard to finish.'

'Fair enough. If you promise to bring along this mysterious husband of yours. Ought to meet him, now that he seems permanent.'

The image of Holmes and Gwyn Claypool circling each other like a pair of wary dogs flickered through my mind, and I had to laugh.

'No promises, Gwyn, but I'll see what I can do.'

I glanced at my wristwatch, then looked more closely in astonishment: We had been at our chat for better than two hours, and if I was to meet Holmes, I would have to scurry. I gave her a card with the flat's telephone number written on it (an extension of which line rang in the downstairs servants' quarters) and resumed my outer clothing. We left the building, embraced, and climbed into separate cabs.

Holmes was not at Simpson's when I arrived, which did not surprise me. I went to their Ladies to tidy my hair-pins, then allowed the maitre d' to show me to one of Holmes' preferred tables.

Half an hour later, Holmes had not arrived, and I was glowering in my seat. At forty minutes my embarrassment and irritation began to crumple under concern. At forty-five minutes the maitre d' came up to the table with a slip of paper in his hand. It read:

KINDLY INFORM MISS RUSSELL THAT HER COMPANION IS AT HIS BROTHER'S. PLEASE TELL HER THAT SHE MUST *NOT* TAKE THE FIRST AVAILABLE TAXI.

The man before me must have seen my face and feared I was about to succumb to some ladylike vapours, but I brushed away his hand and reached for my possessions.

The only reason to avoid the first convenient taxi was for fear it would be a trap. And the only reason to fear a trap – as well as the explanation for why Holmes was not here – was that an attack had already been attempted.

CHAPTER TWENTY-FOUR

I DID, AS IT TURNED OUT, accept the first taxi that presented itself, reasoning that if a cab has just pulled to the kerb when a person comes out of a restaurant door, and if that cab then offloads a Member of Parliament, his wife, and his sister, then a person can feel relatively confident that its driver has not been hovering up the street waiting to pounce upon one. I did take the precaution of giving the driver the wrong address, and splashed through an ill-lit alley to Mycroft's building on Pall Mall.

I trotted up the steps, shunned the lift in favour of the stairway, and pounded on Mycroft's door, slightly breathless. I felt his presence arrive on the other side, where he paused to look through the secret peephole in the centre of the knocker, and then the bolt slid. I slipped past him, shedding raincoat and hat as I went, not needing to ask where Holmes was because I could see his stockinged feet sticking out from the end of the comfortable sofa.

The six-foot-plus man laid out on Mycroft's long settee had at some point since the morning changed into a Frenchman. From his silk-stockinged feet to the sleek part of his hair, his trousers, shirt-front, and even the still-attached moustaches were unmistakably French. He'd even, I noticed from a glance at the suit's coat that lay over the arm of a nearby chair, dug out his Légion d'Honneur. It was honestly come by – Holmes avoided a display of unearned ribbons when he could, even as disguise. The most English things about him at the moment were the squat crystal glass balanced on his chest and the India-rubber ice-bag from the Army and Navy Stores that rested on his head.

A good deal of my apprehension deflated abruptly, leaving me dizzy with relief. Just bruises, then, and perhaps a cracked rib, judging by the care with which he drew breath. And a splint on one finger.

Mycroft placed a glass of brandy in my hand and pushed me gently into a chair. I put the glass aside and sat on the edge of the upholstery.

'You needn't look so mother-hennish, Russell,' Holmes said crossly. 'There's nothing here that some strapping won't take care of.'

'What did they use?' A length of pipe, unless the cut on his jaw came by a fall.

'Brass knuckles and boots, for the most part. One of them picked up a cobble-stone.' He gestured at the jaw. 'But the other ordered him to drop it. They weren't aiming to murder me, just to render me *hors de combat*. Or to warn me off, but if so, the small detail of precisely what it was off which I was being warned was left too late, and omitted entirely when the local constable came pounding and whistling to the rescue.'

'Not robbery?'

'If so, it was secondary to the pleasure of knocking me about.' He shifted in the pillows, and winced. 'If you are not going to drink that excellent brandy, Russell, I shall happily offer it a home.'

His speech and his eyes seemed clear, and the head wounds minor. I handed him the glass. He took a mouthful and made a face; since I was certain that any brandy kept by Mycroft would not make him grimace, I added a loosened tooth to my mental list.

The brandy settled him. After a minute, he went on without prompting.

'Two men, one of them a gentleman or something very near – and yes, I am fully cognisant of the absurdity of that statement, but his voice through its muffling mask had the accents of authority and education, and he commanded the other to drop the stone with the bark of an officer. Unfortunately, that phrase, "Drop it", were the pair's only words – not sufficient to identify the speaker's origins or identity.' He paused to take another swallow, reducing the glass to half its original level, then resumed. 'The authoritative individual was a fit man of around five feet ten or eleven inches – I fear the alley was too dimly lit to allow for any more detail. He had done a certain amount of boxing, I should say, but like most amateur pugilists, he was not entirely familiar with the sensation of hitting with a set of brass knuckles.

'The other man, the muscles of the team, was more street fighter than pugilist. Certainly he was no respecter of the Queensberry rules. He was more than comfortable with a brass weight wrapped between his fingers. Shorter, heavy-set as a stevedore, smelling of beer and bad teeth, wearing a working man's boots.'

Even the sharpest and most disciplined of minds tends to wander somewhat under the influence of a pummelling followed by several ounces of alcohol. Holmes, I thought, could use a gentle firming-up.

'Was the muscle local talent, from London? Or a country boy?'

That made him focus. The confusion at the back of his eyes dissipated as he concentrated on the memories, reaching through the tumult of attack to retrieve the more subtle sensations.

'There must have been three of them, in all, with the third in charge of transport. They were waiting down the street from the door I'd gone through an hour earlier.'

'How did they find you?'

'They may have ears within the War Offices. I had been interviewing there all day, in my guise of a retired French colonel seeking candidates for posthumous awards, and at least three clerks had the opportunity of overhearing the conversation I had with Alistair at Justice Hall regarding our progress, during which I chanced to mention my destination for the evening. I shall give you their names, Mycroft; see if you can turn up any past wrongdoing among them. In any case, my attackers waited up the street, saw which way I was going, and drove past me. As I walked, I noticed two men, their heads ducked against the rain, dash from a private car into a doorway. When I had gone past, they came back onto the street and one of them – the muscles – literally tackled me from behind and ran me into an alleyway. We ended up in the entrance to a yard, with fisticuffs among the dustbins.

'Mycroft,' he interrupted his narrative to say. 'Do you think you might ring down for that light supper you offered me earlier? Soup or a boiled egg for me, although Russell no doubt could do with something more substantial, having had dinner at Simpson's snatched out from under her nose. Where was I? The dust bins, yes.

'The muscular individual was quite aware that a blow to the head induces sufficient disorientation to allow for a more leisurely treatment to the rest of the victim's anatomy. And so it proved.

Against him alone I might have stood; the two of them soon had me down and were, as they say, putting the boots in.

'The muscles was at the most seven inches over five feet, but solid. Wearing an Army greatcoat, newer boots with stiffened toes, steel perhaps – but no, his smell was of city streets and the docks, not of manure and grass. A city tough. He'll have a black eye, but no obvious marks on his hands – he wore gloves.

'The other: not, perhaps, a gentleman in the strict sense, but a man of education. A schoolmaster or high-ranking clerk, perhaps a gentleman's gentleman. Homburg-type rather than cloth cap, although they'd abandoned the actual headgear and pulled on stocking caps, or balaclavas, when they came out of the doorway. His overcoat was good, heavy wool, dark colour but not I think actually black. Neck scarf, also dark, gloves that gleamed in the light, polished lace-up boots. A city suit, I'd say, under the overcoat. No facial hair that I could tell, but I'd have missed a trimmed beard or a small moustache. The gentleman will have a limp: I gave his left knee a good one when I was down. And his overcoat is missing a button.'

With a smile of satisfaction, he worked a cautious hand beneath Mycroft's borrowed dressing gown to the pocket of the shirt, and brought out a silk handkerchief, which he held out to me. I knelt down at the low table with it, and allowed it to unroll. A round of horn dropped out. Wordlessly, Mycroft brought me a small leather kit containing powders, brushes, and insufflators. I raised three partial prints from the surface, and allowed Mycroft to put the object in a safe place, away from the attentions of his housekeeper.

A rattle in the service lift heralded our much-delayed evening meal, with its mixture of invalid food and hearty labourer's fare (for Mycroft, whose brain sweated mightily for king and country).

Mycroft grumbled that the roast beef was dry, but as it was close on to midnight I privately reckoned we were fortunate not to be served shoe leather and yesterday's sprouts.

Holmes looked more substantial after his soup and boiled egg, and I decided not to press for putting him to bed. Not that I would have succeeded; the most I could have hoped for was that he would occupy the sofa while Mycroft and I retreated to our beds. However, I judged that he would stand up to further conversation, so I told him how far I'd got in tracking down the green-eyed Hélène. Which admittedly was not far, so that with the social aspects of my hours with Gwyn left out, my narrative was brief.

'And you, Holmes? Did your crawl through the War Offices records bring you anything? Apart from a beating, that is?'

'Sidney Darling was a staff officer in France, although when I telephoned to Justice this afternoon, neither Alistair nor Marsh could say that Darling and Gabriel ever came into contact over there.'

'I have to say, neither of your attackers resembles Darling in the slightest.'

'Another name did come up,' Holmes continued. 'Also a staff major, also posted to that section of France. Ivo Hughenfort.'

'Alistair's cousin?'

'The same.' He closed his eyes and let his head fall against the cushions, leaving me to glance at Mycroft, see his questioning raised eyebrow, and offer a word of explanation.

'Ivo would be fourth in line to the title,' I said. 'After the boy Thomas, then Alistair.'

'Ah,' Mycroft said, threading his fingers together across his substantial waistcoat. 'I see.'

* * *

Mycroft and I between us succeeded in bullying Holmes to take to the guest-room bed, and we passed a restless night. In the morning Holmes looked worse but felt better, as the bruises coloured richly while the bone and muscle beneath them eased somewhat. Or so he claimed, although his movement remained cautious and he chewed a lot of aspirin. More telling, he did not insist on venturing out into the City in search of further information. He settled before the fire with another heap of unread newspapers and a fistful of tobacco, and dismissed us from his mind.

Mycroft climbed into his overcoat and left at his usual hour – the world of Intelligence never rests – and I rang the Qs to ask that they telephone to Mycroft's number if Gwyn came up with a name and number for me. I then went out myself (rather nervously eyeing all passers-by) to examine closely the site of Holmes' assault. I spent a sodden and dirty half hour in the alleyway that failed to reward me with a dropped calling card or conveniently traceable bespoke hat or boot, then another forty minutes knocking on doors to confirm that at seven o'clock on a wet Tuesday evening there had been no busy pubs or nosey neighbours to witness the event. Without having been set upon by thugs, I returned to Mycroft's flat.

Holmes started up from his snooze on the sofa-cushions and made as if his cold pipe had just that moment gone out. I assembled a pot of tea and reported on nothing.

At one o'clock the telephone rang, with Mr Q's voice shouting down the line to give me a name and address. 'The young lady who telephoned to you asked that you be told that Miss Cobb is not on the telephone, but that she should be happy to receive callers today, or in the morning before ten o'clock. I regret that was the sum total of her message, Miss Russell.'

'That's fine, Mr Quimby. Thank you for phoning the information to me.'

'My pleasure, madam.'

I put the receiver up on its hook and folded the address into my pocket. 'I'm going out for a while, Holmes. Gwyn Claypool found a woman who might know a VAD driver named Hélène.'

'Shall I come?'

'I don't see why. Girl talk will, I fear, prevail.'

'Very well,' he said, but he discarded his newspaper in any event and climbed to his feet. 'I believe in that case I shall spend the afternoon at the baths. Steam and an expert massage are the only means of dispersing a beating. I shall, however, need you to do up my shoes first.'

He dressed, I tied his bootlaces, and we parted.

Dorothea Cobb was the classic VAD ambulance driver, a person I'd have recognised instantly as such if I had happened upon her in the street. The War had presented itself at precisely the right time in her life, when the tedious necessity of marriage was pressing in on her and the excuse of a daredevil lark in the mud of France could be justified as patriotism. She'd started in Belgium, moved down to the Somme, and spent four years wrestling stretchers, staunching wounds, dodging shrapnel, and sleeping with her gas-mask to hand; although she'd come away thin, scarred, gassed, and hearing the groans of the wounded in her dreams, the last five years of civilian life had proven stale indeed.

Dorothea – for such she insisted I call her, two minutes into our acquaintance – was the elder of two girls in a moderately well-to-do family. Her sister, eight years younger, had recently come out, snagged a handsome guardsman, and married, leaving the spinster at home with her parents, dressed in a pair of defiant trousers but sporting her hair in two thick coils over her ears. I wore my own hair long for the convenience of it, but I thought she might be unwilling to face the battle of bobbing hers.

Thus I found her, dutiful on the surface but seething beneath, and gloriously happy for the opportunity of drawing the half-dozen albums of photographs, sketches, letters, and newspaper clippings from the de facto war shrine that occupied one corner of the family sitting room. The room itself was stodgy and stuffy and smelt of dog; Dorothea was a gust of cold air, setting the lace mantel-cloth and fringed lampshades to fluttering. As she bent so eagerly over the photographs, her face came to life, and I wondered how long it would be before she fled the antimacassars. (One could only hope that she wasn't driven to murder her parents first.)

'This is the tent we worked out of when I first got there, and that, if you can believe it, was my ambulance. October 1915. Used to be a butcher's van; I had to paint out the name because I didn't think it a very fortunate image for the poor boys being shoved inside. But I'm sure we didn't have any girls with green eyes in Belgium. The next spring, let's see.' She turned some pages with scarred fingers – nurse's fingers, owing to the sepsis transmitted from their patients' wounds – and I stifled a sigh. At this rate, I should still be here at teatime tomorrow.

'One girl, she was called Charlie, her eyes were green. Yes, this is she.' Dorothea shifted the album so I could see the open, grinning figure, bursting with vitality and the joy of being alive and needed. Her hair was short, curls springing out from under her cap, her light eyes sparkled at the camera, and I could easily imagine a young noble man falling head over heels in love at first glance. 'She died a couple of months after this was taken – the dormitory took a direct hit in '16 and she bled to death. Poor thing; how the boys loved her.' Not Charlie, then. Dorothea turned a page, and another. Nursing sisters in white; surgical wards; two wan doctors sprawled on supply crates with blood on their coats and glasses of beer in their hands; a line of drivers dressed in dusty greatcoats, knee-high boots, and gas-masks, resembling some monstrous insect race; a photograph of a ruined village with a queue of men winding through it, blinded by gas, each with his hands on the next man's shoulders. The War.

Dorothea was seeing only familiar, even loved faces. 'Matilda – I wonder what could have happened to her? Wanda married one of the men she carried from the Front. The twins – identical they were, and didn't they have some fun with the doctors? Did Bunny—? No, her eyes were blue, I'm sure they were. And I heard she married, too. Elsie . . . no. Joan. She died, in Cairo. Gabrielle – no, she was a titch of a thing, could hardly hold one end of a stretcher on her own, though she was a fantastic driver, once we raised the seat for her. You said your driver carried a man?'

'So I was told.'

More pages turned, Dorothea contributing interesting but useless tit-bits about the *personae dramatis* depicted on them. We were now in the autumn of 1917, and I was forced to admit that this would be a lost cause.

And then: 'Wait a minute.' She bent over a small snapshot showing a group of laughing women in greasy overalls and cloth caps, then put the book onto my knees and went to fetch a magnifying glass even Holmes would have been proud to own. She took back the book and leant over it again. 'Yes, I remember her. We only met a handful of times, when we were transferring wounded; she must have worked farther down the line than I did.

But she certainly had green eyes, green as an emerald. How could I have forgotten her? She was as tall as I am, taller even, and she used to wear this fur-lined aviator's jacket under her standard coat – not regulation, but by that time who bothered? I remember admiring it one freezing day, and she told me her brother had given it her; it was what the Canadian flyboys wore.'

Gabriel's diary had made reference to a sheepskin collar. 'Do you remember her name?'

'Her name, her name, what was her name?' she mused, staring into the magnified features. 'A boy's name. Not Charlie, and not Tom – she was in Italy by then. Phil – that's it! Phil, they called her. A nickname, of course; everyone went by nicknames out there. Made a person feel like a schoolgirl again, instead of an old hag who hadn't washed her hair in a fortnight and who walked around with unspeakable things on her boots. They called me Gigi. From my surname, you know? Cobb – horse – gee-gee. Some nicknames were better than others,' she added apologetically. I had silently to agree.

'But what might Phil's name have been?' I asked.

'I somehow think that in her case it was more of a shortening of her proper name.'

Philomena? I wondered. Phillida—Oh, surely not the same name as his aunt; that would be too odd.

'Perhaps Philippa?' she suggested after a moment. 'That seems right somehow.'

As a coincidence, it was not as sharp as Phillida would have been. However, even that close a similarity to the name of a young aunt might explain Gabriel's preference for 'Hélène', whether it was invented as a romantic paean to her beauty (*Is this the face that launched a thousand ambulances?*) or the girl's middle name.

I now had a first name to attach to Gabriel's green-eyed driver. But 'Gigi', it seemed, was not through with her.

'Philippa, yes, and an Irish last name to go with those eyes. O'something. O'Hanlan, O'Flannigan, O'Neill . . .'

I hoped she did not plan on working through the Dublin telephone directory, and reined in my impatience.

'Mary,' she said. I thought she was addressing me, but: 'O'Meary. That was her name. I've always been good with names – I knew hers was in there somewhere. Philippa O'Meary, although she was no more Irish-looking than I am, other than her eyes. And I do remember, she once slung a man over her back all the way through the communications trenches to get him out. Big girl. Slim, but big bones. What you might call farm stock. Not English, though.'

'What, French?' I couldn't picture that.

'American, I think. No, I'm a liar – she was from Canada. Now why do I think that? That aviator's jacket?' She thought for a moment, then shook her head. 'It's gone. May come back, but I picture her as Canadian. She was based near Reims. Had a couple of sisters, I think – lots younger, like mine; we agreed that we hoped it would be over before they could join up. Black hair, she had, shiny and with a little curl to it. She wore it short. Had dimples when she laughed. Good boots – Now why should that come back to me? Someone in her family was a shoemaker. What else can I drag out of this grab-bag of a mind of mine? Fearless driver, had bullet holes – actual bullet holes, not just shrapnel – in her ambulance. Lent me a pair of gloves once – she had two and my hands were ice; I returned them through a friend.

'And do you know, I think she had a ring? We weren't supposed to fraternise, and of course you couldn't be married, but by that time things were too desperate for anyone to pay much attention, so long as you were careful. But I remember the ring – not a gemstone or anything, just a bit of silver, but she wore it on a chain, to keep it hidden. That must have been the last time I saw her, that last summer of the War. It was hot, and the wounded were suffering so, and she looked dreadful herself. The top button of her blouse had come unbuttoned – or perhaps she'd undone it herself, it was that stifling, and one of the nurses said something to her about proper uniform. "Proper uniform", I ask you, with crawling out of a hot bunk after two hours' sleep and working at a run in a world of dust and blood – and the smell! But if Sister had spotted that ring on the chain, Phil would've been on the next boat home.

'Although come to think of it, she may have gone back before the end, since I don't remember seeing her after that week. She wouldn't have been the only one who didn't last the summer, that's for sure.'

'You said she looked sick?'

'Not so much sick as unhappy. Now if that doesn't sound daft, considering the circs we were in, I know. But when the nurse said something about the chain she was wearing, Phil didn't seem embarrassed, like she'd been caught out with a beau. She seemed . . . Well, I guess the nurse was afraid Phil was about to collapse, because she sort of grabbed for her, but Phil shook her off and went back for the next stretcher. And that was the end of the discussion. So . . . maybe her beau didn't make it through.'

Either sensitivity or long experience led Dorothea to the same conclusion that I had reached.

'When would this have been?' I asked her.

She returned to the album as a reference point, and when that proved too indefinite in its dates, she handed it to me along with the powerful glass and took up her personal journal. I studied the photograph, finding it more evocative than informative. A smudge of face, a tuft of dark hair springing out from under the sexless cloth cap, and a rangy shape beneath the shapeless overalls; the only thing I could have said for sure was that her stance shouted self-confidence and strength, and perhaps even a degree of humour, although I couldn't have explained where that last impression came from. Several minutes passed before Dorothea spoke. 'It looks to have been the end of July or the first part of August. Sorry, that's the nearest I can make it.'

Gabriel Hughenfort had been arrested on the twenty-sixth of July and executed at dawn on August the third.

'Where would records of the VAD drivers be kept now?' I asked her.

She wrote an address for me, handed me the paper, closed her photograph album with regret. 'Ask for Millicent,' she suggested. 'Some of the other girls who work there are dead useless, but Millie was a nurse. She'll help you.'

She walked with me to the door, and pulled her knit cardigan more tightly around her as the cold pushed in. I thanked her, for the third or fourth time, and went down the steps.

Halfway down the walk, I stopped. When I turned, she had not moved, in spite of the cold. I spoke without thinking.

'You ought to take up mountain-climbing, or flying,' I urged her. 'Or go on a world tour. Let your sister care for your parents for a while.'

She looked startled, and then in an instant the jaunty daredevil VAD driver of her photo album was standing in the doorway, her head tossed to one side and a grin of schoolgirl mischief on her thirty-year-old face.

'You're absolutely right, Mary. I think I've been good far too long.'

330

And with a wink of understanding, she stepped back inside and gently shut the door. Somehow, I doubted her hair would remain long for many more weeks.

Thursday morning, with Holmes sufficiently recovered that he could do up his own shoe-laces and amble off for a second immersion in the Turkish baths, I set off to trace the green-eyed driver, whose name might be in doubt but who had become a clear personality in my mind.

Millicent, unfortunately, was absent, and the 'other girls' proved as useless as Dorothea had predicted. I dismissed them with empty thanks and pored over the records on my own. By the time the teacart came through in the middle of the morning, I had filthy hands and confirmation of the name. By lunchtime my back ached and I could trace her movements up and down the Front with some reliability. By the afternoon tea break my head was pounding and I knew where she was – or at any rate, where she came from in 1916, and what Philippa Helen O'Meary had given as her home address upon leaving France in August 1918.

Unfortunately, that address was in Canada.

CHAPTER TWENTY-FIVE

I CROSSED LONDON AT ITS wet and dreariest, let myself into Mycroft's flat, found it empty with no indication that either Holmes brother had been there since the morning, and decided that the cure for heaviness of spirit and headache – or at least the only cure to hand – was cleanliness. And as Mycroft had recently installed an elaborate and modernistic shower-bath (I believe it was becoming too much of an effort to heave himself out of the bathtub, although I would never have said anything of the sort), I thought I might give it a try.

With trepidation, I stepped into the closet of this technological wonder and opened all four sprays. I stepped out of it a fervent convert. And beyond the invigoration was the discovery that long hair washed while standing upright did not become the usual mass of tangles. I was humming as I ran the comb through it.

My hair was little more than damp when my companions returned – together, which indicated that Holmes had re-entered the investigation. I watched as he divested himself of coat and hat, and was pleased to see a near-normal range of motion. He had been very lucky; for the moment, all was well.

Dinner – sans business – and a fire, tobacco and brandy for the brothers, and we were ready for work. I sat on the floor with my arms around my drawn-up knees, and watched them speak. Mycroft was, in all things, slow and thorough, where his younger brother flew straight to the core. Together they were formidable, and I could not imagine that many details got past them unnoticed.

It was Holmes who set aside his impatience in order to tell me what they had discovered during the day. That amounted to: One of the clerks who was in a position to know more or less where one inquisitive Frenchman would be at seven o'clock on Tuesday evening had, interestingly enough, left his desk in the middle of the following morning, reporting that he had been taken ill. He had not gone home, however, and enquiries at his doctor's surgery had drawn a blank as well.

The button Holmes had torn from his attacker's coat had been traced to a Jermyn Street tailor, who said the button could have come from any of a hundred such coats the firm had made over the last seven years. The list included nearly a third of the men who had been at Justice for the shooting party, including Sidney Darling, the Marquis, and both Germans, as well as the late duke, Marsh's brother Henry.

The Army records for Sidney Darling gave the picture of a competent officer who took great care to avoid the front lines. Staff officers invariably were granted a greater freedom of movement than line officers and in the spring of 1918 Darling had been based less than twenty miles from Gabriel Hughenfort's new regiment. Because Gabriel's records had been lost – by accident or malice – there was no telling who was responsible for his transfer to the hard-pressed unit he had joined that March, but certainly Darling had been in a position to slip one more such transfer into the machinery of war.

Similarly, he could have been the red-tab major who came to see the condemned man the night before Gabriel was taken out and shot by his comrades. To slip away from headquarters for a few hours in the middle of the night, particularly during the chaos of the summer's shifting Front, would have presented small risk.

However, Ivo Hughenfort's position as a suspect held many of the same points. With his family name to stand upon, he had quickly assumed a place in Paris collating information and writing daily briefings for the Commander-in-Chief. Ivo had been in a position to watch Gabriel, and indeed to nudge him from one place to another, although there was no immediate indication that he had done so, nor was there any sign of an impromptu trip out of Paris in the early hours of August the third.

The records, however, were both voluminous and ill-organised for our purposes. Five years after Armistice, clerks were still filing, and there was nothing to say that another Hughenfort had not been in the wings, a South African son of Philip Peter, say, or the Australian Ralph.

The key element in Gabriel's death, the letter that had driven the nail into his coffin, had been the letter from Haig confirming the divisional commander's sentence of death. That, too, had vanished along with Gabriel's records, and copies of either letter had yet to come to light.

'I've an appointment with Haig himself tomorrow morning,' Mycroft said. 'I cannot imagine he will have forgot a letter such as that.'

I wished I had his faith in the memory, and the sense of moral responsibility, of the commanding officer in question. Still, if the man knew anything about the condemnatory letter, Mycroft was better suited to prise it out of him than any person I knew.

Except, perhaps, one other.

'Have we heard any news of Mah – Marsh, I mean to say?'

'I took advantage of Mycroft's offices this afternoon to place a trunk call to Justice,' Holmes replied. 'He is having a bad time of it, with some blood-poisoning in one arm, but he retains sufficient strength for his voice to be heard from across the room and down the telephone, demanding that we report to Justice Hall without delay or else he will come after us and take matters into his own hands. I quote.'

'Sounds like he's better. Now, do you wish to know who Gabriel's VAD friend was?'

They did, and I described how I had traced Philippa Helen O'Meary through the dusty papers of the VAD. As with most aspects of an investigation, the telling took considerably less time than the doing, and lacked any shred of the dramatic.

At the end of my recitation, Canada seemed farther away than ever.

'I shall write to her immediately,' I concluded. 'Or, as soon as I can compose a letter. How exactly does one ask a complete stranger, "Were you once in love with a young soldier, and did he leave you any letters that might incriminate those who arranged his death?" It is not going to be an easy letter to write.'

I stared into the fire for a minute or so, turning over phrases in my mind, before I slowly became aware that I was seated within a fairly ringing silence. I looked up, and found the two Holmes brothers engaged in a wordless conversation over my head. My husband broke it off first, to lower his gaze to mine.

'Russell,' he said. At the first touch of that gentle, affectionate voice, I nearly leapt to my feet and planted my back against the nearest wall: When Holmes stoops to wheedle, God help us all.

'My dear Russell, how right you are. As always. This is precisely the sort of sensitive query that demands a more personal touch.'

'What do you mean?' I asked, bristling with suspicion while trying to see from which direction the threat was coming.

'Why, Russell, I am merely agreeing with you. It would indeed been excellent idea to confront this O'Meary woman to her face when you ask for the return of Gabriel's letters.'

Now I really was on my feet. 'Oh, no. Cross the Atlantic and half of America to ask some woman if a British soldier had once confided in her? In November? Are you mad? No. Absolutely not.'

'There's a boat for New York that sails tomorrow afternoon,' Mycroft noted, studying his fingernails.

'Don't be absurd. I'm not going anywhere. Except perhaps Oxford. Yes,' I declared, warming to my theme, 'I think I'll take the train up to Oxford and get back to work on my paper. You two can continue to hunt down your red-tab major if you like, but as far as I'm concerned, Marsh Hughenfort can accept that nice boy Thomas as his heir and hie off back to Palestine. You identify who set Gabriel up, the child will be safe, Marsh and Alistair can go back to their tents, I can go back to my books and Holmes to his beehives. How happy we all will be.'

'You can write your paper on the boat,' Holmes told me. 'You're always complaining that you never have the leisure to work properly. You'll be in New York by the middle of the week, take the train to Toronto Thursday or Friday, and be back on board by the Monday sailing. Two weeks, total, to solve our case. Maybe three.'

'You go.' I felt like a rat cornered by two determined terriers; I was not going down without a fight.

And I did not. Go without a fight that is, although in the end, go I did, and on the Friday boat as Mycroft had said. With hastily packed trunks holding clothes scavenged from my flat and Mycroft's guest-room cupboards, and bearing only the most rudimentary books to keep this fool's journey from being an utter waste of time, I was flung onto the ship as by a tornado, the gangway pulling back almost as soon as I had cleared it. I stood on the vibrating deck to watch England retreat into the fog, knowing that I should be very lucky if this exercise in futility were to cost me only three weeks. I put together a complicated Arabic curse worthy of Ali and gave it to the wind; feeling somewhat better, I went below to find my rooms.

As I was shaking my head at the peculiar selection of out-of-date and unseasonable clothing I had at my disposal, and wondering if I might slip beneath the ship's social eye by keeping to my cabin at mealtimes, a rapid-fire knock sounded at my door. If that was a purser bearing propitiatory flowers from Holmes, I swore under my breath, he'd be fortunate to escape with his head on his shoulders. I went back through the rooms, yanked open the door, and felt as if I'd walked into a solid wall.

It was not a purser, flowers or no. Nor a maid, nor a first officer welcoming me on board, nor a boy with a telegram, nor any of the dozen other likely candidates for disturbing me. It was not even Holmes, whose capacity for appearing where he could not possibly be was unparalleled in human experience.

Standing in the corridor was Iris Sutherland.

'Hallo, Mary. I see by your face that the news I was coming along did not reach you.'

'It most certainly did not.'

'Hardly surprising – I didn't know myself until about six hours ago, and there was some question I'd actually make it. You going to invite me in?'

'Of course, please. Sorry – it just surprised me so. But it's an absolute joy to see you.'

And it was. Suddenly this voyage, and the arduous land journey at the end of it, did not seem so much of a burden on my soul.

'My, my,' she was saying. 'This is posh. They've stuck me into a broom closet seventeen levels below the water-line, said they'd try for something with air when they got sorted out.'

My own arrival was nearly as hastily arranged, but either Mycroft's strings or my own chequebook had kicked me upstairs.

'I'll have a word with the captain,' I told her.

'Don't bother, I already have. Using Marsh's name,' Iris added, with a look of mischief. Yes: The knowledge that they had placed a Hughenfort in steerage would set the feathers flying, all right.

I laughed. 'The next knock on the door will be some gentleman with a lot of gold braid telling me ever so apologetically that a mistake's been made, that my room is a nice cosy broom closet, seventeen levels below the water-line.'

'That's all right, then,' she said, gesturing towards the adjoining room. 'We'll make you up a bed on the sofa.'

'How is Marsh?'

'Spitting mad that the doctor and Ali won't let him out of his bed.'

'I didn't even know until yesterday that he'd taken a turn for the worse.'

'He nearly lost his arm.'

'Iris!'

'They couldn't get the infection down. The doctor wanted to amputate – blood-thirsty idiot – but Ali wouldn't let him. Threatened to amputate the *doctor's* arm, in fact. That shut him up.'

'I can imagine.' Particularly if the threat had been accompanied by a blade and one of Ali's patent glares.

'All it wanted was round-the-clock compresses. Ali and I took turns; the infection centralised and could be lanced after a couple of days. Marsh is weak, but he'll be fine.'

'Holmes said he was going down to see them today or tomorrow. I suppose—' I caught myself: We were still standing, as we had been since I let her in. 'Do you want some tea or coffee or something?'

'I'd like a drink, actually. A good old English gin and tonic. Do you have such a thing, or need we call for it?'

'There should be a drinks cabinet somewhere.'

There was, and although I would have preferred hot tea, I joined her in a G and T. She swallowed, and exhaled in appreciation.

'Yes,' she said, picking up on my last statement. 'Justice Hall is a house divided. Phillida is going berserk. She's got this elaborate ball planned for the fifteenth, absolutely refuses to shift it to the London house; I can see her point – she'd be better to cancel it. At the same time, Alistair won't let anyone but Ogilby into the part of the house where Marsh is, which means the entire wing is effectively cut off from the main block. Sidney is irate, because that means the billiards room and the library are in No-Man's-Land, and they had planned to have a few friends up for the weekend. Alistair won't budge, swears he'll empty a load of bird shot into the billiards room if he hears any movement down there. They believe him.'

As would I, I thought, but only commented, 'Sounds like a fine game of Happy Families.'

'An interesting family, no doubt of that. But, Ali told me your husband was attacked on Tuesday. Was it serious? Was it connected with everything else that's going on?'

'Who knows?' Who knew, in fact, what *was* going on? 'He was fortunate – a constable happened on them before it got past the bruises-and-cracked-ribs stage.'

She pulled a face. 'Still, at his age, even that's no small matter.'

I paused, taken somewhat aback. I rarely thought of Holmes as being of any particular age, much less a great one, but it was true: A beating at twenty is not the same as one at sixty. I wondered if I should have insisted he see a doctor, then dismissed the idea immediately. If he'd needed medical attention, he'd have sought it.

We applied ourselves to our glasses and chatted of nothing in particular – flying lessons, as I recall, with Iris asserting that in a few years we'd be criss-crossing the world's oceans in passenger aeroplanes, G and T in hand, and think nothing of it – and I waited for her to ask me for the information Holmes and I had collected since we had last seen each other a week earlier. She did not ask. Once she started me off, of course, the painful flow of facts and images would wash over her in a flood. She knew that, knew there was no comfortable way to ease into the past, and so she hesitated to ask.

In the end, I simply gave her Gabriel's journal. I had brought it with me to search it more closely with an eye to the tall Canadian Hélène whom I would soon be confronting, but it appeared to me more important that Iris read it first. I took it from my locked case, and placed it in her hands.

'This is Gabriel's diary,' I told her. 'Your son's war journal. When you've read it, I'll tell you how we found it.'

She received the battered object with the attitude of a believer accepting the communion host. She bent over it for a moment, then left the cabin without a word.

I did not see her for two days.

CHAPTER TWENTY-SIX

SELECTED ENTRIES FROM THE journal of Gabriel Hughenfort.

10 August 1917

I begin this fresh journal on the train back to Arley Holt, where I shall disembark a different man from the one who climbed onboard early this morning. Today I turned eighteen, and my first act as a man was to enlist. I am now a soldier, returning home to break the news.

I have decided to take this slim volume with me to war, an ornate object that will cheer my drab quarters with its gaudy colour and its reminder of exotic places. My uncle Marsh sent it me, some weeks ago, and I decided as soon as I set eyes on it that it would take its place in my soldier's pack.

For to war I shall be going, and to ensure honest service I have used a false name. I am proud of my true name, but there is no doubt that its syllables make it difficult for people to see the person behind it. Some will need to know, I suppose, but with luck I can keep the numbers down. Henceforth I am Gabriel Hewetson, second lieutenant in His Majesty's Forces.

Pater will storm and Mama will weep, but I can no other. Will Susan weep, I wonder? Or will she be proud of me? I believe I made the right decision when I told her there would be no ring until I return in safety. If I came back horribly wounded, she would feel it shameful not to go through with it. We have an understanding; that shall suffice.

27 August

I dreamt last night that I was walking through the Fox Woods above Justice. It was springtime and the bluebells were out, so the woods resembled a lake with trees growing up from the brilliant blue water. Mama was there with me, and she was crying and crying, saying we'd never pick bluebells together again. Good thing I don't believe in dreams telling the future. I'll have to think on the symbolism of the dream.

Funny, because I haven't been dreaming much since coming to training camp. Probably it's just that I'm so tired at the end of the day, I have no energy for dreaming. I don't even think very often about Susan before dropping off to sleep, even though she let me kiss her and the feel of her kisses stayed with me for days. The dream was probably my mind telling me that when I get back I'll marry Susan and we'll be too busy for me to go blue-belling with Mama, that I'll have grown out of such childish outings.

The first draught of men set off for the Front today, looking eager and deadly. I suppose by the time we go, there'll still be some Jerries left for us. Still, I hope we can hurry up this endless drilling.

30 October

Word today that they'll move up our ship date to France, that it might be before Christmas even. The men are keen but I can see why the higher ranks worry. Without a really solid training, most of these boys won't have a chance. And I say boys because most of them are way younger than me. A couple of them can't be sixteen, no matter what they told the recruiting officer. Of course, there's the old duffers too, conscripts forty and more. How are they expected to carry a full pack through the mud and still be fit to shoot? Children and old men. They'll be issuing rifles to women before much longer.

5 December

Two days' home leave before shipping out. I'm halfway tempted to stay in camp, or go up to London with some of the others for a last fling. But I can't; it wouldn't be fair to the parents. Even though right now I'd just as soon face a German gunner than Mama's tears for her baby boy. Don't I wish they'd had another child, a daughter, to take the pressure off. I wonder how Ogilby would react if I asked him to tie a blindfold on me before I went in through the door. Knowing him, he'd just ask if I wished to use my own, or if I wanted him to fetch one, My Lord.

Christmas Day

Behind the lines, but not far. We can smell it now, and my men are acting the way I feel, like a horse at the scent of smoke, jumpy and white-eyed. Lots of jokes, most of them dirty. They're

*shelling up the line, our guns or theirs, making the earth quiver
like a fractious horse. A few days here, then up to the Front. I
pray God I do not disgrace my family.*

Epiphany 1918

*I had my doubts about this name lark, wondered if it wasn't going
to be more trouble than it was worth, being always on the alert for
an old friend or one of the men spotting the occasional 'Hughenfort'
letter and catching on. Still, I've only had a couple of sticky
moments, and all in all, I think it's been a good idea. Growing
up, close as I was to some of the people on the estate, I knew that
'My Lord' was always in the back of their minds, if not actually on
their tongues. The men here know my class — how could they not? —
but to most of them I'm just another public school boy who doesn't
know the first thing about war, whose job it is to survive long
enough to get slapped into shape, and to transmit orders received,
and to take the heat from above when necessary. When I came, I
was lucky enough not to put my foot wrong too disastrously, and
it must have been obvious that I was pathetically grateful for any
instruction they could give me. When they saw that, and began to
feel that they could trust me a little, they relaxed, and have adopted
me as a sort of pet. Not in the articles of Army discipline, I'm sure,
but I feel I'm coming to know my countrymen in a way I'd never
have in normal times. And I am grateful, to them all.*

28 January

*Never have I imagined cold such as this. Even the frost-rimed
dugout the officers share seems an oasis of warmth. Heaven is*

dry stockings, even if they are caked with dirt. Paradise would be a bed with clean sheets — but that is more than my mind can grasp. The earth no longer holds such things; all the world is half-frozen slime and ear-shattering noise.

A shell hit the neighbouring section of trench today; I went to help a wounded soldier to his feet only to discover he had no legs below the thigh. I shall never lose the sensation of lifting up a legless man. Thank God he was already dead.

And my first thought after the original shock was, I wonder if his feet are dry now. And then I started to laugh. I managed to reach the privacy of the dugout before my nerves gave way and the laughter turned to tears. The first time in days my nerves have gone like that, and not yet in front of the men. The mind toughens slowly.

4 February

Jerry's shelling kept us pinned in our mud-holes four days after we were supposed to go back. There was finally a lull, and we could shift the wounded and trade places with the poor ~~bas~~ souls coming up to take our places. Baths and louse-free shirts and beds that don't jump and twitch under us, hot food and a chance for the ears to cease their endless ringing. But we've pulled a short one this time for some reason — we're headed back into it in three more days. Just in time for the lice to find us again.

Why don't lice get trench foot, or freeze to death? God's mysteries.

345

I've found myself, in recent days, thinking about the dome over the Hall in Justice, with its frescoes of what the prophet Amos calls the Day of the Lord. I have been reflecting that since I was a child, certainly at least a year or two before the archduke's assassination set the spark to the Balkans, I have been aware that there would be a war, and that the War would be a good thing, however painful. I have been remembering those early days, when the older boys and the young men of the estate put on their proud uniforms and clasped to their breasts the opportunity to 'trounce the Kaiser' and 'show the Hun what for'. The nobility of their faces, their shared cause, made my boyish self burn with envy. I raged that they would do the job before I had a chance to join in.

'Why would you want the Day of the Lord?' Amos cries out in horror. Having come here, to the trenches, I understand exactly what Amos means: Why in heaven's name would anyone want Armageddon, if they knew what it really meant, the innocent and the sinner alike crushed underfoot? As if a man fled from a lion to meet a bear, or took refuge in a house to be bitten by a serpent. We lusted after war, and by God, we were given the trenches. The Day of the Lord.

I myself thirst after those waters at the centre of the fresco, for the justice that will flow down like waters, the righteousness like an ever-flowing stream poised above us, ready to sweep through northern France and wash us all away, cleanse the land of howitzers and tanks, half-rotted corpses and gas canisters, filth and blood and terror and desperation.

The land will be empty when the flood has passed through, but it will be clean.

Fancy, I know, but that is what I have been thinking, in recent days.

11 February

Writing this by the Very lights that Jerry's been shooting up over our heads for a week now, one generation of which scarcely fades before the next comes up. I never want to see another display of fireworks as long as I live.

Our howitzers are going now, pounding our bones as we trade death with the men 150 feet away, in their holes, behind their wire. Did I say men? The last group of prisoners I saw might have been thirteen or fourteen. Two of them were crying for their mothers. One of them fell asleep with his thumb in his mouth, for Christ's sake. I saw him. His boots had holes worn through the soles.

The shells are getting closer. Time to choose whether to stay in the open trenches and risk shell fragments, or to get into the dugout and chance being buried.

The sergeant's brewing tea on the fire step, a nonchalant Woodbine hanging off his lip. He reminds me of old man Bloom, who kept a hut in the woods to keep an eye for poachers. The gamekeeper had a cough, too, like the sergeant has, though I suppose his came from the cigarettes and wood smoke instead of mustard gas like Sergeant West's. What I'd give for a nice lungful of wood smoke now, clean and honest. I'd not even mind if

Three weeks ago, the shells suddenly got near enough to make me close this journal and button it into my pocket, and at that very instant, before I could even get to my feet, the world erupted and buried me alive. I woke on the stretcher a different man.

It makes me smile, to think that at the first sight of Hélène I thought she was a man. Her back was to me, of course – no one looking into her eyes would ever make that mistake, no matter how scrambled his brains! – and she was wearing a heavy leather jacket with sheepskin at the collar. Then she turned to me, checking that I wasn't going to be thrown to the floor when we hit a pothole, and thus undo all the work the bearers had gone to. I've never seen eyes like that, green as the hills she was raised in. Heaven only knows what she saw. I could've been a Chinaman for all she could tell, or old as her father or ugly as sin. I was clotted with France, hair to bootlace, and stinking of battle.

A brief flurry of changes, and back I am, in the trenches again. Different trenches, same war.

Two days' quick leave, after hospital and before reporting to my new regiment, and I used it to pay a visit to an aunt who had extended the invitation long ago. I had not seen Aunt Iris since I was in short pants, and her marriage to my uncle Marsh seems to exist in name only, so I had expected a certain amount of discomfort all around. Instead, I came away feeling that I had gained a blood relation, so easy was she to talk to. There were areas into which we did not go — I have my secrets and she very obviously has hers (if indeed one can have an obvious secret; still, I should say her friend Dan is one of those), and I have found it impossible to speak openly about what the War is actually like. No one who has been through the trenches speaks freely with a person who has not done so. When the War is over, a great divide will cut through England.

Nonetheless, Iris seemed to read between my words, and to understand much that was unsaid. She fed me — how, with the restricted civilian rations, I neither knew nor asked — and clothed me and made me feel as if I had another home.

Whole, dry stockings! And two nights cradled by lavender-scented linen! Her flat gleams in my mind as an island of plenty, and of peace, and of all that is good in the world.

So, after a few brief hours behind the lines with my new regiment we came forward, and here I sit again, writing on the pages of my Egypt-leather journal while the shells fall in the distance.

But oh! What a difference from one month ago, for now I need but close my eyes and green eyes gaze back at me. And, is it not fate that my new posting is even closer to hers than the old?

24 April

Terrible news — the entire unit is to shift down the Line, near Reims. Good for the men, of course, since it's a quiet sector for soldiers stretched near to breaking by the continual onslaught of the months past. But that's miles away, miles beyond reach of my fair Hélène. I will find a reason to visit the aid post tomorrow (reasons are always so plentiful – shall it be my feet, or the festering cut on my arm, or the cough?) and wait for her to come in. I must see her once before I go.

2 May

The deed is done. We leave tomorrow at dawn.

2 June

Three weeks of quiet, broken only by the stray shell and the ever-present snipers, and then it all came down on us, hell breaking out anew just after midnight on Monday last. It had been such a lovely holiday, too, with actual fields instead of pitted mud as far as the eyes could see. The trees had branches and delicate spring leaves, there were birds nesting in the church's steeple, the people were still capable of smiling. Birdsong – nightingales – animals other than rats! And one night I heard what I'd have sworn was a dog fox. Then at one in the morning the earth heaved and the sky turned to flame with their guns, and it was back to Hades for us.

Except that this time they've got us out of our trenches and running for our lives. God knows how much equipment we've shed between here and where the front line was 72 hours ago. I managed to hang on to my pack, running through fields with the bullets going zip, zip *over my head, although some Jerry's got himself two pairs of nice new Trench stockings that I'd left drying in the dugout along with my mess kit and entrenching tool. I gave one old pair of stockings to a man who'd run five miles in bare feet, which leaves me with one of Aunt Iris's pairs on my feet and another in my kit that's more holes than yarn. I know what the next letter home's going to ask for!*

14 June

Thank God for the Yanks. The Second Division had been set down not far from where we are now, troops fresh off the boat and spoiling for a fight, and when Jerry got to them, he bounced back like a rubber ball. Not at first, but once they had the feel of it, the Yanks dug in their heels and shoved back. They even retook Belleau Wood, and that seems to be about as far as Jerry's getting this time. But it was close. If he'd had more troops, better supplies, he'd be strolling up the Champs Elysees in the morning.

The guns must have given Iris and her friend Dan a few bad hours. I had a letter from her, one from home, and one from H. – all in the same post today; no doubt they'd sat waiting for us until hdq. could spot where we'd ended up.

Lost only one man – head wound, but he'll live to see Dover. One of the other fellows lost his entire platoon, taken prisoner when he was separated from them. Poor bastard, feels like he lost his mother. Or his sons.

23 June

Back up the line to shore up some weak places in the French fence. Sorry to lose my old batman, he was a great comfort, but I'm closer to H., although I haven't seen her to talk to yet. Spotted her ambulance – I'm pretty certain it was her Ford – scrambling its way down a hill yesterday morning, but she didn't see me, one khaki figure in a hundred.

Holiday's over; we're back in the thick of it. I wonder if Jerry's listening to the nightingales right now. There certainly aren't any around here, just rats.

Shelling heavy tonight, damn them. Makes my nerves jumpy, can't help it. Not even knowing my green-eyed Hélène is near can stop the twitches.

Had a man go bad on us yesterday – not one of mine, thank God, but about a hundred yards up the line. His nerves just crumbled and he downed his rifle and ran. Took a bullet in the shoulder, with luck it'll see him out of trouble, and nobody's saying anything about the fact that he took it in the back. But he'll have to live with knowing he deserted his mates in a pinch. Don't know about him, whether that would trouble him or not, but I know that, once or twice, it's been the only thing that's kept me facing forward, knowing I'd have to live with the shame of abandoning men who counted on me.

Word is, we'll be home by Christmas. They've been saying that since the first winter, I know, but this time it may be true. One way or another.

The padre's just been through. Good man, name of Hastings, too old by far for this stunt but doesn't complain, always a word of encouragement, especially for the young boys. A countryman, Surrey rather than Berkshire but close enough, had some interesting stories about water voles.

Beautiful full moon tonight, brighter than the Very lights. Anyone with nerve enough to peep over the top will catch a glimpse of our own version of the moon, all pitted and lifeless. I watch the real thing pass through the sky over the trench, and think about showing Hélène the lawns under a summer moon. The time Uncle Alistair took me out to Abbot's Clump in the full moon to watch the hares dance. I couldn't have been more than four at the time. Damn the Kaiser.

Front line for going on three weeks, don't know how much longer the men can stand it. One private a week older than I am shot himself in the foot yesterday, trying for his Blighty. Only instead of a boat home, he's in a hole, having missed his aim and hit an artery. Bled to death before they could get him on a stretcher. Probably just as well – it was obvious what he'd done, he'd have been court-martialled for it, and considering the current state of the fighting, probably been shot to discourage others from trying the same. Backs-to-the-wall time, there's no doubt.

Pray God watch over all VAD drivers. Especially those with green eyes.

15 July

No doubt they're partying in Paris today, dancing in the streets outside Aunt Iris's apartment. Not too many bottles of champagne here. Plenty of Bastille Day fireworks, though. Had a blessed three days off the line, baths, warm food, the lice baked out of my clothes, and a chance to see Hélène. She managed to trade with another girl and we sat on a bombed-out building wall and talked and talked while the half moon lay over the poor wounded countryside. I told her about Justice Hall, how I want to show her every corner of it. The Pater'll have a fit. Tried not to let H. know how much of a fit he'd have; time enough for that.

If we lose this bloody awful war, it won't be because of the fighting men, it'll be due to the incredible stupidity of the higher-ups. Still can't believe it – full moon, huge thing brighter than a whole string of Very lights, and down comes the order to take out a wiring party. Insanity! Absolute, blithering idiocy. The men went to ice when they heard it, a sure sentence for the death of ten good men. But they were willing. They'd have done it, for me and for their fellows, but I was having none of it. The order had obviously been sent weeks before and gone astray. Even the daftest old general in London wouldn't send out a wiring party under those circumstances – and when the line's shifting daily and we hardly bother shoring up trenches because we'll be out of 'em in a week? Why wire here at all. Nuts, I said, putting on my best Yank accent. Nuts to you, my men are standing down.

26th

I cannot fathom this. I can't begin to understand. I'm going to wake up now and find it's all one of those loopy dreams. They can't be serious.

29th

This has gone beyond a joke. All right, I could have handled it better, and I understand that they have to stamp on anything that might lose the men from discipline. But this extreme a reaction? They'll look like greater fools when the next level up sees what's happening and sweeps it away.

The things they said in the so-called trial. I was so flabbergasted I could scarcely summon answers. 'Fomenting a mutiny'? Lord, if anything the exact reverse – teaching the men that they can trust their officers not to issue insane orders. It's a fragile trust, yes, so all the more reason to use common sense.

30th

Spent all the night shivering in the heat. I'm in an avalanche. I'm in a train going for a cliff. I'm going to be forced to bring in the Influence. Shameful admission of defeat, to drag in the family name, but I can't see how else to stop the machinery. Maybe I should just take my punishment, even if it's being strapped to a wheel for twenty-one days. Even if it's gaol, surely I can do that? Being stripped of rank would be the worst. Oh, Hélène, what will you do when you find out? God, I hope I can continue to hide behind this name, to keep all this from the parents.

I keep thinking I'll wake up. I don't.

1 August

The Maj. appeared, late last night. Just heard about it, made him insane with wrath, went off to see what he could do short of invoking The Name. Still hopes of defusing the situation under its own power. I told him I'd take a field punishment if it satisfied officialdom's honour, although the image of his fair-haired boy strapped up in the sun for the betterment of the regiment would probably kill Pater. I can't even think about Mama.

I should have just hauled that bloody wire out there myself,
ordered the men to stay behind, and strung it alone. Jerry
might have missed a single figure out there, and I could have
protected my men.

I just never imagined it might come to this. Oh, God, this
is going to be the death of my parents, no matter how it turns
out. A Hughenfort, convicted of refusing an order. Cowardice.
Disgrace.

When I'm alone, I weep. The padre is here a lot, so I keep
myself together for him. Thank God Hélène hasn't come, I
should collapse completely in the agony of it all. It would be a
blessing if she heard nothing about it, until it is over. One way
or another.

August, afternoon

Death? Shot, by my own men? No that's
   God help me, I can't
   Unthinkable. I can't think about it. My mind won't.
   I've sent for the Major, he'll put an end to this.

August, 4:30 a.m.

The Maj. sent a message that he'd come at two in the morning.
I sent the padre away to get some rest, and so I could think.
I knew that if the news had been good, he'd have sent it, not
come himself.

The C in C himself, the Maj. told me, when he heard my
true name, said he was sorry, that it was out of his hands.
That discipline knows no titles. He's right, of course, although

356

I hadn't thought the Army's hold on the common soldier that precarious, to require such an iron grip over its junior officers. He stayed for a long time, from two nearly to dawn. We talked. We'd never really talked before, he never seemed my sort, but it was good to have at my side a man of my own people, an uncle who knew the land and the trees I loved from a child, who understood the difference between the upper lawns and the park, who'd seen the sun rise over The Circles, who had fished Justice Pond in the spring.

He promises me that the Pater and Mama needn't be told. The letter's nearly the same as for an honourable death, now. So grief, but no shame. No blot of cowardice on the name. No dark cloud over Justice Hall.

Under those circumstances, I can—I nearly wrote 'live with this'. And I suppose I can, for the hours left me.

He left a few minutes ago. I asked McFarlane to give him my letters and papers, to hand them personally to my parents on his next leave, along with the letter I wrote to say goodbye and to introduce them to Hélène. This journal I've kept by me, as my private friend. I'll ask the padre to send it home when Pater asks him for it. Pater shall have to judge whether or not Mother is strong enough.

Hélène, when you read this, know that you were in my thoughts to the end. Know that the only regret I hold is that my decision stole the years of joy we would have had together. Kiss my mother and father for me. I know you will love them, given time.

Dawn draws near. The padre prays with me, and sits in silence when I wish to add to these words. He is a good man. I asked him to read to me from the fifth chapter of Amos. He *hesitated, and then did so. When he had finished, I saw tears in his eyes. I have none in mine. I feel only a chasm of regret deeper than any sapper's tunnel, and fear — not of death, I am beyond that now, thank God, but fear that my body will fail me in the morning, and cringe from the wall. Why should shame be such a terrible threat, greater than death itself? A thing you can't eat or drink, all-powerful in a man's life. I suppose because, when it comes down to it, there is nothing but honour and pride.*

It was a blessing to hear the word 'Justice' from the padre's mouth. For a moment, I was home again.

Here it comes. For those I love, for Justice, may I prove myself strong. Justitia fortitudo mea est.

Gabriel Adrian Thomas Hughenfort

3 August 1918

CHAPTER TWENTY-SEVEN

IRIS SPENT TWO DAYS in her cabin, immersing herself in this record of her unacknowledged son's final months and struggling to come to terms with its wrenching emotions and its devastating implications.

The boy had been so alone. That was, I knew, what would hit her the hardest, at first anyway. Transferred from his original unit into another that was then in the heat of battle, and subsequently moved, then overrun, and finally split up and moved again, Gabriel had as much chance of forging friendships as someone attempting to thread a needle in an earthquake. His superior officers did not know him, the padre was sympathetic but ineffectual, and his girl was so rushed, she most likely did not even know of his plight until it was too late. Had he known that his true mother was in Paris, had he ever been told that his true father worked for one of the most powerful men in the British government, he might have sent word, and in an instant the waters of justice would have rolled down into that small and lonely cell and carried him away.

But – and the implications of this would come more slowly

to the woman reading her son's words – Gabriel Hughenfort was given one faint ray of hope, one man who was in a position to stop the juggernaut. Or so the boy believed. He put his hopes in 'the Major', trusted the man to be his advocate among the powerful, even gave that man his most precious letters, to be returned to the family. And the man had gone away, said nothing, kept or destroyed the letters, and finally – the cruellest twist of all – turned Gabriel's own finely honed sense of responsibility and nobility against him, using the boy's bred-in-the-bone consciousness of what it was to be a Hughenfort to keep him from crying the name aloud, using it as a shield to stay the bullets. Use your name, 'the Maj.' had drilled into him that last bitter night, and you might save your life, but the cost? Disgrace for the family name forever. Stay silent, offer your life up to Honour and no one need know. He had held before Gabriel the opportunity to emulate all those Hughenforts who had made the ultimate sacrifice, for one cause or another, to stand with pride beside those demanding ancestors on the walls. And Gabriel fell for it.

With the ashes of that betrayal in my mouth, it was no hardship to avoid the social whirl around the captain's table during our crossing. I probably ate little more than Iris did, and the work I did during those two days, the paper on biblical deductions for the American journal, turned out considerably more caustic than I had originally intended. *Their minds were perverted*, I translated the story of Susanna and the elders; *Their thoughts strayed from the path of God, and they attended not to the demands of Justice.*

For the first leisure hours I'd had since August, these days were proving grimly unsatisfactory.

On the third morning there came a rap at the door. I put down my cup of tea and went to answer it. Iris stood there, wearing the same clothes she'd had on when I last saw her, her face haggard, with dark swathes under her eyes. I pulled her in, took the red journal that she was holding, made her sit on the sofa, and pressed a cup of sweet tea into her hands. I rang for another pot, and some toast, then stood over her until she'd eaten two slices. When she shook her head at more, I drew her a long, hot bath, made her swallow a small whisky, dressed her in a pair of my sleeping pyjamas, and put her to bed.

All without a word between us.

She woke at dinnertime. I was reading, as I had been all that day, when I heard her moving around in the bedroom. When she came out, one of my kimonos belted around her waist, she looked old still, but the dark bruises under her eyes had faded.

'Was Gabriel's major Sidney Darling?' she asked without preliminary.

I put down my book. 'I don't know,' I answered her. 'Would you like tea, or a drink?'

'I don't want anything.'

'Iris, I know how you feel. Not about this – how could I know? – but in general I have stood in your shoes, and I am well acquainted with the all-consuming urge to get my hands around someone's throat. I've felt it, I've seen it, and I know this: You mustn't allow it to consume you.'

She blinked, and seemed to see me for the first time.

'Iris, you need food and rest and time for quiet reflection. In that order. It won't do anyone any good if you stretch yourself until you break. Now: What do you want to eat?'

An omelette was what she would eat, so I joined her. Also toast, and cheese, and water biscuits, and an apple tart, with coffee at the end. I poured a measure of brandy into our cups, in the absence of calvados, and noted with satisfaction the colour in her cheeks. With the coffee, the purser had brought the information that all of Iris's belongings had been transferred to a vacant stateroom not far from mine. Leaving her in my rooms, I followed the purser down the corridor to her new accommodations to retrieve a change of clothing, and when she had dressed I brought out my hairbrush and stood behind her to draw it through her short hair, as a means of giving her the physical contact I thought she needed, in a manner she might permit. She sat stiffly at first, and then more easily, finally allowing her head to loll with the strokes of the brush.

'Ninety-nine,' I said. 'One hundred.'

'Did your mother tell you to brush your hair a hundred times each night?' she asked me.

'Oh yes. Not that I bother, you understand, but she certainly did. My father would sometimes brush it for her.' Now where did *that* bit of ancient history emerge from?

'Well, thank you. My hair has never been so tamed.'

'More coffee?'

'No, thanks. Mary, what are we going to do?'

I smiled as I cleaned the brush of hair. 'I'm glad to hear you say "we".'

'Well, it would appear that we're all in this together.'

'Iris, Holmes is very, very good at what he does.'

'Yes. He'd have to be, wouldn't he? Can he prove it was Sidney who did that . . . I can't even think of a word for such a despicable act.'

'Murder,' I said grimly. 'It was murder.'

She studied my face, and saw there something that seemed to reassure her more than my assertion of Holmes' competency.

'However,' I told her, 'we can't actually be sure that it was Darling, not yet.'

'Of course it was Sidney. Staff major, "my uncle", Gabriel called him. The boy only had two uncles, Sidney and Marsh.'

'He called Alistair "uncle,"' I reminded her.

'Did he? Good Lord, so he did. But to consider Ali as "the Major" is every bit as preposterous as accusing Marsh.'

'I don't mean that Alistair is a suspect, Iris. I meant that Gabriel seems to have used the term "uncle" for any male relative of his father's generation. Marsh, Sidney, and Lionel, yes, but also Alistair, who was sort of a distant cousin.'

'He called Ali's sister Rose "aunt",' she conceded reluctantly. 'I do remember that.'

'And probably their brother Ralph was 'uncle.' Which means that Ivo Hughenfort, who was definitely present in that sector of the Front at that time, might conceivably also have qualified as an uncle,' I reminded her.

'Ivo? Are you saying—oh,' she said. Then, 'Oh, Good Lord. Ivo was at the shoot, the day Marsh—we've got to—'

I broke into her growing panic. 'They know. Marsh has both Ali and Holmes with him. Nothing will happen.'

She did not look too sure about this. Perhaps my voice lacked the requisite note of absolute certainty. I tried again. 'Iris, Marsh and Ali have spent their whole adult lives walking in and out of lethal situations. Both he and Ali made the mistake once of thinking England was safe. Neither of them will make it a second time. Iris, I swear to you: I've seen those two in action. Nothing will get past their guard.'

'You're right. I always forget about that side of them. Marsh is a good friend, and such a gentle person that thinking of him as some kind of behind-the-lines soldier is always difficult. Ali is different – him I can see as dangerous. Not Marsh.'

I did not think it my responsibility to tell her just how dangerous that husband of hers was – in the end, considerably more deadly than Ali. Let her simply settle her mind as to their safety and allow her thoughts to turn again to Gabriel. Which they quickly did.

'I wanted to tell Gabriel the truth, Mary. Those two days he spent with us in Paris. He was talking about his parents one evening, telling me how difficult he found it at times to talk freely with them, how he sometimes felt almost as if they spoke another language from his, and I ached to tell him the reason for that. I couldn't, of course. They were both still alive, and he was Sarah's whole life. Henry, too, but to drive a wedge between the boy and Sarah would have devastated her. And in actual fact, I *was* an aunt to the boy. It wasn't I who raised him and fretted over his childhood illnesses and oversaw his schooling and shaped him into the man he was. But he was so extraordinarily beautiful as a human being, I selfishly wanted to be more in his eyes than just a distant uncle's estranged wife. I couldn't tell him, but I wish to God that I had! He might, just possibly, have used that knowledge in the last days. Might have reached out to ask for the help of a mother as he couldn't do to a scarcely known aunt.'

There was no real reply to that. Nor was there for any of the other painful questions she came out with over the course of the next hours, as she unburdened herself as she had never been able to do before, to anyone. All I could say was, she gave her son a good, loving life, and she had taken the opportunity to lay the foundations of a relationship during his Paris leave. The awareness of Iris as a friend had infused Gabriel's final weeks with a sense of future, at a time when the world was proclaiming there was no future. Faint reassurance, but gratefully received. She went to her new rooms at two in the morning. By later account, she slept better than I.

The next day we spent walking the decks and talking, about matters that often had nothing to do with Gabriel. We discovered that we had been sailing through the edges of a storm since leaving England, and although the rain was now clearing, the ship continued to heave beneath our feet. I told her about my childhood in Sussex and California, she told me about the growing community of artists and writers in Paris – easy conversation, of the sort that takes place at the beginning of any friendship, but which also allowed us to draw breath and permit our real concerns to simmer in the backs of our minds.

I did send a telegram, through Mycroft lest the village post-mistress in Arley Holt prove indiscreet:

WHOM DID GABRIEL ADDRESS AS QUOTE UNCLE QUERY.

The answer came within a message received the next day.

UNCLES MARSH SIDNEY LIONEL ALISTAIR PHILIP RALPH JAMES IVO AND THREE NEIGHBOURS STOP ALL WELL HERE STOP CLERK ARRESTED ADMITS NOTHING STOP HAIG NO MEMORY OF LETTER OR GABRIEL STOP HUNT CONTINUES COMMA GOOD SAILING END.

Philip, I recalled, was the name of Gabriel's grandfather's brother, hence the boy's great-uncle, who moved to South Africa and was never seen again; I thought it doubtful that Gabriel had ever actually met him, although he could have remained an 'uncle' for reference purposes, and his sons, if any, might also qualify for the title. Ralph-pronounced-Rafe was Alistair's brother, who had gone to Australia at the age of nineteen and perhaps died at Gallipoli. Gabriel would have been nine or so when Ralph disappeared, so could have retained an active memory of the man. James, I knew, was the husband of Alistair's sister, Rose, father of the farming nephew who would eventually take over Badger Old Place. All of which made it conclusive that for Gabriel, 'uncle' was a broadly applied honorific. I shouldn't have been surprised had he used it for close friends of his parents, as well.

The huge passenger liner ploughed its luxurious path through the waves and against the headwinds, putting in at New York late on Tuesday. Although we both had friends in the City, we went to our hotel unannounced, and passed out of the City the following day without getting into touch with any of them. Neither of us felt much inclined for light social banter.

The journey north was tedious to the extreme, and I cursed Holmes silently every time the train slowed, halted, and sat waiting for the track to clear. The snow never quite forced abandonment and taking shelter in an hotel, but it did fret us all the way to Toronto. My only bright spot came with a small article in the corner of a discarded day-old newspaper that I picked up, informing its readers of the temporary closure of the London War Records Offices due to an 'infection of unknown origin'. Reading between the lines, I thought the infection bore some names that would be familiar to me: Closing the whole place so that the records might be more readily searched had Mycroft's stamp all over it.

The address I had been given for Philippa Helen O'Meary was in a small town named Webster, to the west of Toronto. I began to worry that the only means of reaching the place would be by dog sled, but in Toronto the storm suddenly tired of us. By Thursday morning the skies were clear and our hotel reassured us, with jaunty Colonial confidence, that we'd have no problem on the train.

Somewhat to our surprise, we did not. The tracks were clear, the carriage warm, and by the middle of the afternoon we were pulling up to a small brick building on which hung the sign, WEBSTER. We climbed down onto the freshly swept platform, took a deep breath of furiously clean air tinged with smoke from the train, and looked out across an expanse of pristine white countryside. After the well-hedged fields of southern England – or indeed the countryside around Paris – the land here seemed to go on for a long, long way. We exchanged an apprehensive glance, and went to find an hotel.

The rooms were basic but clean, the odours from the dining room promising, the arrangement of motorcar and driver nearly instantaneous, but no one knew Philippa O'Meary. Nor Phil nor Hélène. Finally the hotel's owner took pity on us and suggested the manager of the local bank. There was only one in town, he said, so he'd be certain to know anyone with a savings account or a mortgage. We spent the evening in the tiny town, taking dinner in the hotel dining room with the good citizens of Webster, and for lack of entertainment, went early to bed.

Thus, the following morning we were at the bank's door at ten o'clock, and were ushered in to the manager's august presence. I looked at his rotund features, then looked again in annoyance.

'You were dining at the hotel yesterday night,' I accused.

'Why, yes I was. Were you there as well?'

'We were. And the hotel owner knew we were looking to see you today. He might have introduced us then.'

'Oh no. He knows I never work outside of hours. Now, what can I do for you?'

Other than kicking me for the fool I am, I thought, not to

recognise a banker – even of the rural Canadian variety – when I am across the room from one? I resolved never to tell Holmes of my failure.

'We are looking for a woman named Philippa O'Meary,' I told him. 'She may go as Phil, or Hélène. It's about an inheritance,' I added, although it was possible that the only wealth to change hands would be a few old letters. Bankers need to hear that money is involved before they take any interest in a matter.

'I don't believe . . .' His voice trailed off dubiously.

'She has green eyes and was an ambulance driver in France during the—'

'Oho!' the banker interrupted, transformed by recognition. His eyes sparkled, and he all but slapped his knee with pleasure. 'You mean Mad Helen!' And we watched in astonishment as he burst into laughter, then thumbed the toggle on his desk telephone to bring in his secretary. 'Miss Larsen, would you have Booth run these two ladies up to Mad Helen's place?'

'Mr Booth is out at the Grimes farm this morning, Mr Cowper. I could see if Mr Rhoades is available.'

'Rhoades is fine. He can leave the ladies there; they'll telephone to the hotel for a car to fetch them back. Or Mad Helen can, shall we say, drop them there?'

This last baffling remark caused a great deal of merriment on the part of the manager and, to a more subdued degree, his secretary. The latter ushered us out and, obedient if confused, we entered the Rhoades motorcar and were driven out of town.

When we had seen neither barn nor crossroads for a quarter-hour, and I was starting to wonder if Mr Rhoades might not be entirely honourable in his intentions, a barn appeared on the white-blanketed horizon. A large barn – enormous, in fact, although it lacked the normal complement of silos and farm buildings.

All was explained when we turned in to a drive past a sign proclaiming this the WEBSTER AIR FIELD. The barn was a hangar. Rhoades pulled up next to the front of it, opened our door, and then the three of us stopped dead as the sound of a screaming engine came from overhead. We gaped into the clear sky, and there saw a bright red fighter plane, to all appearances out of control and aiming to crash straight into the hangar. Or into the Rhoades motorcar. On it came, roaring full-throatedly, and at the last possible instant it pulled up, passing so close its wind buffeted our hats.

'There was something in the diary about an aviator's jacket,' I recalled. 'And Dorothea Cobb told me that Hélène's brother was a Canadian fighter pilot. That must be he.'

The pilot, having scared us out of our wits, had circled and was lining up his plane with the runway.

'How does one land on the snow?' Iris wondered aloud.

'With care,' came a new voice. We looked at the small door to the barn, over which hung the sign OFFICE, and then lowered our eyes to the figure in the wheeled chair. The hand with which he was shielding his face was slick with old scar tissue, although he grinned as he watched the red machine drop lower and slow in the sky.

As one, Iris and I looked at each other, then at the aeroplane.

'Yep,' said the man. 'You're looking at my sister. Hi, Jimmy,' he added.

Young Mr Rhoades tore his eyes from the flying daredevil and shook his hand. 'Morning, Ben. This here's Miss Russell and Miss Sutherland. They've come looking for your sister. You mind taking care of returning them to town when they're finished? I've got a pile of work.'

'Happy to. Good day, ladies. The name's Ben O'Meary.'

O'Meary's right hand was less disastrously scarred; close up, his face showed signs of a less comprehensive brush with the flames.

'Crashed in the War,' he told us, a phrase so matter-of-fact, he must have begun a thousand conversations with that same blunt explanation. 'They scraped me out and sent me home, to teach my sister to fly. I run the business, she teaches the classes and does the stunt shows. Exactly the opposite of what we'd planned, but ain't that life? You want to come in? She'll be a minute.'

But we chose to wait in the open air for the pilot of the red fighter, and he manoeuvred his chair back through the doorway and left us in the cold.

The aeroplane taxied slowly on the slick surface, neared the barn, and then the engine coughed into silence. In a moment, the plane's pilot climbed out of the cockpit and jumped easily to the ground.

She was a tall woman, as tall as I but broader in the shoulders, and I could well imagine her slinging a wounded Tommy across her back. Then she began to remove the layers of clothing that kept her from freezing. Thick scarf unwrapped from her neck and face, the helmet and goggles. Yes, there were those famous emerald eyes, that ebony hair, but something else as well, a small fact that Gabriel had failed to record.

She was what the boy's parents would no doubt have termed a half-breed. Ireland lay in her eyes and her surname, but those Irish ancestors had intermarried with folk who knew neither freckles nor red hair. She was perhaps a quarter American Indian, maybe an eighth, but plenty to mark her as an odd choice for the heir to one of the oldest dukedoms in England.

She was also extraordinarily beautiful.

She shook her short hair loose of the helmet's marks and shot us a grin of pure high spirits, a grin I recognised instantly from a blurred photograph of overall-clad drivers in France. 'You two ladies looking to learn to fly?' she asked. 'Or you just wanting a quick pass over town? I'm happy to take you, but I hope you'll want to try it for yourselves. There's nothing in the world like it.'

'I can see that,' I told her, speaking only the truth. 'But actually, we've come to talk about another matter.'

'I'm happy to teach your husbands. I'm good with men.'

'It concerns a young soldier you once knew, by the name of Gabriel Hughenfort.'

It was as if I'd kicked her in the stomach. All her high spirits vanished into instant wariness; she even took a step back. In a moment, I thought, she'd break into a run – or reach for a weapon.

'Damn,' she said. 'Damnation. Well, I knew you'd come eventually.'

The man in the chair, wondering perhaps where we had got to, had rolled outside again and now called out, 'Are you ladies going to stand there and freeze to death, or can I shut this door?'

Raising her head, but not taking her eyes off us, the pilot shouted, 'We'll be right there, Ben.' She waited until the door closed, then she leant forward and spoke in a low, forceful voice. 'If you hurt him, if you so much as make him uncomfortable, I swear to God you'll never lay eyes on him again.'

Then she stalked off to the office. Iris stared after her, with an expression that asked about the pilot's sanity, and said, 'But why on earth would we want to hurt that poor man?'

I shook my head, but not, as she thought, from an equal incomprehension. Instead, I was asking Iris to wait, as I propelled her forward by the elbow, trying to keep down my excitement. I could be wrong – those small hints, the odd coincidences; the ring she didn't wear, her willingness to leave France during the last, victorious weeks of the War. I could be mistaken. But the green-eyed woman's attitude made no sense, unless—

I could be wrong.

But I was not.

Iris saw him a split second after I did, standing at the side of the pilot. It took her a moment longer to understand what she was seeing.

A child, about five years of age, with his mother's green eyes.

Everything else about him was pure Hughenfort, from the lift of his chin and his stocky grace to Marsh's raised eyebrow.

Gabriel's son.

CHAPTER TWENTY-EIGHT

IRIS SWAYED, WHEN HER mind finally comprehended what her eyes were telling her, and I seized a beat-up wooden chair and jammed it behind her knees.

'Oh my God,' she breathed. 'Oh my God.'

This reaction quite clearly was not what the boy's mother had anticipated. The child had retreated from the peculiar behaviour of these two strangers, and now stood half hidden behind his mother, her hand resting on his shoulder by way of protection.

'Who are you?' she demanded.

Her brother took it further. 'What the hell is going on here?'

'My name—' Iris began, but I cut in on her.

'Before we get into the details, may I suggest that the boy be excused? That way you can choose how best to talk to him about what we are going to tell you.'

The green eyes thought about it for a while, then flickered over to Ben. 'Would you and Gabe mind going up to the house and starting lunch? The boys will be here before long and they'll be hungry. This may take a while.'

'You're sure?'

'I'm not sure of anything, but I think it'd be a good idea. You go with Ben, okay, Gabe? You can start the sandwiches.'

Iris's rapt gaze followed the boy until the door had shut behind him. Immediately the door closed, the still angry but now confused pilot dragged up another chair and dropped into it.

'Lady, you better start talking.'

'May I ask one question first, Mrs—' I stopped, then apologised. 'I'm sorry, I'm not sure of your name.'

'Hewetson,' she said, then corrected herself 'I call myself Hewetson.'

'Mrs Hewetson, I don't know how to put this so it isn't offensive, so I won't even try. Before we go any further, we have to know: Were you and Gabriel Hughenfort, who was known at the time as Hewetson, legally married?'

She eyed me, thinking about the question's implications – but not, going by her expression, just those that were offensive.

'Why don't you know that already? And if you don't know that, how did you find me?'

By way of answer, Iris reached into her handbag and pulled out the worn red journal. She laid it with care onto the desk between her and Hélène, who had obviously never seen it before. It was equally obvious, blindingly so, that when she opened it, she knew the handwriting as well as she knew her own. She reached out and ran a tentative pair of fingers down one page, as if to touch the hand of the man holding the pen. She then turned to the last page of writing, read for perhaps five seconds, and closed the book.

'How—' she started, but her voice failed her.

'It's a very long story,' Iris answered. 'One that I've come from

England to tell you. But first, please, would you answer my friend's question?'

On the one hand, it mattered not in the least if they had somehow managed to wed on the field of battle. The boy was Gabriel's, and happy; neither of those facts, I thought, would change. On the other, everything depended on it: An illegitimate child could not inherit, no more than a female child could. Marsh's freedom lay in a piece of paper.

Philippa Hewetson raised her head, and I could see the answer before she said it.

'Yes,' she said. Iris covered her mouth with both her gloved hands and made a sound like laughter, with tears in her eyes. I closed my own eyes and found myself saying under my breath, in something remarkably like prayer, *Thank you, God, oh thank you, thank you.*

When I opened my eyes again, the hard, protective look was back on her face, and I made haste to explain our rather extreme reaction. I was not certain just where she perceived a threat, but I knew this was one of those situations where honesty, while not necessarily the best policy, might be the only one possible.

'A legal marriage certificate means that your son is heir to a very large estate and a very important title in England. Gabriel was the only son of the sixth Duke of Beauville. He didn't tell you this?'

'He said his family took its inheritances very seriously. Those were his words. He told me that when I said we didn't need to marry, that I would – Anyway, he wouldn't hear of it, so I asked this priest in one of the villages, an old man I'd gotten to know pretty well. I'm a Catholic, by the way. I thought it was a joke – about the inheritances, that is. Gabriel laughed, that's for sure. I figured his father was the kind of self-made man out to found a dynasty, who'd throw a fit if his son brought home a brown-skinned Canadian Catholic like me.'

'And yet they'd want the boy, eventually,' I concluded. This was the source of her animosity.

'And here you are,' she pointed out.

'It's not quite the same,' Iris objected.

'Isn't it?'

I thought this a good time to throw a couple of facts into the burgeoning argument. 'Iris is Gabriel's mother,' I told her. 'And the reason we—'

The woman's face closed to us as if shutters had been thrown across it. 'No she isn't. She's the aunt Gabriel went to see in Paris. I remember the name. Look here, I don't know what kind of scheme you're trying to pull on me, but it's not going to work. I want you to leave. Now.'

'I am his mother,' Iris told her. 'He didn't know it himself; only six or eight people ever did. And now you. That's part of the long story.'

The green eyes flickered down to the war journal, then back to me. 'You were saying something.'

'I was about to say, the reason we got involved with the string of events that led us here is that someone we both . . . care about needs to know that the succession is secure before he can free himself.'

She was unmoved. 'What if he doesn't? What if I "lose" the marriage certificate, say that Gabe's illegitimate, say we want nothing to do with you?'

'Then your son would be robbed of a heritage that has been a part of England for eight hundred years,' Iris told her. 'You've really never heard of the name Hughenfort?'

The green-eyed pilot shrugged. Shrugged! I pictured the reaction of the Darlings to that shrug, and stifled a laugh.

'I've heard of York and Windsor, too, but that doesn't make Jack York down at the garage into a prince. I don't know. We're happy here. Gabe's got a good life. Why would I want to spoil him by showing him a castle, having people bow and scrape and call him – what would they call him, anyway?'

'Your Grace,' I told her helpfully. 'But they'll call him what you ask. In any case, I'm afraid it's too late. You may choose to have nothing to do with Justice Hall – which is certainly what the current duke would like to do – but we know about you now, and there will be church records.' (If they weren't bombed, lost, or stolen, I added mentally). 'Like it or not, your son is the sixth Duke's heir.' The irony of *forcing* Justice Hall, with all its wealth and beauty, onto not just one unwilling duke, but two, did not escape me. Iris, however, was too close to it to see the humour. She leant forward and stretched out one hand.

'Come back with us,' she burst out. 'Not permanently, just to see it, to meet the family – *your* family.'

'What, now? Don't be ridiculous. I have a business to run.'

'Surely this is your slow time of year,' Iris said diplomatically.

'Christmas!' I said suddenly. 'A Christmas holiday in an English country house. Your son would adore it.' I had to work to get some enthusiasm into that suggestion – personally, I'd rather have been condemned to a week in the trenches. 'And anyway, I'll bet it's been a while since you had a holiday.'

'I couldn't leave Ben here alone.' She was weakening, definitely weakening.

'Bring him, too,' Iris urged, scenting capitulation, but the final unscrupulous blow was mine to deliver.

'Your husband loved Justice Hall,' I told the woman. 'There are pictures of him and his ancestors on the walls, the journals he kept as a boy, servants who watched him grow up. And although I never knew him, I feel confident that the thought of his son there, even on a brief visit, would have made Gabriel very happy.'

Five days later, we all boarded the boat for England.

The voyage back across the ocean, though in truth slowed by weather, seemed to fly, sped on the running feet of an active five-year-old, made smooth by the intelligence and innate grace of his mother. Helen – for so we were to call her – did not let go her apprehension so much as put it to one side, until she had seen and judged all with her own eyes, and made her decision. Before we had left New York Harbour, she and Iris were forever tied, joined by the two Gabriels but also by mutual respect and a very similar way of looking at the world. Both had known hardship, both retained their humour; within days, they began to look like mother and daughter.

Even Ben, who had to be cajoled into making the arduous journey and who could easily have felt even more useless an appendage than his legs were, soon caught the spirit. His laughter as three strong porters hauled him up the gangway was somewhat forced, but once settled into a deck-level cabin his independence and good cheer reasserted themselves, and one night I spotted him on the dance floor, jogging his Bath chair back and forth in time to the music with a giggling young flapper on his lap, clinging for dear life. He caught my eye and winked.

Then we were in Southampton, with ice-slick decks and a low, grey dawn that drizzled sleet and threatened snow before the day was through. We had come without fanfare, with no family to greet us, nothing but a pair of anonymous hired cars arranged by Mycroft. I listened to the complaint of gulls, and asked myself for the hundredth time if I had been right to permit this.

Iris's impulsive invitation, blurted out in the twofold excitement of finding a grandson and freeing a husband at one blow, had caught me unawares. Christmas at Justice Hall for young Gabe and his mother? With its current duke barely healed from a murderous attack and the shadows full of unidentified threat? Surely this was hardly the time to bring a new duke home? That thought had not occurred to Iris until late that same evening, back at the Webster Inn; when it did, when she realised what she had done, she was horrified, and had nearly rung up the O'Meary household then and there. Instead, we had gone out and talked with the two Canadians by clear light of day, and in the end, the four of us had decided to go ahead. It had caused us all a great deal of soul-searching. I could only pray we had made the right decision.

Helen, standing by my side as we were nudged towards the dim outlines of the harbour, had clearly been thinking along the same lines. 'You are sure my son will be safe?'

'This from a woman who takes the child barn-storming?' I replied with a smile.

'One barrel roll, that's all he's ever done with me, and that on his birthday.'

'Yes,' I said more seriously. 'We need to take precautions, but I'd wager Marsh and Alistair against a regiment of guards. The boy'll be safe in that house.'

Watched by hawk-like eyes every instant, no doubt, but he was too young to chafe over restrictions. And we would give it out that the Canadians would be at Justice until Easter, whereas in fact they would return to Canada in early January, weather permitting.

'What is Lord Maurice like?' Helen asked me.

'I met him in Palestine. He's a different man there.'

'A better man?'

'More at home – a part of the landscape, even. The desert burns away extraneous parts of a person. Among the desert peoples, true wealth is measured by what a man carries inside him – his skills, his history, his family. Justice Hall suffocates Marsh. Which is why he will be the first to understand if it has the same effect on you. Keep in mind that the estate can run itself if it has to. Marsh is trapped there at the moment, but not for reasons that affect you and Gabe. Remember that. It's not going to eat you.'

I had been saying the same thing in various ways all the way across the Atlantic. Her wait-and-see attitude prevailed, which was all a person could expect, or ask.

'Oh yes,' I added, 'the rest of the family doesn't know that Marsh and Alistair have been in Palestine. Let them keep guessing.'

'The sister sounds . . . daunting. And the name, so close to mine. Strange.'

'She'll be uncomfortable and protective, but if you let her know that Justice will always be her home, she'll settle down. After all, you and Gabe are no real threat. Her children would never inherit anyway.'

'That really is wrong. Don't you think? Women should be able to inherit. It's archaic.'

'I know. I suppose it'll change, some day.'

Gulls screamed in the cold air, horns sounded, stevedores shouted.

The docks were nearly under our feet now, and we joined the passengers streaming back to their staterooms to collect bags and companions.

'Iris is sure great, isn't she?' Helen commented from behind my shoulder. 'Have you met her . . . friend? Dan?'

'I haven't, no. And yes, I like Iris a great deal.'

'I'm glad you talked me into this,' she said suddenly. 'I'm looking forward to meeting Marsh and the others, seeing the house. Gabriel's house.'

'I did mean what I told you, that he would have loved to see you and the boy there. He revelled in every inch of the place.'

'I know,' she replied. 'You can feel that in the journal.'

Following the mention of the diary, we jostled along the corridor in silence for a time. At her door, she stopped with her hand on the knob. 'I want the man caught, who did that to Gabriel,' she said. 'That staff major.' *I want him torn to pieces*, her eyes said.

'We will catch him,' I told her, meeting her gaze, allowing no doubt to surface.

We had to; any other course was unthinkable.

Disembarking was a laborious business, with three men struggling to keep Ben O'Meary's chair from shooting down the steep gangway. Mycroft had sent two cars, both to give space to carry our trunks and bags and to provide two sturdy drivers to shift them. Ben could actually stand, with assistance, since his legs were burnt, not paralysed, but we were nonetheless grateful for the help. And being Mycroft's men, they would no doubt double as bodyguards, should the need arise.

The roads were an icy slush, and I quickly regretted that we had not tackled the trains instead. Helen seemed oblivious to the skids and slips; the boy duke spent the first part of the journey bouncing from one window to another and the last part asleep; Iris was withdrawn into her own thoughts; and Ben became visibly more and more uncomfortable.

At midday, we stopped at an inn for luncheon. On the way inside, one of the drivers took me aside for a consultation.

'The farther into the countryside we go, Miss Russell, the worse the roads will be. If you want to stop the night and continue tomorrow, just say the word.'

'If this turns to snow, the roads could be completely impassable tomorrow,' I noted. He said nothing, not even to answer my unspoken question, leaving the decision up to me. 'Let's go on after we've eaten. If the driving gets too difficult, that's your word to speak.'

He looked offended, although it was the conditions I was questioning, not his skill. We ate quickly, and upon returning to the motorcar I took the seat beside the driver, to leave more space for those behind the glass. Ben stretched his legs across the seat, Gabe looked at picture books on his mother's lap, Iris stared out the window, and we drove on through the darkness, the drizzle changing to snow in our headlamps, then back to rain.

We passed through Arley Holt and past the deserted train station, and at the turning with the post saying JUSTICE HALL, we went left, spurning the crowded manor house, whose every guest room would soon be bursting, for the quieter spaces of Badger Old Place. These larger motorcars seemed almost certain to become wedged between the tight sides of the lane, but in the end we emerged unscathed. Down the frozen track, through the gates and the outer yard, threading into the lodge-house tunnel and there was Badger's neat gravel, the chapel, and the high Elizabethan windows, glowing with light and welcome.

Gabe had fallen asleep with his thumb in his mouth, and he clung to his mother's side while our two drivers deftly eased Ben into his chair. Introductions were made, and while Mrs Algernon bustled and welcomed like the excellent housekeeper she was, Alistair had eyes only for the boy, this cranky, waist-high snippet of Hughenfort on which so much rested, the futures of two men and of a great house; apart from his distraction, Alistair's welcome was warm (for him) and he waited until we had been given hot drinks and rooms before he climbed into one of Mycroft's motorcars and was driven away.

We changed our clothes, while Gabe pounded up and down the various stairways to rid himself of the tiresome journey. This took a quarter of an hour, after which we sat down to Mrs Algernon's plain and excellent dinner, then adjourned to the Hall, where the child eyed the huge boar's head uncertainly and the rest of us settled into the novelty of a floor that didn't heave or bump beneath us. The entire time, from the moment we climbed down from the car, throughout the meal, and as we took our places before the fire in the Hall, we moved in a kind of limbo. In part this was tiredness compounded by the disorientation of our Canadian companions; but we were also simply waiting. At last our ears caught the sound of tyres on the gravel outside. Ali came in first, and then Marsh, with Holmes behind them closing the door.

Marsh stood in the doorway, a stone thinner but restored in his energies, apparently unaware of Alistair's hands tugging away his coat and plucking the hat from his head. All of Marsh's tremendous powers of concentration were focused upon the woman standing in front of the fire and on the child grown suddenly shy, taking refuge in her skirts. Marsh's fingers went up to his face – not, as I first thought, to trace the scar, as he was wont to do in Palestine when troubled. Rather, his fingers came to rest across his lips, a gesture of such uncertainty, I should not have imagined him capable of it.

Iris eased him into the moment, crossing the room to greet her husband with a very European sort of kiss, then looping her arm through his in order to lead him forward. 'This is Ben O'Meary,' she told him; I doubt Marsh even noticed he was shaking the hand of a man in a wheeled chair. 'And Helen.'

Helen stood before him, straight and proud, her son half hidden behind her. Marsh stepped forward and took her hand briefly.

'Welcome to England, Mrs Hewetson,' he said evenly.

'Please, it's Helen.'

'Helen, then. Thank you. And this is young Gabriel.'

'Gabe,' came an indistinct mutter from the cloth around her thighs.

'Can you shake hands with Lord Maurice, Gabe?' Helen asked the top of his head.

The child seemed to consider this for a minute, then began to unwrap himself from her skirts. He stepped away and looked up at Marsh, chin raised, black hair tumbled.

Marsh's heart seemed visibly to stutter. Certainly the breath caught in his throat – I could hear it do so. His blunt fingers came up again towards his face, and then he noticed the boy's small hand, extended towards him. Slowly, he stretched out his arm and wrapped his hand gently around that of the child, his son's son.

'Oh, Gabe,' he said, his voice impossibly soft. 'I am very, very happy to meet you.'

CHAPTER TWENTY-NINE

LATE THAT NIGHT, WHEN the Canadians had bedded down and the Algernons taken to their quarters, we gathered in the first-floor solar for a council of war. Holmes and I diverted to our rooms to trade our tight collars and high shoes for clothing more conducive to comfort and thought. When Holmes had donned a smoking jacket and I my house slippers, we walked back down the corridor and let ourselves in.

The room was dimly lit and filled with indistinct shapes, an Aladdin's cave of family treasures. My eyes came to rest on the figures before the pulsing flames, and my heart leapt in sudden, startled joy at the image that greeted my eyes – then my vision cleared, and the figure that I had seen as Mahmoud Hazr in Arab dress turned more fully into the light, and it was only Marsh, wearing a long, old-fashioned smoking jacket over his trousers and shirt.

However, as we settled to our places around the fire, I found I could not shake the image of Mahmoud among us. For one thing, he was brewing us coffee – true, using an elaborate glass machine over a spirit lamp rather than the graduated brass pots of the Arabs, and spooning the grounds from a Fortnum and Mason's packet instead of pounding the beans to powder in a wooden mortar, but the scent evoked the ghosts of tents and robes. And carpets – but there, too, the room moved East, for in the weeks I'd been away Badger's plain Turkey floor covering had been overlaid with smaller, more ornate carpets. Like the floor of a tent. The drawn curtains might well have been goat's-hair walls, the fire in the stone hearth crackled with the same rhythm as one laid in a circle of rocks on sand, and the flickering across the gathered faces seemed to darken them, so that even Iris appeared swarthy. The odours of coffee and cigarettes teased my mind, the man squatting before the flames in a tumble of robes, the easy silence before talk began . . .

Abruptly, I stood and switched on one of the electric lamps, and the room was jerked back to Berkshire. The others blinked at the sudden glare, and reason returned. We took our coffee in porcelain cups with handles on their sides and saucers beneath; we were in chairs, not on the floor; the tobacco the others lit was Turkish, not the cheapest black stuff of the desert smoker. I breathed a sigh of relief, took a swallow of Piccadilly coffee, then glanced over at Marsh.

And saw Mahmoud in his eyes, in the hidden amusement of that private, all-seeing gaze, acknowledging what my illuminating efforts meant, why I had needed to do it. His gaze held me in my spot, and then I found myself smiling slowly back, that same warm, intimate sharing of a private joke.

I do not know that I have ever felt more at peace with the world than at the moment when Mahmoud returned.

Ali, of course, had known it before anyone else – probably before Marsh himself. His hands had sought out a scrap of firewood and his folding penknife, and were shaping the wood into one of the incongruously childlike figures he had used to carve around the camp-fire. This one was perhaps fated to become a giraffe, although at the moment it was little more than two lumps connected by a long neck.

Iris, who had never seen these two in their alternate personalities, was looking puzzled, even slightly alarmed at the unfamiliar currents running through the room; Holmes, however, took it in at a glance, nodded approvingly, and drew out his pipe and tobacco pouch. It was he who broke the silence.

'I suppose it hardly needs saying that the boy is who he seems to be?'

'There could be no doubt,' Marsh answered. I peered across at him: Had that been a faint accent I heard, a faintly Semitic placement to the R?

'He is the very image of Gabriel at that age,' Iris confirmed. 'The boy Thomas may be a fake, but not Gabe.'

'I agree,' said Alistair, not looking up from his carving.

'Very well; that settles the problem of inheritances,' Holmes said, and made to go on to the next item of business on his agenda. I, however, was not so sure.

'It may settle the question of the title,' I cut in, 'but I wouldn't assume it settles the future of Justice. Helen is by no means clear in her mind that coming here would be best for the boy.'

Holmes was already shaking his head dismissively. 'It matters not. If the boy is Gabriel's son, born in wedlock, then he *is* the seventh Duke. What his mother decides to do about the child's living arrangements may require lengthy negotiations, but that element of the problem lies in the future. Are we in agreement?'

It was somewhat unusual for Holmes to consult with his

partners before tying off his conclusions, but then, this was hardly his usual sort of case. However, the once and (potentially) future duke, his wife, and his cousin were all in accord: the strawberry leaves, at least, had been lifted from Marsh's head.

'We are still left with the question of Sub-Lieutenant Hughenfort's untimely death. I take it we agree that the man who arranged his death is still at large, and that he must be dealt with before we can all feel free to return to our natural orbits?'

'The child wouldn't live to see mid-summer,' Alistair growled, and sliced a vicious strip from the knot of wood in his hand. Iris winced at his words, Marsh sat silent, but we all agreed: The five-year-old Duke of Beauville could not be left vulnerable.

'From the early days of this case,' Holmes resumed, flaring a match into life and setting it to his pipe-bowl, 'we have been confronted with a choice of villains, coming down eventually to two. And before you interrupt me again, Russell, let me say that the three of us occupied the War Records Offices for a solid week – very solid, taking into account the state of the sofas on which we slept – and after scouring the files, we came up with no definitive evidence, not a shred that would eliminate either man from consideration.'

I raised my cup to my lips, to hide the smile I could not help: Normally it was Holmes who managed to snag the more interesting and productive path of an investigation. This time he had sent me off on a boat into the frigid Atlantic, and I'd come up with gold while he had uncovered only a lot of dust. A few years before, I might have pointed this out; now, I merely took a swallow of coffee and kept my eyes demurely on the fire.

Rather sourly, Holmes continued. 'There are two prime

candidates for Gabriel Hughenfort's murder-by-proxy. Sidney Darling came most immediately to hand – a man with deep ties, both financial and social, to his wife's family home. Even before the War, Darling had a lot to say in the running of the estate and the tenant farms. Since the War, Darling has been virtually running the place. The proposed stud is his project, the Hall and the London house are his freely to use, he has position, authority, everything but the title. All that would have changed were his nephew to have inherited, when Lady Phillida would have been issued an income and become a guest in the Hall, not its mistress. As for opportunity, Darling's position in 1918 was such that he could readily have arranged for Gabriel's transfer and, later, the condemnatory letter. Darling had considerable interest in preserving the *status quo* at Justice Hall. Similarly, when Marsh came, he too represented a threat. Little doubt, then, when handed a golden opportunity to replace the seventh Duke with the malleable child of a half-educated Frenchwoman by the simple mechanism of a stray shotgun shell, he might have been sorely tempted.

'Thomas was clearly Darling's protégé. We know Darling has been to Lyons, to coach the mother and convince the boy. However, we must not place too heavy an emphasis on this scheme, for he might well have been motivated by the simple knowledge that if he could provide Marsh with a satisfactory heir, Marsh would very probably retreat back into whatever hole he'd been occupying since Cambridge, leaving Darling to continue as before. Self-interest does not invariably lead to homicide.

'Our other candidate is Ivo Hughenfort. Means he had, for he too was in a position to act as voice for his superiors and insert orders of transfer or letters of condemnation. Motive could be had by the realisation that in the past few years he had been suddenly and unexpectedly moved from eighth in the line of succession to fourth. In January 1914, there were so many men before Ivo, the possibility that he might one day be duke might well never have occurred to him. Such a catastrophic upheaval of the natural order would have been unthinkable, until the War. Lionel died in May of that year, and the son he left might well not stand up to a legal battle. Then Ralph, the sixth in line, was apparently killed in Gallipoli, and Philip Peter was reputed to have died without children. Marsh and Alistair had not been heard from in years, and could well have got themselves killed in some dusty land. Remember, Mme Hughenfort told us that some family member came to see the boy during the War? That could well have been Ivo, confirming for his own eyes that Thomas was arguably no Hughenfort. Suddenly, in the space of a few years, there was by all appearances only one boy, a vulnerable young soldier already on the Front, standing in the way of Justice Hall.'

Holmes allowed silence to fall while he fiddled with his pipe, then started up again. 'This is, however, entirely speculation. Either man had an equal opportunity to sabotage the wheels of justice, either could have been Gabriel's "uncle" the red-tab major, who said he would lodge an appeal and did not; who in the final hours convinced the boy that a noble silence would safeguard the family honour in the face of disaster; who took away with him the boy's precious letters and papers – including the secret marriage certificate – and ensured that none but his generalised night-before-battle letter ever saw light of day.

'It could have been either,' he said, his summation coming to a close. 'It could have been both, working together then as they occasionally do now. It could, I will admit, be another party altogether whose spoor I have entirely overlooked, although the likelihood of such a possibility is near to infinitesimal.

'How, then, do we lay hands on our villain?'

As if in answer, a penknife flashed through the air, to sink its point into a waiting log and stand there, quivering. Iris flinched; I looked at Alistair with new respect: A penknife is no throwing blade. One glance at his features, however, and the words of praise died away from my lips.

The knife had not been Alistair's irritable comment: It had been Ali's answer to the question of how we were to reveal the villain. Ali the cut-throat sat in the room with us, holding the gaze of his brother Mahmoud, both of them cold, and ruthless, and far, far away.

'No!' It was Holmes who spoke loudly, but I had been saying it internally. I had once witnessed Mahmoud and Ali get a piece of information out of a thief by threatening to blind him with a burning cigarette. They'd have done it, too, had he not given way

Marsh blinked, and tore his eyes away to look at Holmes. After a moment, Marsh wavered, glanced involuntarily at Iris (who of course had not followed the silent discussion going on under her nose), and then looked into the flames. 'Harsh times, harsh methods,' he said. 'Let us hope it does not come to that here.'

That was as much of a promise as Holmes could elicit. With a final glare at the cut-throat nobleman, he turned his attention to me.

'One of the difficulties we encountered while you were on your Atlantic cruise was that both of the gentlemen in question had removed themselves from view. Darling was in Berlin for most of the past ten days, overseeing the hiring of staff for the offices of his new business there, and only returned to London on Monday. Ivo Hughenfort simply vanished, taking his manservant with him and leaving word only that he planned to return to Berkshire in time for the ball this weekend.

'I need hardly add, I think, that careful searches were conducted of the houses and grounds of both men. Four safes in total between them,' he noted, the tedium of extended safe-cracking clear in his voice, 'and not a cache of letters to be found. A variety of illegal activities, particularly on the part of Mr Darling, but nothing to connect either with Gabriel Hughenfort.'

'The letters may have been destroyed.'

'It is always possible, although it is my experience that the criminal mind is generally loath to destroy an object which might be of future use.'

'So what do you propose?' I asked, although I thought I knew.

'A trap,' he replied. Marsh, Alistair, and Iris looked interested.

'Something to send him to his hiding place?'

'Precisely. It is a method I have used before – with, I will admit, varying degrees of success – but more often to bring an object to light than to confirm its existence. Success will require a minimum of four people, two on each suspect. I do not usually possess such riches.'

'What about me?' Iris objected.

'Have you any experience in what they call "tailing" a suspect?' Holmes asked her.

'No, but how difficult—'

'Then you shall be our support staff. We are dealing with a clever man here, and it cannot be expected that he will break immediately from cover. The more caution he possesses, the longer the process will take. You shall be in a central position near a telephone, with a motor and driver to hand, in order to bring whatever equipment or assistance we might require.'

'Such as what?' she demanded, certain she was merely being humoured.

'Anything from a change of disguise to a stick of dynamite.'

'Oh, very well. Although I had rather be of more use.'

'Your position, should it come into play, requires resourcefulness, steady nerves, and the ability to move quickly. I was under the impression that you possessed these characteristics.'

That cheered her. 'I'll do my best.'

'The bait for the trap?' Alistair enquired.

'I should think the marriage certificate would be the best. A witness to the document, perhaps, has come to light.'

'What about the priest who performed it?' I suggested. 'We could say that Marsh has heard a rumour that Gabriel married a French girl, so he's going to France next week to see—'

'No.' It was Marsh, looking unmovable. 'The ball is intended to welcome the seventh Duke to Justice. It will do that.'

'Oh, Marsh,' Iris exclaimed. 'You can't put the boy in harm's way!'

'I must. He will be removed immediately thereafter, and he and his mother will be sheltered until the matter is resolved.' I did not much care for the grim way in which he pronounced the word *resolved*, but Iris did not seem to notice. He went on. 'However, Mary's suggestion remains valid. I will let it be known that we will be searching for the church register. Whichever of the two breaks for the Continent first . . . will be our man.'

CHAPTER THIRTY

SATURDAY'S BALL WAS TO be fancy dress, its theme Tutankhamen's Tomb, which had been opened the previous winter and instantly plunged the world into a state of raving Tutmania. While I was away in Canada, Justice Hall had been transported to the Valley of the Kings. With the minor complication of weather most unsuited to the Egyptian desert, in a dim light one might suspect one was in the archaeological dig that had just resumed for the season in Luxor, three thousand miles away. The final doors of Tutankhamen's inner tomb lay ripe for the opening, but Phillida Darling had anticipated the event.

Wire and papier-mâché palm trees now lined the drive; the pelicans of the fountain had somehow become ibises; crocodiles made of wood and rubber inhabited Justice Stream and its new forest of reeds and papyrus at the shallow beginning of the pond. Huge sheets of painted canvas had been suspended from the battlements, obscuring the house's front façade with row after row of enlarged Egyptian tomb paintings. A trio of stuffed camels sheltered under the portico of the stable wing; an enormous cage, its wire cunningly disguised under vines, occupied the portico on the side of the kitchen block. A closer look at the cage revealed two depressed-looking apes huddling in one corner. The lawn and terraces had either been dug up or had temporary mounds of soil heaped on top, with the odd shovel and barrow sticking out of the caps of melting snow to indicate work in progress. Three men were working up at the rooftop, fixing what looked to be torches along the battlements. Down below, the big double doors of Justice now resembled the entrance to a royal tomb, guarded by two enormous stuffed crocodiles, rearing up on their hind feet and tails. Blood-curdling shrieks came from within, either some terrible human sacrifice or a flock of parrots.

I could only stand in awe near the newly ibised fountain, wondering that Justice Hall did not collapse in mortification.

Iris had either been looking out for me or happened to be passing near one of the few unobscured windows, because she came out of the tomb door, dressed in reassuringly normal trousers, and grinned at my slack-jawed state.

'Quite an effect, isn't it?' she asked.

'Words fail me.'

'Wait 'til you see the Hall.'

'I don't know that I'm strong enough.'

'Well, I shouldn't recommend standing out here too long. Phillida's animal man seems to have lost one of his crocodiles; it's walking around loose, or crawling, or whatever it is crocodiles do.'

'Probably lurking under the bridge, hoping for a deer. Or one of the dogs.' Still, I thought I might go inside, away from concealing shrubbery. As we passed through the tomb-painted drapes, I asked, 'Do you know if Phillida has asked any stray scholars of ancient Egyptian to this bean-feast?'

'Haven't any idea.'

'It's just, I believe that string of hieroglyphs there says something extraordinarily rude about the reader's mother.'

Ogilby held the door for us, dressed, I was relieved to see, in his usual butler's black formality. At least he had not had an Anubis mask placed on his head or been stripped down to the loin-cloth of Egyptian servants.

The Great Hall, on the other hand . . .

The cavernous stone expanse had undergone a complete metamorphosis; I was now standing within a vast tropical grotto, moist-aired and with no hint of an echo. Every corner was thick with head-high reeds and ponds filled with flowering water-lilies; the upper gallery was a jungle of vines that neared the floor; every accessible surface was a riot of lapis, gold, carmine, and emerald scarabs, hieroglyphs, and lotus flowers. A family of disturbingly realistic mummies guarded the inner door. (They had to be papier-mâché; surely Phillida couldn't have persuaded the British Museum . . . ?) Three parrots on high perches screamed their fury, frightening the ape a man was attempting to coax onto an artificial tree. A crew was moving half a dozen monumental statues into place, with a fifteen-foot-high cat-headed god the current object of their attentions. A flock of seven flying ibises had been suspended from the dome. One of their stuffed companions had settled onto the outstretched arm of the classical athlete.

It was absolutely breathtaking.

'How on earth did she do this?' I wondered aloud. 'Look – those lotuses are actually blooming. Shouldn't they be dormant this time of year?'

'Some of them are silk – all the vines are – but she did have two or three dozen pots forced in a hot-house. And Marsh wouldn't let her paint directly onto the marble, so all the columns are covered in canvas.'

'It's even warm in here.'

'The radiators and fireplaces have been blasting away for three days to get it to this point.'

'Extraordinary. I shudder to think what this must be costing them.'

'Justice hasn't had a new duke in twenty-one years. Phillida thought it only right to welcome him in a style worthy of the title.'

I met Iris's eyes, and found them dancing with the same secret pleasure I felt in my own. I glanced around to be sure we weren't overheard, then said, 'I wonder if she will appreciate the surprise we have in store for her?'

'It will be a shock, but in the end the additional news value will make up for it. Justice and the Darlings will be the talk of all Europe for weeks.'

'How many guests are expected?'

'No one seems exactly sure, but the special train they're running from Town holds around two hundred. That's probably more than half of them.'

The logistics were appalling. 'Where on earth are they all going to sleep?'

'Oh heavens, they won't sleep. It's dancing 'til dawn, a breakfast of eggs and champagne, then back on the train, or however they got here.'

'I'm exhausted already.'

Iris looked surprised. 'Surely you've been to a fancy dress ball before?'

My entire life, at times, seemed to be fancy dress. 'Since the end of the War, I've been rather occupied with other things.'

'Well, as parties, they tend to be somewhat . . . uninhibited. There's a freedom in wearing costume. Normal mores and attitudes are set aside.'

'Three hundred uninhibited Young Things. I hope Phillida's hidden away all the breakables.'

'More to the point, she's borrowed strong young manservants from every house in the county, to keep things from getting too out of hand.'

'I can only hope she gives the servants a week off when they've survived this.'

'Oh, Ogilby is in heaven, and Mrs Butter is having the time of her life. Not a one of them would miss this for the world.'

With a last glance at the fifteen-foot-high statue of Bast (plaster, I guessed, by the ease with which two men were carrying it up the stairs), I followed Iris past a trio of stuffed flamingos and through the corridor of outraged marble busts wearing gauze headdresses, ending up at the library, which was miraculously free of Egyptian fetters.

Marsh Hughenfort looked like a man whose fever has broken, leaving him clear-eyed and clear of purpose for the first time. He greeted me casually, but with Mahmoud's hidden meaning behind his eyes, speaking of appreciation and the anticipation of action. He sat in his chair, completely relaxed in the way he had once been when reclining by a camp-fire, and it came to me that he looked more a duke now that he had been supplanted than ever he had when that title had actually ridden his shoulders. Seeing his dark eyes full of life again made my heart glad.

'My brother's guests, they are well?' he asked me.

And Alistair had been restored to 'brotherhood', I noted. 'They slept well, and were fed to repletion by Mrs Algernon. When I left them, the boy was being led off into the meadow on a disgustingly fat pony by Mr Algernon. They seemed to be plotting out the most effective spot for a snowman, if the snow comes back.'

'Mary, I . . . thank you. My entire family is in your debt.' There was a lot of weight behind that statement – the entire weight of the Hughenfort name, in fact. It was a concept both English and Bedouin.

'I was pleased I could be of service.'

'And yet, I find that I must now ask a further service of you and Holmes.'

'You are my brother,' I told him. In Arabic.

He inclined his head, acknowledging not only that he understood the statement, but that he saw the truth of it. 'I wish to make the announcement tonight, during the dance. I wish to introduce the rightful duke before matters become any more complex.'

'What does Helen think?'

'My s—my nephew's wife is a woman worthy of him. She understands that there is no safety in Canada that is not to be found here. She regrets you ever found her, she is angry with herself that she did not have the foresight to conceal the boy from us, she detests the idea of revealing him to public scrutiny and the inevitable acclaim and uproar that will follow, but she also sees that it is the best way. The boy cannot hide forever. Best it is dealt with here and now.'

'By "dealt with" you mean . . . ?'

He met my gaze evenly, 'I mean that I am no longer a duke. I am a commoner, with different rules of behaviour. I mean that I may be required to take brutal action in order to protect my duke. My five-year-old liege lord. I believe you take my meaning.'

'And the service you require?'

'Not to stand in my way.'

The eyes opposite me were dark with warning and with purpose. I had seen those eyes before, and I did not really want to know precisely what he had in mind to wrest the truth of the matter out of its participants. I knew him well enough to be certain that if atrocity could be avoided, he would do so; but I also knew that if brutality was the only way to protect the boy, he would not hesitate for an instant. I nearly opened my mouth to say, *I won't help you, and I don't want to see it,* but caught back the words. He knew that I wanted no part in torturing information out of a man; he would not force me to help, or to witness it.

Unless it proved necessary.

I felt that in the brief minutes I'd been in the library, we had carried on a lengthy discussion. Holmes and I often communicated in such a manner, to all intents and purposes reading the other's mind, but it happened rarely with anyone else. I could only nod, to show that the discussion was over and that we were, however unhappily, in agreement.

'So when do you propose to tell Lady Phillida that she is giving a party for the wrong person?' I asked.

'Not until the last minute. However, strictly speaking, the invitations say merely that we are to honour Justice Hall's seventh Duke. That is precisely what we shall be doing.'

'Even though the menu would more appropriately be fizzy lemonade and sausage rolls, followed by an eight o'clock bed-time. You'll bring him to the dance?'

'My brother Ali will do so, when the evening is under way. In the meantime, the boy is safe with him.'

'And afterwards?'

'I will make the announcement. I will tell the entire room that this boy appears to be the legal heir, even though the actual marriage papers have yet to be found. I will say that on Monday morning a delegation from Justice Hall will leave for France, to seek out the village where Gabriel and Helen were married, and there they will make enquiries from the priest as to the ceremony. That will cause one of two things to happen. If our culprit has already destroyed the copy of the marriage certificate he took from Gabriel – which any sensible person would have done in those circumstances – then he will depart for France with all due haste, there to remove any register in which the priest might have entered the ceremony. And possibly to remove the priest himself. If, however, he is stupid enough to have kept the stolen paper – or overly confident, which amounts to the same thing – then he will make haste to retrieve his copy, either to destroy it or to be absolutely certain that it remains where he hid it. In either case, we shall be at his heels, to see which way our man breaks from cover.'

'This sounds like one of Holmes' plans,' I said uneasily.

'We collaborated.'

'I thought so. He's used it before, this idea that when threatened with destruction, a person retrieves what is most valuable first, be it baby or the instrument of blackmail. I have to say, however, that isn't always the case. A person in a panic is as likely to grab a toothbrush as a diamond necklace, just as a cold-blooded person will control the immediate reaction to fly to the object of desire. The cases Holmes has tried this on haven't invariably turned out quite as he would have wished.'

'I see. Well, failure lurks outside every gate. If this does not succeed, we shall be forced to try . . . harsher methods. In any case, if we do not have our man by Monday night, the boy and his mother will leave the country. Our friend Mycroft Holmes has some plan for them. It involves an air field, so they will feel at home.'

I would not ask how long he planned to wait after Monday before giving up on the idea of the villain's breaking from cover. He would set beaters around the shrubbery after his game, and if that technique failed, he would go in after the man himself. I suppressed a shiver.

'How do we divide them up?'

'You and Holmes will watch Ivo Hughenfort tonight, after I have made my announcement. Ali will be with Sidney. When I have finished and handed the boy over to his mother, I will relieve Holmes and send him to Ali. You and I will then follow Ivo, Ali and Holmes will watch Sidney.'

I thought about it. He clearly considered Sidney Darling the more likely suspect, since Ali's powers of surreptitious pursuit could be surpassed only by the suspect's own shadow. I wondered if Holmes agreed with his assessment.

'You are to watch our suspects, Holmes and I are to watch your backs,' I clarified.

He grinned. 'It is a role you have played before, Amir.'

'And until Monday night, how do you intend to ensure the boy's safety?'

'Iris and the boy's mother will be with him.' Before I could formulate a polite way of saying that the two women were completely without experience in the finer arts of body guarding, he smiled. 'Along with one of your brother-in-law's people, whom your Holmes is bringing from London. A kindly grey-haired woman, very deceptive, very competent. I see what you are thinking, Mary, and I agree: I had rather spirit the boy away this instant and keep him beneath my robes than expose him to danger. But he is a Hughenfort, and we have been soldiers for a thousand years. However, I believe that if the boy's legitimacy can be rendered null, there will be no reason for our culprit to murder him. The risk would be great, and the alternative too simple. No; this is the only way.'

It was not the only way, but it was the most direct, and in any case the situation had been firmly taken out of my hands. I could merely await my orders and pray all would go well.

'I am your humble servant,' I replied. In Arabic.

'Servant you may be,' he rejoined. 'Humble I sincerely doubt.'

Iris came in then, and dropped onto the settee with a cigarette and a shake of the head. 'Marsh, I shall remain forever grateful to you that I am not called upon to mastermind an affair such as this. Planning a dinner party for six stretches my abilities.'

'Phillida seems to find it a pleasure,' he mused.

'She's quite mad. I found her arguing with the stuffed-animal man that he'd brought an alligator with the crocodiles. I ask you, how did she know? And what does it matter?'

'Only to another alligator,' I said.

'What are you going as, Mary?' she asked me.

'It's a surprise. I mean, to me as well. Holmes is in London, and said he'd bring something back for me.'

'You don't sound too happy about it.'

'Holmes has a dreadful habit of allowing his sense of humour free rein at times like this. Once he dressed me as a lady of the evening. Another time I wore a water-butt.'

'A water-butt? You're joking. And I thought you said you'd never been to a fancy dress ball before.'

'No ball, just disguise. A barrel under a drainpipe. A very damp and draughty disguise.'

'Well, I am sure if what he comes up with is too awful, the costume box is still there – isn't it, Marsh? Mary could come as Napoleon. He tried to conquer Egypt once, didn't he?'

'More or less. But he's a few thousand years late for the theme of this ball.'

'You honestly think that will make a whit of difference to the guests? Half of them won't even know where Egypt is.'

'I could always decapitate one of the stuffed ibises in the Hall, put it on my head and come as Thoth.'

Still, I couldn't help wondering what sort of costume Holmes would show up with.

Our council was interrupted by the door's flying open and Lady Phillida's stepping in – a harried-looking Lady Phillida who had neglected to put on her face that morning. The thin lines of her plucked eyebrows were nearly invisible, giving her a look of naked surprise that did not agree with the tension in her jaw.

'Have you seen the children?' she demanded without preamble.

'We have not,' Marsh said.

'That feeble Paul woman is the most useless governess. I should have left them in London.'

'If they come here, I shall ask them to report to you instantly,' Marsh told her.

She turned a glare on him, her forehead puckering with the suspicion that he was laughing at her concerns. Some other thought seemed to occur to her as well, triggered by her belated awareness that her brother was in an unusual state of mind, and that on a day such as this, any new factor could prove catastrophic.

'Are you all right?' she asked sharply.

'I am feeling very well indeed.'

'You're not drunk? Oh, God, Marsh, you can't be drinking today! Iris, can't you—'

'I am not drinking, I have not drunk, I will not drink.'

'Look, Marsh, I know you must be concerned about tonight, but really, there won't be anything to it. Sidney will stand up after dinner and introduce you, you'll say thank you for coming, and then everyone will get back to the dancing. Just a brief moment so as to introduce formally the seventh Duke. I know how you hate a crowd, but you can do that, Marsh, can't you?'

'Alistair will make the introduction.'

'No, no; Sidney's got his speech all ready.'

'Phillida.' That was all Marsh said, but the unaccustomed note of complete authority in his voice got her attention. She blinked, and took another step inside the room as if to see him more clearly. Her antennae were quivering; she knew something was up here, just not what it was, or how it would affect her.

'But Sidney—'

'No. I want Ali.'

'I don't have the time for this,' she fretted. 'Oh, very well, Alistair it is. Just tell him that all he has to do is introduce the seventh Duke of Beauville. Surely he can handle that.'

'Don't worry,' Marsh told her. 'The seventh Duke will have his introduction.'

Now she was certain that he was hiding something from her, and it worried her deeply. 'Marsh, what do you have planned? You're hiding something. I swear, Marsh, if you do anything to spoil this evening, I'll—'

'Phillida, I will not spoil your evening. Your guests will go away happy.'

She might have pursued the matter – not that it would have done her much good, since her brother clearly had no intention of explaining further – but shouts and a crash from somewhere back in the house caught her attention. 'Oh, Lord, what's happened now? I have to go. Iris, Mary, keep an eye on him,' she pleaded, an attempt to enlist the sensible minds in the room onto her side – a futile attempt, as our faces told her. She threw up her hands, left the library, and then stuck her head back inside. 'If you see the children, tell them to go to Miss Paul instantly, or I shall be quite angry.'

The door banged shut, and I made to go as well, but stopped when Marsh said, 'Angry with me, do you suppose, or angry with the children?'

'Both, I should think,' Iris told him.

'In that case, perhaps I should have mentioned to her that they're in the conservatory.'

Iris and I turned sharply in our chairs, to look through the billiards room to the glasshouse beyond. Indeed, after a few seconds, the anaemic vine jerked as if its roots were under attack.

'I merely told her that I hadn't seen them,' Marsh explained placidly. 'Which I hadn't.'

'Marsh, you're terrible,' Iris scolded.

The liberated duke just shrugged. He looked so pleased with himself, I could have hugged him.

Chapter Thirty-One

Taking pity on lady Phillida, Iris and I went out through the conservatory.

A rattle of half-dead shrubbery followed our opening of the door, followed by an exaggerated stillness.

Iris spoke into the damp, mildewed air. 'Your mother wants you to go back to your nurse.'

'She's our governess,' protested a voice from the dead palm.

'I don't care if she's your headmistress, your absence is troubling your mother, who has quite enough on her mind without you two adding to it.'

After a minute of whispered consultation, the bushes disgorged two very untidy children, leaves in their hair, soil to their knees, and rebellion on their grubby faces.

'They've taken over all our hiding places,' Lenore complained.

'Even the cabinet in the drawing room,' Walter added.

'Can't you play somewhere else?' Iris asked.

'We're forbidden to go in the stables wing, and Mrs Butter told us that if she sees us again near the kitchen, we won't eat for a week.'

'That leaves a lot of the Hall to hide in. This whole wing.'

'It's all bedrooms upstairs, except the old nursery, and all the rooms on the ground floor we've been told to keep away from, too.'

'I see your problem,' Iris said solemnly. 'Shall I ask your uncle if you might be permitted, just this once, to make use of the billiards room, when no one else is using it, and the Armoury, if you promise not to touch any of the weapons?'

'Oh, yes, please!'

'But first you report to your governess and let her know you're all right. Then ask if she would mind if you just kept to yourselves, but reported in to her once an hour. That may be an acceptable compromise. *If* you keep your side of the bargain. And brush yourselves clean before she sees you!' Iris called after their rapidly disappearing figures.

A first-rate shot and a woman with negotiating skills – I was amazed that Mycroft had not kept her as one of his own. When the children had left us, Iris lingered, clearly wanting to talk, but not sure how to begin.

'It should go all right,' I said, more to provide an opening than from any enthusiasm for Holmes' proposed trap.

'Do you honestly think so?'

'Well,' I said, 'the whole thing sounds uncertain, but it has been my experience that the more solidly constructed a plan looks to be, the more vulnerable it is. This one has the virtue of simplicity: Whoever is behind this, he *will* want that evidence of marriage, whether it's Gabriel's certificate that he has locked away in a bank vault somewhere, or the actual church register in France. And we do have sufficient manpower to go after him. Both those factors work in our favour.'

'And if he's already destroyed both the certificate and the register?'

'Then in a few days we let it be known that Helen has a copy, and where, and lay the trap that way. It's not perfect, Iris; such things rarely are. But if any group can lay hands on this particular culprit, it's this one.' There was no point in letting her see my uneasiness; if the plan blew up, we should have to deal with it then. As a reassurance, however, it was inadequate, and Iris went off not much satisfied.

I spent the rest of the morning doing a certain amount of hide-and-seek myself, exploring the crannies and crevices of Justice Hall that I had not seen before. In this search I was aided by the librarian Mr Greene, to whom I had brought another sprig of winter-tough rosemary and who in return had lent me the original plans for the house. The volume was bound in green leather with gilt embossing, and was too cumbersome to be of any use while moving about the rooms and corridors, but I borrowed the big desk in Marsh's rooms, and in that relative privacy made copious notes. What the servants thought of this friend of their duke's creeping up the servants' stairways and through the corridors on the wrong side of the baize doors, I hated to think, but most of them were far too busy to enquire, or even take notice.

I saw the Darling children once or twice, and was cautious about opening passages, lest they follow me inside, but they seemed happy enough with the Armoury and later constructed a fortress beneath the billiards table.

By the afternoon I was satisfied that I knew the ground as well as anyone could who had not been born and raised in Justice Hall. I even knew where the secret passages had to be, the concealed doors and the remainder of the spiral staircase, although lacking keys I could not investigate other than on paper. I returned the bound drawings to the library and went downstairs to take my leave of Marsh. To my surprise, he stood up from his conversation with the head butler.

'If you could wait a minute, Mary, I'll join you. Are we finished, Ogilby?'

'Thank you, Your Grace.'

Poor man, I thought; what confusion would reign here on the morrow, when 'Your Grace' would be a waist-high child with a Canadian accent. 'I'm happy to wait.'

'Have one of the cars sent around, if you would, Ogilby. I'll be at my cousin's house for tea. If Lady Phillida starts to worry, tell her I promised to be back here in good time.'

'Very good, Your Grace.'

'Come, Mary. Let us escape before we find ourselves pressed into service as Ra and Hathor.'

Mrs Algernon provided us with a plentiful tea, on the theory that food would not be had for hours (no doubt true) and that we should at any rate be having too good a time that night to bother eating (which, having spent the afternoon teased by the rich odours from the Justice kitchens, I truly doubted). Afterwards, Marsh, Helen, and the child bundled up in their thickest coats and went for a long walk; when they came back, Marsh was carrying the tired boy and Helen was joking with the older man as if she'd known him all her life.

There were snowflakes on their hats, and Algernon appeared before they had completely divested themselves of garments to say that he didn't think the snow would last for long, the sky looking none too determined about the matter, but that maybe we'd want to move ourselves over to the Hall sooner rather than later, just in case. Mrs Algernon insisted we take another cup of tea, which involved our third meal of the afternoon. As we were sitting down in the solar before the fire with our cups, Holmes blew in, looking remarkably disreputable, a number of large parcels in his arms.

'Have you brought my costume?' I demanded. His mouth was already filled by one of Mrs Algernon's sustaining little meat tarts, but he waved me towards the pile of things he had deposited just inside the door of the solar. I went over, and determined which was mine by the method of holding up each one and waiting for a shake or finally, a nod. The brown paper wrapping and crude twine gave me no great hope, but to my astonishment, what I pulled out was a more elegant version of the boy's costume I had worn all through Palestine those years before: loose head-cover, baggy trousers, and long over-shirt, even a heavy sheepskin coat to go over it all. All that was lacking were a curved knife for my belt and the torturous sandals Ali had inflicted on me in the beginning – which had in any case soon been replaced by the very boots residing in Alistair's guest-bedroom wardrobe. In these clothes, I would be 'Amir' – with rather more embroidery and a lot less dirt.

'This costume is anachronistic to a theme of ancient Egypt, Holmes,' I commented, but he did not take it seriously as a protest, as indeed had not been intended. Besides which, no doubt the nomads of the desert had dressed in much the same manner for the whole of their existence. I eyed the other packages. 'Is yours . . . ?'

'The same,' he answered. Which explained why my constitutionally tidy partner had neglected to shave this morning, that he might present a more ferocious visage.

Perhaps, I decided, this fancy dress ball wouldn't be too bad after all.

Donning our costumes was a quick matter, with the

arrangement of my hair beneath the turban taking the longest, as it was a skill I had forgotten. When Holmes and I met in Badger's Hall, I laughed aloud in sheer pleasure. Helen seemed to find our costumes somewhat disappointing, given the ornate possibilities opened up by the Tut theme, but Mahmoud and Ali merely exchanged a glance of amusement.

We piled into the car, Holmes, Marsh, and I, to be driven by Algernon to Justice Hall. Algernon would bring Alistair and the Canadian contingent later, so as to keep them under wraps until the last minute. I had to feel a moment's pity for the unsuspecting Phillida, whose elaborate party was going to be completely eclipsed by her brother's announcement.

The special train had obviously arrived at Arley Holt: We passed a steady stream of motorcars coming away from the Hall empty, returning to the village for the next load. This time Algernon circled around to the delivery entrance of the kitchen wing, so that we might enter Justice without having to push through a hundred excited guests. Marsh took himself off upstairs to consult with Iris concerning the arrangements for Gabe's care during the evening, Holmes disappeared in the other direction with my notes of Justice Hall's hidden passages, and I stood alone in the corridor of the western wing, torn between the tumult of voices spilling out of the Great Hall to my left and the peace of the library above me.

First, I decided, I should like to remedy the one lack in my costume. I was, in fact, armed with a slim throwing knife that rode in the top of my left boot, but a true Bedouin male would not be caught dead without an impressive blade at his belt. Not that I had any intention of using the thing here – I would actually be happy with just a decorative hilt in an empty scabbard – but the costume cried out for it.

The Armoury was the obvious place for decorative knives. Also for pikestaffs, crossbows, claymores, and broadswords, but those weapons fit neither in the theme nor in a press of merrymakers. I walked to the Armoury door, let myself inside, closed the door behind me, and then froze.

One thing about old stone buildings: The sound of rats is generally confined to the wooden rafters, yet I could have sworn that I heard the characteristic quick scuffle of movement from against the wall. From the enormous waist-high chest, in fact, which on closer inspection seemed to have its lid slightly lifted. I fought a smile, frowned at the walls as if choosing my weapon, then went over to the chest and clambered up to reach a foot-long jewelled scabbard hanging above it. I jumped down to the floor and arranged the knife in my belt (where it proved remarkably uncomfortable), stamped noisily across the room to the door, opened it, shut it, then crept back to the chest and waited.

The heavy lid rose up, an inch, then two; I stuck my hands in my belt to face the growing gap. An inch more, then a startled gasp and it banged shut. I stepped forward, wrestled the massive lid open, and glared down at the two figures inside.

'It's all right, sir,' Lenore Darling gabbled. 'We have permission to be here, really we do, and we weren't hurting anything, and never touched the weapons, honest.'

'Honest,' the boy echoed.

'Come on out of there, you two,' I said, and held the top for them. 'How on earth did you get this lid open in the first place? It weighs a young ton.'

'We had to sort of prise at it – I think it scratched it a little, but it has a lot of scratches anyway. Are you one of the guests?' she asked, trying to distract me from my examination of the great

413

gouge along the side where they had levered it open, which was, indeed, only the latest gash among the many time-honoured wounds of its long career. A bit of shoe polish or lamp-black and no one would be the wiser, I thought.

'I am a guest,' I told the girl, 'but we've met before. Mary Russell.'

They gaped at me, frankly admiring. 'Zingers!' said Walter, and 'Is that really you?' said his more sceptical sister. I pulled off my head covering to give them the benefit of my hair, and both agreed it was their uncle's guest.

I was not, however, finished with the chest. They had agreed with Iris not to touch any of the weapons in the Armoury, and although I had no wish to turn them in to the authorities, I thought it best to be sure that they had kept their part of the bargain. Every object I could see capable of prising open that lid had some kind of blade attached to it; I lifted the lid up enough to let light inside, and saw what they had been using.

It was an old tyre-lever, which was now transferring rust to a collection of moth-chewed wall hangings someone had stored in the chest and forgotten. Marsh's mother, or grandmother even; certainly they'd been in the chest so long, I thought, that rusty metal or children's shoes could not do them much damage. Which was more than I could say for the children's clothes – one of Miss Paul's chief duties was undoubtedly overseeing the changing of their clothes several times daily. I stretched to prop the heavy lid against the wall and then hitched my upper body over the side to retrieve the tyre-lever (realising that I probably ought not enquire where they had found the object, seeing that they were forbidden the stables wing as well). As my fingers touched the pitted metal, my sleeve brushed against something that was neither ancient wood nor moth-eaten wool. I handed the lever to Lenore, then went back on my toes to see what the foreign object had been.

Papers, it looked like: a packet of letters bound in a tired blue ribbon, a folded piece of heavy paper, and a single letter in its opened envelope, with a crumpled oilcloth wrap that they had been in. I pulled them out, eased the lid down again, and glanced at the solitary envelope. It had been sealed, then opened with a sharp blade; the envelope had neither the black Post Office stamp nor the red mark of the censor. One glimpse of the handwriting, and I nearly ripped the letter out of its envelope. *Dearest Pater*, it began.

I was holding in my hands Gabriel Hughenfort's final letter to his father, the letter written the night before his execution. A letter, I saw, containing no word of the young officer's true fate, but which held instructions on thanks to be extended to various individuals, including the batman Jamie McFarlane and the Reverend Mr Hastings. Most important, however, and the reason it had never reached Gabriel's parents, was the startling news of his battlefield wife, Helen, his love for her, his apologies for the haste of the marriage, and his knowledge that they would love her as their own. Gabriel's other 'final' letter, that time-stained sheet with the gentle and uplifting words intended for his mother's eyes, had gone through; this one, from the heir to his duke and meant for the father alone, had been given to a trusted family confidant to deliver personally. I sorted quickly through the bound packet of envelopes, all of which were in a woman's hand (Helen's, I thought), then unfolded the heavy paper of the other loose document: a Certificate of Marriage, between Gabriel Adrian Thomas Hughenfort and Philippa Helen O'Meary. To my relief, it did not look as if Lenore and Walter had got as far as reading them.

'Did you find these in here?' I asked them, keeping my voice casual.

'They were under the corner of those dirty cloths,' Lenore informed me, anxious that I should accept the inevitability of their find. 'We just climbed in to hide – or rather, I did, and when Walter couldn't find me he started to blub—'

'Did not!' the boy exclaimed in outrage.

'—and so I let him in with me, and then we could only get the top open a little way and we found these when the cloths got messed up, so we thought we'd sit and read them while we waited for Miss Paul to come looking for us, and then we heard you and got frightened that we might be in trouble and—'

'Oh, I shouldn't worry about it,' I reassured them easily, folding the papers away into an inner pocket. 'I won't tell. Although if I were you, I shouldn't say anything to anyone about having been inside the chest. Parents worry, don't you know, about children getting trapped and being unable to get out. They might decide to keep you in the nursery for your own safety. Too, that way, by the time someone notices the great gash you put into the side of it, you'll be safely back in London.'

I felt remarkably guilty at the manifold threats I was holding over their heads, but I couldn't take the chance of their chattering to their parents or any adult in earshot about being inside the chest where Gabriel's papers had been hidden away. The apprehension on both faces told me they would keep silent, at least long enough for the matter to be resolved.

'How long has it been since you reported in to your governess?'

'We probably ought to go now,' Lenore admitted.

'Dust yourselves off first,' I suggested.

'We're allowed to dress up tonight, too,' Walter informed me.

It was on the tip of my tongue to ask if he planned to come as a character from Mr Barrie's hated play, but I hadn't the heart. 'Good,' I said. 'Have fun.'

They left, the clamour from the Hall rising and cutting off abruptly with the closing of the stout door. I felt the packet of papers through the layers of fabric I wore. My immediate impulse was to shut myself into the nice heated lavatory and read every word on every page, but I had to let go that impulse almost as quickly. The papers belonged to Marsh; it was his decision if any other eyes saw them. Irritated at my sense of fair play, I settled the papers more firmly in the inner pocket, and went to find Marsh.

There had to be two hundred people already in the jungly Great Hall, spilling among the papyrus and shouting at each other beneath the suspended ibises. Bare arms on the women, bare torsos on some of the men (including a number who really oughtn't have), colours and face paint and an impressive effect overall.

And daunting. How was I to find Marsh in this crush?

I spotted a vaguely familiar face, smiled, and then turned back so hastily my head spun: Ogilby, wearing what appeared to be the contents of a washing-line. In fact, all the servants in sight were in similar raiment, Phillida's decorous version of an ancient Egyptian servant's uniform. I looked closely at the two figures standing beneath an arching silken palm tree, and recognised the hair-dressing Emma talking flirtatiously with a similarly draped individual who was not, I thought, one of the Justice staff. One of the strong young men borrowed from the neighbouring houses, no doubt. I settled my head wrapping and went over to the housemaid.

'Emma, have you any idea where I might find Lord – I mean, His Grace?'

She did not notice the familiar face under the costume, even though I had retained my own spectacles, and responded as to a stranger's enquiry. 'I don't believe he's come down yet, sir. I mean, *effendi*.'

'Er, thank you.' The strange servant – whom I now recognised from the day of the shoot, his crooked nose being unmistakable even if the rest of him was hidden by costume – had faded away into the fronds with his drinks tray as soon as he saw me approach. He moved with a slight limp, which spoke eloquently of toes crushed by the guests; I was grateful Holmes had not inflicted sandals on me. Emma, too, took up her tray again and pushed into the throng. I, however, turned towards the peace of the old wing and made my way up the 1612 stairway to Marsh's door.

'Who is that?' he called in answer to my knock.

'Mary,' I answered. Iris opened the door to me, with a drink in her hand; neither she nor Marsh were in costume, unless she proposed to join the party in lounge pyjamas. She looked at me uncertainly, then her face cleared with delight.

'Oh, that is very good, Mary,' she exclaimed. 'You look like a boy.'

'When first she wore that clothing,' Marsh remarked, 'looking like a boy was the idea.'

'It certainly succeeded. And that knife looks fierce.'

'I borrowed it from the Armoury,' I said to Marsh. 'Hope you don't mind.'

'Of course not.'

'Which is where I found this.' I fished the packet from inside my robes.

He unfolded the top page, saw the writing, and sat down abruptly. I poured myself a large dry sherry and took a chair while I waited for him to read it. When he looked back at me, his eyes took some time to come into focus.

'Have you . . . ?' he asked.

'No, just enough to see what it was.'

'Where did you find this?'

'Straight out of *The Purloined Letter* – one hides a thing too close for the person seeking it to find. In this case, it was inside that enormous studded chest in the Armoury. There are some old hangings or curtains or something inside – it doesn't look as if it's been opened for half a century, other than to deposit those.'

He looked at the papers in his hand without seeing them. 'We used to hide things in the Armoury,' he mused, not really thinking about what he was saying. 'In Long Tim's helmet, inside the chest. All the time. When we were boys.'

Iris could take no more. 'Marsh?' she asked. 'What is it?' Mutely, he handed the papers to her. She took them, looked curiously at the ribbon-bound packet, and then opened Gabriel's letter. 'Oh my God,' she murmured, seeing the greeting. She read the remainder in silence. Tears were quivering unshed in her eyes before she came to the end. When she had finished, she handed the letter to me, and I read it.

3 August 1918

Dearest Pater,

I know not how to write this, my last letter to you, but write I must. My uncle waits for me to put it into his hand, and from his hand it will reach yours. He is patient, but he is due back.

The verdict arrived just 12 hours ago. My first reaction was . . . nothingness. The world retreated, and my ears seemed not to hear the sounds of the men passing outside or the constant guns up the line. And then the world rushed back in on me, a tumult of memories and voices, long-forgotten tastes and smells fresh on my tongue and in my nose, as if the mind wished to gather together all the disparate moments in my life and heap them into my arms, to savour at once.

It is given to few men along this bullet-ridden strip of land to know the hour of their death. Most of us have lived so long with the possibility, it has become almost unimportant. One of the first things one learns here is that if one hears a bullet, there is no point in ducking, since if it was going to hit you, it would have. It is given only to the lawfully condemned to hear the bullet coming, to be given a time in which to look over one's life, to hear the voices of friends and tutors, to feel the comfort of parents' hands, to feel one's life narrowing down to a small, quiet centre.

One of those voices has been that of old Pyeminster. Remember the summer we did Henry VI. He and I acted all the sailors in various dialects. And I was Suffolk, emerging from his disguising rags to declare defiantly that true nobility is exempt from fear. Two or three months ago, I'd have laughed hysterically at such a conceit, knowing it unlikely that I, for one, could bear more than the Huns dared to hand out.

Now, however, I stand with Suffolk. I rage at the stupidity, the smallness, of the men who condemned me. I give you free permission, after the War ends, to pursue the injustice of my case, in the hopes that in the future, no man refusing an insane order must pay for it with his life.

I die knowing that my action saved the lives of ten good men. I die in the sureness of my righteousness, and knowing, in the words of St Paul, that being judged by a human court is a very small thing.

The padre no doubt waits, his finger lodged in that fourth chapter of Corinthians. I ask that you look him up, later, for he has been good to me. I ask that you similarly embrace my uncle, who has helped me through these final hours.

But most of all I ask that you welcome your daughter Helen. If any regrets are left me, it is this, that I will have no life with her. As you will see from the enclosed, she is truly your daughter. I have no means of explaining her sudden presence in your lives, but to say that she was a gift from God, and that she saved not only my life, but my soul. The details of our meeting, our wooing, and our brief marriage you shall have to hear from her lips. I leave it to you, to choose whether or not to show her this letter. In the unreal fog in which I have moved this past twelvemonth, Helen was the only clear place. Love her, because I ask it. Love her because she brought your son laughter at a time when laughter was in short supply. Love her because I do, now and forever.

As I love you and Mother.

Your son, Gabriel

P.S. Another text I studied with Pyeminster, one of the odes of old Horace, keeps running through my mind. It is not the rich man one should call happy, he says, peiusque leto flagitium timet, *but the man who fears dishonour more than death, and who is not afraid to die pro caris amici aut patrias – for beloved friends or country. By his definition, I am a happy man indeed.*

With love and gratitude to you, my beloved friend, and my country,

Your faithful Gabriel

When I had reached the end, I felt as if his patient and dignified words had been seared onto my brain. I gave the boy's letter back to Iris, the mother he had not known. She folded it reverently back into its envelope, and handed it to Marsh, along with the handkerchief she had borrowed. She then picked up the other documents from her lap, looking at the packet of letters wrapped in ribbon. 'Isn't that Helen's handwriting?'

'I should think it would have to be,' Marsh replied. 'And this . . . their marriage certificate? Oh, that utter bastard.' Marsh, however, was already looking at the means of turning his anger into action. 'This will simplify things somewhat,' he said grimly.

'I agree,' I said, with feeling. Instead of having to watch the crowd of nearly 350 guests and servants to see which of our suspects made for the exit, then track him unnoticed through house and countryside, by motorcar and train, until he led us to his hiding place, we could now simply wait in the Armoury for him to show. Ali might shadow a nervous hare across a barren hillside unseen, needs be, and would have no problems in the corridors of Justice Hall, but with the hiding place known, the potentially disastrous complexities of Holmes' plan were sliced through like the Gordian knot. It was a tremendous relief.

CHAPTER THIRTY-TWO

THE TIME HAD COME; the inevitable could be delayed no longer; I had to join the party.

Life has ill prepared me for finding any enjoyment in a press of merrymakers. My parents had entertained a certain amount in my childhood, but those were quiet affairs, with intelligent conversation the main interest. Conversation in the Great Hall was far from intellectual; the level of hilarity was already such that a stentorian bellow was required to make polite response of one's name. A band had started up in one corner of the gallery, jazz music loud enough to be appreciated in New Orleans and punctuated by the cries of the distraught parrots. Painted Cleopatra danced with laurel-leafed Caesars (never mind that they were thirteen hundred years too late for Tutankhamen), archaeologists with belly-dancers; women with elaborately outlined eyes linked arms with men wearing masks of various creatures that obscured vision as well as visage and had already begun to be pushed onto the tops of heads. Six men with eyes like Rudolph Valentino's and wearing little more than loin-cloths (their eyes, unfortunately, bore the only resemblance to the actor) were clustered together, attempting to invent an Egyptian dance-step, eliciting gales of mad laughter from a dozen equally heavily painted young women in gauze drapes. Drinks of many unlikely hues rested (briefly) in glasses of various shapes, and I could only anticipate that the place would be reduced to sprawled heaps of comatose human beings in masks long before that eggs-and-champagne breakfast to which Iris had referred. I settled my *abayya* on my shoulders and resolutely pushed my way out into the pulsing mass of humanity.

If I regarded the exercise as an investigation into the social dynamics of crowds, I found, I could keep from being overwhelmed. If I smiled vacantly and nodded at the shouted attempts at conversation of my neighbours, if I kept an untasted drink in one hand so as to forestall a dozen others being pressed on me, if I kept my elbows clamped against my sides so as to protect my ribs, and most of all if I kept moving along the edges of the room, the sheer hysterical energy of the place did not come crashing in upon me and send me gibbering for the open air.

The band added a weirdly humming stringed instrument – to simulate Egyptian harmonies, I supposed – and fifty people joined the six Valentinos in their dance. With a splash and a chorus of whoops, a nearby thicket of papyrus began to leap about violently as a dripping Caesar rose from his lily-pond: jumped, pushed, or fallen? It hardly mattered, to him least of all. A young woman danced by me with one of the artificial jungle-vines wrapped around and around her diaphanous costume, which she may have intended as an exotic belt but which made her look as if she had just escaped from being tied to a post. A redheaded boy went past, doing a brisk fox-trot with one of the stuffed crocodiles that had reared up at the front doors, and I was nearly flattened by a pair of women in brilliant coral-hued gauze jumping on pogo-sticks, more or less in time to the music.

A six-foot-tall scarab beetle (*what* an uncomfortable costume!) was deep in conversation with two blonde belly-dancers; three men in golden masks argued over the proper technique for taking a fox's brush; and an ibis-god on stilts gazed down in solitary splendour at the activity going on around his knees.

And all this before dinner.

With that thought, perhaps forty minutes into my circumnavigation of the floor, a subtle shudder seemed to move through the mass, and it began to thin. At first it seemed the result of a distant earthquake followed by the instinctive search for open space, but then I realised it was the rumour of food in the adjoining rooms. We were to dine buffet style, with a hundred tables set up for people to occupy with their filled plates, and there seemed little point in being among the first rush. I leant against a marble column that was dressed as a palm tree, and took a swallow of the warm liquid in my glass.

'Drinking heavily, are we, Russell?' said a voice in my ear. If I hadn't been so fatigued, I might have thrown my arms around him; as it was, I gave him a tired smile.

'Hello, Holmes. Where have you been?'

'Here, for much of the time. I saw you a few times across the room, but by the time I reached your place, you were gone.'

'You look remarkably fresh. And terribly Bedouin.'

'Better than being dressed as a Caesar.'

'Or Rudolph Valentino, although you have applied the kohl, I see.'

'Marsh told you the plan?'

'I'm not certain if it was Marsh or Mahmoud but yes. Did he tell you—'

'—about the papers?' he interrupted, speaking in a voice so low

I could barely hear it myself. 'He did. He's got them squirreled away now, and wrapped some newspaper inside the piece of oil-cloth to put back in the chest.'

'Any number of people could have hid those papers in the chest,' I noted.

'Anyone who knows Justice Hall,' he agreed.

'Ali will take up his position in the Armoury after Marsh has spoken?'

'Once he's introduced Marsh, he'll slip away. While Marsh is talking to the guests.'

'Ought we to keep an eye on the two men anyway?'

'You know my methods, Russell.'

By this time in my life, his methods were mine.

Dinner was an odd assortment of the familiar and the conscientiously foreign, crab puffs next to bits of bright yellow lamb on skewers, tiny marinated aubergines nestled amongst the iced oysters. This time, there was sufficient quantity to satisfy the mob, even though by the time I surveyed the table of offerings, the most popular items (those of recognisably English heritage) were rather sparsely represented. Holmes had gone off again, and I settled into a corner table. Halfway through my pomegranate-stuffed pigeon, I glanced up, and confronted a vision.

Mahmoud and Ali Hazr stood in the doorway. Mahmoud entered first, dressed in dramatic black and gold, on his face the customary all-seeing expression I had once known. Ali stood at his shoulder, glowering and clothed in all the colours of the rainbow. His hand was resting on a close facsimile of the knife he had used to such lethal purpose, and when he spoke briefly in Mahmoud's ear, I could see that his front teeth were again missing. I choked on my mouthful and stood up; Mahmoud's eyes caught the movement, and he gazed at me across the crowded dining room. His mouth quirked, briefly, at my reaction, and then something behind him called for his attention: I saw, as I pushed my way to them, that that something was five-year-old Gabe Hughenfort, his pale face slightly dubious and his hand clinging tightly to his mother's, but his green eyes glowing with wonder at the sights and sounds of Justice Hall in its festivities. He was dressed – how else? – as the young son of a sheikh, with gold *agahl* holding his snowy *abayya* over those dark Hughenfort curls, his white robes gleaming against the pool of Mahmoud's black. Yes, by God he was a Hughenfort; it was a wonder the entire room of revellers did not rise as one and proclaim it.

And he was more than just a Hughenfort, I decided as he moved into the room: The title had already begun to settle down onto the child, the awareness of responsibility and eight centuries of tradition – unconscious still, but felt in the glances and the voices of the adults closest to him. The responsibility of the title had nearly smothered Marsh, but on this boy it seemed to be having the opposite effect, giving him stature, adding authority to his open good nature and obvious intelligence. In reflecting back the respect others had for the name and the title, this five-year-old had already begun to take into himself those qualities which justified the respect. On this Hughenfort, the weight of the title looked as if it might ride in his bones, not on his back.

Helen leant down and said something to her son; at his nod, they went forward to the buffet, where she helped him choose the only familiar item in sight, a crustless sandwich. I glanced at Mahmoud and Ali: Mahmoud was watching the boy, Ali the crowd. Then Ali's crimson-gold-and-lapis-embroidered elbow jabbed into the black arm beside it, and both dark gazes were drilling the room opposite.

moved, and saw Sidney Darling, his long, slim figure evoking a Hollywood sheikh, his turban nonchalantly tilted on his blond hair. I looked back, Mahmoud caught my eye and jerked his head minutely towards the Hall, and then the Hughenforts were gone, child and all.

I hastened to follow them, looking around for Holmes, who materialised at my side as soon as I came through the doorway. 'I have Ivo Hughenfort,' he murmured in my ear.

'I'll take Darling,' I responded. Holmes faded off into the gathering crowd.

It took some time for the guests to realise that it was time to toast their new duke, but gradually, in groups of two or twelve, they trickled back into the Great Hall, drinks in hand at the ready, not silent but prepared to fall so. I could see Ivo Hughenfort towards the bottom of the stairway, which would be the front of the crowd when Mahmoud began to speak. Holmes was behind him, but with his height, he had no trouble watching Ivo. One of the imported servants – he of the crooked nose – came up to speak into Hughenfort's ear; he listened, nodded, spoke for a moment in response, and the servant went away.

Then Marsh was mounting the stairs, a swirl of midnight black against the pale stone, his right hand holding that of the white-garbed child. Alistair, Helen, Ben, and Iris stayed at the opposite side of the stairs from Ivo Hughenfort, along with a middle-aged woman who would, I thought, meet the description of Mycroft's kindly, deceptive, and competent attendant. I looked again for Darling's insouciant turban, found it unmoved a dozen feet away, and looked back at Marsh. At Mahmoud.

Halfway up the stairs, the black figure turned and stood, waiting for silence. The voices fell to a murmur, and still he waited, until all was silence, and every ear could hear his words.

'Thank you for coming to Justice Hall this evening. You honour my family with your presence.' There was a mild murmur of amusement at that un-English sentiment, and he paused for a moment until the hush returned.

'My sister Phillida made this festivity for the express purpose of welcoming the seventh Duke of Beauville. At the time, she, along with everyone else, assumed that man to be myself.' He held up his left hand to cut off any reaction. 'You may be aware that my brother Henry, the sixth Duke, had a son. His name was Gabriel, and he was killed in the War as so many others were. Only in recent weeks have we begun to suspect that before his death, Gabriel provided himself with an heir. A legal heir, contingent only on locating the certificate, either through a close search of the house, or by means of the church records of the village in France where Gabriel and his bride were secretly wed. A delegation will set out on Monday to locate that legal record, but I thought it best to anticipate their success by allowing my sister's festivities to go on, albeit with the minor change of its honouree. I should like to introduce to you Gabriel Michael Maurice Hughenfort, seventh Duke of Beauville, fourteenth Earl of Calminster, seventh Earl of Darlescote, formerly of Toronto, Canada.'

He picked the boy up and held him, less to reveal him to the people than to comfort him against the applause that would ensue. And after a long, shocked moment, it did: a huge wave of clapping and a babble of voices, amazed, gratified, and well aware of the social coup each one had garnered by being present at such an event. All of London – half the world! – would be talking about this in the coming days, the voices were exclaiming to themselves, and we were there, with those two dramatic Arab costumes on the formal staircase of Justice Hall.

I looked for the white Darling turban, as I had approximately every five seconds since it had come into the Great Hall, and found it moved slightly to one side. I started to push towards it, but it came to a halt again, so I contented myself with watching it with one eye and looking up at the stairs with the other. The boy had been startled at the sudden volume of noise, but Mahmoud spoke quietly to him, and whatever he said had the desired effect. Little Gabe allowed himself to be held there for a minute, and then his mother came up the stairs and gathered him into her arms. Iris was there too, and the deceptive matron, and all three ascended the stairs to escape the acclaim.

At the top, however, Iris stopped and said something to the boy and his mother. He shifted in Helen's arms to look out at the sea of people below, then waved to them. A cheer of 'Hip, hip, hoorah!' shook the frescoed dome, and the women and the child slipped away.

As had Sidney Darling. Oh, the turban was still there, but the hand that came up to push it back into place was paler of hue and blunter of finger: Darling had transferred his turban to another head, and escaped me.

I set my shoulders against the crowd and shoved forward to where I had last seen him before the turban changed places; no Sidney.

I dashed into the dining room, where servants were clearing the remnants of the meal. 'Have any of you seen Mr Darling?' I asked, cursing the invisibility of known figures at a costume ball.

'No, sir,' three of them said; 'No, ma'am,' said the fourth, so I turned to him as the most observant of the lot. 'A tall man in white, bare-headed, in the last few minutes?'

'Through there,' he replied, pointing to the western door.

I went through it at a fast trot, scanning the still-empty rooms as I passed – salon, breakfast room, music room – and then I was entering the corridor of the western wing. I swung right, and at the far end there he was, disappearing through a doorway. The Armoury, if I wasn't mistaken.

I was not.

I found him standing all alone in the middle of the ancient hall of the Hughenforts, surrounded by scores of lethal instruments. He turned at my entrance.

'Miss Russell?' he asked, sounding a bit uncertain.

Damnation, I thought; I'd hoped to catch him with his head in the chest.

'Mr Darling.'

'Was it your message?'

'Which message was that?'

'One of the servants brought me a message that someone wished me to come to the Armoury, but she didn't know who that someone was. Silly sort of a trick.'

'Which servant was that?'

'One of the housemaids. Don't remember her name. Did my wife's hair once,' he added, sounding as if he did not fully approve of this aberration of a mere housemaid's arranging Lady Phillida's hair.

'Emma,' I suggested, and a small alarm began to ring in the back of my mind.

'That it? You may be right, though I don't know that it matters. Dashed annoying; now I have to hunt the silly thing down in that press and ask her who—'

'I know who it was,' I blurted out, and before he could ask me I raised my voice to shout aimlessly into the room, 'Ali! He's a diversion – it's your cousin!'

A guttural curse echoed across the Armoury stones and the wooden screen-wall gave a violent shift an instant before the multi-coloured Ali rose up in the gallery above. He vaulted to the floor, startling Darling into a fruity curse of his own, and stalked across the uneven stones towards us, hand on knife and his eyes threatening all sorts of damage if my premature springing of the trap should have lost us our prey; but I had no concern for threats, merely grabbed his arm and hurried him out of the room.

'It has to be your cousin Ivo. He was speaking with a servant just before Mah – before Marsh's speech, both of them using a very familiar manner, such as indicates a long-time relationship.' I was stumbling over my words as it all came together in my mind – the servant's limp and his fighter's nose; the fact that he and Ivo had left before Holmes returned to dinner on the Saturday of the shoot, so that Holmes had recognised neither of his assailants; the number of telephones in the house and the ease of overhearing conversations – I went on. 'It's not the first time I've seen the housemaid Emma flirting with the man – who was limping, which could have been from Holmes' defence of himself last month. And it was Emma who sent Darling to the Armoury just now, and it must have been she, through the servant, who gave your cousin inside information about the Justice comings and goings. Emma could even have overheard the conversation Holmes had with you on the telephone the afternoon he was attacked, and told her friend where you were.'

While I was offering this logical explanation, which had distressingly little effect on my companion's grim expression, we had cleared the western corridor and re-entered the Hall. Ali, thrusting aside guests left and right, made straight for the stairway, from which height we peered down on the confusing crowd, searching for the figure of Marsh, Holmes, or Ivo Hughenfort.

Ali grunted and started down the stairs towards Mahmoud, who had just appeared from the direction of the dining room, but before

I could join him there was a commotion behind me on the stai–
I looked past yet another Caesar and Cleopatra and saw Helen,
searching the Hall. I called to her, and she hurried down to me.

'What is it?'

'Is Gabe with Marsh?' she demanded.

'I don't know,' I told her. 'He's just there . . .'

We both followed my pointing finger: Marsh, but no small
snowy figure at his side. I flailed my arm in a wide circle. He caught
the motion in the corner of his eye, saw instantly that something
was wrong, and ploughed through the crowd with a speed that
made Ali look like a polite old man.

'Tell me,' he commanded.

'Helen doesn't have the boy.'

'The children wanted to play,' she gabbled. 'I said they could,
but Lenore went one way and Walter the other, and Gabe must
have been with Walter, because he vanished in the blink of an eye.
You don't think—?'

What I thought was that the younger Darlings' desire to initiate
their new duke into the hide-and-seek potentials of Justice might
just have killed the boy. But Mahmoud did not answer; he wheeled
to bound up the stairs, his black robes boiling up around him, Ali
at his shoulder and me at their heels.

The solitary figure of Holmes, coming out from the long
gallery, told me all I needed to know.

'Hughenfort went into the lavatory and was out of the window
before I could get around the house. The boy?'

'Gone.'

'We must split up and search. From which room did he
disappear?'

'Walter and he were last seen going in the direction of the

ninese bedroom, at the far end of the long gallery.'

So much for the grey-haired competent matron, I thought darkly. Mycroft would be mortified at her failure.

There were any number of guests in the rooms we swept through, all startled at the sudden interruption of their private moments, but we found no small figure in the white robes of a sheikh's son. In the Chinese room, however, angry cries and furious kicks shook a seemingly delicate wardrobe. Ali did not pause to look for the key, merely drew his knife from its jewelled scabbard and drove it into the exquisite centuries-old wood, jerking the haft sideways. The door splintered open; Walter Darling blinked at the sudden light, tears streaking his face.

'Which way did they go?' Ali demanded.

'I didn't see!' the boy answered furiously. 'I was locked in here.'

'You have ears. Which way did they go?'

The flat assumption in Ali's voice steadied young Darling. He frowned, dashed his fist against his teary eyes, and decided, 'Not through the gallery.'

'The window?' We were up on the main block's first floor, but a brief roofline lay not far beneath the window-sill, the portico over a side entrance.

'No, I'd have heard that. They just went. I think the man was carrying Gabe.'

'Good lad,' Ali said, and left the room at a run. Even so, Mahmoud was before him.

But they were not in the next room, nor in the corridor that led back into the long gallery. We were now nearing the old part of the house again.

'Isn't there a—' I started to say, the diagrams of Justice clear in my mind, but Mahmoud had already darted into the other end of the corridor and leapt up a flight of six stairs to a small door tha looked to be a service room, but was in fact the upper end of the ancient spiral staircase that led down to Marsh's bedroom and into the Mediaeval chapel with the Roman tiles below. Mahmoud had the key out and the door open in an instant, and then he went still as a statue, listening with all his being for sounds, above or below. None came. Mahmoud snatched up two candle stubs and a box of vestas from the stone niche over the entrance, lit the stubs and thrust one at Ali, then started up the stairway with his hand cupped to shelter the other. I picked up the skirts of my costume and followed on his heels; Holmes plunged into the depths after Ali.

This upper level of stairs was less worn than those Alistair had shown me on our tour, but retained the shape of the others, a tight, shoulder-hugging spiral that ended at a small, sturdy door. It was not locked; Mahmoud blew out the candle and eased the door open.

Icy air rushed over us, blowing snowflakes and the stink of the rooftop torches. The heaving flames reflected off the day's snowfall, giving a degree of substance to the roofs, and Mahmoud moved off with confidence into the shifting darkness. I went after him, trusting his childhood knowledge of the Justice leads, praying that he could see well enough to keep from stumbling into Ivo Hughenfort. As my eyes adjusted I could tell that the snow had been trampled – but that must have been by the servants, lighting those dramatic torches along the roofline. In the furious leap and ebb of the flames I glimpsed the roof as flat expanses of white cut by the sharp dark lines of chimneys and sections of pitched roof, with the dark wall of the crenellations surrounding the whole. Mahmoud's night-dark shape moved silently before me, and then went still.

I too stopped. The flaring torches obscured as much as they

lluminated, but I thought the movement across the snow fifty feet or so away was cast not by the torches, but by a moving figure. *Two* figures, one of them emitting muffled cries of fury and fear. They neared the wall of crenellations, and in an instant the air in front of me was empty. A shadow flew across the patches of light and dark, to merge with the other in a scuffle and exchange of shouts, and I slithered and stumbled my way across the intervening space in time to see Mahmoud sweep the boy behind his robes, the small white patch hidden by the black, and face their attacker, teeth and knife bared.

Then the pulsing light caught on the dull gleam of metal, as the figure facing Mahmoud drew a gun. I was too far away to use my throwing knife, even if I could have hit him in the uncertain light, so I did the only thing I could: I shouted. I don't even know what the string of words that tumbled out of me were, I merely had to let him know that he had a witness, that where he might have hoped to arrange a convenient accident for one Hughenfort, or even two, the problems had expanded beyond that.

The tableau froze, the leaping flames and the rising breath clouds the only signs of movement. I began to inch forward, hoping to get close enough to hit him with my throwing knife, knowing that a cornered man is at his most dangerous when he senses the heavy hand of failure descending onto his shoulder, knowing that the frustration of seeing his long years of planning turning sour might explode into pointless destruction. Knowing that there was not a thing I could do, should he decide to shoot Mahmoud. Knowing I had to try.

Then, seeming loud against the whip of the flames, came a small metallic noise from off to my right, a noise that would have been inaudible inside the house or had a wind been blowing, but a noise that broke the stillness of the rooftop like the gunshot it preceded.

Ivo Hughenfort was enough of a soldier to react to the sour of a rifle bullet being chambered behind his back. He jerked, half turning; I darted forward, but before I had taken two steps, the rifle went off with a flash that imprinted the stark image on my retinas: one man in the instant the bullet took him, a man and a boy behind him, braced for battle. Hughenfort and his gun both landed on the snow-muffled leads, and then I was on him, tumbling him face-first onto the snow. He struggled, but in a moment the rifle's barrel was pressed into his cheek; when I looked up, I was somehow not surprised to see Iris, murder on her face and her finger ready on the trigger.

Mahmoud had not moved from his position in front of the boy. He had been closer than I to the revolver, close enough to dive for Hughenfort's feet and grapple for the gun. Had the child not been present, I knew, he would not have hesitated an instant; instead, he had stayed where he was, using his broad body to block the young duke from a bullet.

Seconds later, Ali and Holmes erupted from the door onto the roof. Ali was all in favour of tossing his cousin over the side, giving to Hughenfort the fate he had intended for the child; it was Mahmoud who restrained him.

Instead, we handed Ivo Hughenfort over to Mycroft's men for safe keeping, to bind his bleeding shoulder and spirit him away to London.

And then we went back to the ball.

CHAPTER THIRTY-THREE

ON THE TWENTIETH OF December, the Thursday after the fancy dress ball that shook an Empire, Iris, Holmes, and I took the train from London to Arley Holt. A car met us at the station to transport us through the wintry countryside to Justice Hall. The house was silent, restored to its alabaster splendour but cavernous in its absence of family, and we took our subdued evening meal before the fire in the so-called library.

Afterwards, Iris settled with a book while Holmes went to wheedle the crypt key from Ogilby (a very hangdog butler, who had taken the treachery of the maid Emma personally). I knew that if I went down with him, I should find myself pulling up Mediaeval tiles with my bare fingers, so instead I wandered the room, looking closely at the collections of artefacts as assembled from the house and grounds: Roman coins, Saxon axe-head, a clot of woven reeds that I decided had been a sandal. Twice servants came in to ask if we needed anything, and we sent them away. With the police gone, the excitement over, the house clear of Egypt, and the family gone to the London house for the

Christmas festivities, the remaining Justice staff was sleepy and bored.

The Darlings had packed up and driven away the day after the ball, prematurely scattering the guests and taking with them Helen, Ben, Gabe, and most of the servants. Marsh and Alistair went with the family to see them settled in, and had then mysteriously vanished.

Iris abandoned her book to stare into the flames. After a while, she asked, 'What do you think are the chances of Ivo's trial?'

I sighed deeply, and returned a scrap of elegant Samian ware back to its shelf. 'He's claiming that he was rescuing the boy from falling off the roof. That the children were playing hide-and-seek, that he saw Gabe dash through the door that opened onto those stairs, that he went after him to bring him back to safety, and that his holding a gun on Mah—on Marsh was the same thing: that he believed the child was being attacked by a robed stranger.'

Iris knew most of this already, but it made her freshly angry each time the topic came up. 'Complete nonsense. He hasn't a chance of getting away with it. Has he?'

I did not wish to answer, saying merely, 'His manservant may be convicted of attacking Holmes, because of that fingerprint he left on the button Holmes pulled off of his assailant's overcoat.' The coat had proved to be a cast-off from the late duke's wardrobe, given to Ivo's servant, found by the police in the man's room, still missing its button. 'The maid Emma is willing to tell all, although what she knows isn't enough to convict anyone but herself. And I'm afraid that the attack on Holmes will be difficult to tie in with the attack on young Gabe.' As for persuading the Crown prosecutors to try Ivo Hughenfort for the death by firing squad of Gabriel Hughenfort, considering that most of the records were nissing, I thought the chances minuscule. In fact, Ivo looked to be a frustrating and potentially dangerous loose end, dangling and threatening to trip us up. Mycroft's influence in the legal system, I reflected, might have to be summoned. Still, I tried to give Iris some encouragement. 'Ivo will be tried, and the evidence is fairly strong. He is not behind bars at the moment because of his name, but that won't save him at trial.'

'It had better not.'

'Let's go to bed,' I suggested. 'We'll need to be up early.'

The sky overhead was pitch black when we three left the house the next morning, hours before dawn. Fitful clouds trailed their skirts over the big white moon and ten thousand stars beat down at us, while ice-crisp blades of grass crackled beneath our boots. I was dressed in my heaviest clothing, but I did not feel warm until we had topped the first long hill out of the Justice valley.

'Any news of Marsh?' Iris asked, breaking the silence for the first time.

'Nothing,' Holmes grunted.

'He and Ali must be back in Palestine by now.'

'If not yet, they soon will be.'

'I wish I'd had the chance to say goodbye,' she said. 'I don't know why he had to race off like that, without a word to anyone other than Gabe.'

Marsh and Ali had entered the London house late on the Monday following the costume ball, in order to say goodbye to young Gabe. No one knew about it until Wednesday morning, when the boy happened to overhear his mother talking about the odd disappearance, and he had told her that 'Uncle Marsh' had come to his bedside, wakened him, and they had talked for a while about England and Canada, and the life that awaited Gabe

440

here. 'Uncle Ali' had been with him, but had stayed near the d⋯
saying nothing. When Gabe had begun to feel sleepy again, Mar⋯
had bent down to kiss the boy's forehead, and told him to take care
of his mother and Justice Hall, in that order. He then gave Gabe
Hughenfort two objects: one, a cleverly carved wooden bird with a
long beak tucked against its breast; the other, an old silver pocket
watch inscribed with the phrase *Justitia fortitude mea est.*

Both uncles, Gabe said, had been wearing costumes like those
they wore to the ball.

The stars faded, objects assumed shape around us, and then we
had cleared the last rise above the dim outlines of the overgrown,
lichen-encrusted stubs of granite that were The Circles. We took
up our places on the trio of smooth boulders, digging into our
rucksacks for the thermal flasks and bread rolls we had brought
with us, and sipped our steaming beakers of coffee while we waited.

The sky grew light, then pale blue, the wisps of high clouds
assuming a tinge of pink. The hill to the east of us glowed, and
we emptied our beakers and walked around the stones to the
eastern side of The Circles, taking care that we should not block
the light. There we hunkered down. The line of sunlight curved
onto the hillside above the three boulders and started to flow down
the frost-rimed grass, turning it first white, then gradually dark as
the ice melted. It hesitated over the hollow that held The Circles,
seeming to hold itself back, and then with a great flash the sun
shot through the two easternmost stones to hit the tallest standing
stone on the west, turning it to flame. It also, just for an instant,
brushed the stone that held the remains of our picnic, the central
smooth boulder. Marsh Hughenfort's stone.

Then the sun filled the hollow, and The Circles were just a
double round of worn rocks sitting beneath an English dawn, as

had done three-quarters of a million times before.

We finished our coffee, ate our bread rolls in a feeling of communion, and walked back across the sun-warmed hills to Justice Hall.

Iris and I paused on the last hill, as we had the time before, to examine the Hall while Holmes walked slowly on, deep in his own thoughts. Justice Hall was a sad building today, despite the sunshine, lonesome and a little embarrassed: The groundsmen had taken advantage of the family's absence to drain the Pond. Ogilby had informed us, abjectly apologetic, that this procedure was done every other winter in order to clean the bottom and service the fountain and dam at the far end. The house's dignity was severely challenged by its current setting overlooking a mud-hole.

'The place looks bereft, without the water,' Iris said.

'You think she'd rather we didn't see her like this?' I asked.

Iris giggled unexpectedly. 'Like a very grand lady whose knicker elastic has given way.'

I joined in her laughter. 'Repeating to herself, "One must not look down!"'

Iris stood for a while with this imaginary conversation going through her mind, and then her smile grew sad. 'I have a cousin who's just had to tear down his country house. It was such a lovely place, but with death taxes, it had to go. I'll admit, I hope Justice can survive. She's a pompous old thing, but she is very beautiful.'

'When she's got a lake at her feet,' I added.

Iris chuckled, and moved off down the hill. I started to follow her, then looked up sharply: There had been movement behind the Justice Hall battlements. I strained to see. At first I thought it might be Mahmoud looking down; then my eyes caught the shape and drab colour of the man's clothing, and for a brief instant I imagined

a youthful second lieutenant, honour restored, come home to ⎦
beloved Justice to find his wife and young son. I blinked, and ⱦ
was neither Gabriel's shade nor his unacknowledged father's figure,
merely a workman clearing the remains of Egypt from the Hall
roofs.

We left Justice two hours later, none of us knowing if we should
ever return. Holmes had gone off to look at something while I
went to take my wistful leave of Mr Greene's riches; when I came
down again I found Iris in the Great Hall, saying a long goodbye to
Ogilby and Mrs Butter. Holmes swept in from the western wing,
his eyes sparkling as if someone had just told him a great joke. He
took my coat from Ogilby; as he was settling it onto my shoulders,
he leant forward to whisper in my ear.

'Go take a look in the Armoury.'

Puzzled, I made my way out of the Great Hall, past Christopher
Hewetson's bust of the third Duke and the heavy-laden porcelain
cabinets and assorted grim Hughenfort ancestors, to the room that
had been the centre of the house for generations of Hughenforts,
and for the monks before them. I walked into the thick-walled
museum of arms, and looked around for what had so amused
Holmes.

I spotted it as soon as I faced the door: The sunburst of Saracen
blades arranged against the wall was missing the small, decorative
element in its hub. Mahmoud's knife was gone from Justice Hall.

EPILOGUE

THE FOLLOWING WEEK, THE day after Christmas, Holmes and
I read in *The Times* that a body had been found on Saturday
in the lake at Justice Hall, the day after we had walked with Iris to
The Circles. The corpse had been identified as Mr Ivo Hughenfort,
recently implicated in a disturbance at the Hall. Police were
speculating that Mr Hughenfort had wandered in (without,
unfortunately, having notified the Hall staff of his presence) to
explore the temporarily drained bottom of Justice Pond, unaware
that the repairs had only that morning been completed. He
appeared to have become trapped in the sticky mud; when the
Justice waters rolled down and flooded back into their bed, they
had swept him away, drowning him.

There was, *The Times* reported, no suspicion of foul play.

Justice Stream continued on, ever flowing.

And in England, no more was seen of Mahmoud Hazr and his
cousin Ali.

EDITOR'S AFTERWORD

O N JUNE 21, 2001, the Shot at Dawn memorial was unveiled at the Memorial Arboretum in Staffordshire, England. It depicts a seventeen-year-old private who was condemned to death, without defence, in the summer of 1915. Behind the blindfolded figure stands a forest of 306 wooden stakes, each representing an executed Commonwealth soldier.

The death penalty for desertion and cowardice was abolished in 1930. In 1997 a review of the cases of the 306 Great War condemned men was begun. In 1998 it was suggested that the names of the executed soldiers might now be added to the country's war memorials. On Remembrance Day 2000, relatives and supporters of the executed soldiers joined the march and the two minutes' silence at the Cenotaph in Whitehall. However, the Secretary of State for Defence later stated that there would be no posthumous pardons for the men and boys who were shot at dawn.

LAURIE R. KING
FREEDOM, CALIFORNIA

GARMENT OF SHADOWS

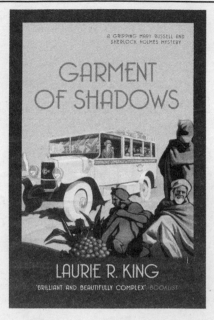

In a strange room in Morocco, Mary Russell is trying to solve a pressing mystery: Who am I? She has awakened with blood on her hands and soldiers pounding at the door. She discovers herself strangely adept in the skills of the underworld, escaping through alleys and rooftops, picking pockets and locks. She is clothed like a man, and armed only with her wits.

Meanwhile, Holmes is pulled into the growing war between France, Spain, and the Rif Revolt led by Emir Abd el-Krim – who may be a Robin Hood, or a power-mad tribesman. Holmes badly wants the wisdom and courage of his wife, whom he's learned, to his horror, has gone missing. As Holmes searches for her, and Russell searches for herself, each tries to crack deadly parallel puzzles before it's too late for them, for Africa, and for the peace of Europe.